Remember WHEN...

SCARLETT FINN

Also by Scarlett Finn

NOTHING TO...
NOTHING TO HIDE
NOTHING TO LOSE
NOTHING IN BETWEEN: ONE
NOTHING TO DECLARE
NOTHING TO US
NOTHING IN BETWEEN: TWO
NOTHING TO SAY
NOTHING TO GAIN
NOTHING IN BETWEEN: THREE
NOTHING TO YOU
NOTHING TO THIS PREQUEL: ONE WILD NIGHT
NOTHING TO THIS
NOTHING IN BETWEEN: FOUR
NOTHING TO DO
NOTHING TO FEAR
NOTHING IN BETWEEN: FIVE
NOTHING TO DENY

GO NOVELS
GO WITH IT
GO IT ALONE
GO ALL OUT
GO ALL IN
GO FULL CIRCLE

KINDRED SERIES
RAVEN
SWALLOW
CUCKOO
SWIFT
FALCON
FINCH

EXILE
HIDE & SEEK
KISS CHASE

THE EXPLICIT SERIES
EXPLICIT INSTRUCTION
EXPLICIT DETAIL
EXPLICIT MEMORY

THE FORBIDDEN NOVELS
FORBIDDEN DESIRE
FORBIDDEN WANT
FORBIDDEN WISH
FORBIDDEN NEED
FORBIDDEN BOND

WRECK & RUIN
RUIN ME
RUIN HIM

MISTAKE DUET
MISTAKE ME NOT
SLEIGHT MISTAKE

THE BRANDED SERIES
BRANDED
SCARRED
MARKED

TO DIE FOR...
TO DIE FOR TRUTH
TO DIE FOR HONOR
TO DIE FOR VIRTUE
TO DIE FOR DUTY
TO DIE FOR LOVE

RISQUÉ & HARROW INTERTWINED
TAKE A RISK
FIGHTING FATE
RISK IT ALL
FIGHTING BACK
GAME OF RISK

FORBIDDEN PREQUEL DUET
ALL. ONLY.
ONLY YOURS

LOVE AGAINST THE ODDS STANDALONE COLLECTION
SWEET SEAS
HEIR'S AFFAIR
RESCUED
MAESTRO'S MUSE
GETTING TRICKY
THIRTEEN
REMEMBER WHEN...
RELUCTANT SUSPICION
XY FACTOR

LOST & FOUND
LOST
FOUND

ONE

"IF ANYONE KNOWS of any reason, lawful or otherwise, that this couple should not be legally wed, speak now or forever hold your peace."

That part of the ceremony was supposed to breeze past quickly. Claire didn't expect to hear anything and neither did her groom, Calvin. He smiled at her and took a breath like he was ready to move onto the vows.

"I object."

The booming voice echoed through the church. Murmurs rose in the congregation as she and Calvin turned to look for the source of the interruption. At the other end of the aisle stood a guy who had to be six four. Muscular and rugged with dark hair and stubble, he was imposing and unmissable. Despite his confidence, Claire only saw a stranger. She didn't recognize him at all, and he wasn't the type to be easily forgotten.

Two other men rushed up behind him, forcing the daunting man to take a step forward.

"What do you think you're doing?" Calvin asked, edging her backward as he moved a few inches down the aisle. "Who the hell are you?"

"I'm her husband."

The room gasped.

Claire took a reflexive step backward.

Her husband?

***

THE NEXT FEW minutes were a blur. Someone took her hand to lead her from the altar to the wings and into the large room where she'd donned her gown. The screen in the far left corner covered the spot where she'd changed her clothes. Not so long ago, she'd stood back there believing her marriage was about to begin. She could never have anticipated such a different turn of events.

Couches lined the far wall under the tall intersecting tracery windows. Full-length mirrors stood in a semicircle by the door she'd just been put through. Claire fixated on the sight of herself in a flowing white dress. Her wedding dress.

It was supposed to be the happiest day of her life. So far, it wasn't going that way.

Others piled into the room behind her, interrupting her reflection.

"Just what the hell is this?" Calvin demanded.

Grabbing her hand, he pulled her toward the couches, urging her deep into the corner of the room. His mother and best man, Diane and Boyd, came over to flank her. Protecting her, maybe. Claire wasn't a fan of the tension pulsing through the beautiful space.

The interrupter and his two cohorts came in and closed the door. The three of them stayed close to the mirrors, ten feet away.

"Shane Warren," the interrupter said and offered her groom a hand.

Calvin refused it with a snort. "I don't think this is the time for introductions. You just ruined our wedding day."

"I know," Shane said.

The man to his left spoke up, "That couldn't be helped. What alternative did we have?"

Claire kept her head down. She and large groups didn't agree with each other. Everything was beginning to feel overwhelming.

After a short silence, she glanced up to catch Shane looking at her, straight past Calvin. He and the other two men were fixated on her.

"It's good to see you, Gin."

That shook something loose. "You know my real name," she said and tried to move closer.

Calvin put out an arm to prevent her from passing him. "How do we know these people are who they say they are?" he demanded.

"That's true," Diane said, going to her son's side. "You're not the first people to claim to know our Claire."

"Her name isn't Claire," the man on the left said. "Her name is Ginger." Ginger. That didn't sound familiar. Not that anything did. "She went missing sixteen months ago, after a boating accident."

"Boating?" Calvin snickered and took her hand. "Claire hates the water."

The man on the left spoke up again. "Actually she doesn't. She's a strong swimmer. She's always loved the beach."

Calvin was shaking his head. Shane frowned and turned to whisper with the most vocal man on their team. They exchanged some words that she couldn't make out and the third turned to murmur along with them.

"We should call the cops," Boyd said.

Claire didn't want anyone to call the authorities. Though it was distressing to be in the current situation, she wanted to know where she'd come from. She wanted to know who she was during the big blank space that was her life before Calvin.

Except while watching the three men talk to each other in secret, she realized that knowing more about them was important too.

"How did you find me?" she asked.

Everyone in the room stopped talking to look at her. Finding her voice had taken time and it sounded meek in comparison to the strong male tones that had dominated so far.

"We never stopped looking," Shane said, leaving his group. Calvin wouldn't let him get too close and kept himself in front of her. "I've been looking for you for sixteen months."

"What happened? I mean, I…"

"What do you remember?" the guy to the left asked. She took a breath, at a loss again. "It was this, your wedding that brought us here. We have a program that's been running, searching the internet for mentions of you."

Calvin blustered. "Mentions of her, we don't know her real name, she knows nothing about her past, how could—"

"Everyone thought she was dead," the man on the left said, getting emotional. "Four bodies were pulled out the water, hers was never found and this guy." He hit Shane's back. "He wouldn't give up. He wouldn't give up on my sister until—"

"Your sister?" Diane said.

Claire's jaw fell. "You're my brother?"

Nodding, he smiled, though his eyes were wet. "Yes, I'm Owen. Your big brother."

"And he's a lawyer," the third man said.

"This is Murphy," Shane said, introducing him. "He's my brother."

Despite her wedding being a bust, it was still a momentous day. It had always been supposed to be memorable, just not in that particular way.

"And we're here to tell you all to back off," Murphy said, looking meaner than his brother, something she hadn't thought possible. "You don't know the first thing about Ginger and she's not marrying anyone today."

"That's not for you to say," Diane said.

"Actually it is," Owen said, putting his briefcase on a side table to open it up. Inside were a bunch of files and folders, but he only took one out. "This is a copy of their original marriage certificate."

He opened the folder and handed it over to Calvin. Claire, or as she'd been revealed to be, Ginger, peeked past Diane and Boyd. There it was, with their names on it. Ginger Leyland was her maiden name. Their wedding had been witnessed by Owen Leyland and Murphy Warren.

"Do I have a mother?" she asked, looking to Owen for an answer.

Losing some of his professional edge, he glanced at Shane. "You do. She's been sick. She's in the hospital. I told her… I told her you'd visit, when we found you, when you were ready. I said we'd let you know where she was."

"And a father?"

"Your dad died when you were fourteen, Bit," Shane said, edging nearer.

Calvin tensed. "This is all lovely but complete bullshit."

"We have no way to prove if any of it is true," Boyd said, supporting his friend.

Ginger's head was spinning; she didn't know what to think. For sixteen months, she'd been an amnesiac. Calvin and his family had gotten her through;

they'd supported her even through the toughest of times. But she couldn't dismiss these men until their veracity had been proven.

Another more pressing matter had to take precedence. "We have two hundred guests out there."

"Want me to talk to them?"

Instead of the groom asking the question, it was Shane. She inhaled and opened her mouth, even without a clue how to respond. It didn't matter because Calvin got there first.

"Our wedding has nothing to do with you!" he exclaimed. "You don't know a single person out there. Why the hell would we let you talk to them?"

"I think it's wrong for you to let Ginny worry about them," Shane said. "Someone should already be out there telling those folks it's not gonna happen."

"Shane," Owen said, taking his turn to calm the man. "I'm sure he wasn't going to send his bride out there to talk to them."

"Ginger hates talking to large groups," Murphy said.

She made eye contact with the man she'd just been told was her brother-in-law. What he'd said was true and something she hated about herself. Turned out something from her past had carried forward into the present.

"I can excuse them," she said, though she didn't have a clue what to say.

The people out there were Calvin's friends and family. Most of them knew about her history, or lack of one, but she didn't like to talk about it.

"I'll excuse them," Calvin said.

"You're getting married today," Diane asserted. "You *have* to get married today."

"You can't get married if she's already married," Boyd said and glanced at everyone. "It's illegal for her to be married twice. Your marriage would be void."

"Boyd is Calvin's lawyer," Ginger said and got glared at. Why that would be a secret was a mystery.

Everyone went back to talking amongst themselves and at each other until voices were raised and the whole room was filled by the din.

When she'd woken up in hospital, doctors told her that her amnesia may be temporary. Unfortunately, it hadn't been. Calvin had been the one to find her at the side of the road. He'd stood by her through everything and encouraged her to make a new life for herself instead of chasing the old one.

There in the room was not just one man from her old life, but three of them. In addition to their presence, they'd brought paperwork that could prove she'd made different choices in the past.

"I want to talk to Mr. Warren alone," Ginger said, her voice loud enough to silence the others although she hadn't shouted.

Every person was again focused on her, so it was important to be confident. Her anxiety wouldn't let her look at Shane, so she focused on Calvin. That didn't help because her request wasn't going over well according to his expression.

"No!" he said. "I cannot allow—"

"You have to tell the guests to leave anyway," Owen said.

Murphy closed in behind Owen. "And this is just beginning," he said. "You're not going to get rid of us easily... You can't come between a man and his wife."

Calvin leaned closer to them, turning his back on her, blocking her from their view. "They're not married, not really. She's my bride, not his. I won't leave him alone with her. If he feels entitled... if he touches her—"

"She said she wanted to talk, not fuck," Shane said, his voice deep and husky. "I swear I'll keep my cock in my pants."

Her mouth fell open. She was glad that Calvin was giving her cover from the room because her cheeks warmed, suggesting they reddened. Calvin and his family didn't talk that way. They were a nice family, a rich family; one who made their money in chemicals. They were traditional and conservative. Well-dressed and proud of their affluence.

In comparison, Shane wore a crumpled shirt over a dark tee-shirt and worn jeans that hadn't seen a washer for a while. Maybe he was used to trash talk, but she'd barely heard a curse word in sixteen months.

"Unless she begs," Murphy muttered. Ginger covered her mouth to conceal her shock. "He never could say no to her... on anything."

She peeked around Calvin to see Murphy nudge his brother. Shane threw a smile at him but was serious when he turned back.

"I'll say no this time," Shane said.

"If you even think about touching her..." Calvin said and began to move.

Ginger ran around him to prevent the men from coming to blows.

Spinning around, she faced Calvin. "Just a few minutes, please."

Calvin wasn't happy, she could tell from how his jaw popped to the side.

He inhaled. "I'll tell everyone there's been a change of plan... Boyd will stay right outside the door. If anything happens, scream."

It took a minute of whispering and shifting expressions for everyone to get out the door in an orderly fashion. Diane took some convincing, but eventually left.

Murphy was the last one still present. Hanging in the door with one hand on the handle and the other on the frame, he made eye contact with his brother. "We'll be right out here too, bro."

He glanced at her before he went out.

Ginger was alone with Shane. Her husband, apparently. Her palms began to sweat, stealing all the moisture from her mouth it seemed because it was dry as a bone all of a sudden.

"I won't bite," Shane said. She took her time to lift her chin. "You were never into that."

When his hand rose as though he intended to touch her face, she backed away, hit by another surge of worry. "I… I don't like to be touched."

Not only did he stop his advance, but he bobbed his head and put his hands in his pockets.

"Okay," he said. "Whatever you need, Bit." His smile slid upward. "I'm just grateful to see you again… You look beautiful."

Well it was her wedding day, people were supposed to say that to her. Except as she peered into him, she sensed he was looking at something other than the dress or her figure.

"Tell me more about how you found me."

He swallowed, getting more business-like. "As Owen said, we had a program running continuously. It picked up stories about women who had unusual pasts, who'd been in accidents or been found in unusual circumstances. Amnesia was an idea floated by one of the doctors we had on the case, so the program flagged those stories too. As you can imagine, we would get several hits a day. Not too many that we couldn't eyeball them… Then we got the story of your wedding, it was run in a local paper. A business tycoon like Calvin, his wedding was big news around here."

She remembered the local media interviewing Calvin. She'd been around but hadn't said much. It was hard to answer questions when your life's narrative was filled with blanks.

Instead of being agreeable, she kept her guard up, remembering what Boyd had said. "How do we know you are who you say you are?"

There was one obvious way she could find out but wasn't ready to go that route yet.

"Damn," he said, but was smiling like he enjoyed this. "You never did take people at face value… For one thing, Owen will submit to a sibling DNA test. Believe me or not, he is your brother." It would be helpful to find out if Owen was indeed her brother, but it wouldn't prove Shane was her husband. "Why would I lie?"

He must have sensed she didn't buy it yet.

"I don't know," she said. "I… this is just so… unusual."

He gestured to the couch. "Why don't we sit down and I'll tell you everything you want to know."

"Everything?" she asked.

The swish of her gown as she turned toward the couch reminded her what she was wearing. A pointless garment given she wasn't going to get married and one she couldn't sit in. The dress even stifled her breathing, which was why she pressed her hands to her abdomen, trying to help her taxed lungs.

Shane was on his way to sit. "I'm an open book."

"Do you mind if I get changed?"

He shook his head after sitting on the couch and stretching his arms along the back of it. "Go right ahead."

The clothes she'd worn that morning were behind the screen to her left. Back there she'd be able to change concealed from his view. Except she couldn't get out of the dress alone. Awkward as it was to ask a stranger to undress her, there weren't any other options. If she called someone else in, she'd never get the chance to vet this man.

Going toward him, she turned her back and

pointed to the lace at her lower back. "Can you unlace me, please?"

Looking over her shoulder, she expected him to be shocked, but he wasn't.

One corner of his mouth curled upward. "Sure," he said and sat up to pull the lace at the bottom. "I'll even do it without touching you... I expect points for that."

But he was touching her, even if there was no skin-to-skin contact. She was asking him to do something intimate and although her heart was pumping, her head was too overwhelmed to read too much into it.

"There's a hook under the satin and the lace is—"

"I know," he said. "I took you out of the first one. I remember how it works."

Oh, right, that made sense if he was her husband. Course, he could be married to any woman. Helping someone remove their wedding dress didn't prove he'd married her and taken hers off. His gentleness surprised her, she'd have expected such a bold guy to be more ham-fisted, but he was delicate about freeing her.

"Thank you," she said when the bodice loosened.

"No worries," he said and sat back again.

Ginger went behind the screen to slip out of it. After tucking the gown back into the dress bag, she bent to retrieve her clothes from the bag put there for her essentials.

"You cut it fine, didn't you, Mr. Warren?" she asked. "When did you see the article?"

"It was published two days ago but hit our system yesterday. I'll be honest, Bit, this is further out than we'd expected you to be. You're a long way from home."

Home, wherever that was. "Have you never heard of a phone?"

"The picture in the article was small, although we

were sure it was you, we weren't a hundred percent. And I know how pissed I'd have been if someone stopped my wedding day on a whim. Anyway, Calvin isn't an easy guy to get on the phone and you're not listed."

"I live at the house with him and his mother, Diane," she called out, zipping her strapless dress beneath her arm. "You're right, it's not listed. I don't have a cell phone… who would call it?"

Coming around the screen, she tucked a ringlet behind her ear. When he saw her, he sat up, leaning forward with a look on his face that suggested he'd forgotten how to breathe.

"Damn, baby…"

So the simple short dress did more for him than the wedding dress? When she glanced down to try figuring out what got him so interested, she noticed the top of her garter belts peeking from beneath it. There she was trying to be more conservative and have a normal conversation and she'd just asked him to undress her then given him a glimpse of her lingerie.

Instead of being embarrassed, she laughed and relaxed further when he joined in. "I didn't mean to—"

"You're making it hard for me to keep my promise."

"Your promise?" she asked, wondering if he'd made some promise to her while they were together.

"About keeping my cock in my pants."

"Oh," she said and suddenly wasn't so amused anymore. "I'm not… I'm not comfortable talking about sex."

He got serious as he sat back. "Okay, but I figure you didn't ask to talk to me alone so we could discuss your phone number."

Shaking her head, she went over to join him on the couch. Luckily, it was long enough that she didn't have to sit too near to him.

"This is awkward," she whispered.

"Not awkward," he said and moved closer. When she tensed, he stopped and held up his hands in apology. "Bit, there's nothing you can ask me that I won't answer. I'll tell you anything it's in my power to tell you. We don't have to talk about sex, but if you want me to prove I am your husband… I can tell you that you have a freckle on your pussy, right at the edge of—"

She held up a quick finger at the same time her chin dropped again. "That's too much."

"Okay, you tell me what you want to know… Anything personal, you won't remember. Physically, I can tell you everything about your body… I can tell you that you make a little squeaking noise when you orgasm, is that easier?"

Much as she was mortified, a smile faded onto her lips. Ginger let herself peek up at him though she couldn't raise her chin. "Do you enjoy making me uncomfortable?"

Leaning in, he lowered his voice. "I don't mind seeing you blush."

"I'm not blushing," she argued, though knew it was a lie.

He held up his thumb and forefinger. "A little… just a tiny bit, Bit."

As she became more comfortable, her chin began to rise. "You could've started with the freckles on my feet."

"You don't have freckles on your feet… and that would prove I've seen you in strappy shoes."

"What about my breasts?"

His eyes dropped. Their obvious interest made her teeth seek her lip.

"Sure, we can talk about those," he said. "They're perfect… what else is there to say?"

Okay, talking about them wasn't any easier. Odd

but Ginger was more relaxed now that they were pushing boundaries. Although he was interested in her figure, he wasn't sitting close enough to intimidate or threaten and he wasn't leering.

They couldn't make jokes all day. Someone had to keep them on point.

"My doctors told me my memories might come back one day," she said. "They said I could talk about what I know, but… if anyone from my past came into my life, they said I shouldn't… that I shouldn't ask too many questions or hear too many stories. They said there was a risk of false memories."

He didn't argue her gear change, just listened. "So you can't ask questions and I can't offer information… Doesn't that make it hard for you to learn about where you came from?"

It was frustrating and confusing and exhausting. Her impulse was to run her hand through her hair so she could find a tendril to curl around her finger. Problem was, her wedding do was up and her hair was drenched in so much spray it was crispy. All she could do was brush her hairline with her fingertips.

"I don't know the rules here," she said.

He came an inch closer. "Bit, you and me were never very good at playing by the rules."

Reaching over, he took a ringlet from behind her ear and laid it over her finger like he knew she'd needed hair to play with.

"Thank you," she whispered, lost in his gaze.

"Giving you what you need," he said. "It's what I'm here for."

The door opened. Calvin came back in with his mother and the others who'd been outside the room. All of them paused when they saw her and Shane on the couch. Sitting close, his hand was suspended near hers, but there was nothing untoward going on.

"What's wrong with your faces?" Shane asked, maybe pissed off, his tone was certainly abrupt.

Murphy grinned and Owen leaned in to say something to him.

Calvin marched forward. "You took off your dress?"

Oh, that was why everyone was surprised.

Ginger smiled and stood up, pulling her dress down in an attempt to cover her garter belts. "I changed behind the screen," she said, pointing at it.

Diane approached behind her son, displeasure all over her expression. "You can't get out of that dress alone."

Murphy laughed. "I think you're safe. We were only out the room for five minutes. Sex between those two always took longer than that."

"I don't know," Owen said, folding his arms. "It's been sixteen months for him, at least. He probably went off like a rocket."

The two men laughed.

Embarrassed and terrified, her cheeks were aflame. "I didn't have sex," she said to Calvin, appealing to him as Diane and Boyd glared. "I promise you, I'm sorry I—"

"She's not on trial," Shane said. Although he was tense and probably meant well, his coming to her defense didn't help. "You trust your woman or you don't."

"And not to be blunt, but they're married… he has seen her naked before. They have been intimate, were intimate for years," Owen said. "Shane's clocked more miles on my sister than you have."

Wasn't that a lovely analogy? Ginger cringed, but it didn't matter, no one was looking at her anymore.

"Yes, but she doesn't remember it," Diane said. "So it never happened."

"Is that the rule around here?" Murphy asked.

"You don't remember, it didn't happen? Is that why you never encouraged her to find out the truth about who she was?"

Everyone started to talk again. There were too many strong opinions in the room; it got overwhelming fast. She didn't know what to do or how to handle the situation. There were still considerations that she hadn't even begun to deliberate yet.

Going to Calvin, Ginger took his hand, which calmed him enough to stop arguing with the others. "We can't stay in the church all day. Did you tell everyone to leave?"

"Yes, I did."

"And the reception? What should we do about that?"

For once, no one had anything to say.

Someone had to break the silence. "You paid for dinner for two hundred," Owen eventually said. "I don't think the staff would mind reducing that to a seven cover, right? We're not going away. Sitting down to dinner like civilized people seems to be the best course of action. We can make a plan… We don't want to turn this into a legal battle."

"Custody over a grown woman," Diane sneered. "Don't be ridiculous."

Squeezing Calvin's hand, Ginger wished she had him alone. He was always more pliable without his mother around. She just had to hope he was focused.

"Please," Ginger said. "We can't just forget this happened. Let's have dinner with them. Dinner can't hurt."

TWO

SHANE WAS AT the bar with Owen and Murphy. They had arrived at the country club ahead of Ginger's group and the possibility of being stood up still existed. It didn't matter if they didn't show, he'd found his wife and wouldn't let her go without a fight. If he had to track her down again, it would be easier to do with the narrower search area... and the confirmation she was alive.

Calvin Bishop had called ahead to the wedding reception venue, so the staff knew what to expect. Being the only three people to walk into a room set for three hundred was odd. Turned out more guests were invited to the dinner than the wedding. People were probably looking forward to being there for the celebration that his arrival had shot to shit.

They'd given staff permission to clean up the places that wouldn't be used. So the employees were scurrying around the room putting silverware and linens away while he and his posse drank at the bar.

"What do we do if they disappear?" Owen asked. "They could take Ginny out of the country."

"Then we leave the country," Murphy said. "We did it. We found her. We know she's alive. Do you think we would give up now?"

"No," Owen said. "But they have the means to take her anywhere."

"And we have the means to follow them," Murphy said. "We know who has her now."

Shane sipped his scotch and kept his eyes on the glass door. It opened onto a second-floor deck that acted as the main entrance to the function room they were in. Before they came inside, the Bishops and Ginger would have to park and ascend the stairs to the deck that wrapped around the upper floor.

Owen and Murphy carried on their conversation. Shane was listening, he was just more interested in anticipating his wife's arrival.

"Has her?" Owen said. "You say that like they kidnapped her."

"Didn't they?" Murphy asked. "She's been staying with them. This Calvin guy convinced her to marry him and she doesn't even know who she is. Who does that? You think if you found a woman at the side of the road you'd lock her in your parent's mansion and make her marry you?"

"You think he forced her?" Owen asked.

"I think he didn't try to heal her. He should've helped her find out who she was."

"At the side of the road," Owen muttered. "I hate that… reading that article gave me chills. It can't be right though, right? I mean how did she get from the ocean to a road two miles from shore? It makes no sense."

"None of this makes sense," Murphy said and hit Shane's shoulder. "What did she say when you were alone?"

Shane couldn't take his eyes from the door; he

was desperate to see her again. It felt odd to leave her with another man, to drive away from the church and wait there without her. He'd always taken care of her… until that night on the boat when he'd let her down. He'd promised himself that if he found her again, he'd never let her out of his sight.

But Ginger was adamant about him going ahead from the church without her. She said they would meet there and he'd believed her sincerity. She'd fought for them to have the dinner. Still, from the level of her obvious anxiety and how she'd avoided looking at him, he felt like she was hiding something. He couldn't begin to guess what it was and he didn't care. He'd accept her no matter what.

"I love her," Shane muttered.

"Did you think you didn't?" Owen asked.

Still, watching the door, waiting for her to come to him, Shane was consumed by her. She was all he thought about. All he had thought about since… as long as he'd known her. He couldn't lose her again. Being apart caused him pain, actual physical pain.

"I've always loved her," he said. "But today… I don't care who this Calvin guy is, I won't leave her."

"We wouldn't expect you to," Murphy said, patting his back in a consoling gesture.

The sound of a car engine approaching piqued his attention. Although they couldn't see the car, he closed his eyes, listening for it to go off. A second later there were footsteps ascending the stairs and then he saw her.

The bar where they were in the back corner had a lower ceiling than the rest of the space. The lighting was dim too, so although Calvin and the Boyd guy looked around inside, they didn't seem to notice the trio at the bar.

Outside, Calvin stopped his group to address his

mother and Boyd, leaving Ginger alone a few feet behind him.

"You see the way he turns his back to her," Shane muttered. "He shouldn't keep her out in the cold. They should've strategized in the car."

Owen and Murphy were enjoying their own drinks, but came into his periphery, signaling they were intent on those on the outside deck too.

"She looks nervous," Owen said. "Look at the way she's twisting her own wrist."

"You think he makes her nervous?" Murphy asked.

"I think this whole thing makes her nervous. Remember, we're being discreet. We're not going to overwhelm her," Shane said, registering Ginger's isolation. "He should be comforting her. He shouldn't leave her standing there on her own."

She was in the corner of the deck, three feet away from the huddled group. Her eyes darted around as she curled her hand around her wrist and shifted her feet. She was cold. She was anxious. And she was alone.

"She looks small," Owen said.

She did and it pissed Shane off as much as it hurt him. "She said she doesn't like to be touched."

Murphy scoffed. "You two could never keep your hands off each other."

"Have you noticed that he doesn't touch her? They hold hands, but that's it. He doesn't put an arm around her, doesn't touch her arm, or her body," Shane said, analyzing what he was witnessing.

"Are you complaining?" Murphy asked. "You used to hate any guy touching her, even me or Owen. You were always selfish with her."

He was and had no intention of changing that. Throwing the rest of his liquor into his throat, he slammed the glass onto the bar and wiped his mouth with the back of his hand.

"I'm going to get her."

Owen caught his arm and his attention. "They'll argue she's not yours to get."

That truth infuriated him. He whirled around to aim that rage at the wrong person. "If he was doing his job, I wouldn't have to do it for him!" he said. Owen was stunned. Damn, Shane knew he shouldn't be taking out his stress on his friend. Pulling his arm away, he slapped a hand onto Owen's shoulder to lean down and look him in the eye. "I looked you in the eye like this on the day I married your sister. I told you I would never let anything bad happen to her. I promised you. Remember?"

"Yeah."

"I failed… It doesn't matter how many times I say I'm sorry, it means shit. I'm going to spend my life making it up to her… and to you… Until she tells me to go to hell, I'll be on her… I'd give my life for hers, you know that, right?"

Owen nodded.

Murphy nudged them both. "My brother the romantic… who knew?"

"Ginny knew," Owen said, but Shane barely heard him because he was heading for the door.

Before he got there, Calvin came inside with everyone else in his wake.

"Okay, we're going to sit down and talk," Calvin said.

"Yeah," Shane said, noticing how Ginger's head was down, though she kept stealing glances at him. She had to be curious. He couldn't imagine how terrifying it must be for her not to have a clue who she was or what she'd been through. Yet, there he was, stomping into her life with her brother and his, telling her he was her lover. "That's why we're here."

"We've called a specialist doctor for Claire,"

Calvin said. "He's the best. He's going to meet us at his offices tomorrow."

"Tomorrow," Shane said and chose to look at his wife instead of the guy doing his best to keep her in the background. "Bit, if you want docs here now, I'll get you docs here now."

"You can talk to me," Calvin said. "And stop calling her Bit, she's not your Bit anymore."

It was habit. Shane would stop as soon as Ginny told him to, not a minute before. "Ginger, do you want medical help?"

"I said you should talk to me," Calvin said, crowding in closer.

Shane wasn't known for keeping his cool when pressed. He'd had an even tougher time holding onto his temper since he'd been without Ginger. His wife always knew how to calm him down. This guy was asking for it, standing between him and the woman he loved. Shane had never let anyone do that. No one ever dared stand between him and Ginger. It just never happened; he didn't like that he might have to get used to it.

"And I'm asking my wife if she wants medical help, what's wrong with that?"

"Don't call her your wife," Calvin snapped.

Murphy came in closer, angling his shoulder in front of Shane's. He knew his brother and everyone had to be sensing the tension.

"Please," Ginger said. The gentle tone, that she couldn't know she'd used to calm him before, was immediately soothing. "I'm asking a lot of all of you, I know. I could decide to forget my past and ask you gentlemen to leave."

"Ask away, Bit," Shane said. "Won't make me walk out that door."

Curiosity seeped into her gaze and it wasn't broken even when Calvin blustered. "Uh, we'll call the police if you think about outstaying your welcome."

Shane sensed a shift in her mood when she next spoke. "I could also accept that I should belong with my brother and my husband and leave with them now. Relieving those in my current life of the burden of caring for me."

Oh yes, there was his Ginger. Although he tried to restrain it, his lips contorted to a smile. Nothing would make him happier than if she asked him to take her home. And he'd just like to see this Calvin guy try to get in his way.

"You would never do that," Calvin said and tugged her hand to get her attention back on him. "Would you, dearest?"

Shane scrutinized the look they exchanged. Yes, there was something in that. If Ginger was hiding something from him, Calvin knew what it was.

"Should we sit?" Owen asked, doing his own bit to diffuse the tension.

The circular table had been set for seven. Calvin took Ginger over to seat her at the table between him and his mother. That was fine with Shane because he was directly opposite her and could catch every one of the glances she stole at him. She might not want him to notice, but he did. He wanted her to notice him, wanted her to look her fill.

Wine was poured for everyone at the table, starting with Calvin.

When the server got to Ginger, she put her hand over the top of the glass. "No thank you," she said and the server left.

Ginger picked up the water jug to pour some out for herself.

"Do you want something else to drink?" Shane asked, wondering why Calvin hadn't offered. "You still like rum and coke?"

"Oh no, I…" There again was that look exchanged between her and Calvin. And Diane, his mother shook her head behind Ginger's back. "I don't drink."

"At all?" Shane asked.

Owen laughed. "Since when?"

"Since… ever," Ginger said. "I don't drink. Is that a problem?"

Shane shook his head and Owen curled his lip to silence his amusement. "Nope… just never figured my sister as a teetotaler."

Maybe that was the secret. Calvin seemed to have a lot of control over Ginger and Shane didn't like it. Control could mean intimidation. It could mean violence. Shane had been rough with his girl when it aroused her, but if he found out this guy was touching Ginger in anger, he'd take him apart.

"What's the point of this meal?" Boyd asked, impatient as the first course was served. "We're all here, someone should start."

Ginger cleared her throat, yet it was Calvin who spoke. "We want to know what happened. What happened the last time you saw Claire?"

Shane would answer all of Ginger's questions, but he wanted to be sure it was what she wanted.

"How does this fit in with what your doctors told you?" he asked his wife.

She shrugged. "It's a stalemate. If I can't ask and you can't tell, how will I ever learn anything?"

He looked at Owen and at Murphy. They didn't want to be used for information and then cut out. But they already had their next appointment lined up with the doctor the following day. That was some reassurance at least.

"We were on a cruise," Shane said. "Some buddies had just made a bunch of cash, so we were taking a yacht out onto the water for a few days. On the second night, we hit weather, the boat sank."

So simple when he put it out there like that. A cruise. A sinking. Easy? Not really. If it was that easy, why were they still trying to recover nearly a year and a half later?

"And?" Calvin asked. "You abandoned her out there?"

Shane shouldn't be surprised that the prick was quick to call him out. It was his fault, at least, that was how he saw it.

"Shane was out there longer than anyone," Owen said, defending him. "Ten were airlifted, four bodies were found and Ginny... she was just missing."

"Your turn," Murphy snapped. "Where'd you pick her up? The article online that brought us here said you found her at the side of the road... that can't be right, she was in the water."

"It is," Calvin said, drinking his wine. "I was driving a back road from an associate's cabin and there she was, at the side of the road. I thought at first that she'd been hit by a car. She was unconscious and I got her to hospital. Claire was in the hospital for a couple of months with complications, after that we agreed to take care of her."

Ginger wasn't eating. She was stroking the end of her ringlet between her forefinger and thumb, a sure sign she was anxious.

"What's the last thing you remember, sis?" Owen asked, gently easing her into what they wanted to know.

"We don't talk about that," Calvin said. "Let's talk about you, you said you're a lawyer, are you with a firm?"

"Yes," Owen said. "And you own a chemical company that made you a couple of million last year, right?"

Good on Owen not giving away too much. They had to play this Calvin guy because he wouldn't hesitate to play them. Ginger was still toying with her hair until Diane caught him looking at her with concern. Diane nudged Ginger and whispered something, apparently instructing her to eat.

"And what is it you do, Mr. Warren?" Calvin asked after spouting off some figures to Owen.

"I write," he muttered.

"Write what?" Calvin sneered. "Books?"

"Yeah, sure," he said and sat up straighter to lean over the table. "Ginger, have you spoken to anyone about your memories?"

"The doctors at the hospital were very good," Calvin said. "But we took her to a private facility and brought in our own professionals very quickly. Their treatment was exemplary."

And directed by Calvin and his wallet. Shane couldn't blame the guy for falling for Ginny or for wanting to keep her for himself. Oddly, instead of anger or jealousy, his next pang was pity. Ginger would be returning home with him. She'd fallen in love with him once. Shane was confident that if he could get close to her, get her alone, maybe reawaken her memory, that she would be his again. No matter what, he planned to win the war, even if it meant forfeiting a few battles.

"I don't doubt that," Shane said. "You look healthy… How's your blood pressure?"

The question shocked not only Ginny, but the others at the table too. "Low," she whispered. "How do you know that?"

"You always had a problem with low blood pressure. Your mom and grandmother had it too," he said. "I'm glad you're keeping an eye on it."

"It's just a shame you didn't know that when she was in the hospital initially," Owen said. "It might have given the doctors a false impression of her condition."

"I don't want finger pointing," Ginger said, squirming in her chair. "I hate that this is awkward."

Guilt. She was coping with guilt and still Calvin did nothing to comfort her.

"You didn't do this," Shane said. "To any of us… You didn't ask for the accident or the amnesia. No one here blames you… You didn't ask me, Owen, and Murphy to show up either. We all make our own choices in life."

"Thank you for the pop psychology," Calvin muttered and returned to his food. "Everyone eat."

THREE

THEY FINISHED THE next course in silence and then spent the rest of the meal listening to Calvin talk about his business and his family. Ginger could tell that the new men in her life weren't impressed, but she'd asked Calvin to make sure there was no pressure on her to rush into a confession.

Although she didn't want any resentment between these men, it was important to take her time and do things right. That meant Calvin had to take the lead, at least at that initial dinner. Talking about himself was great cover, which provided her with some time to adjust to the developments.

After exchanging numbers and cards, they'd all gone their separate ways.

She didn't sleep well but did eventually drift off. For a brief few seconds after waking up, Ginger believed her past chasing her down had been a dream. It didn't take long to realize that it wasn't. If it had been, she'd be wearing a wedding ring and departing for her honeymoon.

Instead of jetting into the sun, they ended up seated in a doctor's office. Since the introductions, Doctor Guinness hadn't said much and he wasn't an easy man to read. In a group with Calvin, Diane, Shane and Owen, the doctor had instructed them to attempt to identify with each other. To bond. Murphy and Boyd were asked to wait outside in the waiting room; she hoped they wouldn't come to blows without supervision.

Doctor Guinness had done well to ensure there was little pressure on her. In fact, his first question had been about sharing early memories and he made everyone in the group, except her, share their earliest memory. It surprised her how open everyone was to helping her and to doing what the doctor asked even in front of strangers as most of them were to each other.

With their stories finished, all eyes had just fallen onto her.

"Your situation is different, you won't have memories of growing up," Doctor Guinness said, "but do you think you could try, could you tell us about your earliest memory?"

"I have pictures of childhood," she said, folding her hands in her lap. "I get pieces that I can't put together. I don't know if they're memories or just something I've made up in my subconscious."

"Yes, that does sometimes happen," Doctor Guinness said. "What about the day you met Calvin? The day we'll call the start of your new life… What do you remember about that day?"

"Uh, Doctor, is this a good idea?" Calvin asked. "We don't want to damage her psychologically."

Doctor Guinness was concise, unlike some of the other doctors she'd met. "We still haven't established whether her amnesia is psychological or physiological," the doctor said. "You've waited long enough, Mr. Bishop and… I don't mean to be blunt, but technically… Mr.

Warren is her next of kin. The marriage certificate has been verified, correct?"

Yes, the lawyers had confirmed the marriage that morning.

"Yes," Calvin mumbled.

"So if our patient is willing and Mr. Warren consents, there's no reason not to help her probe into her memories."

She looked at Shane, who was looking at her, he seemed to do that a lot. "If you're okay, Bit, I'm okay," he said. She'd followed Calvin's advice and tried to give the memories time to come back on their own. They hadn't yet, so she was willing to try something else. "But if you're not sure, we'll shut these bastards down, no hesitation."

He was always so quick to make sure she knew her options and that he supported her choices. Every time he swore, Diane bristled. The reaction was comical.

"I remember pieces of that day," Ginger said without second-guessing herself for not breaking eye contact with Shane.

"You can work backwards," Guinness said. "If it's easier... do you remember the road?"

"I remember emotions," she said. "I remember relief when I heard cars... I was in the woods, I was... I remember voices and my feet hurt but most of all I remember..."

"You remember what?" Guinness asked.

Ginger kept her gaze on Shane's. "I remember the cold... I remember being so cold I thought... I thought I'd never move again... I was... exhausted and so cold..."

"That was probably from the water," Guinness said, "if you were indeed in this yacht sinking."

"I don't remember water, I just remember... I remember being scared like... like I needed to do something or that I'd forgotten something… It's all a jumble."

"That's okay," Guinness said when her head fell into her hands. "It's progress; this is part of a process. One that we hope to begin intensively now that you're prepared and we've had this… development." He looked at his watch. "That's been more than an hour and I have work to do. But I wonder… could I have a moment alone with Owen and with Claire? Excuse me, with Ginger… It will help everyone process if we begin to use Ginger's real name."

It would be weird, but no weirder than learning to respond to Claire. A name change was probably one of the least weird things she'd had to endure. Sixteen months ago, she'd had to learn a new identity. Doing it again wouldn't be too big a deal. No doubt it would be harder for everyone else as they hadn't been through the same process.

After they were all gone and the door was closed, she and her brother turned to the doctor again.

"What can we help you with?" Owen asked, moving over to sit beside her.

So far, she liked her brother. He was warm and charming, though a bit goofy, in the most endearing way.

"I want to discuss family medical history," Guinness said. Owen nodded. "I would also like to discuss the next step of Ginger's treatment. It's unorthodox, but I hope you'll support it."

"Anything," Owen said.

***

OWEN HAD BEEN ALONE in the doctor's office with Ginger for a half hour. Sitting next to Murphy with Calvin and Boyd on the perpendicular couch, Shane was getting edgy. Diane had gone off to some luncheon after pressuring her son about something. He didn't know what. He didn't care.

Boyd and Calvin had been whispering since they came out. No doubt Calvin was updating his buddy on what had happened. They'd been throwing dirty looks his way for a while and it was pissing him off.

"If you've got something to say, Bishop, say it," Shane said.

Beside him, Murphy looked up from his magazine.

"Nothing to say to you," Calvin said. "We're making plans for Claire. For what's best for her."

"Didn't you hear the doctor in there?" Shane asked. "Her name is Ginger."

"Yes, well, we're considering a change of doctor."

Tempering himself, he rolled his lips and shifted to the edge of the couch. "Listen, buddy, I know this is tough on you. I'm a guy who came from nowhere and told you I'm gonna take your woman away. You're allowed to be pissed at me. Don't let that affect Ginny's treatment."

"Take her away?" Calvin said, straightening his pants as he stood up. "You're not taking her anywhere."

Oh, so he wanted a pissing contest. Shane stood up, always game to stake a claim on his wife. "That's for her to decide when she's feeling better."

Calvin looked down his nose. "Like I said, we're going to get a new doctor… And Boyd is already working on proxy documents."

"Excuse me?" Shane asked, raising his brows.

"You might be her husband on paper, but you're not in practice. We'll have power of attorney documents written up for Claire to sign allowing me to make medical decisions."

Working his jaw, it was getting hard to hold onto

his temper. "I don't fucking think so."

"Why is it you have to curse?" Calvin sneered. "You don't know how to express yourself? Is that it?"

"Oh I can express myself," Shane said, squaring up when Calvin tried to bulk up.

If he wanted a fight, Shane would give him one.

"Whoa, guys, let's talk about this," Murphy said.

If he wasn't so angry, the idea of his brother being a rational voice would amuse him. As it was, with the adrenaline flowing, he was ignored.

"Yes, and how is that?" Calvin asked, shoving him. "With your fists?"

He couldn't lose his temper, couldn't punch the bastard in the face like he deserved. At least, that was what he told himself until Calvin shoved him again. Shane grabbed the guy's lapel, hauled him to the tips of his toes and ignored Murphy leaping to his feet behind him.

Pulling back his fist, Shane inhaled, ready to smack the smugness from Calvin's sneer.

Then he heard Ginger's gasp at the other side of the room. "No! Boo, don't hit him!"

The room stopped.

Still with a hold of Calvin, Shane turned his head to see her next to the doctor with Owen behind her, tense, her hands covering her mouth.

"What did you call him?" Calvin said, shoving away from him.

Shane's heart was in his throat. "You called me Boo," he exhaled. "It's been sixteen months since you called me that."

Ginger was gaping when her hands dropped. "I... I didn't think about it..." she stuttered. Owen hugged her from behind. "It was... instinct."

"Good instinct," Shane grinned, feeling like he'd just won the Superbowl.

He wanted to go to her, but Murphy was in the way.

She was blushing again and didn't seem eager to focus on the significance of what had just happened. "Doctor Guinness has suggested intensive therapy," she said, licking her lips. "There's a hotel... a lodge that allows prolonged retreats. He says it will help my memory and to integrate my lives if we go up there... He will clear his schedule and join us... he says he'll offer payments—"

"And I said we'd cover it if it was what she wanted," Owen said, eyeing him.

Taking the signal, he jumped on to reassuring his wife. "Yes," Shane said. "Sure, baby, anything you want."

"Don't call her baby," Calvin said, stomping over to her. "You want to go to this lodge place?"

"We had time off for our honeymoon anyway," she squirmed, giving Shane another clue that this bastard might use his hands to hurt her. "I would like it if we could do this... all of us together."

Calvin leaned close to her. Shane lurched forward, ready to shove Murphy out the way if he needed to get between Ginger and that bastard she called a fiancé.

Instead of hissing or shouting, Calvin spoke in a whisper. "What about..."

"I have to deal with it today... I can't put it off any longer," she said.

Although she was back to being nervous, Owen was grinning, which confused the hell out of him.

"You're in for the shock of your life, buddy," Owen said.

Ginger jabbed an elbow back into her brother, momentarily distracting him with the casual sibling banter. That was what he wanted to see, Ginger getting back to normal.

"I don't think it's a good idea," Calvin said. "We don't even know for sure if—"

"I know we don't," Ginger said. "I know that. But it's best to do it now, in the hospital... If I keep hiding it, it becomes a secret... I don't like secrets."

Although clearly pissed as hell, Calvin backed off to allow her space to walk past him.

Shane was too confused to focus on that, Ginger was all he could see. "What's wrong?"

She was clearly nervous, her face was pale and her hands shaking. "Before you decide if you want to come to the cabin, before you decide if you want to help me..."

"Yeah?" Shane asked. "I want to help you. I already know that."

"Before you commit," she said. He'd already married her, they couldn't get much more committed as far as he was concerned. "I need to show you something."

"Show me something?"

She nodded and took his hand. Everything else vanished. She'd just touched him of her own accord. He'd forgotten how small her hand was in his. As long as they were touching, he was ready, for whatever terrible thing she was about to confess.

FOUR

WHILE LEADING HIM to the third floor, Ginger did consider getting deliberately lost even though she knew the route. Putting it off wouldn't help. There was no getting away from what had to be done. Unless she sent Shane away. But she couldn't do that, not yet. It wouldn't be fair and he deserved a chance.

Pushing into an office, Ginger smiled at the woman behind the high desk. "How was he?" she asked.

The woman at the other side of the desk stood up. "Oh, just great," she said. "He hasn't had his banana yet. He was just having too much fun to sit still."

"That's okay," Ginger said and glanced at a frowning Shane.

She signed the book and took him through the door at the back of the room that led into a large soft play area. The floor was padded and there were tunnels and chutes, everything one would expect in a nursery.

"What are we doing in here?" Shane asked, leaning to whisper above her ear.

One of the minders came over. "Oh, you're

back," she said, disappointed until she noticed Shane. "You want the family room?"

Ginger nodded. "Wait here a second," she said to Shane and opened the small gate that kept the kids away from the door to the office. Except there were no kids there. None except the one she couldn't see.

"You're here for a kid?" Shane asked. "There are no kids here."

"He has a thing for tunnels," she murmured and headed for the tunnel a few feet away. She dropped down to her hands and knees, as soon as she poked her head inside, the kid hiding there shrieked and scrambled toward her. He smacked both hands on her cheeks. "Come on, darling."

Picking him up, Ginger was pleased that the minder handed her the diaper bag and pointed to a door in the corner. "His stroller is in there."

Shane was fixated on them. He had to have figured it out, surely. She nodded toward the office and carried the boy into the family room, hoping that Shane would follow. Sitting on the central couch in front of a low table, she kissed her boy's plump cheek and put him on his feet so he could stand on the seat and lean against the back of the couch.

Shane swallowed hard and closed the door before he approached. "Is that... Is... Is he..."

"Shane Warren," she said, straightening her son's sweater. "Meet my son, Cameron... and unless you were lying about the sex or I was cheating on you... your son."

Now it was his turn to gape, Shane stumbled over and dropped onto the couch beside them, staring at the child.

She leaned in to kiss the back of Cammy's head. "Angel, meet Daddy."

Cammy dropped onto her lap and kicked his legs then he crawled over to bop his father's knee.

"Ma, ma, ma!" Cam called out.

"No," she said, "Da da."

It was supposed to be an easier sound, so she figured he would pick it up quickly. He was always good with language and understanding. Ginger believed he was smart, but also acknowledged her bias.

"Da!" he hollered then climbed over Shane's legs and onto the floor.

Cammy crawled to the corner where he knew he'd find toys.

"He's my son," Shane exhaled.

She nodded, braced for his next reaction. At that moment, stunned was still winning out.

"You didn't know I was pregnant?" He was shaking his head, slowly, staring wide-eyed at the child who was banging thick wooden jigsaw pieces together. "I always wondered if I knew before... if I'd told the father before."

"I had no idea," he said and spun to face her. "How old is he?"

"Almost ten months," she answered. "I must have only been a couple of months pregnant when the accident happened... It's amazing that I didn't lose him."

"Fuck," he whispered.

Ginger dropped a light fist to his knee, not unlike what Cam had done. "Don't swear in front of him."

"Sorry," he said, appearing contrite.

Jumping to Cam's defense was instinct, but she had to be humble about this situation too. "I can't make any guarantees, because I have no memory of his conception. If he's not yours, I'm sorry, but..."

"He's mine," Shane said, pulling her hand up to his mouth. As he kissed her knuckles a grin burst to his lips. "There's no fucking way you were screwing around and we were screwing a lot."

She hit his leg again. "No swearing, Mr. Warren."

"You better start calling me Shane damn soon," he said. "And I'm sorry. I swear more when I'm in shock."

She smiled. "I'm getting that." They shared a moment. Their hands were joined. For the first time, Ginger experienced the warmth and security of his grasp. "You don't have any responsibility to him… I mean, don't think I'm introducing you so I can hit you up for child support or anything… it's just… I'm very particular about being separated from him, in fact, I hate it. So, if we do go to this retreat, he'll be coming with me."

His grin got wider as Cam crawled over and used the couch between them to pull himself onto his feet. Cam handed her a jigsaw piece.

Shane hesitated with a hand above his head.

"It's okay," she said, pushing his hand onto Cam's head.

Shane exhaled and ruffled his hair. "Hey, kid… I'm your daddy."

Cam gave Shane the other jigsaw piece and started to bounce.

"He's a really physical boy," she said. "Sometimes I can't keep up… he's desperate to get on his feet. He crawls around the place like a crazy guy."

"I can't wait to… to get to know him."

"He loves fruit, can't get enough of it and he likes to be moving… that's about all you need to know."

Cam dropped to crawl away again. Always on the move.

Shane looked at her. "Can I… Can I…"

"Play with him?" she asked and laughed as she sat back. "Course you can, but I'm not responsible for any bruises."

"Babe… I…" he said.

It was amazing to see how he glowed even though he was lost for words.

Nodding, she smiled too. "Go on… daddy."

Shane dropped onto his hands and knees and chased Cam to the toy box. Instead of stopping, Cam kept going, shrieking and laughing as Shane chased him. He only paused to turn and crawl underneath him. The boys roughhoused for a while and she watched, amazed at what a relief it was to see father accept son.

She'd still ask him for paternity, just in case. That was what she'd meant upstairs about telling Shane in a hospital, where there were needles and people who could do the tests. But she couldn't lie about her child, not when he was her reason for being.

Her link to her past.

Cam was the boy who'd made the journey with her. He'd been with her all the way, her focus and kept her going through the darkest of times. Being pregnant had made her recovery more difficult, but there wasn't a chance she would give up on the child who had, in so many ways, saved her life.

Watching the boys play, she relaxed on seeing no awkwardness between them. Trust Cammy to just accept everything that was going on. The adults were awkward and uncomfortable while learning each other, Cameron somehow recognized his father. Ginger already knew that the paternity would be positive. They smiled the same, laughed the same, moved the same.

Cameron was her litmus test. If he accepted Shane, then it was her job to do the same.

FIVE

GINGER LET THEM play for another half hour and absorbed every second of the bonding. Despite being largely ignored, she loved it. Cameron was shrieking as Shane tossed him in the air then dropped to roll onto his back to blow raspberries on the baby's belly.

Cameron was red-faced, struggling to take a deep breath because he was laughing so hard. She couldn't blame him, witnessing their joy made her laugh too.

It was getting late; they wouldn't have much more time. Sliding off the couch, she crawled around to the other side of the low coffee table and retrieved the diaper bag from under it. Opening it up, she got out a bowl and pulled a banana from the bunch. She mashed up the fruit, preparing it for her boy, then held the bowl up.

"Okay, mommy has to be a spoil sport," she said. Shane tipped his head all the way back to look at her. "He needs his snack."

"Snack, buddy," Shane said like it was the most exciting prospect in the world. "Let's go get a snack."

He grabbed Cam's waist and flipped over,

helping the boy to walk on his own feet over to the table. When he was there, Cam leaned against the edge. Shane lay down on his side, propped on an elbow, behind Cam, with his elbow almost touching her thigh.

"Thank you," she said as she spooned some banana mix into Cameron's mouth.

"Hey, snack is important," Shane said, picking fluff from Cam's jeans.

"No," she said and smiled out a laugh. "Thank you for accepting him. If he turns out not to be yours—"

"Hey," he said, and sat up beside her, still behind Cam. "He's mine."

"I don't have any memory of—"

He smirked. "You might not believe this now, but we were in love and we had a lot of sex."

She didn't need to be reminded of that because it made her blush again. Cameron ate more banana then dropped onto his butt to crawl under the table and stick his face into the diaper bag.

"Still," she said, pulling down Cam's top so it met his jeans. "I guess we can't know for sure unless—"

"You want to do paternity?" he asked. Biting her lip, she nodded, trying her best to apologize in her wince. "No problem." Cupping her jaw, he smiled. "I told you. If it's in my power to give you it, I will. Don't ever worry about asking me for anything."

"Thank you," she whispered so quietly the words almost didn't come out.

Cam spun around and thrust an arm in the air. "Raaa!" he screamed, throwing his stuffed lion at his father.

Shane screamed appropriately and fell to his back to wrestle with the lion against his neck like he was being mauled. It was funny to see such a big guy at the mercy of something so tiny. But he was a pro and kept fighting the beast as Cam crawled on top of him. Shane managed to balance the baby, caring for him and supporting him, while entertaining him.

Cam bounced on Shane's chest and made more roaring noises. But she picked him up to nestle the baby in her crossed legs.

"Let's give daddy a break, Cam," Ginger said because she had only been half-joking about bruises.

"Raa!" Cam said, holding the lion over his head to his mother.

"Yes, Angel... does Raa want some banana?" she asked and pretended to feed the lion before giving Cam some more. "You're very good with him... I guess I should ask... do you have other children? Do... Do we have other kids?"

"No," he said. "No other kids for either of us, together or apart. Cameron is our first."

But not our last. Maybe she made up that last part, the possibility just seemed to hang in the air unsaid.

Trying to move on, Ginger shifted again. "Were we trying?"

"Not actively, though I guess you could say we were actively practicing." He did enjoy trying to make her blush. "We weren't... not trying either... What's his last name?"

Oh, that was probably a big deal to him. Not knowing her married name brought on the guilt, although there was no way she could have known it.

"I was Jane Doe in hospital for a while When you have no name they go generic, so it's Smith, like I am... I was... I don't know what I am now."

"Cameron Smith," he said and seemed relieved though she didn't know why.

As was his way, Cameron interrupted the moment before she could ask for an explanation.

"Da. Ba," Cam said, pointing to the bunch of

bananas on the table then at his father.

"Does Daddy get a banana?" she asked. Cam climbed up to pull at the bananas, she helped him pull one from the bunch, but left it on the table. "We don't know if Daddy likes bananas."

Cam didn't give him much of a choice, he thrust it at his mother and tugged at the top. "Op. Op, mama."

Peeling the banana for her child, she knew it didn't matter if it ended up in the trash. The moment was important for bonding. She was about to hand it back to Cam when her baby pushed her hand toward Shane, who was sitting up again.

Cam's frown was so cute, he was just so serious. "Dada."

Shane leaned forward and bit the top off the banana she was holding. Now she was feeding both boys. There was something far more intense about feeding the larger one, especially when he pinned her under his gaze.

Cam shrieked and clapped, then climbed off her lap to go back to the diaper bag.

"I'm sorry, he's… bossy," she said, her tongue drying when Shane guided her hand close for another bite.

Their son wasn't watching anymore, so she didn't need to feed him.

Still, Shane followed orders. "It used to be I only had to follow your orders," he said. "Now I have to follow his orders too."

She didn't know if that was a complaint or an insult, and frowned, while Shane smiled.

"He's easy to distract," she said. "If he asks too much, just find Raa. The lion is his favorite."

"So far he seems to be doing me a favor," Shane said.

She noticed her son wrestling with a box of raisins.

"Mommy do it," she said and put the banana aside to take the raisin box from Cam to open it.

Tipping the contents into the banana mix, she stirred it up and added a little more milk before mixing again and feeding Cam some.

"He likes that," Shane said.

Cameron ate more then sat in her crossed legs again to pull the bowl down so he could pick out the raisins with his fingers. He ate one. Then another.

"He's a great eater," she said. "And he loves his fruit… He's not so good with vegetables, unless you mush them up. He'll eat just about anything if it's mushed."

"You've done an amazing job," Shane said, leaning closer to run his fingers through Cameron's hair.

Their boy kept picking raisins, happy and content. Ginger wasn't so settled. She couldn't breathe. She'd never been as close to Shane before. The heat of his whole body was scorching hers.

"Da," Cam said, holding up a slimy raisin between his fingers while he examined the mush for another.

"Is that for me?" Shane asked.

"Daddy doesn't want that," Ginger said and tried to push her son's hand back down, but Shane closed his hand around hers on Cam's arm. All three of them connected for the first time, skin to skin. "It's mixed with my milk."

That admission was mortifying. If he hadn't been put off by Cameron's slimy hands, that truth should deter him.

Except the corner of his lips curled and his eyes darkened as he bowed to close his mouth around Cameron's fingers, sucking the raisin free. Their son went back to his food as soon as Shane let him go, but she couldn't tear her eyes from his.

Her heart was pounding in her chest. "Oh God," she exhaled.

"I've tasted every other part of you," he murmured.

Something was happening. Something between them or something to her, she couldn't figure it out. But there was something compelling her heart to speed up while the rest of her loosened. It was disconcerting in its peculiarity.

"Shane," she whispered. "I don't remember being with you."

"Doesn't matter," he said and kept his tone low making her feel even more exposed. "You don't get it… I don't want you to act on how you used to feel. I want you to act on how you feel now, in the present… and in the future."

"How do I do that?" she asked, begged almost. That was the first time she'd asked for honest advice. "I'm so confused… I'm so scared."

"Baby, I'm here," he said, cupping her jaw again, he leaned in. Not to kiss her, he kept on going and bowed to kiss Cam's head. "Neither of you will ever have to be scared again."

He was so convincing, he really believed it.

Ginger smiled. "You're a real alpha daddy, aren't you?"

"Think so," he said, watching Cam stand up and hand off the banana bowl to his mother.

She scraped the bottom and fed him the last of it while he retrieved the banana on the table for his father, all without letting go of her.

"I'm good at doing what I'm told," she said as Cam pushed the banana to his father's lips. Shane took a bite. Cam tried to follow, except the skin was too high, so father took the fruit to peel back the skin. "Cam's not so good at following orders."

"A rebel," Shane said. His mouth full, he shared more of the fruit with his son. "I like it… You never used to be good at doing what you were told either, momma."

Cam bopped Shane's shoulder and Shane prodded a finger into him.

Ginger laughed at the outrage on Cam's face. "I guess I am now."

Shane pulled Cam forward to hug him and prevent further injury. Cam fought for a minute, but quickly changed tack and climbed up over his father's shoulder, with a boost.

"Can I ask you something that's not meant to be judgment or anger?"

"Oh God," she said, tidying up their mess and pulling baby wipes from her bag. Cam got free and picked up the banana. When she caught him to wipe his face, he whined and fussed. "What?"

"Has he ever put his hands on you… in anger?"

"Cameron?" she asked, switching the banana from one baby hand to the other.

"No… Calvin. Has he ever hit you?"

The implication was so shocking that she gasped. "No, of course not. Why would you think that?"

Ginger focused on her son to ignore Shane's assessment of her.

"Sometimes you seem… afraid of him," he said.

Shaking her head, she was trying not to be offended. "He's been good to me, Shane. Very good to me. You might not understand it, but… he accepted me when I had no one. He was there when the doctors told me about Cam. He was there with me when I told them I wouldn't terminate even if it meant killing me. He supported me in everything… I'm not afraid of him, I… I need his guidance."

"You defer to him," Shane said.

Ginger didn't like that he seemed angry about it.

"Please," she said, shifting over an inch. "Be grateful to him, don't be angry with him."

"I am," Shane said.

Though he smiled, she wasn't sure it was genuine. Cam popped up between them and shoved the last of the banana at his father, smudging it over his face.

Cam thought it was hilarious, she wasn't immune to the picture they created either. Although she tried to restrain it, a laugh escaped her. Shane roared and grabbed up the boy to smack a kiss to his face, sharing the mess of banana. It was up to her to pull them apart.

Laughing, Ginger wiped off Cam's face. "You two encourage each other already," she said.

Cam wriggled free "Mama!"

Ginger turned to wipe the banana from Shane's face too.

It was automatic. She hadn't meant to be forward, it just… happened. Her wiping slowed. Her hand was on his face, touching him. In the cocoon between his body and the straight arm he was leaning on, she was closer to him than she could ever remember being.

"Sorry," she whispered, lowering her gaze and folding the baby wipe over and over.

"You're blushing again," he murmured, hooking a finger beneath her chin to lift her eyes. "Don't hide your eyes, baby. Don't be afraid to look at me."

"You intimidate me," she said, provoking a flash of hurt contrition to cross his gaze. "Not on purpose, I… I can't imagine myself with a man like you… I don't know how I handled you."

"You were the only one who could, Bit," he said. She wasn't sure how to respond. Cam chose that moment to grab Shane's leg and climb into his lap. "Yo, Cam, don't you think mommy deserves a kiss too?"

Horror and intrigue collided, flaring her eyelids.

It was too much too soon.

"Don't," she croaked.

His expression remained patient while he examined her. "When you're ready… you take from me what you want, any time, and if you want me to take action…"

"Let's be patient," she said, resting a hand on his shoulder. "I may never be ready."

He didn't seem to accept that, but smiled like it was an interesting idea.

Shane picked up their boy and held him between them. "Cam can take care of the mommy kisses in the meantime," he said.

"He hates mommy kisses," she said and pressed a hard kiss to Cam's cheek.

On cue, he grumbled and pushed her away. Ginger just laughed; she was used to his attitude.

"Oh, man, kid, you're crazy. Mommy's kisses are the best kisses," he said, leaning in to whisper the second sentence into their son's ear.

She was probably blushing again. "I guess mommy is too needy," she said without averting her gaze. "I get all my affection from him." Running her fingers into Cam's hair, she brushed her lips on his ear. Sometimes Cam got annoyed when she kissed him during play time. Sleepy time was a whole other ballgame. At bedtime, he was like a limpet, so it all balanced out. "He's been my cuddly bear every time I felt sad or lost. Sometimes he's okay with mommy needing lots of hugs, but not when he wants to play."

Cam yawned then dropped to retrieve Raa from beneath the table. Her eyes got caught in the snare of Shane's again.

"All your affection?" he asked, stroking her jaw with the back of one finger. "I noticed that Calvin doesn't touch you."

"I don't like to be touched," she said on autopilot.

Tilting his head, Shane's eyes narrowed. "Really?" he asked, grazing a fingertip up the back of her jaw.

He was touching her. He'd done it several times and either she hadn't noticed or it felt good. It was unlike her. Ginger never liked to be touched and always assumed that came from the doctors prodding at her so often.

With Cam as a distraction, Shane had managed to break down that barrier.

"Did I used to like it?" she asked.

While Shane kept stroking, she watched her son, trying to get used to the experience without allowing it to become too intense. Maybe Shane could help her ease in to being less uptight.

"That's a loaded question," he said. "Did you used to like being touched? Sure. Did I like seeing other guys touching you? No."

Cam flopped onto his back, Raa tucked under one arm, his thumb in his mouth.

"It's naptime," she said, moving onto all fours over Cam. "You want to sleep, Angel?"

Cam shook his head, his thumb slurping from his mouth. "Da," he said, looking at her, but pointing at his father. "Da. Da. Da."

"I don't know, sweetheart," she said, stroking Cam's hair from his forehead.

"What don't you know?" Shane asked. "You're amazing. You have like your own language with him."

"Experience," she said. "Sometimes he's the only one I have to talk to." Worried about transmitting a bad impression, she glanced at Shane. "Calvin works a lot."

"Sure," Shane said. "He runs that big corporation."

Swallowing, she wasn't sure if his understanding was genuine.

Sitting back on her haunches, Ginger took a breath. "Cam wants to know if you'll be around. If you'll play with him again." Comprehension made his chin rise. "I guess he had fun."

"So did I."

Shivering, Ginger fought to stay on point. "Now you know my big secret… you know the truth… Do you still want to help me?"

"More," he said. "I never thought I could want you more, but now I want you both."

She had to make sure he understood. "I don't like introducing people into his life who won't stick around. Whatever happens between us, however my amnesia therapy turns out… if the paternity is positive, will you be a father to him?"

"Yes."

And that was it. One simple word. They were sharing a smile when the door opened. In piled Calvin, Boyd, Owen, and Murphy.

Cam sat up to examine the group.

"Sorry," Owen said. "We held them off as long as we could."

"It's been too long already," Calvin said.

"Fuck," Murphy said, staring at Cam. "I'm an uncle."

"Watch your language," Shane chastised.

This time Ginger did hide her smile. His deliberate hypocrisy was a joke, the humor was laced through his voice.

"Aww, he's adorable," Owen said and began to come over.

As he moved, so did everyone else. Cam scrambled to his feet to run behind his parents.

"He's tired," she said, glancing at her boy.

With one hand on either parent's shoulder, Cam used them both as a shield. It was nice that he was showing such trust in Shane so quickly.

"Do you want to meet your uncles, kid?" Shane asked him, without moving from his shielding position, which she appreciated. "You can wrestle them as much as you like. One of them thinks about hurting you and I'll knock them out."

"Lovely," Calvin muttered.

Ginger covered her laugh with a hand and gave Shane a push when Calvin turned his back on them to organize the stroller. Cam squawked and socked her shoulder with the side of his tiny fist. She gasped in fake outrage and rubbed her shoulder. Cam was upset that she'd pushed Shane, his shocked outrage was hilarious.

"Oh, someone's protective of daddy," she said, wriggling a fingertip into Cam's chest.

Shane kissed Cam's head. "He's got my back," he said then whispered in Cam's ear. "Mommy can beat on daddy any time she likes. It's our job to protect her."

Cam twisted to blink at Shane who nodded. "Ma," Cam said.

Shane nodded. "Yeah, we protect her. See…" Stroking her shoulder in an exaggerated soothing gesture, Shane showed Cam what he meant. For effect, she stuck out her bottom lip to show she was sad. "We make mommy better. We don't hurt mommy."

Cam pointed to the stuffed animal on the floor in front of them. "Raa," he said and pushed through his parents to retrieve his lion. He took it to his mommy and pressed it against her. "Raa."

"Is Raa protecting mommy?" Shane asked.

Cam dropped to sit on his father and lifted his legs onto his mommy.

"While Cam sleeps?" she said when he slid down and sucked his thumb again. "Mommy's honored, Raa usually has to sleep with Cameron. He doesn't like to sleep without him."

Bowing, Ginger kissed her son's face; he snagged a handful of her hair to pull her down for another longer kiss. Yep, he was tired all right. It was as she smiled at her son, rubbing her nose on his that she realized her face was in Shane's lap, her cheek just a couple of inches from his groin.

Sitting up quickly, she blinked at him and dropped her eyes. He smiled and touched her chin. Obviously, he'd registered what she'd done, but he didn't say anything about it. Instead, Shane took Raa from her and the thumb came out Cam's mouth again.

Father gave the stuffed animal to his son. "How about Raa looks after you while you sleep and daddy will protect mommy while you have a nap?"

She wasn't sure if Cam understood or not. Either way, he accepted the animal, he did love his lion.

"Laying it on thick with the mommy, daddy stuff, aren't we?" Calvin said, raising a brow at her. "Come on, Cam. Let's go home."

Cam stretched out and yawned but rolled off his father to crawl over to Calvin who picked him up to put him in the stroller. Watching Shane scrutinize the act, Ginger hoped it wouldn't cause bad feeling that Calvin and Cameron were comfortable with each other. Granted, Calvin had never been hands on with Cam, but he'd seen Cam grow up.

Shane didn't say anything, wearing a half-frown, he got to his feet to straighten his jeans. She packed the diaper bag. Shane picked up Raa to take it over when Cam called for him.

Calvin was behind the stroller when she went over to hook the diaper bag over the handle. Cam was already half-asleep. Shane tucked the lion under his arm and kissed Cam's head then hunkered down in front of him.

"Daddy will see you tomorrow, okay?" Shane said, stroking his drowsy son's face. "And we'll play as much as you like."

Cam muttered something and his eyes closed.

Shane stood up. "Thank you."

He wasn't expressing his gratitude to her. Those words were aimed at Calvin. His expression was so stony that Ginger already missed the open, relaxed man who'd been sitting on the floor with her a minute ago.

"They need blood from me?" Shane asked.

"Uh," she said, eyeing everyone else. Everything was awkward again. "Yes. They took Cam's blood when we arrived. The nurse out there, Stevens, she'll show you what to do. I'm not sure what… I think it's just a needle stick."

"Whatever it takes," Shane said and turned to Calvin to offer his hand in a second attempt at a handshake. The first time Calvin had refused. That time her fiancé was so stunned that he accepted the handshake with a slack jaw. "Thank you… for keeping them safe."

She'd told Shane that he should be grateful and there he was, expressing gratitude. It could be spontaneous or he could be responding to what she'd said. His quip about following her orders maybe hadn't been a joke. Stunned, Ginger couldn't believe he was following through.

"You're… you're welcome," Calvin said.

Calvin hadn't been expecting Shane to act that way. Ginger hadn't either. Even Owen and Murphy were in shock if she was reading their expressions right.

Shane turned to his brother. "You got details of the lodge?"

Murphy nodded, still unable to make words.

Calvin unlocked the brake on the stroller and

moved forward a step. She was ready to follow along with him until the back of Shane's finger touched the curve of her jaw, forcing her to look at him.

"I'll see you tomorrow, Bit."

Nodding, she copied his smile before Calvin put her hand on the stroller handle and pulled her along with him. It was going to be an awkward vacation, but it would be an eventful one.

SIX

SHANE ARRIVED AT the lodge in his pick-up with Murphy and Owen. They piled out, deciding it was best to check in before unloading their luggage. Opening the back door, Shane let Owen out, and liberated a surprise of his own surprise. Much hairier and louder than Cam, the dog seemed pleased to stretch his legs.

Striding toward the glass-fronted lobby of the huge stone and log lodge, he was impressed. The place was off the beaten track. There were different activities available around the large forest resort that had a river running through it and a large lake.

As well as the rooms and facilities inside the lodge itself, there were a dozen chalets around the grounds. One of those chalets would be their home for the duration of the trip. He'd confirmed that when he called the previous day to make final arrangements.

Murphy and Owen were nearly at the door when Ginger came around the corner of the building pushing the stroller. She was alone and he was immediately concerned about why she was out in the cold by herself.

He momentarily forgot that the large husky he'd just let out of his truck wouldn't understand that his mommy no longer knew him.

Rocky changed course to bolt toward Ginger and the stroller.

Shane whistled loud and clapped his hands. "Rocky! No!" he hollered and picked up his pace.

Ginger froze and rushed around to put herself in front of the stroller. Only when she noticed him did Ginger relax and smile. Rocky came to a scrabbling halt, wagging his tail and nosing her. The sound of her laugh eased his tension. She crouched down to rub her fists hard behind his ears, something their fur-boy loved for her to do.

Shane grinned. "Sorry," he said, stopping with them. Ginger was already kissing Rocky's nose and scrunching her fingers in his fur. "I didn't think you'd be outside."

He hadn't expected them to come face to face so quickly.

"He's gorgeous," she said, her grin so wide and genuine that his jeans got tight. God, he loved to see her happy. "Oh, Shane, he's beautiful. He's yours?"

"Ours," he said, bending to stroke Rocky's manic tail. She leaned over the dog, resting her chest on his head to run her fingers the full length of him. "He's excited to see his mommy. I guess I should've mentioned him yesterday when you asked about kids."

Ginger wasn't upset or offended, she laughed. "And what's your name?" she asked, going back to rub her nose on his.

Rocky barked, but she showed no fear and laughed again.

"Rocky," Shane said. "His name is Rocky."

The dog looked at him as Owen came over with Murphy.

"Ginger, why are you outside?" Owen asked.

"Someone was fussing," she said, looking over her shoulder at Cam who was straining his arms and legs forward.

"Wooo! Wooo!" he mimicked the bark and screeched, fighting against the straps holding him in his stroller.

"You like him?" Ginger asked, going over to crouch next to the stroller, with a hand on the frame. "You like the doggy, Angel?" To his surprise, she held out an arm to Rocky. "Rocky, come and meet Cameron."

Cameron strained again. Rocky trotted over to sniff at Cameron.

"He won't bite," Shane said, moving over behind the dog.

"I know," she said, without looking up at him.

She stroked Rocky's head, which gave Cameron permission to grab handfuls of Rocky's cheeks. The boy was rough, but not as rough as he could be. Pulling Rocky forward, Cam copied his mother and pressed his nose to Rocky's nose. Rocky was happy to receive the acceptance. With a long tongue, he lapped Cam's face. The boy paused to blink for a minute, then opened his mouth in a huge shrieking laugh.

Cameron pulled Rocky forward and licked his nose.

Ginger scrunched up her face but laughed. "I guess you've got a new friend, Angel."

Rocky licked him again. Cameron was laughing so hard that his little face got red.

"Wooo!"

Ginger stood up, and after checking the brake was on, she came over. "You showed up right on time," she said, standing beside him to watch dog and boy learn each other. "He was starting to get annoyed at being stuck in the stroller."

"Let him out," Owen said.

"The chalet isn't ready yet," she said. "Calvin is inside with Diane trying to figure it out. Doctor Guinness is on his way."

Shane looked at Murphy who read his unspoken instruction. "I'm on it."

Murphy went inside. Shane was confident his brother would take care of business. He wasn't going to have Ginger and Cameron outside without any comfort or security.

Owen came closer. "Can I go over there to see Cameron?" he asked.

Ginger nodded.

"Get to know him while it's just the two of you," Shane said.

Now that Cameron was wide awake and happy, it was a great time for Uncle Owen to go over and bond with him. One on one would be easier.

"I think you've lost your status," Ginger said, leaning sideways as she folded her arms.

It was amazing to be like this, standing beside her like it was no big deal. She was close to him, so close that if it had been a couple of years ago, he'd have his arms around her. Keeping his distance wasn't easy; it was necessary if he didn't want to scare her. She'd let him touch her face at the hospital the previous day. A good start and one he planned to build on, an inch at a time.

"My status?" he asked.

"Cam asked about you this morning, I think he remembered you said you'd see him," she said. "But you brought a dog." Tipping her head back, she drew her eyes up at him. Shane felt so close to her, he considered that it might be a dream. Being with her again was all he'd ever wanted. "Daddies become insignificant when there are dogs… he's always loved dogs. I've always been so worried because he loves petting them when we're out, but you never know, you know? Some dogs have a bad temper."

"You're not worried about Rocky? He's a big guy," Shane asked, curious about her reaction to him.

"You said I was his mommy," she said. "I wouldn't raise a beast... and how can I be afraid of such a handsome thing?"

Rocky left Cameron poking Owen's glasses and came over to circle her legs. He whined and nudged her. She stroked his head, but that wasn't enough. He rose up, putting his paws on her chest. The weight of the canine made her fall back against him.

Shane almost swore. That was her body, his wife's beautiful body, leaning on his. Yes, it had been the sudden weight of the dog that set her off balance, but he loved that he'd been there to hold her up.

Still, he couldn't keep her there at the expense of her fear. "Down," Shane said. "Come on, boy, you've done so well not to scare anyone."

"It's okay," she said, holding Rocky's legs.

Their fur-boy was heavy and her strained voice betrayed that she was struggling. Rocky licked her and whimpered.

"He's missed you," Shane said. When he turned his mouth down, he caught the scent of her hair, and had to fight back a groan. A shiver went through her that he recognized, not as fear, but as awareness. Damn... his Ginger was within reach. Raising both hands, he considered stroking her arms but wasn't sure how she'd react given that Rocky had backed her into this proverbial corner. "He cried for a month after you went missing. I had to take him to the vet. They were worried about him not eating... he didn't want to exercise."

Rocky pawed her shoulder and nuzzled his muzzle against her throat, forcing her head back. "I'm sorry I hurt you, Rocks," she said, kissing his nose again.

His need grew so much that Shane had to tip his own head back. He'd give anything to spin her around, to grab her face, push her back against the column of the portico, and kiss her with every ounce of gratitude coursing through him. There had been times he never thought he'd see her again. Now she was not only there, but her back was pressed into him.

"Hey!" Someone called out and it took him a minute to recognize his own brother's voice. "We're ready. Chalet four on the waterfront, you coming?" Murphy came over. "It's round back, just down the hill."

Rocky jumped down and returned to Cameron who was delighted at the canine attention.

"Take Ginger and Cam down," Shane said. "We'll get the luggage."

Grinning, Owen came over, around Ginger, to block Shane from her. She glanced back wearing a frown as Murphy pulled her toward the stroller. He couldn't blame Ginger for being confused about why he'd dismissed her, but he couldn't be honest.

When they were out of sight, Shane turned away and fell against the portico pillar, facing out into the parking lot, away from the building. Owen was still grinning and wiggling his brows when he came into view. Shane scrubbed his hands over his face.

"Like that, huh?" Owen asked. "Like getting a little bump and grind with my baby sister?"

"Don't," he groaned behind his hands.

"Your jeans sure liked being that close to her."

Great, that was what he needed, his brother-in-law commenting on his boner. "You're a real pal, Owe."

"Like yesterday when she kissed your crotch, that was a hoot."

"Don't," he said again and dropped his hands. With his shoulders pressed into the column, he let his hips arch forward. "How the fuck am I gonna do this?"

"What? Help my sister? You thinking of bailing on her?"

"No," he said, shoving away from the column. "But she doesn't know everything I do, does she? Seeing her now, with Rocky… and with Cameron, it's like… my life is right there. It's right there." He gestured with flat hands side by side. "It's in front of me and I can't fucking do anything about it."

"That's why we're here, to do something about it," Owen said and put an arm around him. "I saw my sister on both her wedding days and I can tell you, she never looked as happy with him as she did with you."

That wasn't much of a consolation. "No one came in and busted up our wedding," he muttered.

"Not only then, I'm talking about at dinner and yesterday. She looks at you like she knows you. She's comfortable with you. Yesterday, when we walked in and saw you both with Cameron, it looked… right."

Okay, Shane had to concede, that was better. "It was incredible… he's incredible. She's just… despite everything, she raised the most amazing kid… She almost died for him, Owen, how can I give her that back? I wasn't there. I wasn't the one holding her hand when she decided to risk it all for a child she didn't know. She had no idea if he was a product of love or a one night stand. She knew nothing about who had fathered her child, but she was willing to give up her life for him."

"That's what mothers do," Owen said. "The doc will help you talk all of this through."

He shrugged off Owen's arm and moved to look into the lobby where he saw Calvin and his mother talking to someone. He still didn't trust that guy but conceded that could be because the man was sleeping with his wife.

"I never needed a doctor's help with my wife before."

"So go down there and tell her like it is. Lay down the law. You tell her, she's your wife and Cameron's your son. You tell her you make the rules. Tell her she's coming home and this Calvin guy can go fuck himself."

Although Owen was doing well with the delivery, Shane smiled when he turned to his brother-in-law. "How do you think that will play?"

"With your Ginger? She'd grab you by the balls and tell you to say pretty please, or she'd drop to her knees and blow you right there. She always did have a thing for you taking control. This Ginger… I don't know."

The reminder that she wasn't quite the same woman he'd married didn't worry him, it upset him. She was missing out on so much happiness from their past and she might never get it back. He went back to watching Calvin and Diane talking to the lodge employee.

"Gin likes to remind me that we don't know for sure if Cam is mine."

Owen scoffed, having much the same reaction Shane had. "Who else got near enough Ginger to sleep with her?" he asked. "I can't… I can't even imagine her sleeping with another guy, and I'm saying that two days after seeing her at the altar with another guy." Owen always had been one of his biggest supporters. "Wait… you're not worried about that, are you? You don't think she cheated on you, do you?"

"No," Shane spat out. If Owen had been anyone else, he'd have hit him. "God, no, Cam is mine, I don't have any doubt."

"But you did the blood test anyway… Why did you do that?"

"Because Ginger asked me to," he said, looking at his brother-in-law. "Did it offend you? I didn't do it because I had doubts, I did it because she wanted to be sure. I figured you'd support it, as my lawyer, you'll have unequivocal proof of who is responsible for that little dude if we ever have any issues."

Owen nodded. "It is important that we have that. It just weirds me out to think you don't trust each other."

"She doesn't trust herself," Shane said. "I trust her completely."

Owen's expression loosened and his brows rose. "You know she's engaged to Calvin. They've probably had sex."

"Yeah, but that's not my Ginger."

"That's an important distinction for you, is it?" Owen asked.

Another vehicle drove into the parking lot. Doctor Guinness was the one to get out of it.

"Go and get a bellhop," he said to Owen, patting his shoulder as he zeroed in on the doctor. "Or a trolley or something."

"You just want rid of me, don't you?" Owen said.

"Head off our mutual friend if you see him heading this way. I'm going to talk to the good doctor."

Owen went his way and Shane went to meet the doctor who he hadn't managed to speak to alone yet. He didn't have much time, but he had plenty of questions.

SEVEN

THE TWO FLOOR CHALET had seven bedrooms. Only one was isolated with its own bathroom. The other bedrooms were paired, flanking a shared bathroom only accessible from inside each of the two bedrooms it served. Each bedroom had their own door to the mezzanine hallway that hung over the living space.

Ginger decided that Murphy was an interesting character. Cameron liked him; she was pleased about that. He carried his nephew around as they explored every room and did a lap of the wrap around porch that surrounded the lower floor. It also extended along the back of the second floor too, linking the bedrooms. It offered a great view of the lake beyond the grass stretching out from the bottom of the back stairs.

It was a picturesque scene with mountains and forest all around the lake. Not that Ginger imagined she'd be going into the water any time soon.

Finding the kitchen fully stocked was a nice surprise. It was all setup with smoothies, full-fat milk, and more fruit than they'd ever be able to eat. There in the middle of the table was a top-of-the-line blender with a bow on top, so they could mush up anything and everything Cameron might want.

She'd made coffee and fruit salad by the time Calvin and Diane arrived. Owen wasn't far behind. It was another ten minutes before the doctor showed up. Shane hadn't shown up. Ginger shouldn't be worried, but she was.

"I have to put him down for his nap soon," Ginger said, fighting with her struggling son who was trying to free himself from her arms to get to Rocky who was asleep in front of the open fireplace that they hadn't lit yet.

Everyone was sitting around the fireplace drinking coffee, eating fruit, being polite. She guessed they were waiting for Shane before anything official was said. But cases were piled in front of the door, no one had even unpacked yet.

"Yes," the doctor said and put his coffee on the table. "Okay, we'll just get started. First of all, thank you everyone for coming."

She hoped he didn't think that Shane had bailed because he was definitely there, or he had been. Maybe he'd freaked and split, though she doubted he'd have abandoned Rocky.

Mumbles went around in response. "I suppose I should be the one saying that," she said, trying to shirk her distracting concern. "Thank you, everyone, for being here."

Cam was still fighting and because she knew he'd be tired, Ginger let him go. He crawled over to bury his face in Rocky, who cracked an eye, but just settled after seeing the baby.

"I appreciate that you have all given up your time for this. It displays how important this is to all of you," Guinness said and pulled a folder from his case beside him. "I have contracts for each of you to sign."

"Contracts?" Calvin exclaimed and thrust his cup to the table. "We didn't agree to contracts."

"They're goodwill contracts," Guinness said. "Not exactly legally binding."

Owen cleared his throat and opened his hand. "May I?"

The doctor handed one over to her brother.

Calvin exchanged a look with his mother. "Boyd had business. I can't sign anything without my lawyer present."

As Owen read it, his frown became a smile. He relaxed more the further down the page he got until his expression was almost amused. "There is no monetary commitment here and it states anyone can leave at any time, so your freewill is intact. This is not a contract for terms of payment. As he says, it's a goodwill contract... My client will sign it."

"Your client already has," Guinness said, taking another page from the back of the folder to show that Shane had put pen to paper. "I saw him in the parking lot."

Owen cleared his throat and put his own sheet on the table. "My client and I will be having words." The doctor handed out the other sheets and Ginger began to read. Owen was beside her and he offered his pen after he signed. "Apparently my advice isn't needed, but you're safe to sign it, sis."

Ginger took the pen and wondered about her relationship with her brother and how that affected his relationship with Shane, his client. Or maybe Shane hadn't been his client before she disappeared, maybe her disappearance had brought them closer together.

The pen went around the room with grumbles of displeasure and protest. When they were done, Owen tucked the pen away.

The doctor gathered the contracts. "It's best to make sure everyone knows where they stand… This is going to be difficult for everyone. We have to make sure that we understand everyone is on the same level. We all have to be respectful of each other's feelings. We have to make sure there's no physical violence—"

"Uh, the only one who has threatened physical violence is the man conveniently absent for this orientation," Calvin said.

Murphy grumbled. "You pushed him first."

Guinness took control. "This is exactly what we don't want. It won't help Ginger, and we also have to be considerate of the child in the room… Usually we don't have children present for these kind of retreats."

"My son and I come as a package deal," Ginger said, jumping onto the defensive. "If he's not welcome, I'm not welcome." Moving to the edge of her seat, she set her gaze on Guinness. "Would you like us to leave?"

"No," the doctor said quickly. "No, I didn't mean that, Miss…" he stopped and eyed the others in the room.

Her vehemence was always strongest when her child was in question. The reminder of ambiguity over her name took them all down a peg, so she sat back.

"Are you going to start using your married name again?" Murphy asked.

"I… I don't know."

"No, she's not," Calvin said.

"All of these issues will be worked through while we're here," Guinness said, quick to calm everyone. "This is a process, and not one that will happen quickly."

"You said 'retreats like this'," Diane said. "Have you done this kind of thing before?"

"Not exactly this," the doctor said. "I have had several amnesia patients before, but your situation is unique." No kidding. She didn't need to be reminded of that. "We'll begin tomorrow. Tonight we'll settle in, eat at the lodge, and get a good night's sleep."

"Which leads to the question of the bedrooms," Owen said. "I assume doctor that you would like the individual room."

The doctor nodded. It did make the most sense as he was the only one not related. "The other six rooms are arranged in pairs with a shared bathroom between them," the doctor said before he cleared his throat and linked his hands. "As you'll have seen in your contracts, we ask that everyone has their own individual room. It seems best while we have the ambiguity of husbands and fiancés. It's also possible that tensions will run high and we need everyone to have a safe space they can retreat to while they are here. All rooms have locking doors, and the bathrooms have two doors, one from each bedroom. Both are lockable from the inside and from outside. So we will all have our privacy."

She looked at Calvin whose jaw had shifted to the side. Ginger tried to be apologetic. It wasn't fair that he was going to have his status seemingly reduced while in this situation. But it made sense. Though it might look like a nice rural retreat, it was in fact a medical intervention. So they shouldn't really be fooling around. It wasn't a vacation meant for fornication. If the trip was supposed to save her sanity, she shouldn't be thinking about sex.

"What are you thinking, doc?" Murphy asked.

"We divide by family," Guinness said. "The Bishops, Warrens and Leylands."

Murphy bobbed his head. "Trouble is, we have four Warrens."

"I suppose he means siblings," Diane sneered. "Ginger should share with her brother."

"Sure, but how will Owen feel about being woken up by Cameron?" Murphy asked. "Shane's got off lightly on the midnight feeds so far—"

"No, I have to object," Calvin said. "You cannot insinuate that—"

"What?" Murphy asked. "Husband shares with wife, why not?"

"It's not like they'll be having sex," Owen said. "Not while we're all in the same house, and Ginger doesn't like to be touched, right? I guess Shane deserves a chance to get to know his son too."

That was what swayed the doctor, he stopped objecting and looked to Calvin. "As I said, I don't usually have to develop minor relationships. But it would be useful for Mr. Warren to have as much contact with his son as possible while he is so young. They imprint deeply at this age."

"So we're now nurturing not only Ginger's health, but that of father and son too," Diane said, almost choking on her real name. "This is becoming ridiculous."

"No," Calvin said, looking at her. "No, it's okay. Let him share a bathroom with them."

She hadn't expected such a quick turnaround. There was something in the way he was looking at her. Something Ginger didn't understand. Was it a test to see if she would betray him or was he really putting Cameron before himself?

"Excellent," Guinness said. "Then let's all get settled in. We have a reservation for dinner at the lodge at five thirty."

"That's early," Owen said.

"Cameron goes down at seven thirty," she said in explanation and no one argued. "And he needs his bath before bed."

"That tiny thing is going to rule all our lives, isn't he?" Owen said.

Turning on her brother, she lifted a finger.

"Complain and I'll…"

Unthreatened, Owen grabbed her finger and shook it. "What, sis? What will you do? Wedgie me?"

Her bluster left and she laughed. Owen pulled her forward and kissed her head, which was unexpected but nice.

"I'll take your suitcase upstairs," Murphy said to her, getting up.

Since he was the bulkiest of the guys there, she didn't object.

Cam was asleep, almost, and she'd take him upstairs as soon as the movement had died down. Nap time was valuable and she wouldn't let his routine be disrupted because his mommy was so screwed up.

EIGHT

GINGER WAS IN her bedroom kneeling on the floor with her suitcase open in front of her when someone knocked on her door. She turned to see Shane in the doorway.

"You doing okay?"

"Yep," she said. "This is the biggest room because it's in the corner. You don't mind if Cameron and I have it, do you?"

Rocky was laid out on her bed, taking up most of the space; Cam was asleep in his lodge-provided crib.

"Nope," Shane said and sauntered in. He went to sit on the end of the bed to brush a hand through Rocky's fur. The dog lifted his head, registered who was touching him and then laid back down again. "Looks like three of you will be sharing."

"He follows me around," she said, taking toiletries and a bag from the suitcase. "I like it."

She put the items in the bathroom and took a second to admire the central claw-footed bathtub. It was the only full bath in the place, which was another reason they got it. Cameron was the only one who needed a bath.

"I don't know if you've checked, but the shower has a fixed head above the tub," she said when she came back into the bedroom. "Watch out for the ducks."

His brows rose. "Excuse me?"

Ginger explained. "Cam's ducks… his bath toys." He smiled in understanding. "You'll want to make sure there are none in the tub before you get in the shower. Some of them are pretty painful to step on and you could end up on your butt. I try to make sure they're all out, but sometimes they get lost in the bubbles and—" She was babbling so stopped herself to take a breath and look at him. "Is this insane?"

"Is what insane?" he asked, leaning back on his hands.

"Us, sharing, like this."

"I have absolutely no problem with you seeing me naked."

He did have a way of making her smile.

With arms folded, Ginger wandered back toward her case. "What?"

"I've seen you naked, so, nothing new there for daddy." He eyed the crib. "As for the kid, well, we can get him a blindfold or something."

Almost tutting at him, Ginger refrained from laughing. "Cameron has no interest in your penis."

"Great," he said, slapping his hands together as he sat up, his smirk growing. "That kind of implies that you do."

Her jaw fell. "It doesn't. I meant that I had no problem with Cameron seeing you naked because he couldn't care less… You're not going to scar him." Changing the subject before he could tease her any more, Ginger lowered her voice. "And no more clapping. He sleeps heavily. When he's out, he's usually out, but we don't make loud abrupt noises that could scare him."

He lifted three fingers. "Scouts honor, sorry, mommy."

"You were never a boy scout," she said and crouched at her case.

There was a pause. "Do you remember that or are you guessing?"

Ginger had to stop and think about it. "Guessing," she said, because she hadn't known it was fact. "How was the test yesterday?"

"Just blood like you said," he said, extending his arm to show her there was nothing there except the tiniest mark. She was more enticed by the width of his solid, tanned arm. "No big deal. The results will take a few days."

She nodded and piled her clothes beside Cameron's. "Cam has no boundaries and believes everything belongs to him," she said. "Make sure prescription drugs are locked away, and illegal drugs—"

"No illegal drugs," he said. "No prescription drugs either."

Pausing with a pile of clothes on her lap, she looked up at him, cringing that she had to ask. "Can you ask Owen and Murphy to make sure they don't—"

"I will," he said on a reassuring smile. "I meant what I said about knocking out anyone who hurts him." She actually believed him. "And the nearest hospital is nineteen point seven miles away... I already checked... I can make it in less than twenty minutes if I have to." She didn't know why he'd done that, but it was good to know that he had. Taking her clothes to the dresser by the door, she put them in the third drawer. "Looks like the kid has more clothes than you."

"Going anywhere with a kid requires a trailer," she said, continuing to put things away.

"Why do you start in the third drawer?"

"Cam gets the top two," she said. "This will have to double as a changing table. I'll put his clothes away and use the smaller drawers at the top for diapers, wipes, cream, powder." Wearing a smile, she turned to lean on the dresser because there were more instructions on her list. "Don't leave food lying around. Don't leave glasses of liquor or beer bottles anywhere he can reach them. He doesn't drink soda either. Anything hot, colognes, styling products—"

"Man, you're good at this mommy thing," he said, rising from the bed. "Your contract is longer than the docs."

"Condoms," she said.

He paused in surprise then grinned. "Didn't bring any. Do I need 'em?"

"Not you," she said, pushing away from the dresser. "Owen and Murphy, can you tell them not to leave them lying around? They're a choking hazard."

He was scratching the back of his head when she passed by to retrieve more things from her case. "You're all about teeing up the puns today, Bit," he said. Ginger smiled, though he wouldn't have seen it because she was bent over her case. "Murphy never introduces the women in his life to the family, so no danger of him bringing a woman here. And Owen is married."

Spinning around, another dose of shock hit her. "My brother is married?"

He nodded and put his hands in his pockets. "Last year."

Dropping the perfume bottle back into her suitcase, Ginger went over to the bed and sat down. "I missed my brother's wedding?"

"It was right after your mom was diagnosed," he said, joining her on the end of the bed. "She wanted to see them married before her treatment. We weren't sure how it would work out for her... we're still not sure...

But Owen's been with Derek five years now… maybe more than that… I think they met the year we got married."

Another surprise. "He's gay?"

Shane laughed and gripped her neck through her hair. "You were the first one he told when you were kids."

"There's so much I don't know," she murmured and cast her eyes toward the crib. "What about your family?"

"Mine?" he asked. "Murphy's my only sibling. He's got no wife, no kids, but he's hetero."

"And your parents?" He didn't respond, which was significant. It was the first time he'd taken his time about being honest with her. When she turned to him, she wondered about his blank expression and the way he fixated on the floor. Scooping a hand onto his cheek, she drew his head around to peer at him. "Shane?"

"We don't get along. I haven't had a relationship with my parents for years."

Something else that had been neglected because of her accident. "If paternity comes back… will you tell them about Cam?"

"I don't know," he said. "Like I said, I haven't spoken to them for years."

"They deserve to know he exists, don't you think?" she asked and had to catch her breath when he stood up; she hadn't expected him to move so fast. "They're his grandparents."

"Don't do this," he murmured without turning to her.

"What?" Ginger was confused, she'd never seen him so closed off and taut. "Don't do what? We should talk about it. If they want a relationship with him—"

Whirling around, his expression was so stern it stunned her. "They can kiss my ass is what they can do," he said. "They're not getting near him. Never. You understand?"

Stunned, it took her a minute to find words. "What could they have done that was so awful?" she asked, standing up. "I always felt so guilty that Cam wouldn't know his blood family and here he is, in a room with his father. His father, Shane. You can't possibly understand what that means to me."

He brought his hand up to her face as he gentled his voice. "And to me. I love him more than I knew was possible."

"You just met him."

"Doesn't matter."

And because she understood that parental love, she smiled. "I know." After they took a breath, she hoped he was feeling more reasonable. "Don't you think his grandparents will love him that much?"

His hand dropped. "No, I don't."

That answer hurt her. "Because there's something wrong with him?" she asked. "He's damaged because of me or something I did to him?"

His eyes flared. "What? No! I'm so proud of you, Bit. You did an incredible job with him."

"But he's not good enough, is that it?"

"You're twisting this around," he said. "I didn't say there was anything wrong with him. There's something wrong with them, they're not... They're not capable of loving anyone except themselves."

"So there was some childhood trauma? They did something awful to you that—"

"Does it matter?" he asked, his volume raised slightly. "I'm saying no. Why can't you just accept that?"

"Because no doesn't work. It's not a reason I can explain to my child."

His arms opened. "Oh, so he's your child now. I say something you don't like and you cut me out? One little thing doesn't fit with the picture you have and—"

"Uh, hello, I don't have a picture," she said. "Amnesia sufferer, remember? All I'm asking is for some help in understanding why the people who raised you are so despicable. Is that too much? You can't give me an explanation?"

"No," he argued. "No, Bit, I can't explain. There. But will you accept that? Somehow I doubt it."

She growled at him. "Don't be sarcastic," she said. "It's unproductive."

"Unproductive," he said, leaning back while his head bobbed. "Right and we hate when I'm unproductive, don't we? Goddamnit, Gin, you can't expect to understand everything in one day. We had five years together, four of them married before you disappeared, and we have the sixteen months we've been apart on top of that. Do you really expect to understand everything that happened in a snap?"

"Now you're being patronizing," she sneered and folded her arms, gnawing on the inside bottom corner of her lower lip.

Again, he raised his hands and drove his fingers into his hair before turning his back. "And she's doing the lip chew, are you that pissed at me? Huh? I won't give you an inch and you cut me out. Is it the silent treatment now? The sulk?" Spinning back, he opened his arms. "'Cause we can't fuck and make up right now. I mean, far as I'm concerned we can, but your fiancé out there might get in a snit about it."

"Don't talk to me like that," she said. Shocked, Ginger didn't remember anyone ever being so blunt with her. "My decision not to sleep with you has nothing to do with Calvin and everything to do with the fact that you're a pig!"

"A pig you had no problem getting naked with for half a decade. A pig you said 'I do' to. A pig who fathered your child."

"Well maybe I didn't have the same perspective then that I do today," she snapped. "'Cause from where I'm standing, you leave a lot to be desired. You're rude and coarse and… and…"

"Unproductive?"

"What the hell, Boo!" she shouted. "Stop being a bastard!"

"What happened to watching our language, mommy?" Oh, she wanted to slap him right across the face. Shane didn't take his eyes away from hers as he marched over and Ginger wasn't about to shrink. Rocky began to growl. Shane just thrust a finger toward the dog. "Don't you start, Rock. Lie down."

The dog grumbled but did as he was told.

Ginger folded her arms. "Maybe he understands that you're out of line."

His head tilted, but he was still sneering. "Oh, he was always your big defender… always a mommy's boy and then you were gone, out of his life, just gone."

Was he really throwing that at her?

Ginger could match his ire, but that didn't mean she wasn't hurt by him pressing on her guilt. "Yeah, 'cause that was my conscious choice. I thought, *how can I hurt Rocky today?*' and made the Gem sink all on my own."

His mouth opened to argue back. Before a word came out, he paused to peer at her. There was less anger in his next question. "How do you know it was called the Gem?"

Had she said that? Had she known the name all along or had someone said it? Ginger tried to answer but came up short and could only mouth and blink for a score of seconds.

"I…" Emotions. Ginger remembered emotions. As another memory flickered up, her chin fell. "We fought that night too."

Hooking a finger under her chin, he brought her eyes up. "What about?" he probed with a desperate hope that tugged on her heart. "What did we fight about, Bit?"

But she couldn't find it. The whisper of emotion flittered away, she gritted her teeth to growl in frustration. "I don't know… I… it was right there."

"It's okay," he said. "Focus… We did. We fought right there on the boat in our cabin… just like this. You and me alone in the bedroom. I said something that upset you… what did I say to you?"

Squeezing her eyes closed, she tried to concentrate but couldn't picture the scene, couldn't remember what the room looked like. All she could remember was the feeling that came before fear.

"I remember the water," Ginger whispered. "It was cold."

"Yes, it was," he said. "The water was cold, very cold."

"It was dark… and I couldn't… I couldn't see."

"That's it," he murmured, stroking her cheek. "Keep talking, Little Bit."

"I couldn't breathe and… I was so scared I… the surface, I remember I… I thought I was dead and then I got to the surface. But I… I was alone…"

"What did we fight about, Bit?" he murmured. "Come on, baby, what were we fighting about?"

All Ginger could remember was the black ink of the water. The icy feeling in her limbs and the weight of her own body as she fought to kick and find the surface. She couldn't remember being a person. It was like being out of body; like she was an entity inside her being rather than her whole self.

Balling her fists, she growled again and bashed his chest in her frustration, not with any intention, or force enough, to hurt him.

"I don't remember!" Ginger felt hollow, desperate, pathetic. As her eyes opened, they drifted, unable to find focus. "God, I'm useless."

"Hey," he said, giving her a shake. "Don't you ever say anything like that again. Do you realize what you just did? You remembered something."

"But it was useless. It wasn't what you wanted me to remember."

Smiling, he brushed his thumb across her lower lip like he was substituting the touch for a kiss. "I don't want you to remember anything," he said. "You remember what I told you about the present?" She nodded. "You were amazing. Look at what you've done and we haven't even been here a day." He glanced toward the crib. "How long until junior wakes up?"

"An hour maybe."

"You want to get some sleep too... or are you hungry?"

"Are you trying to take care of me?" she asked, surprised that he was being so considerate. "Weren't we fighting a minute ago?"

He shrugged. "Baby, one thing you'll learn about us is that fighting doesn't change what we are to each other... You might not know what that is now, but I do... We piss each other off all the time, it doesn't mean anything. So, food, sleep... walk?"

Searching her memory was exhausting. "Sleep," she said.

"Rocky," he said and whistled, but she grabbed his arm as the dog looked up.

"Wait... can't I keep him?"

Another grin. Seeing it relaxed her. "You want to sleep with the dog?"

She nodded, biting her lip, she shrugged with hope. "If that's inappropriate..."

Brushing his finger down her jaw, he looked into

her. "He always did get more love than I did," he joked. Ginger laughed, giving him a nudge that Cam would've objected to if he'd been awake. "Rocky, stay with momma."

Rocky was still snoozing in the middle of the bed and didn't appear to have had any intention of moving anyway. Shane began to retreat.

"Thank you," Ginger said before he pulled the slightly ajar door further open. "You didn't have to come here and... you did and... we're making progress."

"This is just the beginning," he said and stepped out into the hall to close the door.

With a sigh, she checked her son, and then began to strip off to climb into bed with her new furry friend.

NINE

SHANE CLOSED THE BEDROOM door and turned around to see Calvin leaning against the banister at the top of the stairs where it turned to be the railing at the edge of the mezzanine. No one else was out there. He was peering right at him wearing a sinister look.

"Enjoy the show?" Shane asked.

He wouldn't be intimidated or make excuses or apologies for spending time with his wife.

"Don't get comfortable, Warren."

Oh that was just great. He couldn't help but be amused. "Ah, so this is the warning. This is where we square off?"

"No squaring off," he said, pushing away from the banister. "Just a friendly warning… I never lose."

Sliding his hands into his pockets, Shane didn't want to provoke the guy too much. Though he was guilty of smiling as he sauntered over to his adversary and lowered his volume.

"You've never played against me, Bishop."

"That why you're here? You think you can win

her back?"

Calvin was whispering too; the hissing tone matched his. Neither wanted to be caught threatening the other. It was technically against the terms of the contract they'd signed. And with the doctor's bedroom door perpendicular to Ginger's, they couldn't risk rousing him.

"There's no *think* about it."

"Do you really believe that?" Calvin asked.

The point of the exercise was to rile him, so Shane tried to temper his response so as not to give Calvin any satisfaction. But he had an internal reaction all right; he had an overwhelming urge to toss the guy on his ass and kick him down the stairs.

"She's my wife."

"She doesn't remember you," Calvin sneered. "She doesn't want to be with you."

"Then you have nothing to worry about, do you?" he said. "What's your problem? If you're sure she'd never look at me twice, why are you warning me off?"

"I'm not warning you off. I'm warning you not to make a fool of yourself."

Shane's laugh was automatic and louder than it should've been given that they were trying to be discreet. "You think this is foolish? Fuck, Bishop…" Clearing his throat, he prepared to give his opponent a lesson. He hadn't expected to be educating anyone except Ginger about his relationship history, but he'd give this one lesson for free. "I knew Ginny about… a year before I told her we were going to be together forever. We worked together and, uh… the relationship would've been, inappropriate, least that's what people kept telling me. I fell in love with her the first minute I saw her. I turned a corner and there she was, laughing at something and I… got the boner of my life. She was fucking beautiful, but it was her optimism that did me in. She had me there and then. But it wasn't going to happen, 'cause it was inappropriate, right?

"Then one day I thought, *Fuck it.*' I went to her and I said, 'Ginger Leyland, one day you are going to be my wife and the minute you say 'I do' you'll know what forever means.' I promised myself to her and nothing has changed. She thought I was crazy, she laughed at me, probably felt sorry for me. Man, I was a puppy dog; I'd have done anything she said because I was so in love with her. But you want to know why I kept pursuing her when she kept saying no? It was because I knew she loved me too… And, yeah, you'll call me a crazy stalker, but that wasn't it. She had the same voices in her ear telling her it would never work, telling her we would never work out, that it was 'inappropriate.' She wanted it. She wanted to be with me. But she needed me to tell her it was okay. To prove that all those voices were bullshit, that no one knew us except us."

"What an interesting—"

"I'm not done," he said, understanding that he wasn't getting through. The story was the prelude that came with the threat he delivered next in his own sinister voice. "Want to know what happened the night of our first kiss?" Calvin's brows rose, uninterested as his eyes drifted sideways. "I proposed." That got his adversary's attention, so Shane had the right to be smug now. "And she said yes… That was it, Bishop. One kiss and she was mine. Neither of us blinked after that. We defended our relationship, sacrificed whatever we had to… She didn't kiss me until she knew she belonged to me all the way. And she did kiss me, Bishop. She made the first physical move."

Calvin's jaw jutted to the side. Shane could hear his fury though he tried to pretend it wasn't there.

"Am I supposed to be scared?"

"A friendly warning," Shane said, taking a stride back. "I'm telling you, if she kisses me, it's game over for you."

"You think one kiss will bring back her memory?" Calvin sneered.

"I'm telling you that it doesn't matter. She doesn't need her memory to kiss me, and she doesn't need it to fall in love with me. I pursued her for months and it paid off. She kissed me and that was it. I'm not here to sprint with you… I'm here for the marathon. I'll persevere long after you're out of the picture if that's what it takes. I'm not going anywhere." Letting his smile widen, it was wrong that he got so much pleasure out of seeing Calvin slip down a peg, but Shane couldn't contain it. He opened his arms as he prepared to deliver the final blow with the ace he'd always carry. "After all, who's the daddy?"

Turning around, he descended the stairs, leaving Calvin with that thought. It was the perfect reminder. Ginger could get rid of Calvin without turning back; they had no permanent ties. Shane was not only her husband, but the father of her child. He wasn't going to be leaving the picture in a hurry.

TEN

THERE WAS SO MUCH tension. Ginger had felt it at dinner. So much so that she was grateful to get her baby back to bed and slip into her own bed with Rocky and her book.

The new day meant breakfast and dealing with people again. At that moment, a nanny from the lodge was upstairs with Cam. Shane was taking Rocky out back to relieve himself. The dog, not the man.

Everyone else was seating themselves around the fireplace in the living area for their first therapy session.

Ginger didn't know why there was so much tension. It had grown since the previous day, but she hoped to God that the session would help them work some of it out. Shane appeared from the kitchen that was positioned beneath her bedroom and came over to join them.

Ginger couldn't see the dog. "Where's Rocky?" she asked.

"On the porch," Shane said, dropping onto a loveseat with Murphy. There were only three loveseats and an armchair around the fireplace with a central coffee table between them. Doctor Guinness occupied the armchair next to the hearth that he'd angled to face his patients.

Twisting around to focus over the back of the couch, Ginger could see past the pillar that held up the mezzanine and found that the back screen door was closed.

She turned back to address Shane. "The screen is closed."

"So?" Shane asked, brushing dirt from his jeans.

Was he that oblivious? Ginger didn't understand how he could be so glib.

"He can't get back in," she said. "You can't leave him out there. What if he gets cold?"

Shane smiled. "Have you seen all that fur?"

"What if he gets lonely or attacked by a bear or something?"

His brows went up as his mouth opened. Although he didn't actually laugh, she could tell he wanted to.

"A bear?" Shane asked, amusement laced through his voice. "You think he'll be attacked by a bear?"

She didn't appreciate his mocking, even if he was restraining it.

Ginger's worry was genuine. "He could go for a walk and get lost in the woods. Please, Shane, let him in."

He came over all innocent. "I wasn't locking him out," Shane said. "If he wants in, he'll come to the screen."

"And scratch," Calvin muttered. "There goes our security deposit."

Shane's ease lessened. "Who paid the pet deposit? I forget."

"Why is the dog so important to you?" Guinness

asked, transforming their conversation into something else.

Rather than an informal exchange, Ginger suddenly felt like therapy had started.

Everyone was looking at her, waiting for an answer. "I don't want him to get hurt," she murmured.

"No, please don't feel you should withdraw," Guinness said, intensifying his focus. "We're not judging here. It's just curious that you should have such a strong reaction." He addressed the group. "This is an important point that you all must understand, nothing said here is to be judged. We should also do our best to avoid confrontation. Everyone is entitled to their opinion. Honesty is important. So when someone is talking or expressing themselves, we shouldn't interrupt. We can ask questions. But voices shouldn't be raised. We're not attacking each other here, simply trying to make progress. So, Ginger, do you think Rocky will get hurt outside? He's a hardy dog and we would hear him barking if he was in trouble."

"I know," she said, self-conscious about making such a big deal about it. "I just wouldn't want him to think he was unwelcome or abandoned."

The doctor was nodding. "Often we project emotions from ourselves onto others. You said you recall feeling emotions from the past. Do you remember ever feeling unwelcome or abandoned?"

Calvin answered, "We know now that she was abandoned in the ocean."

Murphy sat up straight. "Wait a fucking minute, she wasn't abandoned out there. It was an accident. No one chose to leave her there."

Guinness' focus stayed on her. "Is that it, Ginger? You felt abandoned?"

Coming to the lodge was supposed to be helpful. Their first therapy session was proving how much pressure would be laid on her.

"No, I… I didn't remember anything about the accident until yesterday," she said.

Seated on the central couch, Ginger had Owen at her side. Guinness was right next to the fireplace with Shane and Murphy's couch nearest it. Calvin and Diane's couch was on the other side of hers. That put Ginger in the epicenter of everyone's attention.

"Yes, you mentioned that recollection at dinner," Guinness said. "You remembered something when you were talking to Shane."

She nodded and glanced at Shane. When she'd mentioned it, the doctor had advised her to wait for the session to discuss it further. He wanted to get session one under their belt before widening the forum to discussing things in non-therapy time.

"It happened when we were talking about family," Shane said. "About Cam's family and things got… heated."

That intrigued the doctor. "You argued?" They both nodded. "What did you argue about?"

When it became clear that Shane wasn't going to answer, Ginger did. "His parents," she said, thinking that the group couldn't expect her to be honest and then hide their own flaws.

Murphy laughed and dropped a heavy hand to his leg. Owen didn't do a much better job of hiding his own smirk.

"That's funny?" Guinness asked Murphy.

"That they were arguing about my parents?" Murphy asked. "No, not ha-ha funny… well I guess yeah, it is ha-ha funny 'cause I laughed."

"Why is that amusing?" the doctor asked.

Murphy and Owen shared a look. "Oh, I don't know, maybe because they spent years arguing about, and with, the Warrens," Owen said.

"We're not getting into that, not on day one," Shane said, glaring at his brother and hers.

Twisting to look at him, Ginger didn't miss how her so-called husband avoided eye contact. "Within minutes of us being alone at the church you were talking about my pussy," she said.

Diane squawked.

Owen covered his ears. "Tell me when this part of the conversation is over," her brother said.

Ginger slapped his thigh and he dropped his hands.

She stayed fixated on Shane who had finally conceded to look at her. "You'll talk about that, but not family? Just what do you classify as personal? Some would say talking to a woman about her intimate parts is personal."

"If I offended you," Shane sneered. "I'm sorry."

That was snide. His expression was cutting, his eyes cold like he was unimpressed that this had somehow become about him. Judging by his glare, she guessed he blamed her for that.

Owen took her hand before he spoke, "You have to remember that when we last saw you... you were... well... you. And when we first saw you in the church, you looked like our Ginger, mostly... We didn't realize you were... different. So in Shane's defense, talking about sex with you and your... parts... well that's normal behavior."

"I assure you, it's not," Diane scoffed.

Murphy tsked. "Well, no, it's not normal for a woman with a stick up her butt like you, but it was normal for them, okay?"

"Excuse me?" Diane asked.

Calvin objected with some bluster too.

Guinness held up a calming hand. "If we can refrain from insults, please."

"Sorry," Murphy mumbled.

"He's protective of his brother," Owen said. "As I am of my sister. We've been looking for her for sixteen months. There were times we thought we would never see her again. This… it's an adjustment for all of us. We thought we were looking for our Ginger. We were so focused on that, we never considered what we'd find."

Oh. That was a blow, one that made her slide her hand out from under his and blink her eyes away from Shane's.

"Meaning?" she asked, feeling inadequate.

Owen swallowed and squirmed. "Just… you're different."

"How am I different?"

"Because she doesn't remember?" Guinness asked. "She doesn't respond to you how she used to because she doesn't remember the details of your lives and relationships?"

"Well, yeah," Owen said. "But not just that, she's… she's more reserved, I guess. Her confidence is lower."

"That's understandable," Guinness said. "She's lived through a traumatic event and none of you should kid yourselves that she isn't suffering from PTSD. She will probably always feel the effects of this event, even if all of her memories return."

"What does that involve?" Shane asked.

His tone was so detached and businesslike that a shiver went through her.

The doctor inhaled before answering, "If her memories return there will be more flashbacks. I have read some of her previous psychiatrist's notes. She suffers from nightmares now, mood swings, anxiety attacks… It's not a nice illness. She can be fine one minute and descend into panic and paranoia the next. It's important for those with PTSD to have a secure support network… and the most integral part of that is her son."

Shane's chin rose. "Cam?"

"Yes," Guinness said. "He came through the trauma with her. He might not remember any of it, but he experienced every physical trauma Ginger did. One of the recurrent themes in her therapy has been her guilt over the kind of life her child would have without a past."

Wringing her hands on her lap, Ginger gritted her teeth. Despite her attempts to steel herself, the tears sank from her lashes to skitter down her cheeks.

"Should we be talking about this?" Owen asked.

Ginger could feel her sibling's eyes on her. Everyone else in the room was probably staring too.

"Would you like me to stop, Ginger?" Guinness asked. She shook her head, gripping her hands together. "Ginger knew this would be difficult and that she was asking a lot of you all to be here… she signed a waiver. All of you have some part to play in putting her life back together. She knew she couldn't do that without sharing more of herself than maybe she was comfortable with."

"If you're uncomfortable, why are you doing this?" Murphy asked with a gentle concern in his voice she'd never heard from him before.

"Cam," Shane said. "She's doing this for Cameron… That's why you were so adamant about my parents yesterday."

Raising her head, she met his eye. "I'm sorry," she croaked because the impact of her tears forced her to gasp in for breath.

"Shit," Shane whispered and was off the couch in an instant.

"Uh, if we could keep our seats," Guinness said.

Shane ignored him and came over to crouch in front of her, covering her hands with his. "Bit, he's fine. We're going to make sure he has the most incredible life. I promise."

Her voice was a mess, lost in the upset. "But if you hadn't found us—"

"I did," he said, smiling and cupping her face. "I did find you, baby. I was always going to find you. If it hadn't been then, it would've been tomorrow or the next day. I was never going to stop looking."

"But I never tried to find you," she whispered. "I knew you were out there. I knew he had a father and I… I never tried."

"I think you had enough to worry about," Shane said, brushing her lips with his thumb again. "You stayed alive and you kept him safe, that was what you were supposed to do. You did the right thing."

"We had no idea what kind of man he was," Calvin piped up. "Were we supposed to seek out someone who could've been a pervert or a sex offender?"

Ginger understood Calvin's position on the issue because they'd discussed it before. She'd always carried guilt about not doing more.

The doctor spoke again, "Please, Mr. Warren return to your seat."

Shane wiped the tears from her face. Ginger made herself smile knowing Shane wouldn't do as the doctor said unless she showed him that she was feeling better.

"Okay?" he mouthed and she nodded. "Good girl."

Shane went back to his seat and Owen handed her some tissues from the box on the coffee table.

When they were settled again, Guinness turned to Calvin. "You didn't think it was wise to search for Cameron's father?"

"Where would we have begun?" Calvin asked. "We knew nothing about who she was. She wasn't carrying anything and had no healed scars or tattoos."

Ginger's heart missed a beat. Shit, what did Calvin have to go and say that for? Letting her eyes ascend to the top of their sockets, she watched Shane's head rise slowly as clarity seeped in. He looked right at her for half a second. Ginger closed her eyes. Shit, he knew. She did have a tattoo and he knew it… but Calvin didn't.

At the hospital, in the initial days, when they were talking about distinguishing marks, she didn't confess the secret of what was printed on her body because she hadn't known it was there. It was only much later that she found it. Even then, she didn't want to admit to what it was or its location. The last thing she wanted was pictures of herself like that.

The maternity doctors probably knew it was there later. By then, her history was just another part of the file. No one paid any attention to that history because she and Calvin had been so clear about moving forward, not backward.

"There was no way for us to know who she was," Diane said, defending her son. "There was no jewelry, no significant labels in the clothes."

"What happened to her wedding ring?" Murphy asked.

"She wasn't wearing one," Diane said. "It probably came off in the water."

"It's possible," Guinness said. "Again, we're not here to make accusations or speculate. It's best we deal with facts and our feelings… Ginger, you felt guilty about not finding Cameron's father… Did you resent Calvin for not being more helpful?"

"No," she said quickly. "God, no, he was right, absolutely right. I can feel bad about something without regretting the way I acted. It was possible Cam's father was a good guy, but it was just as likely that he wasn't. And the longer I spent in the hospital without anyone coming to find me, I... I thought maybe it was a one night stand or a nothing relationship, you know? I mean, we knew nothing about the water. No one knew what had happened. As far as we know I was just left at the side of the road. There were so many possibilities and this..." She gestured around to the men. "This was never something we considered."

They kept talking about the early days and why they had and hadn't acted in particular ways. She'd been taken to the hospital unconscious and had no memory of anything before waking up in the private facility Calvin had paid to care for her. Shane and the others gave more details about their search and what had happened in the days and weeks after the sinking.

It was probably a couple of hours later when they stopped for a late lunch that coincided with Cameron's snack. Shane fed him while she went outside with Rocky. While Ginger was reflecting on everything that had been said, she stayed close. As soon as Cam was done, she took him for a walk with the dog, refusing all offers of company.

Everyone was nervous for her to be alone, but there was no problem with her short-term memory, so she found her way back.

Cam was awake when they got back to the chalet. He crawled around the yard with Rocky under Shane's purview until it was time for dinner at the lodge again.

All the activity meant she managed to avoid being alone with anyone except Cam, which was just the way she liked it. They'd got all the way to bath time, precious time that she enjoyed spending with her boy.

Her boy was in his seat in the middle of the bubbly water, separating his ducks into what seemed to be warring factions. Laughing at her son's enthusiasm for the toys, Ginger joined in the war until there was a knock behind her.

She glanced over her shoulder to see Shane propped on the doorway between the bathroom and his bedroom.

"Sorry, do you need in?" she asked. "We'll be just two more minutes."

"No, I'm good," he said.

The smug smile in his voice made her do a double take.

"You look damn pleased with yourself," she said, soaping her hands to run them over her boy.

Shane didn't even bother to hide his smirking joy as he sauntered over and hunkered down beside her. "Oh, I am. I am, baby. Very pleased with myself… and very pleased with you."

Ginger knew where the conversation was going and wouldn't look him in the eye. It was a good thing that she had Cam to focus on.

"Don't," she said. "Okay? Just… don't."

Obviously, Shane had decided not to be a gentleman. "You know what I'm thinking about, don't you?"

"Yes, I do," she said, shampooing Cam's hair much to his chagrin. He kept trying to push her hands away, but she persisted despite his protests. "And I'm asking you not to talk about it."

"Isn't it better that we talk about it now? It's that or it comes up at a therapy session."

"Then let it come up there," she said, styling Cam's hair in a soapy peak.

Shane rested his chin on her shoulder, indicating that he was way closer to her than he should've been. Ginger had General Cameron to keep her busy, so she managed to ignore the man at her side.

"In front of everyone, you really want me to talk about it there?" Her hands slowed in their soaping and descended into the water. "You haven't slept with him."

And there it was. Her eyes closed slowly. "Shane."

"I know," he said, grinning again. "I'm not supposed to be smug about it. I'm supposed to be calm and understanding. No judgment, but tell me, baby… why doesn't he get you hot?"

"Stop!" she exclaimed. Even Cam was startled, to divert her baby, Ginger smiled and blew a bubble with the soap, distracting him into a laugh. "It's not like that and I have slept with him, I just haven't… had sex with him… rather he hasn't had sex with me."

That comment put Shane on his ass. Sitting on the floor next to her, he frowned, pondering what she meant. His confusion gave her a window to lift Cam out of his seat to lay him back so she could rinse the shampoo from his hair.

"I don't even know what that means," Shane said a minute later.

"He's had oral," she said, pressing her lips to a thin smile that tried to be smug but didn't quite make it. "There. Happy that you know that?"

"No," he said, cringing like it was the most disgusting thing he'd ever heard. "No. I'm not happy knowing that… but it's better than what I thought this morning."

Ginger exhaled. "Please don't make this a thing," she said, sitting Cam up and wiping his face. "You might be okay with having dirty thoughts all the time, but not everything is about sex."

"Dirty thoughts?" he asked.

Cam splashed him. "Da!"

"Da has dirty thoughts, did you hear that, son?" he asked. "Maybe I need to wash those off."

Moving onto his knees, Shane grabbed his tee-shirt at the back of his neck and pulled it off in one slick move. Pouncing to a crouch, he took his cellphone from his back pocket and thrust it into her hands.

Before Ginger could say anything else, he leaped into the bathtub, jeans and all, scooping up a screaming Cameron into his arms in the process. The water sloshed, soaking her knees, but she didn't register. The sight of the shirtless father under his bouncing baby who was overjoyed by the craziness stunned her for a second.

Shane was soaked and his jeans would be wringing, but he didn't seem to care. Cam was splashing him, slapping at his chest with his joyful hands and lurching forward to kiss his insane father.

"You're crazy," she said, holding the phone in the air when more water sloshed. "And my hands are wet, your phone will be ruined."

"It'll be fine, it's water resistant," he said. "And I can always replace a phone. I can't replace the precious moments." Like her memories, he couldn't replace them. It was like he read her mind when he clutched Cam close and covered her cheek with his wet hand. "We'll make new ones."

Cam splashed him again. Shane shifted the baby so that he was sitting higher on his chest, giving them room to grab up the ducks to restart the war.

Shaking her head, Ginger smiled at her son. For some reason, her gaze fell to the phone in her hand resting against her lap. The lock screen was lit. It took her a minute to realize that the picture on it was of her, in Shane's arms.

There it was. Evidence of their past. His arms were locked around her shoulders, their faces side by side. His mouth was turned into her hair, his lips by her ear and her mouth was open in a laugh. But it was her eyes that mesmerized her, they were lit and alive. She looked... happy.

"Gorgeous, isn't she?" he asked.

Her attention snapped up; he'd caught her

looking. "I… I'm sorry, I…"

"It's okay," he said and scooped water from the bath to wash bubbles from Cam's back. "There are other pictures in there… you can look, whenever you're ready."

"Pictures?"

"Sure," he said, still stroking his son, he shared a private smile with himself. "Just don't look at anything in the folder labelled *Relations*."

"What's in there?" she said, grinning. "Your porn?"

His smile got wider as his head bobbed. "Yeah. That's the folder I use to get myself off."

"Well you know I have to look now," she said.

Again, he'd diffused a difficult situation, putting her at ease with humor.

Cam wriggled and put a duck on Shane's defined arm. She'd tried not to focus on the fact that the man in her tub was half naked. It got more difficult with him relaxed and the water settled. His body was solid. Each muscle had been nurtured to its perfect peak fitness in a series of grooves and ridges that had once been hers to taste and tantalize.

Blinking, Ginger shook her head and averted her attention. Had she really just been looking at his chest thinking about how it would taste? Her eyes rose again, over the impressive girth of his upper arm to his rounded and capable shoulder. He had dedication to her body that—his body. Shit, he had dedication to his body, to his physique, not to hers. Why had she been thinking about him and her… together?

Her lips were drying, yet her tongue drowned as she turned her lips into her mouth, wondering what he'd do if she leaned over the rolled edge of the bathtub and closed her mouth over that groove at the base of his throat.

"Shit," she whispered.

"What?" he asked, oblivious to her thoughts as he ran his fingers through Cam's wet hair. It was his turn to do a double take, except he was confused, not smug this time. "Bit? Why are you blushing?"

"I'm… I'm not," she said and rose high onto her knees.

His hand shot out to grab her wrist. "Don't run away," he said, frowning.

That his worry was so genuine only made the moment all the more intense. How could a stranger care about her so much?

And why hadn't she turned the bathroom light all the way up? The dimmer switch had been a novelty, but now the lighting in the room seemed intimate.

A thrum between her thighs grew to an insistent tingle. It rose in a roiling heat to her belly, and blood heated her clit, making her more aware of it than she'd ever been. He pulled her an inch closer; his head tilted like he was trying to read her. God that hold, the strength in that grip. It owned her without scaring her. How the hell did he do that?

She wouldn't look him in the eye, couldn't. When he pulled her again, her curled fingers unfurled of their own volition and that was it.

He got it.

But he didn't say anything, he wasn't smug, he just lowered her hand to his pec and pressed it down hard.

Vibration ascended through her diaphragm. Weakness struck Ginger so hard that her knees gave way and her chest relaxed against the edge of the bathtub.

"Is that it?" he murmured. The velvet coating of his voice cascading across her skin closed her eyes as her lips parted in a whimper. "Is that what you need, baby?"

She didn't mean to nod but was sure she did.

Although with her eyes closed and her mind descending into a mist of hormones, reality and fantasy were fluid.

"I should..." she exhaled, unable to put any conviction in her voice.

He pushed her hand up to his shoulder, across to his throat and down until it was touching the waterline. While directing her caress, he didn't say anything, just gave her permission to fulfill her fantasy.

"Do you want to join us, baby?" he asked, releasing his grip, leaving her hand there on his ribs, so he could touch her mouth, smudging his wet thumb against her lips.

Ginger must have been infected by his craziness because she parted them a few millimeters and pressed a deep kiss against the pad of his thumb. When her eyes opened, they met his, which were aflame with the same hue of heat tormenting her insides. She did it again, this time letting his thumb go just a fraction deeper so she could drag her teeth on it in a light bite.

It was nice to see him unnerved and he was definitely that. His Adam's apple bobbed in a shaky swallow and she sank back, letting her hand slip out of the water.

"I guess you do like biting," he mumbled.

Looking to her son, she stood up and put the phone on the side before retrieving Cam's towel. Picking her son up out of the water, gave his father permission to leap to his feet.

But Ginger was already retreating to her room. "Leave your wet clothes in the tub or you'll make a swamp," she said. "Goodnight, Shane."

After closing her bedroom door and locking it from her side, she stood still, trying to process what had just happened and what it might possibly mean.

"Mama!"

Smiling at her son, she kissed his head. Thank

God she had Cam to concentrate on. He was her rock, he needed her, and she needed him… apparently more than she knew.

ELEVEN

HIS WIFE STILL KNEW how to drive him nuts. Whatever last night was, Shane wasn't complaining. In fact, he'd like more of it.

She'd been aroused by him.

Goddamnit. The memory put a real shit-eating grin on his face. It only got wider when he looked down at the picture on his lock screen.

"What's got you so happy?" Murphy asked, coming over to join him on the porch swing. "Therapy this morning was a head fuck."

They'd had therapy and lunch. Everyone had gone their separate ways since then. Calvin was at the lodge with his mother, Ginger, and Cam. Owen was upstairs on the phone to his husband. With the advent of video calling, the less Shane thought about that, the better.

Therapy this morning had been a discussion of childhoods in an attempt to make Ginger feel better about Cam's life so far. He figured she was looking for some clue about what was wrong with his parental relationship because when he didn't reveal any major trauma, she seemed disappointed. His upbringing had been fine and normal; it was in his adult life that the problems arose.

Therapy was a gradual process. Shane was impressed by Guinness' attempts to keep some of the pressure off Ginger, who hadn't shared much that day. She had enjoyed learning about her childhood from Owen. Seeing her smile so much was a boost he wouldn't take for granted.

Looking down at the lock screen picture again, he considered all the memories they'd shared that she might never remember.

Murphy leaned over to look at the image. "When was that?" his brother asked.

"Just a random moment," Shane muttered, thinking those were the ones they'd never get back.

Birthdays she would ask about. Anniversaries, their wedding, she'd ask about all of the significant events eventually. But that picture was from one of those times when they were just happy. It wasn't an event; it was just a day in their lives.

"You've had that on your phone forever… it's been a long time since I've seen you smile at it like that," Murphy said.

Owen came out of the back door to join them, propping himself against the porch railing opposite the door.

"Don't hate me," Owen said, offering each of them a beer.

Shane paused before taking the bottle. "For what?" he asked, given their current situation, anything could be going on.

"You have to go back to California."

Shane laughed and snatched the bottle to take a long drink. "You're funny, Owe. Thanks, I needed a laugh."

"The acquisition is falling apart. Ventura are talking about going a different way… Julianna said the sale was dependent on meeting you and guess what? She hasn't done that yet."

"Look around you," Shane said, gesturing to their surroundings. "I'm on a beautiful lake with my two best friends, my girl, my son, and my dog… Is there any amount of money that will make me walk away from this?"

"Your girl's fiancé and future mother-in-law are here too," Owen said. "Murph and I can hold down the fort; it'll be like three days."

"Nope," he said. "I'm not leaving until she's with me."

"Seriously?" Owen asked.

"I'm not leaving here without my wife and son."

Although he noticed Owen and Murphy exchanging a dubious look, he didn't care. Shane meant exactly what he said.

"You know I'm all about confidence," Murphy said. "But she's with him. I'm not saying you won't win, I know you will, but… we could be talking years. You knew her a year before you told her you loved her for the first time. It still took you like a year after that to get her to agree to go on a date with you."

"And they were married a year later," Owen said.

Shane slurped. "Would've been sooner if she'd been into the Vegas idea."

"Mom would've killed you if you eloped," Owen said and Shane laughed because it was so true. "She needed the year to plan the wedding of the century."

Sharing happy memories helped him hold on, and it was his responsibility to do that while Ginger couldn't.

"Yeah. In the end, it was me telling Ginny to be

patient," Shane said. "By the time we got married it felt like we'd been together forever."

"You had," Owen said. "Fun as history is to talk about, you know if it repeats itself that you have to wait a year before you tell her you love her, then another before she'll agree to date you. It will be a year after that before you're man and wife again… Ventura won't wait that long… this lodge won't be here that long."

That was an exaggeration.

Shane scowled at the innocent Owen, and shook his head. "It won't take us three years to be man and wife again."

"Oh yeah? We taking bets?" Murphy asked and held his fingers away from his beer bottle in turn as he counted. "Let's take into account the fiancé, the mother-in-law, the doc, who I can't figure out… Oh yeah, and the two thousand or so miles between where we are now and where you live… You'll be lucky if it's a year."

"More like two," Owen said.

The guys were so sure. They didn't know what he knew. Last night was a beacon, an encouraging sign of what was to come. Thinking about it, he hid his smirk behind his beer bottle, but not well enough. His friends saw it and eyed each other.

Murphy looked to him. "How long do you think?" his brother asked, his voice full of suspicion.

"A week," Shane said and both his buddies leaped to their feet.

"No way!" Murphy hollered.

Owen crouched in front of him. "What happened?"

"Did you fuck her?" Murphy asked.

Owen hit Murphy's leg. "That's my sister."

"Oh sorry, did you make sweet, sweet love to your beautiful wife?" Murphy mocked.

Shane laughed. "No, I just know my girl… Okay,

maybe we won't be man and wife in a week. Maybe that will take a bit longer. But I think we'll be back... 'there' in a week or two."

"Shit," Owen said, clutching his chest. "I don't know how you do it. I think I'm going to have a heart attack."

Murphy smacked his shoulder and sank onto the swing again. Owen pulled one of the wicker chairs over and they all touched bottles.

"To making memories," Shane said.

All of them drank, pondering that for a moment.

"How's Derek?" Shane asked, leading them into a conversation about life at home.

They were still talking about it about ten minutes later when the screen door creaked open. All three of them turned to see Ginger hanging out the door with Cam on her hip.

"Hey, buddy," Shane said and opened his arms. "Want me to take him?"

"You have an iPhone, right?" she asked and he nodded. "Can you unlock it?"

He dug it from his back pocket and did as she asked. "I'd wait 'til junior's asleep before you look at the porn," he said.

"Steady on, man," Murphy said.

The brothers probably thought he was joking. Let them, he was referring to last night and all he cared about was that Ginger knew it. The way she avoided his gaze was a telltale sign that she did. In truth, he'd welcome her looking at any of the pictures on his phone. After witnessing her response to seeing a single innocuous one last night, he'd be intrigued to watch how she reacted to the more... graphic ones. He went into the settings and took her hand to pull her closer.

Selecting her thumb, he straightened it out. "Here, do this."

"What are you doing?"

"Putting your print in," he said, moving her finger on and off the pad then turning it as required. It registered and he smiled. "There. Done. Now you can get into it any time. Just put your print on the home button."

Seeming perplexed, she took it and disappeared into the house.

"You just hand your phone over?" Murphy asked. "You better not have any kinky porn on your phone, you're trying to make a good impression. Remember, you have to ease them into kink."

As they all laughed, music blasted from the house, triggering them to leap to their feet.

"Geez," Owen said, holding his hand to his ear. "Cam's hearing will be permanently damaged… is that Blondie?"

"Party time," Murphy said, never one to say no to a good time.

His brother was the first inside. Even Rocky came running up the stairs to follow him and Owen inside.

In the living room, they found Ginger jumping and dancing with Cam who was laughing and trying his best to sing along in babbling baby talk. She dipped the baby then crouched and shot back to her feet. Shane hung back just watching her move, that body move, the body he'd felt beneath his hands so many times. The body that had reacted to his last night.

"What's going on?" Owen asked, going to the stereo in the corner where the phone was in the docking station.

Shane got it, she needed music and had said that she didn't have a cellphone of her own. Owen turned the music down. Cam shouted and wriggled away from his mother to crawl at speed across the floor to his uncle.

"He likes it loud," Ginger said as Cam tugged on Owen's jeans. "It's naptime and someone's not tired enough…" Looking at all of them, she shrugged. "If we have the house to ourselves, we dance… We can stop if it bothers you."

"If it bothers them, they can leave," Shane said, going to get his son.

He turned up the music and picked up the wriggling, baby-singing Cam.

"Put him on the floor," Ginger called above the music and went over to get on the floor with him.

Shane took the coffee table out the way to give them more room to dance and play. After Owen got used to the volume he was singing and playing DJ. It didn't take long to learn that Cam had a thing for rock music. Each of the guys took turns putting their phone on the dock to let him hear as much as possible.

When Cam was lying on the floor on top of his mother with his thumb in his mouth and his other hand tangled in her hair, Shane began to turn the music down gradually. By the time it was off, both mother and son were asleep on the floor.

"Man, your kid is fun," Murphy said. "He knocked Ginny out too."

"This whole thing is taking a lot out of her," Owen said.

Everyone was tired, but it was taxing on her in ways they couldn't imagine. The emotional pressure was immense, and she was still a full-time mommy too. Rocky went over to nose her face.

Shane pulled him back. "Upstairs," he said to Rocky who grumbled but turned to go upstairs.

"They're sleeping in his favorite spot," Owen said.

"No," Shane said, bending to carefully scoop both mother and son off the floor into his arms. "His favorite spot is spooning with Ginny… same as mine."

Ginger cocooned Cam in her arms and twisted toward him making it easier for him to carry both of them without fear of dropping the baby. When she rubbed her face in his neck half way up the stairs, he cursed. Great, he was hard again; she really had to stop doing that when he was concentrating.

Rocky was already on the bed when he got to the bedroom. He laid Ginger down and picked up Cam to move him into the crib like she'd shown him.

"Shane," she whimpered as he tucked Cam in.

"Yeah, Bit?" he asked and turned expecting to see her looking at him.

Instead, she was still fast asleep. A grin slid to his lips. Either she was dreaming of him or just had the urge to say his name, whichever way it was, he was winning.

TWELVE

AT LEAST SHANE THOUGHT he was winning until much later that night. The opposite seemed more true when he went into the kitchen and saw through the open back door that Ginger was in Calvin's arms. They were at the water's edge in the moonlight and the bastard was holding her, whispering something and kissing her lips.

Murphy came up beside him. "Want to revise your estimate?"

Shane felt sick. "Would it be wrong for me to go out there and punch him?"

"You could ask the doctor what the appropriate response is," Murphy said, but Shane knew the answer. "She's still wearing his ring, you know, Bishop's. If she wasn't planning on marrying him—"

"I get it," Shane said and turned his back on the intimate scene only to come face to face with a panicked looking Owen.

"Uh, Cam is awake," Owen said. His worry made Shane smile. "I have to get Ginger."

"There you go," Murphy said. "There's your

interruption. Did you train the kid?"

"We don't have to get anyone," Shane said. Although he was new to the fathering thing, the point of him sharing a bathroom with mother and son was so that he could bond with his child. "I'll go to him."

"You will?" Murphy asked.

Both Owen and his brother were surprised, but Shane was liking the dad stuff. Shaking his head and laughing, he left the kitchen and rounded into the living room to vault up the stairs.

Diane went to bed early every night, and he wasn't complaining about that. Except Shane didn't want his son being blamed for waking anyone.

When he opened the bedroom door, he strode in to find Cam was on his feet holding the edge of the crib bouncing.

"What are you doing, dude?" he asked. "You're supposed to be asleep."

As soon as he picked him up, he smelled the problem and then he understood Owen's worry. The fun stuff, he could do, the practical stuff had been all Ginger so far. Although he was worried about screwing up, his son needed him, so he took a deep breath and took him to the makeshift changing table.

***

GINGER WAS TIRED and confused. She just wanted to go to bed. Calvin had been right in most of what he'd said and that meant she had to talk to Shane. The idea of that particular conversation wasn't one she relished. When she'd come back inside, leaving Calvin outside, she hadn't seen anyone so hoped they were all in bed. If Shane was asleep, no one could expect her to talk to him. Maybe she could just slip into bed and worry about the situation later, like the next day later.

Opening her bedroom door carefully, she didn't make a sound so as not to disturb Cam. Ginger paused when she realized her bed was occupied by three slumbering males. Her surprise gave way to a smile as she angled her head to better admire the view. Shane was sleeping with an arm tucked around Cam and Rocky was on the other side of the bed. Covering her laugh with her fingertips, she went to nudge Rocky.

"Come with mommy," she whispered, "come on."

The dog gave a squeaking yawn but leaped down off the bed and trotted along with her. After putting the bedside barrier on the open side of the bed, she took Rocky through to Shane's bedroom. All she needed was a bed. And Shane deserved to know what it was like to wake up to Cam's version of an alarm clock at least once in his life.

Stripping to her underwear, she pulled back the covers and lay down in the bed. Rocky circled a couple of times and then slumped down with her. She stroked him and kissed his head, then closed her eyes.

***

IT WAS SUNNY when she woke up alone. Very sunny. Shielding her eyes with her hand, Ginger rolled over and opened an eye only to see she was right on the edge of the bed and face to face with a crouched Shane.

"Go back to sleep," he whispered and pulled a plug from the wall. "I'm just getting my charger."

But she was awake and it was sunny. "What time is it?" she grumbled.

"Ten thirty," he said.

Sort of half-nodding until his words sank in, Ginger sat bolt upright.

"Where's Cam?"

"Outside playing ball with his uncles." Jumping out the bed, Ginger ran to the window and shook the locked door. "Uh, I wouldn't go outside," Shane said.

She fought with the key she demanded everyone use so Cam couldn't get out onto the balcony.

"Why not? Is he okay? I need to see him."

"Okay but get dressed first."

Spinning around, she was aghast on catching sight of herself in the mirror to her left. All she wore was her thong panties and a plunge bra.

"Right," she said. "Clothes."

"I'm not complaining," he said. "Though knowing you slept like that in my bed won't help me sleep tonight."

She tried to straighten out her hair. "I didn't want to wake you."

"No, I get it," he said. "Sleeping with Cam was great. Thank you. He woke up early." Yes, that sounded like her boy. "He's not subtle, is he?"

She laughed and tried to remember where she'd put her clothes. "Not even a little bit."

"I took your clothes to the laundry," he said and pulled a tee-shirt from a drawer to toss it to her.

"Wish I'd known that was there last night," she said and put it on. "Did you feed him?"

"Cam?" he said, in a daze as he watched her cover up. "Yeah, I'm not sure you can't feed him. He's clear about what he wants. It's impossible to neglect him." While unlocking the balcony door, she threw a glare at him. "Not that I ever would."

Going outside, she was chilled by the air, but it was sunny and probably warm away from the shade of the awning. Just as Shane had said Cam was outside crawling around after a ball with Owen and Murphy under his spell. She watched for a minute and then Cam noticed her and pointed up, so she waved.

"Ma!" he screamed.

Ginger laughed. "Good morning, Angel. Are you being a good boy?"

"Da!" Cam hollered.

Ginger turned around to see that Shane was joining her. He leaned on the wooden railing, just a little closer to her than he should be. But making a big deal of his proximity would draw attention to it. She'd learned her lesson about doing that so stayed still and tried not to be tense.

"Well isn't that a blast from the past," Murphy called, never subtle. Maybe that was where Cam got it from. Was something like that genetic? Murphy grinned and shielded his eyes from the sun. "She naked under your shirt, bro?"

"Oh God," she whispered and turned to dart back inside despite Shane gesturing at his brother to cool it.

"Ignore him," Shane said, coming in and locking the door again.

But it was too late, the damage was done. "I'm not the one we have to worry about," she said and took off his tee-shirt.

Ginger was too frantic to be modest and he'd seen her naked before. He'd alluded to that so many times that it was a given. Her underwear was as concealing as a bathing suit anyway. Though, in honesty, Ginger didn't care, couldn't care, not while she paced and panicked.

"What's wrong?" Shane asked, coming over to take her arm and stall her. "Gin, talk to me."

By accident, she'd fallen into a private moment with him. That was as good a time as any to have the conversation.

"He's jealous of you," she whispered.

"Who?"

For a brief frustrating second, Ginger considered that he might be the dumbest man on the planet. "Calvin," she said, refraining from following it up with an impulsive 'duh'. "We're spending too much time together."

"You're spending too much time with Calvin?"

God, he was thick or playing dumb to rile her. "Us. We're spending too much time together," she said, removing his hand from her arm. "And you touch me too much."

He squinted. "Is that you saying that or him?"

"Him!" she said then lowered her volume and began to finger the ends of her hair. "What was I thinking? He tells me it's too much and then I come up here and sleep in your bed."

"I wasn't in it," Shane said. "If I was in it, then I could understand him being upset… But wait a fucking second, I'm the husband! Shouldn't I be pissed off about your little make-out session in the yard last night?"

Mortified, she sagged. The universe wasn't playing nice. "You saw that?" Ginger whined and he nodded. Her head fell to her hands. "God, this is a mess. He was upset, I had to give him something."

"Give him something?" Shane said, his tone discouraging. He shook her once to make her look at him. "I left you alone because I thought you wanted to kiss him. Are you telling me you were doing that under duress?"

"No! Not under duress, no! Shane, I—"

"I think I need to talk to your fiancé—"

Before he could move her aside, she got in front of him, blocking his way to the exit. "Please, Shane, this is difficult enough. I can't have you two… fighting… I… please."

"Please what?" he asked. "What do you want me to do? Let him force you into kissing him?"

The moment was getting away from her fast. "He didn't force me," she said. "It wasn't like that. I just meant... he doesn't feel good. I wanted to make him feel good."

His scowl didn't scream understanding, in fact it was outright snide. "I don't feel good. What do I get?" he snapped.

If he was going to give attitude, she was going to return it. "You're a big boy, get over it."

"Oh so he's the baby? Are we in agreement about that? He gets a kiss and I get the cold shoulder?"

Shane didn't pout like Calvin did, but his anger made her feel different, so she responded to each man in different ways. She didn't argue with Calvin, not like she did with Shane. It made no sense to her why Shane couldn't see the situation from Calvin's point of view.

"What do you want from me?" she asked, lifting her shoulders. "You want a kiss? Will that make you feel better?"

She picked up his hand and kissed the back of it.

He grouched. "Yeah, 'cause that's the same as what he got."

"I can't give you both the same..." She moved in close so no one could overhear, not that there was anyone else around. Maybe she was paranoid. "Did you forget what happened in the bathroom?"

That relaxed him, but it wasn't supposed to make him smirk like it did. "I didn't forget."

Clinging to her patience, Ginger tried to be clear. "You and me, we're..."

"We're? Married? Yeah, I know."

"Well I don't," she said. His attitude began to accumulate again, she could actually feel it prickling her skin without him saying a word. "I don't remember being married to you, so you can't expect me to do... married things."

"I never asked you to do any damn thing. We're talking about what your fiancé is asking you to do," he said and picked up her hand to show her ring. "And why are you still wearing this? You know you're not going to marry him, right?"

Pulling her hand away, she stepped back. "I don't know that. Why should I know that?"

Bowing, he brought his face close to hers. "To marry him, you have to divorce me… You think I'm going to consent to a divorce? Look at my face, Bit, do I look like I'm open to that?"

She wouldn't be intimidated by Shane any more, not after witnessing how he melted around their child. Ginger could be overwhelmed by him, but she'd never fear him.

"Who I marry is my business and I'll divorce you if I want to. I can argue extenuating circumstances. There isn't a judge in the country who wouldn't consent to a divorce petition given the situation, even without your consent."

He threw his head back in a laugh then sneered at her. "Oh, baby, you do have a sense of humor." Getting close again, he brushed his fingertips down the strap of her bra. "It'll take more than a kiss to scare me away."

Her hands rose to her hips. "Then I'll make sure he gets more than a kiss next time."

Full of horror, Shane inhaled, but the door opened before he could say a word.

Owen stuck his head in but faltered when he drank in the scene. "Are you two fighting again?"

"Yes," they said in unison.

Owen shrugged. "At least you agree on something. I'd tell you to get a room, but… yeah… Anyway, put some clothes on, sis. The nanny is here, it's therapy time."

Spinning around, Ginger marched to her room. "Oh, goodie," she hissed.

THIRTEEN

THERAPY WAS NOT going to be fun. No one was saying much. Maybe because she was in a huff or because Shane was sulking.

Guinness was struggling to get anyone to engage. "I sense heightened tension in the room today," the doctor said. "Should we talk about that?"

"No," Shane said at the same time she did.

"Did something happen between you two?" Guinness asked.

Her foot was shaking in a show of the frustration and adrenaline still lingering from what had happened upstairs. Of their own accord, her eyes drifted to Calvin, probably because some part of her subconscious wanted to know if her mood was obvious.

Her fiancé was already fixated on her. "Did you talk to him?" Calvin asked. "Is he causing trouble?"

"Yo, buddy, I'm right fucking here," Shane said. "If there's trouble, it's between her and me."

"That's not the point of this retreat," Diane said, more smug than usual. "You were told to back off, weren't you?"

"Oh, you spoke to your mommy about it," Shane said to Calvin then looked at her. "You were right, Bit, he is a baby."

Slamming her hand on the arm of the couch, she sat up. "I did not say that!"

Shane scoffed. "You've called me way worse. If he needs his hand held over one bad name, he is a fucking baby."

"Okay, why don't we go back to the beginning?" Guinness said and laid his focus on Calvin. "You and Ginger talked about Shane?"

"Yes, last night," Calvin said. "I told her that I believed she and Warren were spending too much time together… and then she went upstairs and slept in his bed."

At the time it hadn't seemed like a stupid move. Ginger was mad at herself. What had she been thinking?

"I wasn't in it!" Shane exclaimed. "I wasn't in the fucking bed. I was in her bed with our son. Would you rather she got into her own bed with me and Cam? 'Cause that works just fine with me. I'll make sure I'm in her bed every night. And I'll say the same thing to you that I said to her upstairs, I'm the fucking husband! If anyone has a right to be pissed, it should be me. I'm the one with rights to have a problem with you!"

"Okay, this is good," Guinness said. "We need to get to the heart of these issues."

"She's marrying me," Calvin said as though the doctor hadn't said a word.

"She's already married!" Shane exclaimed. "She can't marry you!"

"Until she divorces you," Calvin said and looked at his mother.

"That's not gonna happen," Shane said.

A bang upstairs put Ginger on her feet in a flash.

Before the wail of Cam's cry even hit the air, she was halfway to the stairs. She knew her baby's cries and that wasn't a standard boo-boo cry.

Throwing open the bedroom door, she gasped at the sight of the nanny clutching a screaming Cameron who had blood over the side of his head. Ginger had never known pure terror until that moment. Her whole body clenched in fear.

"Shane!" she screamed until all the air was gone from her lungs.

Grabbing a towel from the changing table, Ginger rushed over to snatch her baby, pushing the towel to the wound.

"I'm sorry, Mrs. Warren! I'm sorry! He was on the bed and I turned around and—"

Ginger didn't have the time to think about the nanny. Hurrying back to the bedroom door, she met Shane coming in. Immediately, he pulled her under his arm.

"Hospital," he said, guiding her down the stairs and into his truck.

They were on the road a blink later. Cradling her crying baby, kissing and soothing him, Ginger tried to see the extent of the wound.

"It's okay, baby," she whispered into him, kissing his soft hair. "Momma's here."

Tears rolled over her lashes in constant streams. When Shane glanced her way, they made eye contact. The worry she read in him made her inhale, but she bit her lip because staying calm was crucial. If Cam saw her upset, he'd get upset too.

"He's okay," Shane said, pulling her hand to his mouth to kiss it. "Just keep him awake, keep him talking."

"Boo," she whispered, her heart sore with trepidation squeezing around it.

Shane glanced at her again. "I promise you, baby, everything will be just fine."

Despite his confidence, when she locked her fingers between his and pulled his hand against Cam's back, she felt that he was shaking just the same as her. "You hear that, Angel," she said into their baby. "You're going to be just fine. We love you so much, we do." Sitting back to look at Cam's pale, tear-stained face, she smiled and kissed his nose. "Cammy, you're a good boy... tell mommy you're a good boy."

"Goo..." he said.

Ginger was so relieved to hear his voice. Although it was wavering, at least it was there.

"That's it," she said. "We're going to get you cleaned up, then we'll take you home and mommy will get you some strawberries. What do you think of that?"

"Num..."

"Yes," she said and brushed the smudged blood from his skin. The wound wasn't bleeding anymore, but the sight of that stain on her precious baby kept her heart pounding. There was just so much of it and a head wound was always serious. "And we'll play with Rocky. You like Rocky, don't you?"

"Wooo."

"Yes," she said and grinned as she kissed him again. "We'll play with the doggy; do you think he likes strawberries?" Cam tried to cuddle against her, but she sat him up again. It broke her heart to see fresh tears welling in his eyes. "Mommy wants to see those beautiful eyes. Who has the most beautiful eyes?"

"Da!" Cam said and pointed at his father.

She laughed a half-sob but smiled and kept stroking and kissing him. "Daddy does have beautiful eyes," she said and they shared another moment. "But whose eyes are the most beautiful?"

"Ca..." he said and touched his own chest.

"That's right," she said. Her concern grew when her baby's eyes got heavy. "Shane?"

"Hey," Shane said, trying to sound upbeat as he put on the radio. "Do you want to dance?"

Cam perked up, so she turned him around so he could press the buttons on the radio, changing stations and settings.

It was probably less than twenty minutes as he'd said, but it felt like twenty hours before they pulled into the hospital. Shane didn't bother with a space, he pulled right up next to the ambulance bay and put the car in park.

"You'll be towed," she said when he pulled her and Cam out of the truck.

"I'll buy a new truck," he said, urging her into the ER. Putting her against the wall by reception, he stroked a hand down her face and cupped Cam's back. "Wait here a minute, baby, okay?"

Shane went straight to a doctor. He didn't even go to the desk or a nurse, he went straight to a doctor who was with a patient, took his arm and pulled him away, draping an arm over his shoulders as they walked. They exchanged some quiet words and then the doctor snapped his fingers and pulled three nurses away from what they were doing to come to her.

"Cameron," the doctor said, reaching for the baby.

Ginger wouldn't give him up. "He hit his head," she said, without any desire to hand over her baby, especially when he was clinging to her tight.

"Yes, he'll be taken care of," the doctor said. "Why don't you bring him to this room along here?" Past all the curtains and waiting patients, they were taken into a private room. The doctor pulled back a curtain to reveal the bed and gestured to it. "Do you want to sit down with him?"

The doctor put Cam through a battery of tests. He was optimistic and friendly the whole time and accommodated her odd, clingy behavior. They gave Cam cat scans, x-rays, and an MRI. When they were all done, she gave him a feed, something she'd been trying to wean him from. Just as she tucked her breast away, Shane opened the curtain.

"Oh, I'm sorry," he said.

Ginger smiled. "It's okay, I'm done," she said, and moved off the bed to lie Cam down. "They said it was okay to let him sleep."

Cam had a bandage around his head and looked like quite the wounded soldier. Shane had been the one with the doctors receiving the final results.

"They're going to keep him in for observation overnight."

She stopped dead, her eyes wide as a fresh wave of panic consumed her. "Why? Oh my God, what's wrong with him?"

Shane smiled and came over to stroke her arm. "Nothing, baby, I promise, he's fine. They said head wounds always bleed like a motherfucker." She scowled so he shrugged. "My word, I'll admit… There is no internal bleeding or swelling. No fracture."

"So why are they keeping him in?" she asked.

"Because I can be a motherfucker too," he said. "Sorry… I asked them to keep him in. He'll get the full service treatment, I promise, and we can stay with him. He'll get his own room upstairs. He'll have a TV and toys, everything he wants."

Her heart rate began to even out though the adrenaline was still sticky and bitter in her mouth. "But he's healthy? You're not trying to protect me? Because I would rather know if—"

"He's fine," he said, brushing her jaw with the back of his finger.

Ginger exhaled. "Next thing is the cost," she said. "Calvin has all of the insurance details—"

"It's taken care of," he said.

She hadn't expected him to say that. "You paid for his treatment? But… that must have been a fortune, they gave him every test under the sun."

"So we know he's healthy. All worth it."

Turning around, Ginger watched her angel sleeping. Her shaking hand went to her mouth. "If anything had happened to him, Shane…" she whispered.

"Nothing did," he said. "Just an accident."

She turned back to him. "Just an accident took me from you for sixteen months."

His smile faltered. "That won't happen again, you have my word."

"I was so worried," she said, her voice breaking.

"Hey, it's okay."

But words wouldn't console her. With Cam sleeping, Ginger could relax, and that gave her tears silent permission to escape. Her baby had been in need. She could've lost him, anything could've happened. Her son was the only sure thing in her life.

Leaning forward, she rested on Shane and he wrapped her in his arms. "Shh, baby, I got you. You don't have anything to worry about. I got you."

Tipping her head back, she saw something more in him than she'd noticed about the desirable man in the bathtub. "You were there, Shane. When I saw the blood, I called for you and… you were there."

He smiled. "Where else would I be?" A kind of concern swept his expression when her hand slid up between them and kept on going until it rested on his face. Grazing her thumb on his stubble, she wondered again what he'd taste like. It wasn't like before when blind desire brought the question to mind. There in that room, it was appreciation and… something else. "I'm yours, Bit. Always. But once we cross the line, you can't ever go back," he murmured, appearing more dubious than she'd have assumed he would.

"I know," she whispered.

Before she could make a decision on whether to cross it or not, the door opened and Calvin came in with Diane and the others.

"How is he?" Owen was the first to ask, rushing over to the bed.

"A wounded soldier," she said, leaving Shane's arms to join her brother. "He's sleeping. We shouldn't disturb him."

"What a trooper," Owen said, touching the bandage. "He takes a hit and still doesn't miss naptime."

She laughed and went into her brother's arms. Shane ushered everyone else out as her brother comforted her. Having Shane around to keep control was invaluable. Ginger would never be able to repay what he'd done for her and Cam that day.

FOURTEEN

OWEN STAYED AT Ginger's side every minute. He was still with her much later in the night as she stood over her son's crib in his private hospital room. The room had a cot and a couch in addition to Cam's crib. Shane had gone on the hunt for another cot, leaving her alone with Owen. Her brother sat on the couch, flicking through kids shows on the TV. It was programmed to only allow kids shows. There seemed to be Disney movies playing on repeat on different channels too.

Everyone else had gone back to the lodge. Murphy was taking care of Rocky and she imagined that it wasn't fun being the only Warren in their chalet.

"You're a good mom, you know," Owen said absently as he channel surfed.

She stopped fixing Cam's blankets to look at her brother. "What?"

"Today, the way you jumped into action. You called Shane and boom, the two of you were out the door. Gone. Spraying up gravel, blasting out of there like Bonnie and Clyde with a score, fleeing in a hail of bullets."

Her brother did see things in a strange way. Content that Cam was safe, Ginger went over to sit on the couch with him as he paused on something Disney, Beauty and the Beast.

"I like this one," she said, putting a hand over his on the remote to stop him.

Their hands and the remote sank to his knee. They watched the muted TV for a minute.

"He loves you," Owen said. "You do know that, don't you?"

Her focus fell away from the TV. Were they going to talk about it? Really? There, like that? Owen wasn't going to be polite and ignore their situation and she wasn't going to play it dumb.

"Shane?" she asked.

"Yes, Shane. I'm not going to be here arguing for the other guy, am I?"

Twisting to face him, she put an elbow on the back of the couch. "I'm in the most impossible position," she said.

Odd as it was, it felt natural to confide in him.

"Why?" he asked. "You love someone or you don't." Sealing her lips, Ginger thought for a second and he seemed to sense her hesitation. "I'm a lawyer, you know attorney-client privilege?" She nodded. "You and I are the fucking Hoover Dam with each other's secrets. Everyone used to joke we had brother-sister privilege that was more sacred to me than attorney-client... Anything you say to me is in confidence."

"I do love Calvin. I was so sure about marrying him. He was my whole world, all I knew."

"Because you had amnesia. You don't even have a job, do you? You don't have friends. You have no social life. He didn't let you find your old life or experience a new one." She wasn't happy with that answer and he seemed to sense that fast. "I'm playing Devil's Advocate… If you want to be with Calvin, I'll still be your brother, won't I? So really, I have no vested interest in whether you choose Calvin or Shane… or no one. You know that's an option too, right?"

"No one," she muttered. "Go out on my own?"

The question amused him. "You wouldn't be on your own, you'd have me. And you'd have Cam… You know you used to have a great life. Even before Shane, you had friends, you had a job. You don't need a man." He cast his eyes upward. "Sheesh, listen to me."

She laughed and took his hand over the remote again. "I don't know what I want, but I feel like… I feel like everyone expects something and I don't know what it is."

"We just want you to be happy," Owen said. "You're really holding court. I mean, you've got two gorgeous guys by the balls, hanging on your every word. You've got the mother waiting for you to pick her son. Murphy ready to take bets on when you'll be back with Shane and…"

"You," she said. "What is it you want from me?"

"I want you to be happy," he said again, drawing a line across her wrist with a fingertip.

"Owen," she said, ducking to make eye contact. "What do you want from me?"

He exhaled. "I don't want to put more pressure on you."

"Please just tell me, I'll hate to wonder."

"Mom," he said. "I'd love it if she could meet Cam."

"Really?" she asked. It was obvious he didn't understand how much that meant to her. "I would love for them to meet."

"You would?"

He grinned and grabbed her into a hug. When he

pulled back, she got her turn to wipe tears from his cheeks.

"You're a lawyer, right?" she asked. He nodded. "You'll have to help me, I don't know the rules about siblings and the law."

He got serious. "I can help you. You need help with the law?"

"I don't have ID. I don't think I can travel without it and I… I don't even know the rules with my name being… I don't know."

Owen patted her hand. "Shane has your passport. The original… you were supposed to take it on the boat, but he left it in the car by mistake along with his. So you have all the documents you'll need to travel."

"Good then… Cameron will need one."

Owen's business face returned. "We'll have to talk about that. Do you have his birth certificate?" She nodded. "I can arrange it."

"How soon do we have to go?"

"Not before Cam's better." Well obviously not before then, nothing would persuade her to take her baby out of the hospital before he was better. "It would work for me if we waited a while anyway. Shane has a business thing I've been bugging him about. If you suddenly declare you're going home to see mom, he'll think I persuaded you to go home to get him back there."

Ginger could see why she'd been so close to her brother.

Joking, like she was serious, she found it easy to relax with him. "Gosh, is Shane Mr. Ego or what?"

Owen tutted. "Yeah, exactly, right?"

They laughed and she steeled herself to ask what she'd been considering since Cam got the all clear.

"How quickly can a name be changed?"

"Overnight," he said.

"And a passport? How long does that take?"

"Whose name are we talking about?" he asked and she glanced toward the crib. "At Cam's age, with the consent of both parents, in a day."

She nodded and took both his hands. "Then there's something we have to do… as a kind of thank you for today."

"Okay," he said, tilting his head and peering at her. "What?"

She grinned. "I think I like having a lawyer brother."

"You always did," he said and pulled her into another hug.

FIFTEEN

CAM WAS RETURNING to his old self. It was as if nothing had happened, except for the bandage covering the wound. At least they had taken off the one that was wrapped around his head and replaced it with sticky gauze that they'd be able to change after each bath. One tiny dissolvable stitch just behind his ear, already he was scarred for life.

Ginger watched her baby sleep and turned on the monitor in their chalet bedroom. Part of her wanted to stay right there, forever. Doctor Guinness had been the one to tell her it was best to get back to normal as quickly as possible and not to let her anxieties about Cam's wellbeing become paranoias that would weigh her down.

It was naptime, and she was going to leave him alone for the first time since he'd hurt himself.

Going down the stairs, she found Calvin and his mother in the living room. Guinness was reading in the corner. The trio of men she was seeking were on the back porch beyond the kitchen.

Bringing the monitor to her ear, she listened for

Cam's breathing one more time. When she was satisfied that he was okay, she headed for the porch, grabbing her jacket on the way past. The three men were laughing before Ginger went out but silenced when she opened the screen.

"More music?" Murphy asked.

She smiled. "No, he's sleeping." Holding the monitor out to Shane, she waited for him to accept it. Instead of letting go of the device, Ginger pulled their joined hands to her chest. "Can I take Rocky for a walk?"

"Knock yourself out, gorgeous," Shane said and whistled. Rocky bounded up the stairs. "Go keep momma safe."

Rocky barked in response and ran back down the stairs.

With a hand on his jaw, Ginger took Shane's attention from the dog up to her. "Will you check on Cam? I mean, will you keep checking on him?"

"I swear it, baby. I'll keep him safe," Shane said.

Ginger lowered her mouth to nuzzle her lips on his knuckles over the monitor before turning to follow the path that circled the water with her fur-baby leading the way.

***

DAMN, HE WAS HARD again, and in the company of his brother and hers. Picking up a pillow from the swing, Shane tried to be discreet about moving it to his lap, but the guys were already jeering.

"Man, you need to get some!" Murphy said, shoving him.

Shane didn't need to be told. He'd been waiting sixteen months for some and the some he wanted was just disappearing into the tree line.

He groaned. "I swear she's doing it on purpose."

"Trying to break your dick?" Murphy asked and gulped his beer. "Your Ginger would totally tease you like that."

His Ginger. "Something… I don't know, something's happening," he said, watching the spot where she'd disappeared into the trees.

He and Murphy were on the swing with Owen on the wicker chair opposite, in the positions that had become their norm.

"What about you?" Murphy asked, giving Owen a light kick. "You spent all night in the hospital with her. You've been quiet."

"Nothing to tell," Owen shrugged and drank his beer.

Drawing his eyes away from the path, Shane was suspicious when he spied his brother-in-law.

"When I came back in with that bed, you were pretty damn cozy on the couch," Shane said. "What were you talking about?"

"Nothing," Owen said.

But he knew his brother-in-law's tells, and he groaned again when Owen drank his beer and averted his eyes. "You fucker! You bonded, didn't you?" he said. "You're back to that brother-sister privilege stuff, aren't you?"

Owen could barely contain his joy when he grinned. "Yes!"

"Well I'm happy for you," Shane muttered.

As much as he tried to sound like he was annoyed, he wasn't. Any return to her previous self was progress as far as he was concerned.

No one was in the mood for therapy that day; they were happy to spend it settling Cameron in. For once, there was a kind of truce. For the sake of the baby, everyone was going out of their way not to get in each other's faces.

Though it would be temporary, Ginger appeared more relaxed. She'd already told him they wouldn't be using the babysitting services of the lodge anymore too. He'd been in the manager's office that morning, it had been nice to play daddy in an official capacity.

"So, changing the subject, do you want me to file papers?" Owen asked.

"We're not suing the resort," Shane said.

Though he'd have thrown the book at them, Ginger accepted it as an accident. She didn't want the tearful college kid nanny to have this on her conscience when it was clear she felt bad enough. The babysitter had come over to the chalet as soon as Cam was back and she'd had a conversation with a surprisingly stern Ginger… Watching her play mommy had been a major turn-on. But who was he kidding? Everything was a turn on to him with her.

"You're not?" Owen asked.

"Ginger's decision."

"God, it's weird," Murphy said. "You've had the company for years and I've seen you act all grown up, but… seeing you and Gin play parents, it's like you're really an adult now."

"Well I'm going into town tomorrow anyway," Owen said. "So if you change your mind…"

That idea just pissed him off. "You're not going into town," Shane said. Ginger needed them there and no one was abandoning her, especially not after Cam's accident. "You're not going fucking anywhere."

"Yes, I am," Owen said, leaning forward and sticking out his tongue.

"Does that argument work in court?" Murphy joked.

"I have a note from mommy, I'm allowed," Owen said.

"Your mom?" Shane asked. It would be his

worst nightmare for something to happen to Ginger's mom while they were so far away. She'd never had to cope on her own for this long before. "Is she okay?"

"Not my mommy," Owen said. "Cam's mommy."

He did the math, but that just led to more confusion.

"You're going into town for Ginger?" Shane asked. Owen nodded. "What for? I can go get her whatever she needs now."

"Ah, ah," Owen said and nodded at the monitor. "You're on daddy duty."

He took the monitor to his ear and listened to Cameron sucking on his thumb. "I can go when she gets back."

Owen's smugness was playful. "You know, she has other friends now," he said. "This is a job only Uncle Owen can do."

Owen might think the teasing was fun, but every comment just increased Shane's intrigue. "Why?" he asked, leaning forward. He didn't like to be out of the circle when it came to Ginger. "What can you do that I can't?" He didn't expect an answer and was really just thinking out loud. "Is it something official? Something lawyery?" Saying nothing, Owen drank his beer and averted his eyes. Enough of a tell to prove to Shane he was right. Sometimes brother wasn't that different to sister; he knew all of Ginger's tells too. "What does she need a lawyer for?"

"Just be pleased she's using yours and not his," Murphy said, tipping his head backward to indicate Calvin.

That was true and an interesting distinction.

Shane was enjoying the puzzle. "Why would she use my lawyer and not Bishop's... Unless it's something that Bishop's lawyer won't do..." He couldn't figure it out. "You come back here with divorce papers and I'll shove them so far up your ass—"

Murphy laughed. "Sounds like a promise."

Owen crooked a brow. "I can't tell you what it is. It's both brother-sister privilege and attorney-client."

Whatever Ginger was doing, she was being proactive. That she was choosing to turn to her brother was a positive, a move in the right direction.

Shane got practical. "Did she sign a retainer agreement?" he asked. Owen just blinked. "I don't think she has her own accounts here. I'll wire the retainer now."

Shane lifted his hips to retrieve his phone from his back pocket.

Owen stalled him. "She's my sister, I don't need a retainer."

It wasn't about the money. "If she wants you to do something official, I don't want any gray areas," Shane said. "I don't want Bishop coming back at her or Boyd poking holes."

Owen scoffed. "Poking holes in my work? I'm insulted!" His brother-in-law could be dramatic. "Besides, I am the Warren family lawyer, so technically I never stopped being her lawyer."

Shane remembered something Calvin had once said. "Wait, this isn't a power of attorney or medical proxy thing, is it?"

"I can't say," Owen enunciated, but winked, which meant no.

"Speaking of which, we need to get Cam onto my insurance," Shane said to both Owen and Murphy.

"You paid cash at the hospital," Murphy said. "I wish I'd been there to see the doctor trip over himself when you told him how much you'd donate." He laughed. "You know how to get things done."

"You took care of that?" Shane asked, pointing

at his brother who nodded. "I'd have bankrupted myself if it meant Cam was safe and Ginny could relax. I've never seen her so scared… I mean, she was amazing. She kept her cool for Cam and kept him talking. She actually managed to keep smiling at him. It was just… she's astounding."

"Yeah, yeah, we get it," Owen said. "You're in love with her."

"Did you tell her that?" Murphy asked.

The words kind of slid out quickly. Shane didn't think anything about them, not until Owen froze, halfway to taking a drink.

Shane leaned forward to rest his elbows on his knees. "You told her I loved her?"

Full of innocence, Owen shrugged. "I thought it was a given."

"What happened to brother-sister privilege?" Murphy asked.

"I told her that before we re-established the privilege," he said and finished his drink.

Shane peered at him, playing the unimpressed brother-in-law again. "Just what else was said before you re-established this special privilege?"

Owen shrugged and picked at the label on his bottle. "Nothing, she just said she was in an impossible position."

Murphy nudged him. "That's good, right? At least she didn't say she wanted you to get the fuck out her life."

"Did she?" Shane asked, intent on Owen. "Did she say that?"

But he knew Owen too well. He wasn't going to betray his sister. Once someone betrayed Ginger, there was no going back and time was too precious. They needed to rebuild these relationships, not help each other break them.

One thing did pop into his mind. It wouldn't exactly be betraying anything if Owen simply confirmed or denied his curiosity.

Shane cleared his throat and tried to be aloof when asking, "Did she tell you what happened... upstairs?"

Both Owen and Murphy closed in around him.

"Yes," Owen drawled, but turned his head a fraction. "Yes, she did tell me. That was quite... interesting."

Laughing, Shane shoved both men away. "She didn't tell you shit," he said and stood up. "I'm going upstairs to hang with my boy. You two can sit down here and speculate."

He wasn't going to give up secrets and he liked spending time with Cam, even when he was sleeping. Owen and Murphy would be a nightmare for a while anyway and he didn't want to hear what whacked ideas they might come out with. So he headed upstairs to keep an eye on the boy he'd promised his wife he'd protect. Letting her down again wasn't on his agenda.

SIXTEEN

CAMERON WAS SLEEPING. Even though it was dark outside, Ginger was restless. Maybe because Shane had taken care of bath and bedtime that night while she spoke to Calvin about the hospital and therapy. That left her feeling like there was something important she'd forgotten to do.

Her conversations with Calvin were becoming more and more benign. It was heart-breaking that there was such distrust growing between them, because he was the man she was supposed to be marrying. She could see he was becoming more guarded and less trusting of her. He was angry at her all the time; she didn't like letting him down.

She'd changed into her satin chemise for bed before she lay down a couple of hours ago. Still, sleep hadn't come, so Ginger considered changing and going for a walk. Though she didn't usually go out in the dark. Leaving Cam in Shane's care was still a new experience that she was trying to get used to. And she'd never left Cam at night. Never.

While it was nice to have some more freedom

during the day, after what had happened with the nanny, she doubted she'd be leaving her son with anyone except his father any time soon.

Frustrated, she threw back the covers and got out of bed to pace and wring her hands together to stop herself from pulling out her hair. Calvin hated it when she played with her hair. It was a habit she was trying to break.

All she wanted were answers. She wanted to know more about the life that Owen had alluded to and what the hell had she and Shane been arguing about the night of the sinking.

Frustrated with herself, pacing around and fretting would never help her sleep. Resolving to get back in bed, she turned only to spot Shane's phone on the corner of the changing table. Grabbing it up, she spun around with intentions of returning it, but stopped before she got two steps toward the bathroom.

Clutching it in both hands, she began to tiptoe backwards toward the bed. He'd said there were images on the device. They might give her clues about her past. Ginger kept going backwards until she was sitting on the bed. Hooking her feet under the covers, she turned off the lamp and lay down, pressing her thumb to the home button to unlock it.

Without looking at anything else, she went into the pictures and was about to go into them when she noticed the 'Relations' folder. He'd told her not to, but she smiled and clicked on it. He'd said that knowing, given half a chance, she would go straight into it. It wasn't violating any privacy when he'd really goaded her into it. She was curious about what he was into and how wild it might be.

Opening the first picture, it took her a minute to realize she was looking at herself in her underwear. When it sank in, she sat up. Oh God, it wasn't a porn folder, it was… them. It was the folder that he said he used to get himself off and it was filled with pictures of her.

Some of them were posed in beds and rooms she didn't recognize, wearing lingerie she didn't remember owning. Then, oh God, there were topless shots. She couldn't look at those, it was too mortifying.

Scrolling past images of her sleeping, and random pictures of her in perfectly normal places doing what she would consider normal things, she froze with her thumb suspended over the screen. She'd spotted what was next… Video.

Turning down the volume, Ginger dived under the covers to hide with the device like a naughty teenager before she pressed play, braced to hate what she was about to see.

It started with a silhouette of a woman standing in a long, tall window, looking out.

"Come on, baby, turn around," Shane's voice came down the phone.

"Not until you tell me you're sorry." Ginger heard her own voice, but it was teasing, they were playing.

He snorted. "Sorry? Yes, I'm sorry you're such a horny little fox that you couldn't stay the fuck away from my cock for ten minutes."

Ginger gasped. But Video-Ginger spun around and leaned back on the floor to ceiling window that showcased an epic view of the distant ocean under glorious sunshine. Her hair was different, way longer and she had thick bangs, but it was definitely her on that screen.

Video-Ginger's shirt was open. She loosened her cuffs then unzipped her skirt before letting it drop to the floor and strutting toward him, slowly, one foot in front of the other. She didn't recognize that confident vixen staring at the man behind the camera with sultry bedroom eyes.

"Did you lock the door?" Video-Ginger whispered.

The camera moved to the side like the operator was more interested in something else, which might explain the kissing noises.

"I don't give a fuck about the door, Bit. We've had an audience before… I need you."

The camera was tossed away and landed with a view of a ceiling.

Her laugh came down the speaker and was soon joined by the sound of someone clearing a desk. Papers cascaded over the screen, obscuring the visual, but the sound kept on going. There was more kissing and she guessed by the sounds of fabric and fasteners that clothes were discarded.

On the video, she shrieked. "Boo," her voice begged. "Oh, yes, sir I'll get right on that."

Video-Shane laughed, his mouth occupied between kisses. "That was cheesy."

"Shut up and fuck me, Shane… Shit… Okay, yeah… Like that… Keep doing that… Oh, God, that feels good."

"Yeah?" Video-Shane teased, his voice deep and guttural.

There was a loud spanking thwack and another female shriek.

"Fuck, Boo, you need to soundproof this office," she panted. "I want to scream for you."

Again his mouth was muffled, but Ginger heard when he said, "Did it the week after we started sleeping together."

Laughing came from the speakers. It sounded like there was another kiss and then she screamed.

"I knew there was a reason I loved you."

It felt weird listening to them having sex,

especially since she didn't remember it, so it was like eavesdropping. Closing that video with a blush, Ginger ignored how her skin shimmered. The chill in her limbs became weakness as her blood rushed between her thighs and to her breasts.

She meant to turn it off and forget she ever heard it. Instead, somehow, Ginger went to the next video and saw an image of Shane lying in bed. The new video didn't seem to be from a phone camera. The feed was coming from a fixed position high in a corner.

Shane was lying, face down in a massive mahogany-framed bed covered in red and black linens. Sleeping on his own, he hugged a pillow to his chest. The sheet was draped over his hips showcasing his beautifully toned back. Wondering if he had always been so particular about his physique, Ginger checked the details for the date and gasped when she read it. The video was created the week of her disappearance. In the video he was oblivious, but it was the week he was going to lose her.

Except, so far, nothing had happened.

The bed was raised on a step and there were more tall windows. The view outside was different to the one in the previous film. Wooden doors without handles on the far side of the screen gave no clue about what was beyond them.

Just when Ginger was about to turn off the video, figuring nothing was going to happen, a blonde appeared at the bottom of the screen. The blonde tiptoed over to the bed like she was trying not to wake the sleeping man.

Ginger was intrigued. Was she about to watch Shane cheating on her? Could she watch that and then not tell him she'd seen it?

The blonde got to the bottom of the bed and grabbed the sheet to yank it from him. Her jaw fell when she saw Shane's tan covered every inch of him, including his tight butt. But that wasn't the most shocking thing. He flipped onto his back and she got a glimpse of his dick before the blonde leaped onto the bed on top of him. She shouldn't but…

Ginger rewound and played the frames to see what he was packing and she almost choked just at the sight of his long, thick member. The shocks kept on coming, the most potent hit when she noticed the line at the top seam of his thigh. Zooming in, she found it read exactly the same as the one she had in almost the same spot.

Oh wow, they had matching tattoos… there. She'd thought *"Bon appetite"* was risqué until she realized it was meant for both of them. What a shame that Video-Shane was about to ruin the arousal that had been heating her by enjoying this random blonde.

Playing the video, Ginger let it continue, but was feeling sick already. The blonde leaped onto Video-Shane though his eyes were still closed in apparent sleep.

Climbing up his body, she rubbed her breasts on his dick and kissed his abs. "Want to play, Boo?"

He cracked open an eye and lifted his head from the bed. When he saw her, he blinked and lifted his head higher.

"Don't think my wife would like us to screw in the marital bed," Video-Shane mumbled. "If she finds blonde hairs in the sheets, she'll figure us out."

The blonde slid down his body and took hold of his dick, which she proceeded to breathe in and again, Ginger coughed. That was quite a mouthful, but when Shane groaned in the video, she whimpered. The blonde worked her mouth over him a few more times before sucking her mouth free and kissing his head.

The blonde woman kept moving her hand up and down his shaft. "You don't like it?" she asked.

"I like anything you do, baby," he said, reaching down to stroke her hair. "Blonde suits you, but I prefer brunettes, you know that."

The woman in the video rose and whipped off the blonde hair. Ginger gasped, it was a wig! The woman on the camera tossed her head forward and shook her hair over his body before tossing it back. He was still half-asleep when she went back to blowing him.

Shane, in the video, stroked her hair. "Bit, you're fucking amazing at that. Goddamn."

Video-Ginger stopped sucking and worked her fist over him again. "But…"

Ginger had heard it too, that unsaid word in his sleepy voice. "Fucking your throat won't get you pregnant… Come up here, let me do it properly… I want to be a daddy."

Dropping the phone, Ginger covered her mouth with both hands and watched herself climb up him to sink down onto his cock. There they were on the screen having sex. She was too shocked to be shocked.

In that video, she was already pregnant. Just a few days later, they'd be in the accident that separated them. That was the proof, if she'd needed it, of what Shane had said. They weren't trying, but he had wanted Cam. Shane wanted them to have a baby and hadn't known their son was already there. Cam was in that shot with them, only neither of them had known it.

"I love you, Boo," Video-Ginger purred, working herself up and down, running her hands through her hair as he took hold of her breasts. "Say it, Boo. Tell me that you love me."

His strong arms came around her and he swept her down onto her back, so they were lying the wrong way on the bed.

He stroked her face and kissed her. "I love you, Bit," he said, brushing the back of his fingers down her cheeks. "The world's got nothing on us."

Her video counterpart arched her body. Grinning at him, she grabbed his face to pull him down into a deep kiss, her fingers lost in his hair. Ginger was transfixed. The sheet was tangled around their lower bodies, they just lay there kissing for three minutes before his hips even began to move again. He was making love to her.

Their mouths never parted. She couldn't stop watching their lips, rubbing together, mouths open, tongues twined... They were in love. They had it all and then... it had been taken away from them.

Tossing the cover from her bed, Ginger got to her feet and began to walk toward the bathroom. Creeping through it, she didn't knock, she just went into Shane's bedroom, not really knowing why she was there or what she was going to do.

He was sitting on the end of his bed, taking off his boots. The guys had been out on the back porch drinking beer. Ginger hadn't even known if he was upstairs yet or not, she just had to be there.

Leaning on the door frame by the bathroom with her hands at the small of her back, she said nothing. Examining him through the low light coming from the nightlight plugged in by his bed, he was a wonder and a mystery.

She hadn't said anything. Neither had he, on pause he was still half-bent over, waiting.

When she remained quiet, one corner of his lips turned up. His eyes went left and right. "Hi," he said, probably amused by her inactivity. Ginger stayed silent; his word didn't prompt her to say anything. It prompted movement. Going to him, she sank down onto her knees between his feet. "Babe—"

"Shh," she said, touching a finger to his lips.

He was still confused. It didn't help that she did

nothing to explain herself. Scooping her hands up over his cheeks, she rose and touched her lips to his. He didn't move or respond, so she kissed him deeper. Then kissed him again. Touching her tongue to his lower lip, she angled her head and exhaled into his mouth. And that was it.

His hands sank into her hair and he tipped the other way to open his mouth over hers to take control of the kiss. Just like the man on that video, he kissed his love and devotion into her, massaging her lips with the tender need of a starving man. She felt treasured and desired and everything she'd missed since he walked into that church.

Inching back, Ginger took a minute to compose herself then she sank a bit lower. Her hands fell from his face, his were slower but did eventually leave her hair.

Resting his hands on her shoulders, he slid them down in a stroke, and gripped her upper arms to draw her higher again.

When he tried to kiss her, she dipped her head back, keeping her mouth from his reach.

"Gin," he breathed, his voice a rasp with desperation.

"We can't," she whispered, touching her fingertips to his lips again. "I just... I wanted to know what it was like... to be her."

His grip eased as his head tilted because there was no way he could know what she meant. Part of her wanted to ask, like the woman on the film, she wanted to ask him to say the words. But what she'd done was already too much. Kissing was so over the line that she deserved a slap. But sitting on the floor between his feet made her feel more complete than she had for a long time.

Rising again, Ginger pressed her mouth to his. He was amazing. Kissing Shane showed her purpose. He stroked his rough palms up and down her upper arms, enlivening and enticing her. Her fingers curled around his shoulders and squeezed hard to experience the strength of the muscles she'd admired from a distance.

But she couldn't stay, the urgency of his touch was growing again, and she wasn't sure she could trust herself. Forcing herself to withdraw wasn't easy. Her eyes were glued shut. Opening them would signal the end of the moment and she didn't want it to be over. It felt like she belonged in that second of time and nowhere else.

His mouth touched hers again and she knew if she didn't leave then, she might never have the strength to do it.

Standing up, Ginger forced their kiss to end.

Shane snagged her wrist before she could walk away. "Stay," he murmured. "Stay the night with me, Bit."

The temptation was immense. Maybe if she was still as strong as the woman in the video, she would. As it was, Ginger touched his hairline and drew her palm down his temple to his cheek and kept on going to his jaw so she could touch her thumb to his lips.

"Goodnight, Boo," she whispered.

He exhaled, resolved that she wasn't going to yield. His hand drifted away giving her silent permission to return to her room and to her bed.

SEVENTEEN

GINGER SLEPT SURPRISINGLY well. But that calm didn't last into the next day. Cam was up early, so she fed him and took him for a walk with Rocky, managing to get out before anyone else was awake. They'd pushed the therapy session to the afternoon to coincide with Cam's nap.

Her boy had an early lunch just after eleven. She fed him in the kitchen and cleared out in time for the others to feed themselves. Avoiding eye contact with everyone was probably conspicuous. Just like her decision to take Cam out again. The others had to be thinking that something was wrong.

Cam had gone down early for his afternoon nap, which was part of her design. With the monitor in one hand and the cellphone she still hadn't returned to Shane in the other, Ginger marched down the hall to her brother's bedroom.

Except he wasn't in it.

"Owen?" she called.

"In here," he replied from the bathroom.

Finding him alone was a relief. Heading in the direction of his voice, she went in and closed the door. Owen was leaning in close to the mirror, tweezers at his eyebrows. The bathroom was half the size of hers, but with only a shower stall against the wall it still succeeded in being spacious.

"Can I talk to you?" she asked, putting the monitor on the vanity beneath him.

"Yep," he said, tweezing. "I'm almost done… Where the hell have you been this morning anyway? You've been nowhere."

"That's kind of what I need to talk to you about," she said, sitting in the chair between the vanity and his bedroom door. "I… I have a problem."

He stopped tweezing to frown at her. Something caught his eye and he bent down to begin tweezing her brows.

"Okay, so this is private therapy," he said, continuing to work on her. "My light is on, what's up?"

"I'm worried I might have slept with Murphy."

With one steadying hand still on her head and the other occupied by the tweezers, he leaned back to blink at her. "What like by accident? Did you slip and fall onto his cock?"

A facetious response didn't make her feel better, so she ignored it. "What do you know about sibling DNA on paternity? I mean, would the test be able to tell one brother from another?"

Folding his arms, Owen was trying to follow what she was saying. "You think you slept with Murphy and Shane and now you're worried the paternity can't tell the difference? I don't know. I guess if they were twins it might be difficult, but they're not. I think you'll be fine." Returning to his tweezing, he smiled. "What makes you think you slept with Murphy? Are you having some memory about waking up with him? Murphy used to party a lot. It wouldn't surprise me if he crawled into the wrong bed a few times. He stayed with you and Shane all the time, so… Is that what it is? You're having a memory."

"No," she said, pushing his hands away to rise and pace toward Murphy's closed bedroom door. "Not a memory. I figured something out."

"Figured what out?" he asked, finishing his own brows.

Taking a deep breath, Ginger was ready to make the confession. "I'm a slut."

Owen's hand dropped a second before he twisted to look over his shoulder at her.

Just then Murphy's bedroom door opened. He started to come in but stopped when he saw them and re-zipped his fly. "I—"

"In a minute," Owen said, rushing past her to push Murphy out. Closing the door, Owen flattened himself against it to gape at her. "You're a slut? How the hell did you come to that conclusion? Sure, you're a slut with Shane, you two are… healthy together. But you never screwed around. You trusted me; you would've told me."

Ginger crept closer, worried and wringing her hands around Shane's phone that had been her companion since the previous night. "But would I? You're close to Shane, maybe I was worried about putting you in the middle."

He exhaled like he was humoring her and then composed himself. "Okay, why do you think you're a slut?"

"I'm married to Shane," she said. "I'm engaged to Calvin. But I'm kissing Shane while in a relationship with Calvin, the man I'm supposed to be marrying." She groaned in embarrassment. "I dream about him."

His brow was down. "Which one? Calvin or—"

"Shane!" she whined. "I dream about having sex with him. I was kissing Calvin outside one night and then it's like next minute I'm kneeling down in front of Shane and—"

"Whoa, wait, is this a dream or real?" Owen asked, closing his eyes and waving his open hands.

"Real! Oh my God, Owe, this is fucked up."

Her brother came closer. "Wait… you and Shane were kissing? When?"

"Last night," she said. "What kind of woman does something like that?"

"And the kneeling, that was—"

Next it was Owen's bedroom door that opened to interrupt them. Shane poked his head in. Silently groaning, Ginger closed her eyes and went around her brother to put her back to both of them.

"Everything okay in here?" Shane asked.

"Yeah," Owen said. "We just need a minute."

"Sure," Shane said. Ginger glanced back just as he ducked out, but a breath later, he returned. "Quick one, anyone seen my phone around?"

Glancing down at the device in her hands, Ginger spun around to face him, hiding the phone behind her back.

"Nope," she said, putting a smile—that probably wasn't too convincing—on her face.

Shane's focus zeroed in on her and he slipped around the door to saunter in. "What's behind your back?"

"Nothing," she said. "Can you go and check on Cam?"

"Already did," he said, snaking around Owen to get up close to her. "He's fine."

"Oh." Damnit, how was she supposed to get rid of him? "Thanks."

He opened his hand. "Phone. Please." There was

no way she could claim not to have it, so she exhaled and slapped it into his palm. "Thanks." Backing off a step, he began to do something on the phone, his thumb moving fast across the screen. "I'm not listening," Shane muttered, loitering in the corner. "Carry on with whatever you were doing."

"Yeah, right," she said. Owen smiled and went back to his tweezing. "We'll wait."

"Seriously, you don't have to worry about me," Shane said and winked at her. "I'm great at keeping secrets."

Owen hadn't seen that exchange, but that didn't stop him from scoffing. "Gin's not as great at it as you think," he muttered.

Shane straightened and locked the phone to return it to his back pocket. "Really?"

"She thinks she slept with Murphy," Owen said.

Ginger gasped and lunged across the room to hit his arm. "Owen!"

"When?" Shane asked, folding his arms and widening his stance. "Today? She has been AWOL for most of it... and Murph disappeared for a while too... They wouldn't screw in front of Cam though."

"Not today, she's not really sure when," Owen said, finishing up with his plucking.

Shane clarified. "Wait, she thinks she slept with him or she thinks she wants to sleep with him?"

The men were talking like she wasn't there. Ginger didn't appreciate the undercurrent of mocking.

"She thinks she did," Owen said and looked at her. "But I don't know, do you want to?"

Murphy's bedroom door opened again and he groaned. "Shit now there's a fucking party in here. What's a guy gotta do to take a piss?"

"Carry on, no one in here cares about you peeing," Owen said, focusing on Shane again.

Murphy actually did go over to the toilet.

On hearing him unzip, Ginger turned her eyes to the ceiling. "Oh God."

Shane moved around behind her and gripped her shoulders in a reassuring massage.

The reassurance was less appreciated when he dipped to murmur into her hair above her ear. "Contain yourself, baby. He'll put his dick away in a minute."

As if it wasn't already mortifying, Shane's dose of accelerant flamed her embarrassment. Murphy flushed. Shane kissed the top of her head and they turned, but Murphy headed straight for the bedroom.

"Uh, wash your hands," Ginger exclaimed. "You touch my child with those hands."

Murphy looked at his hands and shrugged as he went to the sink to wash up.

"You think she just wants to be close to him for longer?" Owen stage whispered at Shane.

Ginger pushed away from Shane when he laughed. "You're all bastards."

Murphy was oblivious as to their conversation, still, he'd been bunched into the bracket too it seemed. Ginger went to snag the towel from the loop beside Owen's bedroom door to toss it to her brother-in-law.

"What you talking about?" Murphy asked, drying his hands.

"You fucking my wife," Shane said like it was the most normal thing in the world.

Her mouth fell open.

Murphy stopped drying to examine their faces. "You're kidding… right?" When he fixated on her to look her up and down, disgust contorted his expression. It made Ginger wish she had something heavier to throw at him. "That's a really disturbing visual."

"Stop visualizing or we'll have a problem," Shane said.

His arms came around her shoulders to pull her back against his torso.

Squirming against him, Ginger tried to free herself, but he didn't seem to get the hint. "Shane," she murmured and managed to get as far as turning around, which he took as an invitation to try kissing her. "Stop! Don't do that!"

"What?" he asked, watching her eye the brothers. "You told Owen. I figured we're public knowledge."

Again, Shane ducked in an attempt at a kiss, but she pushed away. "I… I told Owen, I…"

Owen was peering at Shane and came in close beside them, fixating on something on his brother-in-law's head. Owen reached up with the tweezers to pluck a hair from Shane's brow.

He reared back in an instinctual wince. "Ow, what the fuck, buddy?" Shane said, rubbing the spot he'd plucked.

"Suck it up," Owen said. "That's been bugging me, Ginny will kiss it better."

Shane's hopeful attention flicked to her, but she held up her hands and backed off, coming up against Murphy.

"No," Ginger said. "I can't kiss you again… anywhere."

"Anywhere?" Murphy asked. "Where did she kiss you the first time, bro?"

Running her hands into her hair, she twirled a tendril around her finger. "Oh, this is bad, this is really bad."

"No," Shane soothed, taking her arms to draw her away from Murphy. "No one in here has any problems with us kissing, right, guys?"

Murphy and Owen agreed, but that wasn't the point. Shane didn't get it.

Her begging eyes leaped to his. "The more

people who know, the more chance Calvin will find out."

"He'll find out anyway 'cause we're gonna tell him," Shane said.

Shaking her head, she grabbed his tee-shirt, thinking that was exactly her worry. "No, we can't. We can't tell him."

"Why not?" Shane asked. "The sooner he knows where he stands, the sooner we can start putting our lives back together."

Her head sank into her hands. "Oh God," she wailed.

"Uh, I don't think that's what she wanted to hear," Murphy said. "I feel like I'm missing something major."

"You're not the only one," Owen said.

Ginger sucked in a breath through her nose and stood up straight, backing away from Shane. "Can you give me and Shane a minute alone, please?"

Murphy began to retreat. "Don't they have their own bathroom to screw in?" he muttered to Owen.

Spinning around, Ginger was going to correct him, but Owen was in front of her, interrupting her objection. "Before you have your moment," her brother said. "I have to tell you we have a problem."

That took some of her bluster. "What problem?" she asked.

"That thing you wanted me to do," he whispered, glancing at Shane who was behind her.

"Yeah, what's the problem?"

"I need a signature from each parent." He eyed Shane while Ginger wondered what her brother was getting at. "If I put it down in front of him, he'll read it."

"What's going on?" Shane asked.

Ginger ignored him to address her brother. "Can't you just cover it up?" she asked. "Just put something over the top of it and leave the signature line free."

Owen scowled at her. "Do you know how many times I've lectured him for signing things without reading them?"

"Then let this be a lesson to you," she said. "Wise advice normally, but I guess there are exceptions."

Owen sighed. "So what do you want me to do?"

Pushing her lips to the side, Ginger considered the problem. "Do you have it here ready?" Owen nodded. "Go get it."

Murphy was already in his room. Owen passed them to go into his own bedroom and when he came back, he was hugging a pile of papers to his chest.

Spinning around, she smiled up at Shane. "Owen and I need you to sign something... without reading it."

"I got that," Shane said, peering at her with suspicion. "Something for Cameron."

"What?" she asked. "How did you know that?"

"He said two parental signatures, not spousal signatures."

Nudging Owen, she growled at him. "Good going."

"What is it?" Shane asked.

Owen leaned in to mutter in her ear, "Flash him, that will distract him."

She tossed her response over her shoulder at her brother. "He doesn't care about my breasts, he's seen them too many times."

Shane raised his hand. "Do I get a vote?"

"No," she and Owen said in unison.

Ginger returned to smiling, hoping if she was sweet, he'd be charmed enough to play along. "You have no reason to trust me—"

"Other than the fact that I love you."

"Yes, other than..." Her blood pressure plummeted. "What?"

He traced the back of his finger down her cheek, a real deep, genuine smile on his lips. "You heard me, Bit… You want me to sign it, I will."

"You will? Just like that?"

He nodded. "If it makes you happy then it's what I want too… and Owen's read it, so I know you're not signing away the store." That was going to be her point before he dropped that last bomb. "So if you want me to sign it, I'll sign it… after our next kiss."

Jarring her from the daze of his admission, she had to switch mental gears fast. "What? After our what?" He could make her mad as fast as he could make her laugh. "You're demanding payment per signature?"

"No," he said. "Doesn't matter if it's now or next week. I'll wait. Soon as you're ready to share those lips again, I'll sign whatever you want me to sign."

Owen leaned in behind her again. "We actually need three signatures to cover everything."

That pleased Shane no end. He rocked back on his heels while sliding his hands into his pockets. "Great. Three."

"What about last night?" she asked. "Doesn't that count for anything?"

"That was spontaneous," he said. "A wet dream come to life." Her narrowed focus made him shrug. "Okay, I'll give you one for last night."

"I need to submit this," Owen said.

Ginger gritted her teeth. "Okay," she said and grabbed the document from him to search for the place she was supposed to sign. Shane tried to peek over her shoulder so she snatched it to her chest and covered his eyes with her hand. "You're getting what you want, big boy, okay?"

He smiled and even though she couldn't see his gaze, she felt the heat of it. Grabbing the back of his neck, she pulled him down and pressed her mouth onto his once.

Owen laughed when she shoved Shane away. "Sexy," Owen said.

Shane was shaking his head. "Nope, that's not what I mean," he said and snatched her hips to lift her onto the vanity.

The strength of his entitlement was shocking. He parted her legs and seized her ass to pull her tight against the mass behind his fly without even thinking about asking permission. He wasn't even hard, but the feel of him there, pressed into her intimacy brought a gasp to her lips.

His half-smile was almost sinister; he winked. "That's right, Bit."

"Uh, can you both sign so I don't have to witness this?" Owen asked.

The couple were distracted enough that Owen got away with covering the documents to only reveal the signature lines. Ginger didn't really know what she was signing either. Every time she leaned to the side to sign, she rubbed against Shane. By the time they were done, he was solid and breathing wasn't so simple.

Owen held up the completed document. "Okay, I'll get out of your way for the… payment part…"

Her brother departed, closing the door at his back. Before she even managed to inhale, Shane was leaning in seeking her mouth.

Ginger bowed back. "You're not really going to make me do this, are you?"

"Oh yeah," he said. "It's a step back to normality… We used to trade sexual favors all the time. Kissing is nothing compared to what we used to promise each other."

"That's just it," she said, stacking her hands over his heart. "This isn't normal. We're not normal. Last night, it was…" Shrugging, she found a little bit of confidence. "I was horny."

"And you came to me," he said. Although his eyes were drowsy, they were ecstatic. "More normalcy."

Ginger would have gone to her husband if aroused in the past, sure. But there was something she had to help him understand, even if it was embarrassing as hell.

"There's… something I have to tell you. Something I think you haven't realized yet."

"Okay," he said, brushing his lips on her jaw. "Tell me, Bit."

"I'm a virgin."

He stopped kissing and drew back to meet her eye. "What?"

"Figuratively speaking." Gripping his shoulders, she found comfort and confidence in their stability. "I… I know I have a child and… I have done it before, but I have no memory of having sex." Pushing through the embarrassment, Ginger pressed her calves deeper against his outer thighs. "I can't do anything, you know? I don't remember how to do… stuff."

Sliding his hands up and down her back, he pulled her closer. "I'm a good coach. We'll do fine… is that why you didn't do anything with him?"

Calvin. Shane wouldn't even say his name. That reluctance made sense because the reminder of her fiancé filled her with guilt.

Ginger pushed him away. "I'm not saying that I'm going to do anything with you. Last night was a one off… Calvin and I… we've only been together about six months. I was in hospital and with the pregnancy, I wasn't thinking about sex. Then I had Cam and he… he was my focus, my world. I wasn't thinking about relationships, I just wanted to be with my little boy… I guess I knew Calvin was interested, I just… wasn't sure what I was doing with a man and he kinda had to spell it out."

"And that's when you got together?"

She nodded. "With feeding Cam and getting up in the night with him, there wasn't much time for intimacy and we wanted to do it right. I'll admit that I was nervous and Calvin was really turned off by the whole breast-feeding thing. So… I thought it might be romantic to wait, until the wedding night, you know?"

And then he'd come along and busted up the day, what perfect timing.

"That would be romantic… but we've had our wedding night," he said.

A wedding night she didn't remember. Ginger didn't want to talk about sex anymore; her mind was so screwed up about everything.

"I can't have sex with you, Shane."

"We'll do it properly the first time, not like this in our brothers' bathroom… all I want now is a kiss."

"A kiss," she said, touching his lips with her fingertips. "Just a kiss."

Even that was too much. Except when he bowed forward, she parted her lips and let him slide his tongue between them. Ginger fitted against him, warm and natural. Her legs slid higher, coiling around him. She rubbed their centers together, stimulating parts of herself that had been neglected.

His hand skimmed down her back and up, heating her, teasing her, touching her everywhere. Folding her hands one over the other at the back of his neck, holding him closer, tugging him hard, Ginger angled her mouth to take his breath into her lungs. His thumbs were first to pick their way under her top at the small of her back, then they were moving up, sending little sparkles through her as they ascended.

Her bra popped loose.

Gasping, she pushed him back to glare. "Boo!

Did you just unhook my bra?"

"Oops," he said, wearing a grin a chancing teenager would be proud of.

Her legs had to tighten as she reached around and hook it again.

Murphy came in and stopped in the doorway again. "Fuck, are you not done yet?" He examined them and laughed. "It been so long you've forgotten how to take a bra off, bro?" he asked and reversed out still snickering.

Shane gestured at the closed door. "Now you have to let me take it off."

To an observer, it would look like she was unfastening it for him rather than re-hooking it. Still, his brother's teasing wouldn't be enough to relax her boundaries.

Scratching a fingernail on his stubble, she enjoyed the primal sensation. Her hips began to move, her body responding to all the new feelings.

Fighting that curiosity, when Shane came close for another kiss, she pressed a hand on his chest. "We have to cool off. We can't be doing this… it looks like we're…"

"Like we're what?" he asked, putting his weight on his hands on either side of her thighs. "Being man and wife?"

"Having an affair," she whispered.

"Murph and Owen won't say anything… But we are together… right?"

Exhaling, she examined his face and had to admit that whatever they were doing, it was unfair to Calvin.

"Maybe," she said. "No." He frowned. "I don't know."

Shane was quick to take control while soothing her at the same time. "If you're worried about telling him, I can deal with it. You can stay right here and I'll deal with everything."

Yeah, 'cause that wasn't a ridiculous idea. "Hide in my brother's bathroom? No. What about Cam?"

Shivers joined her when his hands began to tease her neck and shoulders beneath her hair. Anytime he touched her, anywhere, it did something to her. Something she'd never experienced in the past... not that she remembered.

"I'll protect him. No one hurts my family... Are you concerned Calvin will hurt our son? I can get round the clock protection for you both, if—"

"No, of course not, don't be silly." With her fingernail, she drew a line around his pec through his tee-shirt, distracting herself while she confessed something else. "Boyd is coming in today... He'll be here any minute... might be here already."

"I have Murph behind me, we can take them."

He'd missed her meaning and jumped straight into assuming there would be a physical altercation. "No... he'll bring the paternity results."

The envelope would be sealed, so they'd have to wait to find out the truth of Cam's paternity. Maybe that was why she was so edgy.

Instead of being anxious, he smiled. "It will finally be official."

His eagerness concerned her. Doubting herself, Ginger considered that maybe they should've waited for the results before sending Owen off with the legal documents that would change her son's name. If the results came back negative, asking Shane to call Owen to stop him filing would be awkward.

"Everything could fall apart when we open that envelope," she said.

He tipped her chin up. "He's mine. I'm not worried."

The ease of his confidence was sweet if nothing

else.

Stretching her arms around his neck, Ginger smiled. "Maybe it's me who should be telling you off… you were the one cheating on me after all."

Although he frowned, he didn't relax his hold on her. "Was I?"

She nodded and bit her lip. "The blonde in your bed… in our bed."

It only took him half a beat to catch up.

Shane laughed, hooking her hair away from her face. "Yeah, my bad, she was too hot to pass up…" He kissed her lightly and brushed his nose on hers. "That's what you meant about feeling like her… and why you were horny last night?" She nodded, her nose bumping his. "How many did you watch?"

"Just a couple," she said. "I can't believe we… did that."

"It was just a wig. You've worn crazier stuff in bed—"

"No, videoed ourselves. There seem to be a lot of them."

He shrugged. "We have security cameras in every room of the house and in the office. We have dash-cams too that film inside and out our vehicles. Sometimes we use them for… recreational reasons."

"I never thought I was the kind of woman to… do that. Video? That's risky, isn't it? What if someone hacked us or something? That's a thing right? What if they got out?"

His wide smile and bold laugh were too exaggerated and knowing, leaving her feeling like she was missing something.

"Don't worry about our security, baby. No chance of anything electronic getting out there without us knowing."

They'd been cooped up in there for quite a while.

Ginger eased him back and slid down off the vanity to put some space between them. Shane groaned in protest, kind of like Cam would do if she took his toys away.

"We've been in here too long. Murphy needs his bathroom."

"He can pee in the yard," Shane said, trying to take her waist, but she dipped away. "If it's good enough for Rocky, it's good enough for my brother."

"I have to go find Calvin," she said.

Hope made his brows rise. "You're going to tell him?"

Ginger patted his chest, meaning to dampen his expectations, but when she made contact with the solid muscle beneath his shirt, she sighed and bit her lip. "I have to hit the gym before I get naked with anyone," she muttered, thinking aloud.

Yanking off his own tee-shirt, Shane erased her resolve like he knew just how to manipulate her by flashing his form. "I saw your body come out of my bed the other morning," he said, ducking in a swooping motion to taste her neck and push her against Owen's bedroom door in the same move. "It's perfect."

The breathy words made her whimper. Her body wasn't hers; it was reacting to his like it was an extension of his form.

Boneless and powerless to resist, Ginger moaned when he kissed around to her throat, and back up to her ear. "Oh, Shane…"

"You're mine," he growled.

Her mouth opened wide in a yelp and she grabbed the back of his head to haul his mouth up to hers. Bending his knees, he scooped her up, guiding her legs around him. Their kiss grew ferocious as it deepened. Supporting her weight with one arm, his other came around to massage her through her panties with his fingertips.

"Shane," she whispered.

"Let me go down on you," he mumbled on her mouth, tasting her again. "Please, baby. Let me eat your sweet pussy. I'll make you feel so good."

"Let you…" Her eyes opened on their kiss; she seized his shoulders to give him a shove. "Shane… no, we can't."

Ginger was sure. Reality demanded that she be strong and resist, right up to the second he pushed his fingers against her opening through her panties. Forgetting every woe, she gasped, failing to catch a breath. Pushing up, her nails dug into his shoulders, and she smiled instead of protesting, because wow, that one pulse of sudden pleasure had felt good.

"I remember how to do stuff," he said. "When you're ready."

Shane put her on her feet and she didn't know if she was more disappointed or guilty. A whine on the monitor that had been pushed to the other side of the vanity brought her back to her senses.

"I have to make sure he's settled," she said, struggling to switch back to mommy mode. "Cam has to stay down until we find out what Doctor Guinness wants to do about therapy."

"Will there be a session after Calvin finds out?" Shane asked.

But Ginger was sure of one thing. "No one will be making any big announcements today, okay? This is supposed to be… medical not recreational."

He dug his hands in his back pockets. "So we're not telling him we're together?"

She was tired and frustrated. "Please, Boo, don't push. Just… be patient. We have to figure this out one day at a time and today it's paternity results, okay? If they come back negative… I guess we'll need therapy."

"Okay," he said, squeezing her shoulder.

"Whatever you want, Bit." She retrieved the monitor, but he took it from her as she passed him. "Go see if Boyd is here with the envelope… I'll check in on our boy."

Searching his eyes, Ginger was as worried as she was sorry. That could be the last time Shane went to Cam thinking he was his. If the results were negative, that was it, over. Nodding, her smile didn't go far enough to allay her concerns. As was becoming his habit, Shane read her worries and kissed her head to console her as he passed to go to Cam.

Straightening her clothes, Ginger looked at her reflection in the mirror and touched her reddened lips. She was something else, something different. The same woman was looking back at her but there was something different in her aura. She just hoped Calvin wouldn't see it before she got the chance to talk to him.

EIGHTEEN

BOYD HAD ARRIVED. Ginger found him and Calvin in the dedicated dining room located in the back corner of the lower floor. The door was open and she went over but didn't get a chance to say anything.

Calvin noticed her and stood up. "Come in," he said, gesturing to her.

He came over to take her hand and led her inside, leaving the door ajar. Boyd stood up. A buzz in the air betrayed that there was something going on.

"What is it?" she asked, wondering which of the men were going to fill her in. "Did the results come back?"

"Yes," Calvin said, pushing some papers aside to pick up an envelope that she noticed was already open.

"Well?" she asked, reaching to take it.

Calvin was reluctant to hand it over and kept hold of it even after her hand was around it. Ginger couldn't tell why he was reluctant, nothing in his expression gave it away. Her heart got faster as she began to panic that maybe it didn't say what they expected it to say. Maybe she was a slut after all.

When Calvin let go, she ignored her urge to bury her head in the sand and slid the paper from inside.

"It's positive," Calvin said.

"Oh, thank God," she exhaled.

Relief made her grin as she unfolded the sheet to see that yes, Shane was Cam's father without a shadow of a doubt. Spinning around, Ginger intended to go to him and share the news.

Calvin spoke again before she made it one step. "Boyd brought something else."

Facing Calvin again, Ginger registered his grave expression. It turned out that her relief had been premature. He gave her a thick stack of documents.

As soon as she began to read, an inhale of shock took her eyes to his. "Dissolution of Marriage?" she asked. "You wrote divorce papers?"

"Boyd did," Calvin said, stepping back to gesture at his lawyer and to pick up a heavy pen from the table. "All you have to do is sign and then we'll get Warren to—"

"Sign?" she asked. "Now?"

In one hand she held a document proclaiming her son's true family. In the other was the document that would sever her ties to that family.

"Yes," Calvin said. "Why delay? If we sign them today, Boyd can lodge them with the court… The sooner you divorce, the sooner we can marry."

"I—"

Sound from beyond the dining room carried to them. Shane and Murphy were coming down the stairs together, laughing about something, in a good mood. Oh no. The moment had the potential to be explosive. She turned to rush over to the door intending to close it, but Shane and Murphy rounded the bottom of the stairs and saw her in the doorway.

"Well?" Shane asked. "You ready to hear me say I told you so?"

"What?" Ginger snapped, panicked because she had no idea what to do. This situation was a powder keg. Calvin was going to have to force Shane's hand if he was going to get him to sign the divorce papers. Trouble was, she wasn't sure if she wanted to sign them either. "Oh, the paternity, yes. Yes, you're his father."

Ginger went to close the door, but her abrupt answer had been a stupid move. Her panic hadn't been missed. Shane was worried, she saw it in the way his expression grew stern as he came toward her.

"What's wrong?" Shane asked.

"Nothing," she said.

Before she could close the dining room door, Calvin and Boyd were behind her, moving her out of the dining room and into the living area beneath the mezzanine.

There they were. Calvin and Boyd just a few feet from Shane and Murphy, and she was right in the middle. The doctor was out somewhere, Owen was on his way into the city, and she didn't even know where Diane was. It was just her... and them.

"Can I see?" Shane asked, holding out a hand to her, though his glare was fixed on Calvin.

"Uh, sure," Ginger said, stepping over to hand him the paternity document.

He and Murphy both read it, then Shane folded it and put it in his back pocket.

"We'll need that back for our records," Calvin said.

Shane ignored him and nodded at her other hand, the one clutching the wedge of documents at her chest. "What's that, Bit?"

Shit. "This?" she said, glancing at it and then holding it closer. "Nothing. This is... nothing."

"It's something we'll need you to sign," Calvin said, taking the papers from her trembling hand. "I don't believe in beating around the bush."

Shane took the stack but kept staring at Calvin for a few seconds before lowering his attention to the papers.

His scowl got deeper in a flash. "Divorce papers?" he snapped at her. "You knew about this?"

"No!" she said. "No, I—"

"I had Boyd write them up. It saves time, don't you think?" Calvin said, taking a pen from his inside pocket. "If you could just…"

Shane's demeanor shifted. Calvin must have noticed it too because he trailed off. As Shane went through the pages, he paused and his scowl loosened. He glanced at Murphy who had been reading over his shoulder, and they exchanged a knowing look.

To her utter surprise, Shane smiled… he actually smiled and then… he laughed. A loud, fully expressive laugh that pushed his head back as the laughter grew and his brother joined in.

"I fail to see what's so funny," Calvin snapped, unhappy at their reaction.

Instantly the humor left him and was replaced by fury. Shane held up the document to shake it at Calvin. "This! How long have you known, you fucker?"

She seemed to be the only one at a loss. Murphy closed in next to his brother.

Calvin's anger became a sinister smugness that Boyd mirrored. "A while," he drawled.

"What?" she asked, searching the men. "What's going on?"

"Five hundred million in settlement and half a million a month in child support," Murphy said, not to her, but to Calvin. "You're in this for the money, you fuck."

"What?" she shrieked and marched over to snatch the document. Murphy was right, that was exactly what it said. She spun to Calvin. "I don't understand." Did he not want the divorce to go ahead? "How is anyone supposed to afford this? Who could—"

"Maybe the man responsible for WarNet, one of the most successful mapping software companies in the world. The man who also owns one of the biggest security software firms in the world," Calvin said. "The guy's worth thirty-something billion dollars… and if the Ventura takeover goes ahead, he could add another ten to that. Right, Warren? He's lucky it's not more."

Ginger stood frozen for what might have been an eternity. It seemed her whole body was turning to ice. Her eyes blurred, not with tears, just with the sheer implication of what the revelation meant. Slowly, she turned around. When her focus came to stop on Shane, all she saw was a stranger.

"You lied to me," she whispered. Shane's fury blinked away; she didn't even care that he was suddenly at such a loss. "You're… you're…"

"Not what he told us he was," Calvin said, putting an arm around her. "I'm sorry you had to find out this way. I was shocked too. He told us he writes books."

"I write code and develop outdoor electronics," Shane said. "You said books, not me… and baby, I never lied to you—"

He tried to come over to touch her, but she backed away, moving out of Calvin's grip and away from Shane's.

"He's the one gold-digging. Yell at him, not us!" Murphy said. "Your fiancé, Gin, look at that damn document! You're a money train. You sign that and he gets control of half a billion dollars!"

Half a billion dollars. She didn't even know what

that looked like, couldn't even begin to comprehend what life would be like with that kind of money. But she didn't care. She couldn't care less if he was worth ten cents or ten trillion dollars.

Tears finally found her eyes. She couldn't trust anyone. Murphy could be right. That was a lot of money for Calvin to ignore. But Shane… Why when she tried to focus on him could she no longer see the man who'd rolled around on the floor with their son? She couldn't see the man she kissed last night or the one she'd confided in upstairs just a few minutes ago.

"I am not! The settlement is reasonable," Calvin said. "There is no reason not to sign it!"

Fixated on Shane who was looking at her, he was waiting for a reaction she couldn't give him. Anger and hurt made her feel so weak. Taking control… that was the only way to be strong.

"Get me a pen," she said, her voice flat.

"No!" Shane exclaimed. "You are not signing that fucking thing."

"That's not your decision," Calvin said, holding out a pen to her.

Ginger snatched it from him and went to Shane, who was still holding the divorce papers.

"No," Shane said, a pain in his voice that didn't affect her. "Baby, you don't want to sign these. You're upset. Think about this before you do something permanent."

Grabbing the settlement page, she tore it out and ripped it to shreds before tossing the pieces to the floor. Calvin and Boyd both called out in protest, but she kept her eyes on Shane.

"I don't want your money, Warren. Cam and I will be just fine without it."

"I'd give you every cent," he said and tried to touch her, but she ducked away. "You can have it all, Bit.

It means nothing compared to you and Cam."

"We have another copy of the papers in the dining room," Calvin said, snapping his fingers at Boyd who scrambled away.

"I don't want the money," she said. Calvin's insistence that it was important sickened her. Sneering at all of them, Ginger yanked off her engagement ring and tossed it at the stuttering Calvin. The only thing that would make her feel better was getting away from them and being near her baby. "Go to hell. All of you."

Spinning around, she marched to the stairs, needing to put space between her and… everything.

NINETEEN

SHANE WANTED TO follow her, but Murphy put a hand on the front of his shoulder before he got the chance to chase Ginger up the stairs.

"Give her some space," Murphy said.

Trying to think of how he could fix this and erase that look of disgust from her face, Shane was reminded of the instigator when Calvin laughed. Whipping around, it took all of Murphy's weight to hold him back. All he could think about was ripping the guy apart.

"Come on, Warren," Calvin said, still smiling after he picked up the ring and put it in his pocket. "Hit me… I'll sue you for every cent you just promised my fiancée. You know, it's a good thing she ripped up that page. After that promise I think we'll triple the settlement, maybe quadruple it."

"You used her for money, you sick fuck," Shane said, having never felt such rage. "You put her through all of this, made her jump through all these hoops at this fucking retreat, not because you love her, but because you knew she'd clean up in a divorce… You wanted to make sure I would give her and Cam everything, didn't you? Is that why you let us share? To make sure I was pliable for your settlement?"

"I don't know what you're talking about," Calvin said, glancing at Boyd who came back to join the group.

"You're going to pay for this," Murphy said. "We're going to make sure you—"

"On the contrary," Calvin said. "That piece of paper in his back pocket promises he's going to be the one paying through the teeth for at least the next eighteen years."

Shane growled and lunged forward, Murphy hauled him back.

"You bastard," Shane spat. "The paternity was never for Ginger, it was never for Cameron. You needed it for the divorce settlement. Soon as you had irrefutable proof he was mine…"

Murphy exhaled a laugh. "Funny thing is, Shane never denied Cam and never would."

"No," Shane said. "I'll take care of my son, don't worry about that, Bishop. I'll take care of my wife too… and I guarantee you'll never see a dime."

Calvin laughed again. Shane ground his teeth together watching the bastard and his lawyer exchange a smug look.

"Ginger will marry me… she'll come back to me," Calvin said. "I understand her, the woman she is now. She doesn't even know who you are, we have sixteen months together."

"Sixteen celibate months," Shane sneered, glad he had the chance to slap him with that.

Calvin hadn't expected it, but Shane's satisfaction didn't last.

"Maybe. But she has such a talented little mouth… I bet you remember."

Growling again, Shane fought against his brother

to try to get his hands on Calvin. It might be worth being sued just to pummel the guy.

"We're not paying him a cent," Murphy said, throwing him back a few feet and whirling around. "How long have you known, Bishop? Before we came here? Before the meeting at Guinness' office. How long?"

"A while."

"A while," Murphy sneered. "What the fuck is that? Did you know before dinner at your fucking country club?"

Calvin didn't flinch and a chilling thought crept up on Shane as he read the calculating look in the bastard's eye. "You've known all along, haven't you, Bishop? You knew before the wedding, didn't you? Before we ever showed up, you knew exactly who she was."

"Fuck," Murphy exhaled, catching up with his thinking. "That's why one of the richest guys in the country couldn't find his woman no matter how much money he threw at it or how much publicity he got. That's why you kept her locked in your Minnesota mansion, didn't let her have a phone or money, she doesn't even have a computer or a tablet. Has she used the internet at all in the last sixteen months? You kept her from finding out who she was because you wanted to get your hooks in."

Calvin said nothing, neither confirming nor denying the charge. Though there was an angry acceptance in his eyes. Either Murphy was right, or the accusation that he could be so cruel was getting to him. In that minute, Shane could only believe his brother's narrative.

"She was unconscious when you picked her up," Shane said. "That's what you said. Did you know then?"

He exhaled and drove his fingers through his hair as he realized the kidnapping charge wasn't far from accurate.

Murphy shook his head. "The private facility. You said you put her in a private facility with private doctors. Your doctors. People you paid. All so you could control the flow of information, right? What were you waiting for? Were you going to call in a ransom? Wait until we cranked up the reward?"

The trouble with the reward was that all kinds of cranks called because they just wanted money. Shane had set up a department at his offices to process and investigate every call, but they'd all ended up as dead ends... with these revelations, he understood why.

"You don't know what you're talking about," Calvin said and tried to turn away.

Shane wouldn't let him off the hook so easy. "Makes sense now. Nobody finds a person at the side of the road and ends up marrying them, not a rich, selfish bastard like you." Calvin was rich all right, probably thought of himself as quite the mogul with his few million in the bank. Shane had never measured himself by the yardstick of money like it was clear Calvin did. "If she'd been some crack whore, you'd have dumped her at the hospital and driven off. So you figured it out fast... how fast? Huh? Our campaign wasn't national, not in those first few weeks. Is that when you paid to have her looked after by a select few? Once you realized she had amnesia, you picked men who wouldn't push her to remember or think too hard about her past. It wasn't about moving forward; you weren't doing what was best for her. You didn't want her to know."

"Did you just decide to keep her forever?" Murphy asked. "Why the hell did you hold her for sixteen months?"

Shane couldn't figure that out either. The plan must have been fluid, decisions made spontaneously. Calvin picked her up and took her to people who had no idea who she was. Calvin may have assumed he'd get a reward from a grateful husband, then the amnesia had changed his strategy.

Frustratingly, if Calvin, or a proxy, had called and asked for a fortune, Shane would've paid it. But money was short-lived, it ran out… unless it was a regular payment. As the truth struck him, it was so surprising that he fell back against the pillar holding up the mezzanine.

"Cam… You found out she was pregnant… Shit, Murph… they were going to give her back until they found out she was carrying my child… This was all about child support."

"I'll deny everything," Calvin said, the superior sonofabitch looking down his nose. "I love Ginger very much."

"Maybe now you do," Shane said. "But this didn't start with altruism."

Murphy laughed. "He doesn't love her. He's just sticking to the plan. He talks her into divorcing you and she marries him and that's it. You have no choice. You have to send the money and he's got her so brainwashed that she'll let him control it all… Must be easy to control an amnesia sufferer. You convince her she has no friends and family, that she doesn't need any contact with the outside world. You fill her head with your story, your version of events. She is a blank slate, so she just absorbs it all."

"Who would call it," Shane muttered, remembering what Ginger had said about not having a cell phone. Murphy was right. He was bang on the money. Squinting, he shook his head. "One thing I don't get, how did you know I'd show up?"

"He knew you'd show up eventually," Murphy said. "And that press article… geez, was that a fucking plant? There were no other media articles about the mysterious woman found at the side of the road by the millionaire… You found her in Washington and brought her back here to your state. You kept her hidden and then right when you were ready to collect, you did the interview. She wasn't questioned by the reporter, only you were, so you could control what was revealed. Again, it's all about control. And the picture… that was the first picture of her ever released."

Calvin glanced at Boyd. "I think we're done here."

"Yes, sir," Boyd said. "I think we should collect your fiancé and depart."

Shane was so angry. All he could do was sneer out a laugh. If he did anything else, he'd murder the bastard. "Over my dead fucking body… You're not taking my wife anywhere."

TWENTY

THE SECOND SOMEONE knocked on her bedroom door, Ginger grabbed for the shoe she'd just put in her suitcase. When it opened, she hurled the weapon at whoever was intruding and was mortified to see the doctor duck to avoid it.

"Oh my God, Doctor Guinness, I'm sorry!" Leaping up, she rushed over to guide him into the room. "I'm sorry, I didn't mean—"

"I can see emotions are running high here too," Guinness said, clearing his throat and taking a moment to compose himself. "I came back from my walk to find Shane and Murphy arguing with Calvin and Boyd… There seems to be a bit of confusion?"

"No confusion," she said, but he looked past her.

"Yet, you're packing your things."

"Yes," she said. "Thank you very much for your help. The retreat has been… helpful."

Maybe not in the way she'd anticipated. Still, Ginger had a more accurate picture of who was in her life and how she'd been set up.

"But you're leaving? We haven't completed our journey."

She didn't want to be rude but was at the limit of her patience. "I understand. With everything that's happened, I think the group will disband. There is no need for us to be here. Shane and I will be getting a divorce," she said and looked at her naked ring finger. "Calvin and I will not be getting married either…" She took a breath. "I will wait for my brother to come back from town. When he does, Cam and I will be leaving."

Ginger was pissed at her brother too; he hadn't been forthcoming either. The blame didn't only belong to others. She was angry at herself as well for ending up stuck in a corner. She had no money to her name and doubted the DMV would give her a driver's license when she couldn't remember passing her test. Ginger couldn't walk out the door with Cameron, she couldn't even afford a bus ticket. At least, not yet.

Owen had said she'd had a job and he'd known about her passport. Her hope was he might be able to help her find out if she'd ever squirreled away any money.

"I'm sorry to hear that," Doctor Guinness said. "What is the cause of this upset?"

So many things. As Ginger looked at the doctor, she was too tired to explain it all.

"Shane has money. A lot of money. Calvin found out and didn't tell me then he wrote this crazy settlement into divorce papers I didn't ask him to solicit."

"That is an abuse of trust," the doctor said, directing her to sit on the bed. "But if Calvin loves you and wants to marry you, perhaps he is eager to see you make a commitment to him. That begins with divorcing your husband. You have to prove to him that you are ready to move forward. You said yourself in one of our sessions that he felt threatened by Shane."

She had been wishy-washy about divorcing

Shane and Calvin wouldn't want to be made a fool of. Of course, making out with Shane in Owen's bathroom was kind of making a fool of the man who'd taken care of her for sixteen months.

"But that… that doesn't explain the money."

"Shane is worth a lot of money," Guinness said.

She huffed. "You knew too?"

"I make it a rule to do some background on all my clients," he said with a smile and covered her linked fingers with his. "You can't be too hard on them. Calvin probably thought he was doing a good thing, taking care of an uncomfortable issue. Relieving some of the pressure for you by dealing with the practicalities while you are rehabilitating. Your injuries may be invisible, but you live with a disability. He probably sees it as his responsibility to take care of you."

Just as he had for the last sixteen months, she began to feel sick. Maybe her response was an overreaction.

Pressing her hands to her gut, she recalled the papers. "That doesn't explain the settlement. It asked for half a billion dollars, doctor. I can't… I can't even think about that kind of money without getting dizzy."

He laughed and patted her. "He didn't choose your husband, you did. And from my understanding Mr. Warren is worth much more than that… If Mr. Bishop was only interested in money, he could've asked for half of Shane's whole fortune, especially taking Cameron into account. Half a billion is actually a modest amount."

Sheesh, he was right. If all Calvin wanted was money, he could have asked for so much more. Half a billion was like the lowest possible amount he probably could ask for. It wouldn't make sense to ask a man of Shane's means for twenty bucks… Calvin also had medical bills to recoup, he'd paid hers and Cam's before they were on his insurance. And he'd fed and housed them both, providing everything they needed.

Growling, she put her feet on the end of the bed and dropped her forehead to her knees. "Shane is the bastard for not telling me the truth," she murmured, turning to look at the doctor for confirmation.

The doctor tipped his head and winced. "Well..."

"What?"

"We haven't covered education and occupation yet," the doctor said. "I haven't heard him talk about what he does. But I haven't heard Calvin or Diane talking about their careers either. Neither has Murphy. We talk about this being a process, about answering questions and not overloading. And well, I did lay it on quite thick with him in the parking lot on the first day about not going into too much detail about your life together too quickly. It's important to try and stimulate your own memory, not to simply ask and be told."

She'd been told that by other doctors too. "Oh..."

"Maybe he could have been more forthcoming, but we don't know anything about bank balances or material possessions... I'm not sure when it would've come up... Has he actively gone out of his way to hide his means? Do you think he was trying to subvert a divorce settlement if there was to be one?" The doctor frowned and then spoke as if to himself. "I don't know what reason he would have to conceal the truth. You share a son. You would have found out eventually. Even if divorce proceedings were done through mediation and courts, there would have been full financial disclosure."

Oh great, so she'd overreacted there too.

Ginger sighed. "How could I have married a billionaire?" she whispered, believing it unlike herself.

Doctor Guinness smiled. "I would like to think you married the man and not his money."

Upon arriving at the lodge, she'd been open to learning about her past and accepted that her knowledge was limited. Since spending time with these people, she'd believed that while getting to know them, they were forging relationships. It was those relationships she felt had been betrayed when in truth, it all came from a false sense of security. Her subconscious knew these people and that made her feel connected to them, but they owed her nothing.

Doctor Guinness had said more than once that it was a process. For some reason, she'd decided to skip the whole damn course to try rushing to the end without giving everything its due focus. Ginger took a deep breath.

"Will you stay?" Guinness asked, squeezing her hand.

Smiling at him, she nodded. "But we have to make some changes."

"Okay," he said, becoming professional. "I am open to suggestions of what will make this easiest for you."

"I want to know these people, who they are now, and I want to be able to ask about who I was. I need answers."

He nodded, considering her request. "Okay… then I have a suggestion."

***

AFTER HER PRIVATE SESSION with Doctor Guinness, Ginger did feel better, and was ready to give everyone a chance again. Cam woke up, interrupting her and the doctor. They were done anyway, so she prepared her son and took him down stairs to find Calvin and Boyd in the living room.

"I'm sorry," she said. Both men sat up. "I

overreacted and I shouldn't have been so hasty."

"That's okay," Calvin said, glancing at Boyd. "We understand your condition."

Maybe her PTSD had been to blame, her mood swings often were extreme. "Will you stay?" she asked them.

"Yes," Calvin said. "If the doctor believes it's for the best."

"Thank you," she said.

"What about Warren?" Boyd asked, looking toward the back of the house.

Exhaling, she followed his line of sight. Both Shane and Murphy were on the back porch, though only the tops of their heads could be seen beyond the kitchen window. "I need them to stay too. I need them all to stay. Everyone has to have a private session with Doctor Guinness tonight. Cal, would you… would you mind going first?"

"Of course not," he said and stood up, he came over and kissed her and Cam too.

His smile was weak, but she appreciated it all the same. "He's in his room."

Calvin nodded and looked at his lawyer again before going up the stairs. "You're doing the right thing," Boyd said.

Taking another breath, Ginger shrugged. "I hope so, Boyd. I really do."

Heading for the kitchen, struggling to contain her wriggly son, Ginger was pleased that he calmed as soon as she pushed open the back screen. When she stepped outside both Shane and Murphy sat up straight, clearing their tense expressions of annoyance to look at her with contrite hope.

She didn't even know where to begin. There was some hope. Shane. She recognized him again and that was more of a relief than she could express with words.

"Hey, buddy," Shane said to Cam.

When he raised a finger toward their boy, she twisted the baby away to prevent contact much to Shane and Murphy's surprise.

"I'm sorry," she said, finding that apology harder than the one inside.

"You're... You're sorry?" Shane asked. "Baby, I'm sorry. You have nothing to apologize for."

"Doctor Guinness and I had a conversation. He thinks it would be beneficial for everyone to have a private session with him. Calvin has agreed to stay and is talking to the doctor now." Rolling her eyes upward in an attempt to restrain her emotions, Ginger hid her mouth in Cam's hair for a moment to calm herself before she spoke again. "I need to apologize to you both and ask if you are willing to stay and keep working."

They shared a look. For a second, she thought they were going to say no. Ginger didn't know what she would do if they did.

"We're here to the bitter end for anything you need, Bit," Shane said

His polite smile gave her some hope that maybe there was something for them to build on.

"Owen said you had business to deal with," she said, kicking herself for not asking about the office in the times it had been mentioned.

Having spent some time thinking about it, she realized how free Shane had been with money. He'd never hidden his means. He paid Cam's treatment at the hospital, spoke about buying a new car, offered to pay for the lodge stay too. Focusing on the clues she'd failed to pick up on wasn't productive, they had to move forward.

"I didn't realize how important it might be. If you have to leave—"

"Nothing is more important than this," Shane

said.

She believed him but had to be honest. "My memories aren't worth ten billion dollars."

"No," Shane said, leaving his seat. "They're worth a hundred times that much."

Looking at him or letting him touch her could bring her emotions to the fore again, so when he tried to reach for her face, she backed off a step.

"Shane…" she started, except her voice cracked.

Fighting to hold in her emotion, Ginger dug her teeth into her lip.

"You don't like to be touched," he said, disappointed and resigned.

Raising her eyes to his, a tear slid from her lashes. "I'm sorry," she whispered.

"It's my fault," he said, struggling to contain the annoyance simmering behind his tone. "You did nothing wrong… I promised myself I wouldn't hurt you again and I… I fucked that up, didn't I?" She didn't even correct his cursing. His tongue moved on the inside of his lip. "Excuse me."

Shane marched off but didn't leave their sight. He went down the porch stairs and kept on going until he reached the edge of the grass just before the lake's perimeter path.

While watching the back of the stoic man, another tear slid free. It should be a happy day; Cam had official notification of his father's identity. Instead, Shane had been threatened with divorce, told he was being used for his money, and kicked out of her life.

The sadness welled because she had no idea if they would ever get their rapport back. She would have to be more guarded. It wasn't his fault that she'd leaped in with both feet and got burned. But he would suffer the consequences because she couldn't let it happen again.

"There are things you have to know," Murphy said.

Ginger spun around, having almost forgotten that he was there. "I know," she said. "I mean, I know that now."

"He never wanted to hurt you."

"But I got hurt," she said. "Even if it was my own fault, it happened."

"You can't keep him from his son," Murphy said. "It's not fair, they adore each other."

She looked at Cam to see he was staring at his father's static figure. "I... I wouldn't, I..."

"Shane tried to touch Cam just now and you pulled the little guy away like his father was poison."

Oh God, she was fucking up over and over again. "I had to say my piece, that was all," she said. "Doctor Guinness said I shouldn't do anything else until I apologized and asked you all to stay."

To console Shane in the way she couldn't, and to prove she had no intentions of playing games with their relationship, Ginger took Cam onto the grass and put him down.

"Go get daddy," she whispered into the top of his head and kissed him before letting him go.

Watching him in his racing crawl for a few feet until she was happy he was headed in the right direction, she went back up the stairs to flop onto the seat beside Murphy.

"You know how to keep things interesting, Gin..." her brother-in-law said. "You always did."

The grass was only about fifteen feet wide. Cam was three quarters of the way across when he stopped to sit. "Da!" he called out and quickly got to crawling again.

Shane spun around, surprised by the proximity of the call. As soon as he saw Cam, he crouched and gestured him over. "Come on, buddy."

When his son got to him, Shane swept him up into his arms and held him high above his head. He brought him down for a kiss then tossed him up and caught him before running around with Cam stretched above his head.

Seeing the joy on her child's face brought a smile to hers. If nothing else came of their retreat, she had made the right choice of father for her son.

"I'm so happy it was positive," she murmured.

"I told you. They adore each other," Murphy said. "None of us thought this was going to be easy."

"No," she said. "But I didn't think it through. I've been passive, letting everything come to me when I…" Ginger wasn't going to do it anymore; she couldn't put her destiny in others' hands and then cry when she didn't have a full picture. Leaving the bench, she went to the porch railing. "Shane?" He turned around. "You got him?"

"Sure," he replied.

"For about an hour?"

He swept a hand through Cam's hair. "As long as you need."

"Where are you going?" Murphy asked when she began to head inside.

"To the lodge," she said. "It's time I got myself an education."

***

GINGER HAD BEEN gone for more than an hour, but there was a lot to take in, more than she could ever have imagined. WarNet started as a mapping device for outdoor types. She didn't really understand how it worked, but it sent out pulses that registered every environment in 3D. It collected the data and uploaded it whenever it came into contact with any Wi-Fi and could be plugged into other devices too.

There was a whole range of hardware from watches to bulky, mechanical looking things that were used by scientific sorts, with prices ranging from a grand to a hundred grand. Over the years, the devices had grown and included all sorts of extra features. There was also a WarNetwork too which connected all sorts of people who enjoyed outdoor pursuits. They shared the data from their devices on this massive social network allowing for changes and updates to be made all the time. People could communicate, keep in touch, check in with relatives, as well as share photos and status updates.

People could plan their trips and routes, right down to taking into account the latest fallen tree. But it wasn't just used by survivalists and boy scouts. WarNet had government contracts and were apparently working on some joint venture with NASA and another with the Navy. The device's range was ever growing and they could be used to communicate. In fact, WarNet offered a whole range of sat phones that were apparently the world's most reliable.

As for Shane, his love for the outdoors was what inspired the device. He was an avid mountaineer who'd summited some of the world's highest peaks, including Everest. He tested all devices himself, making sure they were durable and fit for purpose, taking them to their limits.

WarNet worked to provide information to ski resorts and other weather reliant services as the devices could also collect data on humidity, air quality; a whole host of things.

Ginger couldn't even begin to read up on everything, she'd just started to read about the securities company Shane had acquired five years ago when she noticed the time and had to run from the internet café at the lodge to get back to the chalet.

Shane had Cam ready for dinner by the time she got back. Everyone else was ready, waiting for her. Holding her printouts under her arm, Ginger went over to kiss her baby and then headed to the stairs.

"Sorry, guys, I'll get changed, just give me a minute," Ginger said, starting upstairs. She paused to turn and look back at the group. "Calvin, can I talk to you?"

"Of course." He left Boyd and followed her up to her bedroom. Grabbing a dress from the closet, Ginger stripped out of her jeans and shirt as he closed the door. "Is everything okay?"

"Yes," she said, applying moisturizer and deodorant. "How was your session with Doctor Guinness?"

"Productive," he said. "He has some good ideas. I like the change to how therapy will work."

"Me too," she said, putting on her dress. She grabbed her brush from the drawer to run it through her hair. "I haven't seen your mom today, is she okay?"

Really Ginger wanted to know how Diane was handling the explosive day.

"She's going back to the city," he said. "Boyd will remain here."

He was probably more useful and with the changes in therapy, there would be less need for Diane to be present.

"Could I ask you for something?" she asked, spraying perfume.

"Anything."

"I need a computer."

He blinked, like he hadn't expected her to say that and frowned. "Uh, okay… I can arrange to have one delivered. A laptop?"

"Thank you," she said. "I'd appreciate that."

Going over to him, ready, Ginger took a breath

and smiled.

"Doctor Guinness said you were going to make a decision," Calvin said. "That I shouldn't push about the divorce papers for a few days."

She shook her head and wrapped her arms around him. "I know this is complicated and I appreciate you being patient... he suggested that on top of our regular therapy Shane and I should sit with a lawyer, you know, like mediation... I need to talk to him about it tonight."

"I would prefer you not talk to him alone." Nodding, she relaxed when he put his arms around her. "Doctor Guinness said I should be honest about my feelings on your relationship with him, before the fact if I can."

Communicating was better, honesty was better. Ginger was seeing more of the Calvin she knew. "He said the same to me. About being honest when I was going to be with Shane... but we can save this for therapy tomorrow. I just wanted to ask how your session went and to tell you that I might need to find a minute alone with Shane tonight."

"Do it at the lodge," Calvin said. "Before we come back here... and keep your door locked when you're in your room. I know he has to be in here for Cam. But he should never be in here with you, do you understand?"

"I do," she said, widening her smile. "I feel better talking to you about this."

Calvin seemed relaxed. It was reassuring to be over the bump. "And I feel better that you're talking. I didn't like the not knowing. We're better when we strategize together."

"Absolutely," she said and accepted his kiss. "We should get downstairs. Everyone is waiting."

But he wasn't in a rush. "We could ask Warren

to keep an eye on Cam tonight… you could join me in my room."

Normality. Being with Calvin was what she knew. Ginger told herself to stop being seduced by novelty.

"If you like," she said. "But Shane has never had full responsibility for Cam overnight… I don't know if he's comfortable enough for that yet."

"He's confident with Cam," Calvin said. "I don't see why he would have a problem." As much as she wasn't sure she was ready to be spending the night in bed with anyone, Ginger also felt guilt for what she'd done with Shane. Calvin deserved to be given his place with her. Having confessed the full truth to a shocked Doctor Guinness, he advised her not to tell Calvin until they were in session where reactions could be monitored and controlled. "It won't hurt to ask."

"No," she said. "It won't… I'll mention it when I talk to him tonight."

"Good," he said and kissed her again. "Now, let's go to dinner."

Ginger hooked her hand inside his elbow and allowed him to lead her out of the room. Being the only female left, she was grateful for Doctor Guinness being there to witness the tension. With all the testosterone zipping around, it was like living in a pressure cooker. Their experience that day proved she couldn't control it alone.

TWENTY-ONE

DINNER WAS LOVELY, as always. The lodge were getting used to their motley family group. Ginger always sat between Cam and Calvin. Shane sat on Cam's other side. With the high chair between them, they didn't have to look at each other if they didn't want to.

Owen and Murphy sat on Shane's other side. Doctor Guinness sat opposite her at the circular table separating Boyd and Owen from each other.

Cam was trying to pick up the slices of banana she'd put on his high-chair tray for him while she wiped chocolate pudding from his lips. The little guy kept trying to push her hands out of his way.

"Want me to get that?" Shane asked her.

"Sure," she said, but didn't return his smile when he took the wipes.

"Come on, buddy, let's get you clean," Shane said and began to wipe off Cam's face and hands.

There hadn't been time to talk to Shane alone. Talking over the top of Cam and in front of an audience, wasn't an option. She couldn't do it when they got back to the lodge because that would mean going to one of the bedrooms and Calvin didn't want them to be alone together.

Glancing around the room, she considered inviting him to the bar for a drink. Problem was, she didn't drink and getting away would be difficult.

Calvin leaned in at her side. "Ask him to dance."

Twisting, she looked at the dance floor that had been occupied since the band had started. They played every night, background music that allowed couples to enjoy some romance during their stay.

"I don't—"

"I'll keep an eye on you," Calvin said. "You'll be alone without having to be alone."

"Okay," she said. Having just told Shane that she didn't like to be touched, she was about to ask him to hold her. The situation wasn't ideal. Dancing was all they had to work with. Standing up, Ginger took her napkin from her lap and put it on the chair. "Make sure Cam eats his banana."

"Of course," Calvin said, moving across a chair. "Remember tonight."

She nodded and passed Cam to get to the frowning Shane who was fixated on Calvin. Probably because he used a fork to pick the banana from Cam's tray when both parents just used their fingers.

Ginger laid a hesitant hand on Shane's shoulder and cleared her throat when his surprised attention leaped to her. "Will you dance with me… please?"

Shane tossed his napkin backwards as he stood up. It landed on Murphy, distracting him from his conversation with Owen and probably confusing him too.

"Hell, yeah," Shane said and took her hand to kiss her knuckles. He began to lead her toward the dance floor but glanced back. "We can bring Cam if you want.

I can hold both of you."

Having decided not to talk over her son at the table, she didn't want to substitute the table for the floor. "He's fine," she said.

On the dancefloor, Shane tried to take her into his arms. Rather than something more intimate, Ginger took his hand in hers and directed his other to her hip, eyeing him in a way meant to convey her invitation hadn't been a prelude to romance.

"Uh oh," he said, giving her a squeeze as they began to move. "Guess I shouldn't have read too much into you picking me over Calvin."

"We have to talk."

Dancing was much better than drinking at the bar because she could focus on his chest instead of having to look him in the eye.

"Another uh oh," he said. "You're about to say something I'm going to hate."

Truth was, there was too much to say. Ginger didn't know where to begin in their limited window of time. "Did you talk to Doctor Guinness?"

"Yes, after Calvin… I took Cam in with me, he was fine playing on the floor. You can leave him with me any time and I'll always—"

"I know. I think you're a good father and I'm sorry if my actions earlier implied anything else."

He tried to pull her closer, but she resisted. "Why are you talking to me like that? In that tone? Why won't you look at me? Baby, I'm sorry for—"

"It has to stop." She'd known the conversation was going to be difficult, but this was a million times worse than she imagined. "Doctor Guinness spoke to me about prioritizing, about taking control and making decisions."

"Yes," he said. "Everyone will be entitled to a private session, but we can invite another into our session if we want. No more group sessions in front of the fire… unless that's what you want."

"Yes, but…" Ginger couldn't let herself be led, she had to be clear. Doctor Guinness' words rang in her head, strength. It was all about strength "My priority is Cameron."

"Good," he nodded. "Mine too."

"Doctor Guinness suggested that we should sit with a mediator, a lawyer, someone who can help us draw up a plan for him. I have questions about some practicalities."

"Okay," he said. "I've already taken steps to set up a trust for him and college will be taken care of, of course. Anything he needs—"

"No, it has to be more specific than that. I don't want airy promises. We have to put a clear structure in place for his support."

Glancing up to see how he was taking her determination, she was surprised to find him smiling.

"Anything you need, Bit. For you and Cam, nothing is enough."

Maybe she wasn't being clear enough. "You're the father of my child."

His smile glowed. "I know."

"No, I mean… that's it. That's all you are. You're Cam's father." His smile faltered. "We have to draw a line. My life now is with Calvin. I've done a lot of damage to my relationship with him in the last twenty-four hours. It was selfish. Doctor Guinness will sit down with me and him tomorrow and I'll tell him everything. Everything, Shane. I'll tell him that I kissed you. I'll tell him about what happened in the bathroom… both of them. I'm only going to be honest from here on out."

That declaration put a scowl on his face. Although he still held the position, Shane stopped moving to the music. "You have to listen to me, he hasn't been honest with you… There are things you need to know."

Shaking her head, Ginger closed her eyes for a second and took her hands from him. "No… I know you don't like him, but—"

"No, this is more than that. It's nothing to do with me, well, it's nothing to do with us. I have to tell you—"

"If you have some big secret to share, invite me into your private session with the doctor. You and I will not be having any more private conversations alone in bedrooms and bathrooms. From now on, everything is witnessed."

"Because you don't trust yourself?" he asked and stole a glance at the table. Exhaling a laugh, his hand rose to his forehead. "That's what the dance is for. He's watching, isn't he? He wants us talking somewhere he can keep an eye on you."

"All Calvin wants to do is protect our relationship. He wants to protect me and Cam."

"From me?" Shane snapped. "Why am I the only one who remembers that I'm your husband? It's my job to protect you and our son, not his."

More anger. Shane was used to working on instinct and not rationale. "Calvin has been very understanding," she said, losing her patience. "He hasn't commented on how much time you've been spending with Cam even though it must be tearing him apart."

"To see me bonding with my son? He doesn't give a crap about Cammy; all he wants is the child support and—"

"Stop it! Stop talking about money like it's the be all and end all. No one cares about your money." Clenching her jaw, she exhaled because somehow he was making her lose her rationality too. "Do you know what I did today?" He shrugged. "Research… I know who you are Mr. Warren. I know where you live. I know about the Ventura deal. I know how you made your money."

"Good," he said. "I never wanted to hide anything from you. I wasn't the one who refused you the right to use a telephone line for sixteen months."

"I saw the campaign. You spent a fortune trying to find me. You made appeals all over the media."

"And I'd do it again," he said.

"Well you've found me and…" Ginger didn't want to be cruel but reminded herself to be clear. "And I don't want any part of it, Shane. I'm sorry."

"Any part of what?"

"The money. The circus. I don't want to be paraded around in the media, hailed as the infamous wife come home. I don't want to do interviews and exploit myself and I sure won't exploit my son."

"Is that what you meant about a plan? You want to keep him out of the media?"

"Part of it," she said. "I don't want his picture plastered—"

"Neither do I," he said and widened his stance as his shoulders hunched and he peered closer. "How much research did you do into our lives before I lost you?"

"I…" That took some of the wind from her sails. "I…"

She'd researched his biography and the companies that were related to him, but she hadn't gone into great detail about the nitty gritty of their lives.

"We never did interviews. I bet you'd struggle to find one picture of us together online. You always hated if someone tried to take our picture. If I had to go through digital backdoors and take them down for you, I did. You didn't even come on stage at conventions or releases. You stayed in the background and everyone respected that because it was hard enough for them to get me to talk or even show up. We threw everything at the campaign because I wanted you back… Cam won't be exploited and neither will you… I promise."

It was so easy for him to sound certain, but his memory for details wasn't that good. "Like you promised yourself you wouldn't hurt me again?" she asked.

The words impacted him with such force that he took a step backward and his hand went to his chest.

But he recovered quickly. "If I'd known that not being upfront about the company would've hurt you, I'd have told you everything… I swear, there's nothing I'm keeping from you on purpose. No secrets."

"The Ventura woman," she said and because they were conspicuous as the only couple not moving on the floor, she let him take hold of her so they could dance again. "She's beautiful."

His brow twitched down. "Julianna? Uh, I guess… I've never met her."

"Ever?" she asked and thought that was quite an extreme position.

"Ever. In fact, that's why the deal's not going to happen. She wanted to meet and I said no dice."

There was no logic in that. "Why not?"

"Because I'm here," he said.

Oh, so it was on her, just what she didn't want. "I told you that you could go back to work," Ginger said. "I won't have you missing out on a deal because of my issues."

"Your issues are my issues."

"No," she said, frustrated that he wasn't listening. "That's what I'm telling you. You're Cam's father. That's the only tie you have to me. And he can live without you for a few days… He's never used video calling, but Owen was telling me at the hospital that it's a thing, right? Maybe Owen can set it up for you and Cam to talk on video."

"And you? How do I talk to you? I won't be a

Skype dad."

"I don't even know what that means," she said. "I'm trying to be reasonable. To show you that I won't obstruct your relationship with him… I don't know anything about technology, so I can't do it, but Owen can."

His patience was being stretched again. "We can stop talking about this because I'm not going anywhere. I'm staying here… How will we have our mediation sessions about Cam's future if I'm not here?"

That was a good point and one she pondered for a minute before coming up with another idea. "Then invite her here."

Shock made him blink. "What?"

"Not to the chalet." That was a laughable idea. "It's nuts down there and we don't want her seeing any part of that. But this is a hotel too. You can arrange for her to have a suite and they have conference rooms. You can have your meetings here at the lodge."

"That's… that's… not a bad idea."

See, they could both be reasonable. If they stayed detached and didn't get emotional. "You can have dinner and drinks, maybe you could invite her to—"

"It's business, not social," he said like he was suspicious of her motives. It would make Ginger's life easier if his romantic interest switched to someone else. "I'll talk to Murph about it, he'll set it up. Thank you, Bit."

"You don't have to thank me. I will support your business and accommodate what you do providing it doesn't interfere with Cam's wellbeing."

"Nothing ever will."

"Good," she said. "Then I think we're done."

"The divorce papers," he said before she could turn away. "Don't sign them."

"I tore up the settlement."

"It's not the money. I don't care about that, just… don't sign them."

Exhaling, she wasn't sure she'd got through to him at all. "You're Cam's father—"

"And your husband," he said, stopping to cup her face to tip her head back. "I'm not asking you for a commitment… I'm not even asking for a kiss." He smiled and touched his thumb to her lips. Ginger fought herself to stay detached. "All I'm asking is that you don't put pen to paper. Please. Make me this one promise."

It was a big one. The biggest one. Divorce papers needed signatures of both spouses, although given the circumstances, hers may be enough to convince a judge to force the issue.

"Doctor Guinness suggested we stick a pin in the issue for a few days anyway. Calvin's agreed with that."

His hands dropped and his scowl returned. "Oh, well, if Calvin's agreed."

"He's going to be a part of my life, which means he'll be a part of Cam's. You have to find a way to get along with him… just like I'll have to find a way to get along with whoever you end up with."

Pissed, Shane left reasonable behind to become snide. "You might have self-esteem issues, but I'll love you enough for both of us."

She wanted to scream. "Shane, you have to let this go. You're not listening to me! There's nothing between us anymore. Our marriage ended sixteen months ago. Calvin is—"

"He's in it for the money. He wants to marry you because you're worth a fortune."

"Okay then," she said, folding her arms. "If you believe that, go on over there and offer him money. Offer him money to walk away."

His chin rose, either angry or intrigued by the idea. "Cam's at that table," Shane said. "I'm not starting a fight in front of our son and I don't trust myself not to punch the guy in the face if things get dirty."

Rolling her tongue, Ginger tutted. "Great, use our son as an excuse. You won't do it because you know he wouldn't take it. You could offer him ten billion dollars and he wouldn't leave me for it. He loves me, Shane. I don't know why you can't believe that."

"Because after you left this afternoon, Murph and I figured out the truth, and baby, it's not pretty."

"Secrets," she said and turned to walk away.

Shane scooped an arm around her waist and hauled her back to him. "Truth," he said, hunched so his face was just an inch from hers.

Searching his eyes, she saw that certainty. He hadn't heard her or if he had, he had ignored what she was trying to tell him.

Maybe a cold hard slap was what he needed. "Will you sleep in my room tonight?" she asked.

His certainty flashed to surprise then he slowly grinned. "I thought you'd never ask."

"Cam shouldn't wake up, but I'll make a bottle for him just in case. You can use the warmer that's in the drawer. It's electronic, you're good with that stuff, right? You'll figure it out, there's only one switch."

The instruction confused him. "Okay."

"You know where his diapers are… and I don't mind Rocky in the bed in the morning. But if Cam ends up in with you, can you keep Rocky on the floor? I don't want Cam trying to suck on his fur while he's sleeping."

"Okay, but I don't—"

"I'll only be in Calvin's room, so if there are any problems—"

Letting her go, Shane stood up straight, shaking his head. "No… no. You want me to…" He dipped to hiss, "You want me to babysit so you can go to him and get laid? Not a chance."

Typical that he should be the one to use Cam against her when she'd just been clear about not doing the opposite. "We're not going to have sex."

"Oh, baby, don't be naïve," he snickered, sneering at her breasts. "If he gets you on your back, he'll be taking you all the way."

Pushing his chest, she wished he wouldn't look at her with such a leer. "Why? Because that's what you would do?"

"I don't have to rush. I have forever with you, baby. He's running out of time."

He infuriated her. "You're so arrogant," she hissed. "Hear what I'm saying. You're. Not. Getting. Me. Back."

When he lunged forward, she gasped thinking he was going to kiss her. Instead, he grabbed her chin and thrusted it upward. Ginger yelped when he sealed his mouth against the artery in her neck and sucked hard. She punched his shoulder with the side of her fist and shoved him back as he released her.

"There," he scowled. "Little something for him to focus on while he fucks you."

Her hand rose to her throat as Shane strode off the dance floor to return to the table. He didn't sit down, he scooped up Cam and slung the diaper bag over his shoulder. His sideways nod was enough to get Murphy and Owen onto their feet. Though they were surprised by the sudden departure, neither man abandoned their friend.

Ginger was still standing there in the middle of the dance floor with her fingertips on the bruise Shane had left on her neck. She watched as he marched away from the dinner table, their son in his arms, Murphy and Owen in his wake.

Calvin was coming over to her, but she couldn't stop staring at the door. He'd marked her body and taken her son. She'd asked him to take responsibility for Cam so she could be alone and he had. So why did she feel so bereft?

TWENTY-TWO

"THANK YOU," Ginger said, standing in Calvin's bedroom doorway with him, accepting his kiss.

"We can't be patient forever," Calvin said.

Ginger sighed. "I know, just… give me a little more time."

He rolled his eyes and bent to kiss her. Pressing her into the wood at her spine, he pushed harder than usual until she was struggling for breath and had to jolt him back. Tilting her head in silent request for an explanation, he smiled.

"I want you badly."

Kissing him once more, Ginger slid away from the doorway. Calvin dropped her hand and went inside, closing the door, leaving her alone in the darkened hallway of the upper mezzanine.

Everyone else was in bed. She and Calvin had stayed at the lodge. They'd drank and danced, but as the bruise Shane had left on her neck darkened, so did Calvin's mood. Eventually, it became clear to them both that they were not going to be spending the night together.

He did try to take her to his bedroom, but she had stopped in the doorway. It had been hours since she'd seen Cameron. Though she was confident in his safety, she felt uneasy about the way dinner had ended and just didn't feel in a sexy mood.

Shane would be asleep in her bed and it hadn't worked out so well the last time she'd slept in his. Another person had been neglected that day. With ideas of remedying that, Ginger went down the hallway and past Murphy's bedroom door to knock on the next one.

Ginger didn't wait for a response because she didn't know if he'd be asleep. Just to check, she poked her head around the door and saw Owen sitting up, reading by lamplight.

"Hey," he said, taking off his glasses and putting them on the bedside with his reading tablet thing.

"Still talking to me?"

He smiled and opened his arms, so she went in and closed the door. Rushing over to him, she was pleased to be accepted by her brother.

After their hug, he pulled back his covers and welcomed her into his bed. "What the hell happened? I left to file those papers in the city and then... what the fuck?" Owen asked. "I came home to World War Three."

Ginger actually envied him for missing most of the drama. "I don't know what happened," she said.

The day had been so crazy that she was still trying to figure out how it had all gone down. Lying on her side, Ginger gave the pillow a punch and blew her hair from her face.

Owen settled down to lie facing her. "I thought you were going to bed with Calvin."

Squeezing her lips together, she winced and shook her head.

Tipping her head back, she pointed at the hickey. "I think this killed the mood," she said. "Calvin wanted to tear after Shane… I can't believe he… that Shane… Calvin was talking sexual assault and—"

Owen grumbled. "Course he was, he wants to sue."

Pushing back, she narrowed one eye. "I guess Shane told you what he thought then."

"Murphy actually," Owen said. "He gave me the run down while Shane was playing with Cam when you were up at the lodge today… I was going to come and find you but I was just so shocked… Is it true Calvin knew who you were the whole time?"

She hadn't heard Shane's full accusation and didn't like the creepy feeling that tickled her shoulders. "What? No! Calvin didn't know who I was," Ginger said. "He was as surprised as I was about you guys showing up at the church."

"Then why did he ask for such a hefty settlement? He knew exactly who Shane was."

She couldn't argue that he knew, the settlement clause made that obvious. "Yeah, now he knows. But he didn't know then… how could he?" She'd told Shane she didn't want any stories, that all of them should be kept for the session. Going any further would be playing by two sets of rules. "Was Cam okay when you got home?"

"Shane took him straight into his bath," Owen said. "I heard some hilarity, but I haven't seen either of them… I'm sure you can go and look in on them. Shane won't mind seeing you."

Gnawing her lip, she shook her head, snagging her hair with a finger. "No, I can't… I don't want Cam to see us fighting."

"Why would you fight?" Owen asked. "You seem to do that a lot."

"I know," she said. Ginger wasn't oblivious to

the fact that she fought more with Shane than she did with anyone else and he was supposed to be the one who wanted to bond with her. "I'm pissed at him."

"Why?" he asked and she pointed at her neck again. "Okay, yeah, you're maybe a little old for hickeys but his intention was good."

Her mood wasn't just about the bruise. "You didn't hear what he said to me," she said, rolling onto her back. "He's always so... rude."

Owen laughed and squeezed an arm around her. "You used to love it when he talked dirty to you."

Yeah, she'd seen that on the video. But she wasn't used to that language. Calvin didn't use it and they'd made out plenty of times.

"I'm not talking about that stuff. He's arrogant and—"

"Uh, I think Calvin gets the award for most superior. Shane doesn't even iron his clothes and his boots are scuffed to hell. Calvin comes down in a three piece suit every day."

She nudged him. "He does not! He wears polo shirts and chinos."

Owen laughed. "I'm not sure Shane even knows what chinos are."

That was probably true. Ginger turned her face to her brother's shoulder. "How could I have been attracted to such different men?"

Owen had an explanation. "You're attracted to strong men... usually the strongest man in the room."

"I am not," she said and thought about it. "Am I that easy?"

Her brother seemed sure. "It's the reason you fell back under Shane's spell so fast. He's definitely stronger than Calvin."

Comparing the men wasn't fair, especially when she'd taken Shane out of the running. "I must have an amoeba brain," she said.

"At its earliest stage of development, definitely," he said and she pinched him. "I meant, you're an amnesia victim, so you're innocent. You don't have the benefit of all your romantic experience. Your body reacts before your brain tells you it's not a good idea."

A good point, well made. "Making out with Shane wasn't a good idea," she said, settling against him, and pushing her hair out her face. "But it's okay. That's done now."

"Done?" he asked. "Forever."

"Yes," she said, yawning. "I have a child to think about, I can't be messing around with different men."

"You don't think it's a smart idea to have a good relationship with the father of your child?"

"Yes," she said. "Absolutely, we will have to put up with each other for the next eighteen years."

"And the rest," Owen said. "You'll have Cam's college stuff, his wedding, you'll share grandkids…"

"You know what I was thinking about today when I was reading about Shane's success," she said, rolling to her side again to tuck her hands beneath her chin. Owen raised his brows to prompt her. "My children are never going to like each other."

"What?"

"If Calvin and I have kids, I mean, they'll be happy but you know what kids are like… Calvin and I will get kid two a Mini Cooper as his first car and Cam will rock up in the Ferrari his dad just bought him." Owen laughed. "I mean it! Think about it," she said. "Cam is going to be a brat, there's just no way to avoid it. You've seen what Shane is like with him. He won't just take him to Disneyland, he'll rent out the whole park for a week for a private experience."

Owen leaned in, his face contorted with mocking. "Don't worry, I'm sure Shane will invite you."

She gave him a shove. "It's going to be a nightmare."

"Shane's not like that. He'll respect your wishes. Trust me, whether you end up with him or not, he'll still bow to your every whim… I wouldn't be surprised if he buys all your kids a Ferrari just to make your life easier."

She groaned. "How do you live with all that money? I don't get it. I don't… see it."

"When you look at him?" Owen shrugged. "He just… doesn't care about the money. He cares about the code and the summit. He loves a puzzle and a challenge. His father was a professional gambler, his mother was a cocktail waitress. It was a professor who saw his talent. The guy was at the school giving a talk about something and he gave the kids a bunch of instructions and set them a puzzle. No one was supposed to solve it. Shane did. After that, the professor began to tutor him. Shane resisted until he realized it was all a puzzle, and he loves one of those.

"The outdoor stuff started much younger, he won some competition his mom entered him in 'cause he was always hyper and became part of a mountaineering club when he was like five. He fell in love with it and had an uncle who took him camping and stuff. I actually think he started his first company because he wanted to bankroll his mountaineering."

"So his home life… He said in therapy that they were happy. Murphy turned out okay, but went through a rough phase. The house he described was normal, they had a car, normal holidays… least that's how it seemed."

"It was the professor who got Shane into college on a scholarship, but he was already building his company by then. His father did okay with the gambling, so yeah, they grew up okay for money, but there was no stability. They weren't rich or anything. I guess you can take the boy out the ghetto…"

She tsked. "He did not live in a ghetto."

"You know what I mean. He got in his share of fights at school. He and Murphy were quite the duo, always had each other's backs."

"He said that in therapy," she said, thinking about the team defending each other. "Murphy works with him now?"

"He's his right-hand man, he takes care of the details… I deal with the official stuff."

"Will you help us with the mediation?" she asked. "I think Boyd will just rile Shane, not on purpose, he's a good guy, but just his presence will—"

"Of course," Owen said. "I'm still the Warren family lawyer."

Peeking at him, she wasn't going to let that slide. "You know where all the bodies are buried?"

He grinned. "I do."

That was encouraging, and she shifted higher. "Do you know if I had my own bank accounts? I mean, did I just live off Shane? You said I had a job, right?"

"You worked with Shane," he said. "You were at WarNet for two years before you started dating him. Murphy was actually the one to hire you as one of his intern assistants in your last year of college. You didn't meet Shane until a couple of weeks later. He said he fell in love with you the first time he saw you. He turned down one of the corridors at HQ and saw you talking to someone and that was it."

"That's not true," she tutted never believing in such a thing as love at first sight.

"He kept his hands off. Everyone told him that screwing with young underlings was a bad idea. His family thought he could do better, so he stayed away… for a year anyway. Well, I say he stayed away, you were socializing with us by then. I don't know what happened in that year. One day he just decided to go for it and he pursued you for another year before you gave in… A year later you were married."

"And we were married for four years?"

"Yeah, the accident was just a couple of weeks after your fourth anniversary… you had a party because Shane promised you'd be alone somewhere tropical for your fifth… that didn't exactly work out."

"I don't remember any of that," she murmured.

"I know it must be frustrating," he said, rubbing her arm when she lay down and hugged the comforter against her.

It was, but she shouldn't be talking about Shane. In bed with Owen wasn't therapy and she was over her husband.

Ginger took a big breath. "Tell me about Derek."

Owen grinned. "Why don't we get ready for bed and I'll tell you whatever you want to know."

Sleeping with her brother was a better option than going to Shane's bed and she wasn't going to kick him out of her bed when she'd asked him to occupy it. Cam would be sleeping and she didn't want to wake him either. So Ginger got out of bed and changed into Owen's tee-shirt. A sleepover with her brother was just what she needed to reset the needle.

TWENTY-THREE

PART OF SHANE hoped that Ginger would be in his bed when he woke up. She wasn't. Trying to put her out of his mind, Shane got himself and Cam ready. It sort of surprised him that she'd managed to stay away from Cam for so long. He'd kind of hoped she'd come in to see their baby when she got back from the lodge so he could take one last crack at preventing her from going to bed with Calvin. That had backfired because he hadn't seen her.

Cam ate his breakfast like a pro and Shane got a new appreciation for how lonely being a single parent could be. Spending time with his son was incredible and enjoying each other in these crisp early hours was a treat. There was something intimate about it and he began to recognize how Ginger and Cam had developed such a strong bond. They really were best friends. But it was hard work and isolating to be the only adult awake, tiptoeing around a house full of sleepers.

Rocky stayed out in the yard after Shane let him out for his pee. Although Shane told himself that he was worried about Cam making noise, the truth was, he was wound too tight to sit still. He needed someone to talk to, someone to vent to. It was making him itch to know that his wife was in Calvin's bed and there wasn't a damn thing he could do about it.

With Cam under his arm, Shane ran up the stairs and stormed along the corridor, choosing to walk into Owen's room. He didn't trust himself not to keep on going to Calvin's room at the end to demand an explanation if he went as far as Murphy's.

"Okay, I'm going fucking insane," Shane said, striding past the bed to pull open the shades to let some light into the dark room.

Despite knowing that Owen liked to stay up late reading or talking to Derek, Shane couldn't even bring himself to care that he was being rude by waking up his friend.

"What's wrong?" Owen croaked.

Shane kept his back to the bed giving his friend a chance to cough and wake up. "I—"

"Mama!" Cam shrieked and began to struggle. It broke Shane's heart that he couldn't let Cam see his mother, but using his son as an excuse to rouse her from Calvin's room was cheap. He sure wasn't going to let Cam into Calvin's bed. "Mama! Mama!"

"Oh, Angel, come see mama," said a sleepy female voice.

Whirling around, Shane was speechless at the sight of Ginger there in the center of Owen's bed under the comforter. With her eyes half-closed, and her hair rumpled, she looked delicious. Cam was still struggling, so Shane put him down on the floor.

Cam scrambled across the floor and tried to climb up on the bed. Owen was on the other side, sitting up, rubbing his face and retrieving his glasses. Ginger flopped over, reaching her son and dragging him up onto the bed. She was wearing one of Owen's silk V-neck tee-shirts. The comforter stayed low on her thighs when she returned to her back and closed her eyes.

Hugging Cam to her chest, Ginger smiled and kissed his head. "Oh, baby, momma missed you… you smell like daddy."

Was that a good thing? He couldn't tell from her expression, but she was still asleep enough that she might not even have known she said it aloud.

"Mama!" Cam said and turned his face to rub against her breast through the tee-shirt.

She loosened her arms so the baby could climb up and nuzzle her face. She laughed and didn't even bother to wipe the slobber from her lips after his exuberant kiss. Cam wriggled away down her body and pulled up her tee-shirt. Her taut belly came into view and Shane was happy to watch his son try to stick his head beneath her shirt; he'd be doing the same if he was allowed to get close enough.

"No," she said, taking the bottom of the shirt to pull it back down. Cam squawked and persisted. "No milkies in Uncle Owen's bed." Cam protested and squashed his mouth to her diaphragm. "Stop that." She laughed again. "You won't get anything from there and if you keep on rooting, I'll leak."

"Okay, eww, keep the shirt," Owen said.

Though her eyes were still closed, Ginger smiled and prodded her brother. Her distraction gave Cam the opportunity to drag the shirt upward with the top of his head and the underside of her bare breast came into view.

"Cam," Ginger said, more insistent in her tone. She cracked an eye and turned to him, squinting against the glare of the sun. "Shane, did you feed him?"

"No, I thought I'd starve him," Shane said and immediately wanted to slap himself for being rude. "Yes, sorry, I don't know why I—he had oatmeal and fruit."

"She slept here all night," Owen said, yawning. "You don't have to be pissy that you didn't get any, neither did she."

Sitting up and yawning, Ginger pulled Cam into her lap as she tugged her shirt down. "Can we all watch our language around precious ears," she said in a happy mommy voice as she glared at each of the men. "I'm going to introduce a swear jar."

"Did you need something?" Owen asked him.

Shane's reason for coming in was moot, but that didn't mean he wanted to leave. Watching mother and son reunite was mesmerizing.

"Did Cam behave?" Ginger asked, holding Cam's waist as he stood up. "Did he wake up?"

"Once," Shane said. "He had a drink and went back down."

She nodded. "Thank you… I could've done it, but I didn't want to disturb either of you."

"No, we had fun," Shane said.

Caring for his son was fun. The lying in his wife's sheets part was torturous. Thinking of her in another man's bed made him want to set the building on fire. But when his anger got to critical mass, he went to the crib and watched Cam sleeping. It was amazing the effect such a small thing could have on him. Cam gave him a determined purpose. There was nothing he and his wife couldn't come back from and Shane had resolved himself to doing his best by his son. Ginger was right, Cam was the most important thing.

"Da! Da!" Cam called and reached toward him. "Da! Cam! Cam!"

He didn't know if he was saying his own name or commanding his father to come over. But he pushed away from the window and wandered toward his boy.

"Need something, sire?" Shane asked, noticing the smile flash on Ginger's face at his joke as she ran her fingers through Cam's hair, admiring him like he was the most precious thing in the world, which he was.

Cam reached higher and Shane took his hand. Cam gave him a tug. "Da… Da…" Cam ordered and pulled on him so Shane sat down facing the end of the bed. Cam clambered over his mother's leg and into Shane's lap. Shoving his father's chest, bouncing back and forth to push harder and harder, it was clear that Cam wanted him to lie down, so he did, keeping his legs off the edge of the bed.

Shane was just thinking about how odd it was to be lying in bed with his wife and brother-in-law when Ginger yelped. Cam's fingers were tangled in her hair. He gave a yank, pulling Ginger back fast, faster than Shane could react though there was nowhere to go. One of his arms was under his wife and the other was around Cam. The back of Ginger's head smacked into his cheekbone with bruising force.

"Oh, baby!" she cried out.

Shane didn't know if she was talking to him or Cam, but his vision was speckling, so he just blinked.

Ginger twisted, endeavoring to untangle her hair from Cam's fingers. She managed to free herself and while their son laughed, she pounced higher to curl her fingers around his jaw.

"Oh, Shane, I'm sorry," she said.

"No," Shane said. "No, it's fine."

"Oh, no it's not," she cried out and touched his cheek. "I'm so sorry, does it hurt? Is it broken?"

"No, no, baby. We're good," Shane said, still a little in shock. His arm stayed around Cam to ensure the little one kept his seat on his father's chest. Curving the other up Ginger's back, Shane rubbed the back of her head. "Are you okay?"

"I'm so sorry," she said.

He was just coming around to how mortified her

expression was when she rose and pressed her lips to his cheekbone. His awareness morphed to something else and on instinct his body reacted. He was holding his wife and his son; he wouldn't care if an anvil dropped on him right then.

Cam was still laughing and bouncing on his stomach. "Da! Da!"

"If that bruises you can sue for domestic abuse," Owen said, not doing a great job of containing his amusement. "We'll have plenty for a countersuit." Shane didn't know what that meant, but Ginger obviously did because she scowled at her brother and slapped his chest. "Oh, look, she's on a rampage… Watch out, Cam! Take cover!"

Shane smiled at their ease, but when Ginger looked back at him the pain of apology had returned to her eyes.

"I'm so sorry," she whispered.

"Really, Bit, I'm fine," he said, gathering her hair back from her temple.

Cradling the back of her skull, he considered whether he'd get away with trying to kiss her when she yelped again and grabbed her boob.

"Ow! Cam!" she said, seizing his pudgy hand. "No pinching."

The kid was having all the fun this morning. Ginger sat up, fondling her breast while wearing a look of discomfort.

"Gin kissed your boo-boo better, Shane," Owen said, nudging his shoulder. "You want to kiss hers better?"

Shane's brows rose as he turned his eyes to hers knowing that his gaze was full of mischief.

She sneered, but it was good natured. "No, thank you," she said. There was momentary groin contact when she climbed over him to get out of bed. "One night with his daddy and my baby's turned violent."

Shane might have objected to that statement, except Ginger stretched her hands to the ceiling. Her yawn closed her eyes, giving him the opportunity to admire the line of her legs, and her tiny panties below her lower abdomen. God bless Owen and his tight tee-shirts. As if that wasn't enough to enrapture him, Ginger turned to the window and Shane got a view of her ass too.

Stretching his legs onto the bed, Shane put a hand behind his head while admiring her tush. Owen slapped his shoulder, but Shane swatted his brother-in-law's hand away and exhaled. It started as the second worst day of his life, but this day was turning around fast.

"Da!" Cam said, rising to bounce on his stomach again making Shane 'oof'. "Wooo!"

"Mommy will take Rocky out," Ginger said, wandering to the window to look down at the yard. "It's dry, looks quite nice out… What have we got on today?"

"Therapy, therapy, and more therapy," Owen said, getting out of bed leaving Shane alone with Cam who chose to roll onto the middle of the bed where his mother had been. "You want to do that mediation thing this morning, sis?"

"Maybe," she said. "We should finish our conversation first."

"Okay," Owen said. "I'm going to shower before Murphy goes in… He takes an age."

Owen left the bedroom and locked the bathroom door. She stayed at the window for a while; Shane was in no hurry to go anywhere.

"Is there internet here?" she asked.

"Wi-Fi?" he asked. "Yeah, didn't you use it at the lodge yesterday?"

"Yeah, but here I mean," she said, turning around to lean on the ledge where he'd been before.

Glancing at Cam, Shane saw him trying to pick

up Owen's Kindle, so he pulled his son to the middle of the bed again and took his phone from his pocket to hand it over to his son.

Ginger straightened up, wearing a look of panic.

Shane smiled. "It's a phone and he likes it. Doesn't matter if he breaks it."

"He'll slobber on it," she said and rightly enough, Cam tried to put it in his mouth. She rushed over and leaned across him to take the phone from Cam's mouth. "He has a tooth coming in… I put some carrot sticks in the freezer for him."

"He'd probably prefer apple, something sweeter."

She shrugged, showing Cam where the pictures on the phone were, not the risqué ones, but the regular ones, though she didn't look at them. Cam enjoyed babbling at the faces.

"We're out of apples."

"When he's done with the phone I can change that," he said.

She pinned him with an unimpressed look. "With all your money?" That sounded like a kneejerk comment, much like his had been this morning. Sure enough, she exhaled a minute later. "Sorry… we'd appreciate that."

"No problem."

Cam tossed the phone aside and clambered over him to climb onto his mother, but he just used her as a bridge to get to the floor. He began to crawl to the door.

"The Wi-Fi thing," she said, standing up to watch Cam. "Is it hard to set up?"

He was curious and confused. "No… there's a laptop in my room if you need—"

"Calvin said he'd have a new one delivered for me today," she said.

There was optimism in her eyes when she looked at him. Maybe she thought she was proving something because Calvin was allowing her contact with the outside world.

"Nice of him," he muttered and she crooked a brow. He shouldn't be such a dick, but it was difficult to see her thinking highly of the guy he knew was a snake. "I can set it up for you… if you'd like."

"Calvin has… he has people who do that kind of thing, I don't know if—"

"It's not a problem," he said, leaving the bed to stand up close to her. "You just tell me what you need and I'll deliver." She just looked confused. He smiled and brushed his finger down her jaw. "What you need it for and I'll make sure all the programs you need are on it."

She nodded. "Thank you. I'd appreciate that… Did you talk to Julianna?"

"Murphy did last night. She's coming later tonight."

"Wow, you're important," she said. "A big CEO drops everything to rush to you." Was that jealousy in her voice or was she making fun of him? "I hope you don't greet her with a black eye." She dug her teeth into her lip as she reached up to touch his face. When she touched him all he felt was joy, there was no pain. "I really am so sorry."

"Wouldn't be the first time we've exchanged bruises," he said. Horror spread on her expression, so he touched the hickey on her neck. "Sex games gone awry, not domestic abuse."

Her hand fell and a panicked look overcame her face. "Oh God," she breathed.

"What?"

He smiled and tried to take her hand, but she backed off.

"I… I have to go." That was weird. She'd told him not to touch her before, but she'd never appeared so scared. Rushing away, she swept up Cam from the floor and dashed to the door. Just before she closed it, she turned to him. "We're not supposed to be alone anymore… ever. Don't…"

Was she going to tell him not to tell Calvin about that morning? That wouldn't be hard because Shane had no intention of talking to the snake ever again if he didn't have to. Except he wouldn't lie about spending time with his wife.

After how he'd left her on the dance floor last night, her trust in him was probably wavering. Maybe that was why she didn't bother finishing her sentence.

She inhaled, sagged, and walked out without saying anything else.

***

GINGER'S SESSION WITH Doctor Guinness was productive.

When she came downstairs from the doctor's room, Cam was with Shane and his uncles in the living room and Calvin was on the phone at the bottom of the stairs. She ran down to him and took his hand.

"One sec," Calvin said into the phone. "You need something?"

"You're next with Doctor Guinness," she said and he nodded before returning to the phone.

A knock at the front door took her away from Calvin. As Ginger went toward the entrance, she waved at Cam who was sitting on his father, something he seemed to like to do a lot. Rocky was whining at Murphy; she guessed he was hiding dog treats somewhere on his person.

She opened the door to find one of the lodge employees on the other side.

"Can you sign for a delivery?" the employee asked.

Ginger was examining the basket of apples when she took the clipboard and signed. The employee grinned and handed over the basket then picked up a box for her. Her computer! She was admiring the laptop box while the delivery boy glanced at the clipboard.

"Thank you, Mrs. Warren. Enjoy!"

"What?" she asked, surprised at that use of her name.

"Mrs. Warren," the employee said, looking at her like she was peculiar… but she was acting weird. "Right?"

He turned the clipboard and she saw that she had actually signed Ginger Warren. She hadn't even been paying attention, it had come from the pen automatically in some kind of weird show of muscle memory.

"Thank you," she murmured and went inside.

Kicking the door shut, she wondered if she should read anything into her absentminded signing.

"You ready?" Calvin asked from the bottom of the stairs.

She snapped from her daze. "Oh, you want me to come with you?" she asked and he nodded, like that was obvious.

Taking the apples to the table, she put them down and Cam shrieked. He clambered off his father and she rotated the basket away.

"You can have one if daddy cleans it and cuts it up for you," she said to Cam then looked at Shane who was still lying on the floor. "That okay?"

"Yep," he said.

Ginger turned the laptop box over to Shane who'd said he'd set it up for her and he sat up to take it from her.

"I won't be long," she said to him. "I know you've had Cam for ages."

Because she couldn't resist, she went over to kiss

Cam's head, but he was busy trying to climb over Rocky so he could get around the table to the front of the apple basket. Her boy squawked at her and shoved her away.

"Ah, love," Owen said.

Ginger stuck her tongue out at her brother and ran over to take Calvin's hand. "Sorry, honey, let's go."

She'd have a crazy day because she guessed that she'd have to be in Shane's session too, at least part of it. They had to have their mediation session as well. The new rules meant crazier times for her, but Ginger was invigorated. Finally, it felt like they were making progress. It was just a shame she missed her baby so much.

TWENTY-FOUR

SHANE HAD OFFERED to put Cam down for his nap. Although Ginger was eager to get back to mommying her baby, she wasn't going to argue when Cam was already in his father's arms. She asked Shane to meet her and Owen in the dining room when he was done. That gave her the chance to finish her conversation with Owen before they had to start their mediation.

Ten minutes after he left, Shane came into the dining room, hooked the monitor on his belt and held up his hands like guns to blow on his fingertips.

Ginger smiled as Owen laughed. "Done?" she asked.

"I'm getting good at this dad stuff," Shane said, coming in and closing the door to round the table.

He went past her and Owen to sit at the head of the table and put the monitor in prime view for them all.

"Yes, you are," she said, wondering what Shane looked like at the head of boardroom tables. "We only have a few minutes because Doctor Guinness is waiting for you."

It was a long day for the doctor too, but he was dedicated and hadn't complained about the increase in workload.

"My turn at bat?" Shane asked and she nodded.

"And don't forget that Julianna will be in at five," Owen said, pressing his hands to the table to lean past her as Shane looked at his watch. "You have to meet her at the airport."

His attention shot up. "At the airport?" Shane asked, his hand falling to the table in a thump. "Why the hell do I have to go to the airport? I'm not going to the airport."

"Yes, you are," Owen said. "She came all this way for you."

"Did we send the jet?" Shane asked and Owen nodded. "Thank fuck for that, she'll be in the private lounge then… Does she mind the pick-up?"

If Julianna was a rich, classy woman, she probably wouldn't expect Shane to pick her up in a dirty truck.

But Owen was prepared. "I rented you an Audi… And you are going to put a shirt on," Owen said. Shane huffed. "A proper one. I ironed one for you, it's hanging in your bedroom."

Shane smiled. "You do know my son is alone up there right now. If he gets out his crib…"

Owen tensed and almost leaped from the table until she put her hand over his wrist. "Cam won't get out his crib… and even if he did, daddy won't have left the bathroom door open, will he?"

She glared at him.

Shane grinned while holding up his hands. "No, I didn't. Cam is safe. I had to scare Owen… He's making me wear grown up clothes and drive a clean car."

Owen looked at his fingernails while muttering,

"I pressed slacks for you too."

Shane narrowed his eyes. "Are you trying to sneak me into a suit?" Owen enjoyed his chance to grin, but Shane shrugged. "Can't... I didn't bring cufflinks."

Owen's eyes flared in panic.

Ginger looked from her brother to the smug Shane. "Calvin has cufflinks," she offered.

The men switched expressions. "Uh, I am not wearing anything of his," Shane said.

"They're not infected with anything," Owen said. "They're cufflinks."

Ginger guessed Shane was going to accept the offer because he grumbled but didn't say anything else about it.

They were short of time, and had important things to address

Yet, Ginger couldn't resist asking, "Do you really have your own jet?"

Shane stretched in the chair and glanced to the window. "It's a rental," he said and scratched his chest as he yawned. "I could've laid down with Cam... I'm beat."

"It's not even two in the afternoon," Owen said.

"He gets up early," Shane said, and swept his arm in an arc on the table top to snag her hand. "I don't know how you've done this full-time for ten months, almost eleven... alone."

Why was he touching her again? Shane was always touching her.

"I've not been alone," she said, fixated on their linked hands. "Calvin helped."

"With midnight feedings and diaper changes?" Owen asked.

She sensed tension from Shane. "Kind of," Ginger said and shook her head. "We're not here to talk about that. We have to be quick."

"Right, yes," Owen said, sitting up straighter. "Ginger needs new cards for all her accounts."

With his hands spread flat on the table, Shane nodded once. "Okay."

That was it? Ginger was surprised, Shane didn't even blink, he was just fine and relaxed. "My accounts," she said, pressing a finger into the back of his hand. "Just my accounts, you understand? Not yours. Owen said I was paid a salary. I must have put that money somewhere."

"You were paid a salary," Shane said, turning her hand over to cup it in his, then he frowned at Owen. "Did anyone ever take her off payroll?"

When Owen shrugged, her jaw sank. "What?" Ginger gasped. "You can't pay me for work I didn't do!"

Shane smiled and leaned down to meet her palm with his lips. "I'm kidding. I'm sure we terminated your contract the day of the accident."

Taken aback, she found that particularly cold. "Really?" she asked.

Typical that Shane should smile. "I have no idea," he said, tracing the lines on her hand, but she pulled it away.

It didn't matter how many times she told him not to touch her, he was always doing it. It felt too nice, too good. She relaxed wondering if it could really hurt to let him stroke her like that.

No! Ginger tensed and mentally chastised herself. She wasn't doing things just because they felt good, not anymore. She was not giving in to childish impulses. She was being sensible, smart, and rational.

Ginger reminded herself by asserting their connection aloud. "Father of my child," she said.

But Shane didn't get it. "Yes, mother of my child?" he asked, folding his hands in front of him.

Nothing could faze him, he seemed so at peace.

"Is this a sexy thing you do?" Owen asked like he didn't get it.

Shane smiled at him. "It's actually a major turn on to see her with Cam… I never figured it would be, but it is."

The conversation was edging toward the slippery slope and was beginning to sound like flirtation. Somehow it had just gone that way all on its own. Ginger couldn't figure out how it had happened.

"No," she said, waving at each man. "I meant, you are just the father of my child. You're not supposed to be holding my hands and kissing me."

"Okay," Shane said, not that she was sure he heard her.

He infuriated her… again. "Don't dismiss me," she said.

"Please don't fight again," Owen groaned. "I don't like witnessing your foreplay up close."

Shane got serious. "Do you want me to transfer the savings to your checking account, Bit?" he asked. "And there must be half a dozen credit cards in your name, do you want them all or just the black one?"

Ginger didn't know what the black one was. Before she could ask, another thought hit her, forcing her to sit upright. "Oh my God, are they overdue?"

Was she in sixteen months of debt?

"No," Shane said and she thought he might be laughing at her. "I know for a fact they're all at zero."

"How do you know that?" Ginger asked.

Owen answered, "Because he pays the full balance on all the cards every month. And we had to keep checking if there was activity on any of your cards."

"You thought I ran away?" she asked. "Like Sleeping with the Enemy? Do you have scary sex music?"

Again, Shane snickered. "No, but we knew if you were picked up there was a chance someone could coerce you. If you needed money, I wanted to make sure it was there."

"Shame she never remembered her PIN or maybe we wouldn't be in this mess."

That seemed sort of like her brother was implying that Calvin could've been paid off. Ginger wasn't even going to entertain their jibes; they didn't have time.

"So I got a salary, but you paid the bills?" she asked. "How did that work?"

"Always worked for us," Shane said. "It's not like we have any huge bills. We live in an apartment."

"You own the top two floors of the most coveted high-rise in the city," Owen said.

Shane hissed at him like he shouldn't play it up. Being where they were and knowing how much Shane liked the outdoors, she kind of couldn't picture him living in an apartment.

"We don't have a yard?" she asked, then shook her head. "I mean… *you* don't have a yard?"

"You own the roof," Owen said. "Pool terrace and everything. It's beautiful."

"The roof?" she asked, her concern switching to her son. "You're going to put Cameron on the roof of a skyscraper?"

They weren't supposed to judge each other, but she couldn't imagine for a second how that could be safe. He'd be up there, in the wind… there could be a railing, but—

"Yeah, it's me." Glancing around Ginger was surprised to see Shane on the phone. It hadn't been in his hand when she was last looking his way. Since then, she'd been too busy imagining the worst to notice anyway. "Yeah, yeah, been a while, we're great…" Shane said into the phone. "Listen, I want you to sell the penthouse."

The guy was apparently determined to give her a heart attack. She'd just been a person talking and he was… she didn't even know what.

Grabbing Owen's wrist, Ginger hissed, "What's he doing?"

Owen looked up from his notebook to Shane and then at her. "Making you happy," he said like it was obvious, he'd been infected with the nonchalant bug too. "It's what he does."

"Yeah, I need something with land," Shane said, still on the phone. "I don't care… Yeah, send pictures… No, not the cabin. We like the cabin, we're keeping that… I need something near the office. Something…" His eyes flicked to her before he twisted away and lowered his volume. "Something kid-proof… Yeah, you heard me… Nell, don't give me shit, just do it, please… Thank you."

Shane disconnected the phone and put it back in his pocket as Owen laughed. "Ah, you've set the tongues wagging… she'll never let that go."

"Nell's good," Shane said, drawing a fingertip down the line on the table where two planks met. "So are we done? I'll get the cards couriered to us, you can have them tonight."

Still in shock, Ginger started to feel guilty. "You didn't have to sell your house because… because of one comment."

Owen's arm touched hers. "One comment from *you*, Gin. He's made bigger life decisions based on your facial expression after something he's said."

"Okay," she said, overwhelmed, she took a breath and held up both hands. "Are you both listening to me? This is a business meeting, official, you get it? Shane is Cam's father. That's it. I am not making decisions for him. We do not make joint decisions. We do not have a relationship."

The men were looking at her, yet it didn't seem to matter that she was stern. They just ignored her conviction.

Owen proved that when he took a big breath and turned to Shane. "How do you feel about sperm donation?"

"If I'm donating to Ginny, I love it," Shane said, locking his fingers behind his head. Gritting her teeth, Ginger growled aloud. The men just smiled and carried on. "Why?"

"I was thinking we should set something up," Owen said. "Ginny is worried her kids won't like each other unless they're all yours."

Shane's interested brows went up while she was left gaping. "Wha…" she gasped. "I never—uh—"

"Do you want more children, Mr. Warren?" Owen asked, licking the tip of his pen and then theatrically posing to write.

Like he was in the midst of an interview, Shane was concise, "A bunch. My wife and I spoke about having four or five."

"Hmm," Owen said like he was enthralled and he started to write something.

Ginger attempted to peek at his notepad, but her brother pulled it away and curled an arm around it. "What are you doing?" she asked, trying to tug his arm out of the way. "You're supposed to be writing about Cameron's care."

"We are," Owen said. "Any parental contract should always include the provision for further children. What if you write this now and then have another four kids and they're not alluded to? That could cause all sorts of legal problems."

These guys were enjoying riling her and she was being stupid enough to give them the satisfaction of reacting.

Slumping back, Ginger folded her arms. "I'm getting my tubes tied," she muttered.

"That's pretty much the only way to be sure you won't be having more of Shane's kids," Owen said, again suggesting she'd get with Shane, which he seemed to enjoy doing too.

"Guardianship," she said, appealing to them. "Can we at least cover one serious thing before you two have more fun?"

"Guardianship?" Shane asked. "What if—"

She sat up. "Who do we want to care for him if we're both dead?"

It was obvious that Shane didn't like the morbid thought because he sneered. But given what had happened to her, she was more cautious.

"She has a point," Owen said. "If it had been both of you on that boat a year later with Cam on shore…"

"I don't think we'll be attending many social functions together now," she said, smirking at them both. "But Shane does enjoy some risky pursuits."

"I don't climb half as much now as I used to," Shane said. "We do spend a lot of time together in the domestic wilderness though… I guess anything can happen out there."

More reference to them being together, Ginger was struggling to restrain an urge to scream. "We don't have to die at the same time," she said. "It's good to have in black and white what we both want in case one of us goes after the other."

Owen nodded and repositioned his pad. "Yes."

"Do we have to sign something to say the other gets him?" she asked. "You know, if I die tomorrow, should I sign something to say Shane gets full-custody?"

The men shared a look she didn't understand. "Does Calvin have a problem with that?" Owen asked.

Oh, shit, she hadn't considered how Calvin would react. "I… I don't think he'd fight for custody," she said, trying to play that future through in her mind.

"If you're still planning to marry him, he might," Owen said. "This could be years down the line. If Cam has been living with him and going to school in his area, Calvin might have a claim… Especially if you sign something to say you want Cam to stay with him… Does Calvin travel for work?"

Planning Cam's future was going to be far more complicated than she'd originally thought. "Sometimes," Ginger said. "Not much… But he does work long hours."

"Shane spends all day goofing off," Owen said and Shane threw him a mock laugh. "But he does travel a few times a year. That would go against him in a custody hearing."

Shane was quick to emphasize, "If I had Cam, I wouldn't be going anywhere."

She exhaled and flopped back in her chair. "This was supposed to be the easy part."

"It is easy," Owen said, taking her hand. "I can write a contract, if you want Shane to have full-custody in the event of your death, then that's all we need. If anything happens to you, we present that to a judge as your wishes."

Her brother began to write. She lowered her chin and fixated on the table wondering how it would go across with Calvin.

"Ginger?" Shane asked, a thread of severe wariness wavered through his tone. She lifted her eyes while coiling a strand of hair around her finger. "You will sign it, won't you?"

She winced. "I'll have to talk to Calvin."

Shane smacked a palm on the table and surged to his feet, turning his back on her to stride to the window.

Owen leaned in. "You can't want Calvin to have full-custody. You can't want him to have any custody," her brother said. "Do you think he and Shane will be able to work out amicable visitation?" That would be a joke. "You've seen how Shane is with Cam. He's a great father. You shouldn't worry about—"

"I know he's a great father," she said. Her hesitation wasn't about Shane's suitability. "I told Shane that. I don't doubt he'll do what's best for Cam."

"So what's the problem?" Owen asked.

She sighed. "I just... with everything else that's going on... Calvin... he's insecure and I... I don't want him to think we're plotting against him."

Owen tapped the pen on the desk.

Chills swept across her shoulders, Shane still hadn't turned or said a word. "I'm sorry," she murmured.

All she seemed to do these days was hurt people.

"You know," Owen said to her in low volume. "I can write it and you both can sign it and Calvin never has to know... I can keep it in a file somewhere and the three of us, we'll never mention it to anyone. I can have it anonymously notarized. The chances of anything happening to you are slim, and once Cam is a teenager the court will listen to his wishes about where he wants to live. If, God forbid, something does happen to you, Shane and I will deal with the fall out with Calvin and you—"

Shane spun with open arms. "Why the hell are we even talking about this?"

Owen squeezed his pen. "I know it's a difficult subject, but it's smart to be prepared," her brother said. "Especially if we think there might be a challenge to your guardianship. If we can get the mother's support from be—"

"No," Shane said, coming to the table. He dropped both hands onto it. Keeping his arms straight to bear his weight, he fixed his stern eyes on her. "I love you, Bit. I love you. I don't know how many other ways I can say it."

Oh, God, he was doing it again.

Ginger tensed, but quickly relaxed because after panic came pity. "Shane—"

"No! We're going to be together," he asserted. "I know it. Owen knows it. Murph knows it. Hell, I think even Cam knows it."

Invoking their son was not a wise move. It squeezed a raw nerve and all she could do was react with instinctual anger.

"Do not bring him into this!"

"You don't think he wants his parents to be together?" Shane asked, returning some anger of his own.

"He wants us to be happy."

"The only way I'll be happy is if we're man and wife again, in every way."

Ginger sat back. Stretching her legs beneath the table, she crossed her ankles. "So this is about sex again?"

Shane squinted and bowed his head, shaking it once like she was insane. "No, fuck sex, this has nothing to do with sex... This whole conversation is pointless because Bishop is a non-factor in our lives. He's not going to be around when Cam is a teenager. Hell, I'd be surprised if he makes it to Cam's first birthday."

That was just a matter of weeks away and an insult. "I don't—"

"You guys are late for therapy, maybe you should take this upstairs," Owen said. "I feel... underqualified."

But Ginger could be confident in her return, "I'm not late," she said. "Shane is. It's his session... and he hasn't asked me to be a part of it."

Shane grabbed the baby monitor then came around the table and took her hand to haul her up to her feet.

"Everything in my life is about you," he said. "You're coming with me."

He pulled her up the stairs and into Guinness' office where the doctor got a heated recitation of what had happened downstairs. They came to no conclusions before Shane announced he was going to tell her everything that he'd heard after she left him with Calvin, Boyd, and the divorce papers.

The story was... shocking to put it mildly. At least it was at first until he carried on and on and got so ludicrous that it became entertaining. Ginger had no choice except to become incredulous. Was he really so desperate to get her away from Calvin that he would concoct a tale with his brother to poison her mind? It was just so... fantastical.

The doctor's bedroom was good for these private meetings. The doctor's view was over the side of the building. He had two chairs arranged next to each other at one side of the window with his own chair opposite, it was like a real couples counselling session. She and Calvin had joked about it during their session that day. She didn't feel much like joking with Shane.

With her legs crossed and her arms folded, Ginger was just waiting for Shane to talk himself out. The doctor asked questions and showed signs of concern as Shane answered them. In fairness, Ginger was concerned too, for Shane's sanity.

"These are quite shocking revelations," Guinness said. "Ginger, how do they make you feel?"

"Feel?" she asked the doctor. "It's ridiculous... and insulting."

It irked her that she saw pity in Shane's expression. "I don't know if Bishop loves her now," Shane said to the doctor. Her so-called husband was leaning forward, one hand curled around his other fist, his elbows on his knees. "Murphy's convinced that he doesn't. I… I can't understand how any man could live with Ginny and not love her."

"But you do think that he is still interested in money?" Guinness asked. "Forgive me for saying, but the divorce settlement was… modest given what you could provide Ginger with."

The crazy person she'd apparently married didn't let that truth dissuade him from his fantasy. "Maybe it was an opening bid," Shane said. "I could provide more, yes, but it's likely if they married, I would be a source of financial support for Ginger… I would never say no to her."

"Hmm," the doctor said like he might be considering that as an actual possibility.

"No," she said, slapping her hands on the arms of the chair. "This is crazy! Forget about the money! Even if Shane's right that Calvin's in it for the money, who cares about that! He's accusing Calvin of sinister… evil plotting! I've lived with the man for sixteen months, I've seen him almost every single day. How could he know exactly who I was that whole time and never tell me?" It was insane. "And Shane says there were doctors involved as well! How can that be possible?"

"Well doctors are bound by confidentiality, so they would not announce who their patient was anyway," Guinness said. "Especially if they were told that you were in some kind of danger or not to be declared for your own safety. And they may have been assured that the issue was in hand."

"Even if the patient was a missing person?" Ginger asked.

"They would inform the police," Guinness said. "If there was a report made… did anyone report that a Jane Doe had been found?"

Ginger couldn't remember talking to police, but

she'd been unconscious when she was found. Even after she woke up, she was out of it for the first few days.

"I... I don't know," she said. "I can't remember."

"I suppose I could request all of your medical records," Guinness said. "I was brought in for my expertise in amnesia, I only read the psychological report... We had never met before your husband came into your life."

Shane jumped on that. "Yeah, you're a new doctor," he said. "Funny that Bishop chose to call up the amnesia expert after we were back in her life. Why did he get rid of all the old docs, huh? Worried one of them might flip sides? If he's offered them a tasty sum, I can double it. What do you think I'll get for that? The truth?"

Ginger didn't find the new side of Shane attractive at all. "Why are you being like this?" she asked. "Why can't you just accept that I'm happy? You said that's what you wanted."

"Because I don't believe he does make you happy. You're not happy with him like you were with me... You're not in love, not with him."

That was about as subtle as a freight train. "Oh, so I'm in love with you?"

The position of being side by side made it more difficult to see each other. Maybe that was why it was so easy for him to spout his drivel. Except he wasn't shy.

"Yeah," Shane said, twisting around to look at her. "As a matter of fact, you are. You're just denying it to be stubborn... 'cause that's what my Ginger is like. Maybe his Ginger is different, but my Ginger likes arguing. She likes making her point. Likes making me work for it. She enjoys teasing and playing..." He glowered at her. "And for damn sure, my Ginger wouldn't be afraid to sign anything without my permission. She'd sign it, flutter her eyelashes at me later, and I'd find a way to work everything out."

How could he be glib at such a time? "We're talking about the life of our child."

"Yes," he snapped. "Exactly! *Our* child. Cam is nothing to him… why should you have to ask that fucking snake's permission? He hasn't had anything to do with Cam. Don't get me wrong, I'm fucking fine with that, I don't want the prick anywhere near my son. But it does kind of limit his right to have any input in Cam's upbringing."

The doctor explained. "If Calvin is going to be a part of Cameron's life, you will have to get used to him being present. He'll be at Cameron's birthday parties. He'll be part of decisions that Ginger makes throughout her life."

Shane threw up his hands. "Weren't either of you listening? We can't let him make decisions about Cameron! He kept the truth of who Ginger was a secret! He wrecked all of our lives! Kept me away from my child! For months! I lost my wife and my son! I spent a fortune trying to find them! I can't get those early days of Cam's life back and who knows? Maybe if the fucking snake had been honest and I'd gotten to Gin sooner, she could've got the proper care and she wouldn't be suffering now!"

A mumble on the monitor broke the tense moment. Then Cam grumbled and called out, "Ma! Mama! Da! Dadeeee!"

They all blinked at the monitor. "I have to go to him," she said and stood up. "Finish your session, Shane. All of this is confidential…" Ginger stepped over Shane's legs to head for the door. That was another thing about him, he always managed to get in her way. All the time he was just there. Always just… there. "I wouldn't even know how to…" With her hand on the door handle, she paused. "Did you say any of this to Calvin?"

"All of it," Shane said.

It was unbelievable that he could be so blatant and lack any kind of shame or remorse.

"God, Shane," she hissed and growled. "Well don't say it again, either of you, this is… enough, okay? Just… enough."

Leaving the bedroom, Ginger had to steel herself before she went to her son. Shane could be a larger than life character, but he'd never seemed… unstable. The accusations were insane and she couldn't even begin to think about how to process them.

TWENTY-FIVE

AFTER TAKING CAM from his crib, she changed his diaper, and took him and Rocky for a walk. By the time she returned to the back porch, she was much calmer. At least she was until Owen came out the back door flapping his arms around.

"What's wrong?" she asked, hurrying up to him.

"Everyone is out," Owen said. "Shane and I can't go into Calvin's room, he'll accuse us of stealing or something."

"I don't understand what—"

"The cufflinks," he said. "We need the cufflinks."

Was that all? She was worried someone got hurt or something.

"Oh," Ginger said and put the brake on the stroller. "Take Cam out of his seat and bring him inside, I'll run up and get them."

Shane would have to leave like that minute if he was going to make it to the airport to pick up Julianna. Ginger's head was clearer that it had been earlier. She should have retrieved the cufflinks before going out for her walk. She should've asked Calvin's permission to take them too, but he'd been working at the lodge, so there was no time to find him to ask.

Running upstairs, Ginger saw that Shane's bedroom door was open a few inches, but she didn't seek him out. The last thing they needed was to delay him further by fighting more. And fighting seemed to be the only thing they excelled at together.

Ginger went straight into Calvin's bedroom and to the dresser where she knew his cufflinks would be. He had a chunky leather box that he kept all his accessories in while travelling. There was a spot for his watch, for cufflinks, and other compartments for knick-knacks. Placing it on top of the dresser, Ginger popped open the lid and lifted out the internal tray that showcased his cufflinks.

Once, a while ago, she'd heard the box rattle. That was when Calvin told her that he kept his less-used items beneath this tray in a secret space.

Giving Shane a less important pair of cufflinks from somewhere Calvin didn't often check was just smart. Calvin would be less likely to miss them and she didn't want to risk giving Shane anything too valuable. If she gave Shane the most expensive pair, not that she knew how much these things cost, and he lost them, there would be hell to pay. Though she didn't believe for a second that he'd do something like that on purpose.

Tipping the box over onto its side, Ginger dug around at the cufflinks that fell out and picked a discreet pair that she had given Calvin for his birthday a few months ago, under Diane's instruction. Calvin never wore that pair anyway, so she didn't think he'd notice them missing.

With the cufflinks in her palm, Ginger began to put the other scattered items away. The last thing she picked up was a small dark velvet pouch. Curious about what was in it and if there might be a better pair of cufflinks for Shane, she loosened the drawstring and upended the bag.

But there weren't cufflinks inside.

Two rings rested on the heel of her hand. One had a brilliant square cut solitaire set on what had to be platinum because it matched the narrow plain band of the second ring and both were heavy.

Why would there be two rings in a pouch she'd never seen? The tip of her thumb slipped inside the plain band and grazed an impurity. Turning it to the light, she looked inside and saw an engraving, "This is forever, Bit."

Gasping, Ginger almost dropped the rings. Why would Shane's pet name for her be written inside a ring secreted in Calvin's drawer?

Confused, the discovery was so unexpected that she couldn't even begin to figure it out. "Bit?" She heard the word, but thought it was in her mind. "Babe, you okay?"

Spinning around, Ginger held her clasped hand to her cleavage and gaped at Shane who was loitering in the doorway, looking rather worried. "Shane, I…"

"You okay?" he asked.

He had a meeting. He was late. The discovery meant… she didn't know what it meant.

Spreading a smile on her lips, Ginger turned to clear up the mess. "Yes, of course, I… just wait out there. I'll be one sec."

Putting everything back as it had been only took a second. Glancing at the rings again, she couldn't bring herself to put them in the drawer, so she put them in the pouch and dropped it into her pocket.

Holding only the cufflinks, she hurried out of Calvin's bedroom, herding Shane further into the hallway. "You sure you're okay?" he asked.

Grabbing his arm, she fastened one cufflink for him and then did the other. "Yes," she said, her mind spinning. "Yes, why wouldn't I be?"

"You seem freaked," he said. "Are you still pissed about therapy? Babe—"

"Shh," she said, pressing a finger to his lips and gazing up into his eyes.

He did look familiar and not just from the last few days. She could see something beyond his exterior. It was always there when she looked at him, that deep longing, the innate concern… the love.

"Gin," he murmured.

Maybe he was right about her feelings. Why else would she feel like she was looking into her home whenever she met his eye? Right then, it seemed like maybe he was the only one she could rely on. But she couldn't be selfish about her needs. Their therapy session was still plaguing her mind, adding what she'd just found… whatever the new discovery meant.

Shane's meeting was important. So she took a breath and did what he would do in return, Ginger prioritized him over herself.

"We'll talk about that later," she said. "You have to get going."

But he wasn't quick to go. "If you want me to stay—"

Smiling, she shook her head and pressed a hand to the line of buttons on his chest to admire him. "You look good," she said and narrowed an eye. "Weird, but good."

"Weird?" he asked, straightening his cuffs. "Why weird?"

"You just look… grown up."

He grinned. "Yeah, I guess you're used to seeing me rolling around with Cam and Rocky."

"I like seeing you rolling around with Cam and Rocky," she said without thinking through her words. Before he could respond, Ginger changed the subject. "I haven't spoken to Calvin about the cufflinks, but he won't care. I got those ones for him a million years ago and he's never worn them, he won't notice they're gone."

"Okay, I don't know what time we'll be back. We'll probably get dinner in the city."

Nodding, she was actually sorry to see him go, especially since she could do with a hug.

Struggling to keep it together, Ginger tried to project happiness. "We won't wait up."

"Hey," he said, hooking a finger beneath her chin. "This isn't like that. I'm coming home to you… I always come home to you."

She nodded. Maybe he noticed the wobble in her lower lip because his gaze became more acute, peering deeper into her.

"Uh." She cleared her throat. "Don't forget to kiss Cam goodbye, he'll miss you at dinner."

"I'll miss him too. I'll miss you both… If Rocky is too much—"

"Please. He's my baby too. We'll be fine."

Shane seemed to like it when she acknowledged the dog as hers, and she had become quite attached to him.

"You'll probably be asleep when I get back," he said. "If anything happens, I want you to call me, okay? Don't hesitate, don't think about the deal, just call."

"I don't have a—"

He handed her his phone. "Owen and Murphy will be with me; their numbers are in there. So if you need anything… I don't care if it's a glass of milk… you call me and I'll come pour it for you, okay?"

Oh, he was going to push her over the emotional edge. Until not long ago, Ginger had thought she was having a productive day. As it turned out the more intensive therapy was flagging up a whole bunch of new demons.

Ginger nodded. "I will."

He peered again. It was really unsettling that he kept doing that while she felt so unstable. Funny that she'd considered Shane the crazy one earlier when it turned out she was the bigger wreck.

"You sure you're okay?" he asked.

"Shane!" Owen hollered from the bottom of the stairs. "We have to get moving!"

Shane winced and began to hurry off. "Sorry, Bit, we'll talk tomorrow, okay?"

"Kiss Cam," she said as a reminder when he was at the top of the stairs.

Waving at her, Shane winked and ran down the stairs. Ginger looked over the railing to see him going to the fireplace. He ruffled Rocky's fur then scooped up Cam who was trying to climb up Rocky's back.

Owen was at the door trying to hurry Shane out. "Do not get dog hair and baby drool on those pants," Owen instructed.

She hid her smile.

"Should I ask Ginny for lipstick on the collar for the trifecta?" Shane asked, kissing and nuzzling Cam, showing no signs of being in a hurry.

Her brother wasn't impressed but found the time to tease his friend. "You're a real family man now," Owen said. "You're getting old, Shane, my friend."

"And loving it," Shane said and she sighed.

He said a long goodbye to his son making it obvious that he didn't want to be parted from his child. Ginger's heart lightened, until her hand slid down and touched the edge of her pocket. The reminder of what she'd found hardened lead around her heart. The weight couldn't be shifted even with the medication of watching father and son doting on each other.

Shane put Cam down and glanced up at her; he stopped and held eye contact for a minute. Ginger had to hold back her tears. She had to. Otherwise he'd never leave. Why did Shane have to be so… him, all the time?

Just when she was losing the ability to hold her breath, Shane turned away and rushed out with Owen. Ginger had the place to herself. Her baby was healthy and life was supposed to be good.

Except she was beginning to wonder if everything she'd known for the last sixteen months was a lie. If Shane had been right about that all along, what else had he been right about?

TWENTY-SIX

CAM WENT DOWN like a dream.

Her son was a great distraction through dinner while Ginger did her best not to look at Calvin or Boyd. Every time she did, she found herself suspecting them both. Doctor Guinness was in good spirits, but having him around always made her feel scrutinized. She just couldn't breathe.

An employee snuck up at dinner to hand over an envelope addressed to her, luckily Calvin was on the phone when she opened it. Inside she found the cards that Shane had promised her, all emblazoned with the name: Ginger Warren. She was officially her again and apparently had means; though Ginger had no idea what she wanted to do with them. She felt stupid and insecure and couldn't focus; speculation ran rife through her mind.

As soon as she got back to the chalet, she got into the bathtub with Cam and played with him for longer than she should have. Being with him helped to keep her thoughts away from what she'd found in

Calvin's room. After their bath, she took the gauze from his head to let his healing injury breathe and had some fun with her baby and the camera on his daddy's phone. They filled it with more pictures and videos of Cam than Shane would probably ever need.

Cam started yawning and got snuggly, so she settled her baby to sleep in his crib much later than he would usually go down.

Ginger had listened to everyone else go to their bedrooms and the house descend into silence. First Calvin and Boyd went to their beds. A long time after, Shane came back with Murphy and Owen. The men did their best to be quiet, said their goodnights in the hallway.

The house was silent.

Yet, Ginger was still awake.

The nightlight intended for Cam gave her a view of her ceiling, and of the rings she held in her hand. Squeezing them in her palm, Ginger closed her eyes tight and told herself to forget about them. They couldn't possibly mean anything. It was some coincidence. Maybe Calvin had found something Shane had dropped when they arrived. Or maybe the pet name meant nothing and she was reading too much into it.

Lying there, trying to convince herself of something that could be easily cleared up was dumb. Ginger was just too afraid to confront it, except she was supposed to be taking control of her life. When she'd been afraid before, she signed her life over to Calvin and allowed him to make all of the decisions.

After the divorce paper debacle, she'd told Doctor Guinness she was going to go with her gut and be proactive. That she was going to do what was right and be decisive for the sake of her son.

If she didn't clear up the mystery, she would never sleep. She'd be a mess the next day. Everyone would know something was wrong, which could lead to another blow out. Ginger didn't want that to happen in front of Cam.

Drawing in a breath, Ginger sat up, deciding that she wasn't going to wait any longer. After checking on Cam, she locked her outer bedroom door and went through the bathroom to get to Shane's bedroom, leaving both bathroom doors open in her wake.

Shane's room was dark. The only light came from the dim nightlight in her room. He'd been home for a couple of hours and was fast asleep on his front, lying on the edge of the bed with his arm hanging off. From the gentle snore, she knew he was asleep. He looked so peaceful that she considered leaving him. But when she squeezed the rings again, she decided there was no way walking out was an option.

Locking his main bedroom door without his permission, Ginger crept over to his bed, past his loose arm, and crouched next to his face.

Brushing his hair from his forehead, she smiled. For the first time that night, she felt calm. One way or the other, she was about to find out if her worst fears were coming true.

"Shane," she whispered, scratching a finger over his cheek to his lips. "Boo, honey, wake up for me." He grumbled as she switched on the nightlight in the outlet beside his charger. "Shane?"

Leaning forward, she touched her lips to his and eased back to watch his eyes open to slivers. "Did you just kiss me?" he mumbled.

"Can you look at something for me?" she asked. "Tell me if it means anything to you."

He licked his lips and his eyes closed again. "If this is a dream," he murmured. "It never stops at looking."

Making her laugh in that moment was quite an

achievement, the man was barely conscious. "Please, Boo, just look for one second and I'll leave you alone again."

"Then I'm definitely not looking, 'cause I want you to stay." He was a kidder when he was sleepy. Running her fingers through his hair, she took a breath and rested her face against his perpendicular cheek. He hummed out pleasure. "Good dream."

Talking him into this wasn't working, so she took a different tack. Twisting around, Ginger turned his hand over, palm-up, and put one of the rings into it. Curling his fingers around it, she tried to read his features as they moved in time with his fondling of the object.

"What is that?" he murmured and bent his arm to open his palm beneath his nose. Shane blinked at the too close object and pulled his head back. She was biting her lip, tugging on a tendril of hair when he finally focused. In that instant, he became fully awake. "What the hell?"

He leaped into a seated position as he shouted the question.

Ginger reared up high on her knees to press her fingers to his lips. "Shh!" she said. "It's late, everyone's asleep."

"Where the hell did you get this?" he demanded.

All traces of sleep were gone. Shane was furious and confused, just like she'd been.

"Do you know what it is?" she whispered.

"Yes," he said. Holding it between his thumb and forefinger, he scrutinized the stone then blinked his angry eyes to hers. "It's your goddamn engagement ring." And that was it. Sinking down to sit on her feet, Ginger didn't know if she should be relieved or devastated. All emotion drained out of her. "Where did you find this? Your wedding ring should've been—" On a sigh, she held it up, though the rest of her body was too heavy to move. She'd first shown him the ring without the inscription on purpose. Except he'd identified it, so she didn't need to conceal the second ring. "Fuck, Bit, where the fuck..."

He snatched the wedding ring from her too and she balled her empty fists. Free of the jewelry, but not free of the demons.

"You were right," she mumbled.

"What? Gin, where did you find them?"

Her head fell back because she was too weak to hold it up. "In Calvin's drawer," she murmured. Shane began to rise. Fury burned through him, lighting his eyes and hardening his form. Shaking her head, Ginger clambered up to clasp his shoulders to keep him seated. "No, you are not going through there now. He's asleep. More importantly, Cam is asleep. Do you want to wake him up with shouting? You'll scare him."

Although Ginger could see the tick in Shane's jaw and the tightness radiating in his body, he didn't fight her.

Instead, he settled for baring his teeth to growl. "Ginger..."

"I know," she whispered, stroking his bare shoulders. "I know, baby. I'm sorry. You were right. I'm sorry." Still stroking, she pushed him back into bed. "Lie down, just be calm, okay?" Climbing over him, Ginger got onto the bed beside him and guided his arm around her as she coiled herself against him. It was instinct, nothing else she could think of would make her act that way. "There. Doesn't that feel better?" Whispering the words against him, Ginger stroked a soothing hand up and down his sternum. She moistened her lips. "Easy, Boo. It's good. We're good."

He began to relax. The weight of his arm was reassuring when it eventually rested around her. "The fucker knew, the whole fucking time."

It was a good thing that Cam wasn't there to hear his father's language or witness his rage. But Shane's reaction was understandable, Ginger couldn't judge him for it.

"I guess he did," she said. Pain and embarrassment closed her eyes. She'd believed Calvin loved her, believed that he wanted to be with her forever. Ginger had risked everything in her past to be with a man who'd manipulated her every single day. Coming to terms with that wouldn't be an easy process. "How did the meeting go?"

"Meeting?"

"With Julianna?"

"Seriously?" he hissed. "I don't give a shit about that."

"Maybe not," she said, lifting her body so she could make eye contact. It felt important to be looking him in the eye, like it might help with calming him down. "But I give a shit, I'm asking, so tell me."

Her command surprised him. It surprised her too. In spite of that, Ginger didn't back down… even as her heart began to race.

"It went fine," he sighed. "She's full of herself, loves money, figures speak to her. We have negotiations planned at the lodge tomorrow; she's leaving the following day."

"Okay," Ginger said, laying her cheek on his chest. When he began to stroke her arm, she lost her train of thought and wriggled out from under his arm to lie on her back separate from him so she could think. "We can't say anything to Calvin while she's here. If I tell him that…"

"Tell him that, what? He's a lying fuck who's going to spend the next few years in jail?"

Rolling to her side, Ginger wasn't surprised to see Shane scowling again. "He didn't break any laws…

did he? I wasn't locked up in a tower… I have to talk to him. To find out what he was thinking and—"

"No," Shane said, flipping over to scowl at her. "You're not going near him. You're going to—"

She put a hand on his chest. "We're going to play this smart," she said. "We don't let on that we know anything, to anyone, until Julianna is on a plane."

"But why wo—"

"Because I don't trust him not to screw up the deal," she said, making it as plain as possible. "Calvin will make a scene or say something inappropriate. He understands business, he values it. He'll think the easiest way to hurt you is to hurt the business."

Shane wasn't swayed, but he was too angry to understand sense. "I don't give a damn about the deal or the business. I—"

"Do you want to give him the satisfaction?" Ginger asked, sliding her hand up to his throat so she could touch the groove she'd once thought about kissing. "I don't want complications and I don't want anything to hurt Cameron. So we deal with one thing at a time. You charm Julianna, get the deal done, and then we'll… deal with Calvin."

"You're not marrying him."

Ginger scoffed and flopped onto her back. "No kidding," she said, covering her eyes with a hand. "God, how did we end up here? How could I have been so blind? I let that man near my baby."

Soothing her seemed to center him somewhat. "You're okay now," Shane said, sidling up to her side, the weight of his hand on her belly was reassuring. "You know the truth. You found out before there was any permanent damage."

Dropping the hand from her eyes, she focused on him looming above her. "We don't know that yet," she whispered and touched his lips.

"Cam is fine," Shane said, grasping her wrist to kiss each of her fingertips.

"And you?" she asked, seeing that love emanating from him again. "God, Boo, what did I do to you?"

Wearing a smile, his head tilted. "That sounded like... For a minute there you were... her."

Ginger knew that she had to be clear with him about their reality, despite the new revelation. "I'm not her, I can't... I can't remember our life together," she said. "But I see what you've done for me. That you were right all along and I was... bull-headed."

"Just like my Ginny," he said and dipped to kiss her forehead. "Are you going to sleep there?"

Was that hope in his voice? "No," she said and his body loosened in disappointment. Ginger was so tired of letting him down. Pushing him onto his back, she returned to her previous place, pressed against him with her head on his chest. "I'm going to sleep here... unless you object."

Shane laughed and kissed the top of her head. "Doesn't sound like me, does it?" Stretching to turn off the light, he returned to his place and held her tight. "Good dream."

At least he'd relaxed and didn't want to beat on anyone anymore. Her eyes were closed by the time she had a thought she probably should've had before.

"Boo?"

"Hmm?"

"Are you naked right now?"

The mischievous smile on his lips was audible in his tone. "Yep... Want me to put something on?"

She should say yes. Ginger was the woman who'd blushed at anything close to sex talk and there she was in bed with a virile, naked man. A man who wasn't shy about claiming to want her.

After processing the possibilities and realizing what her gut was feeling, she smiled. "No… I don't."

Shane kissed her head again and fumbled with her hand, she wasn't sure what he was doing until she felt the slide of two warm metal bands around her ring finger. He'd just put her rings back on. Ginger would have to take them off before they left this room, but if it made Shane feel better to put them there, she wasn't going to object. If nothing else, it felt nice to cleanse her hand of Calvin's ring and she needed some… normalcy.

TWENTY-SEVEN

SHANE DIDN'T KNOW what time it was when he woke up. There was light coming through the crack at the edge of the roller blind over his window, not much, but enough that he could figure out it was morning.

When he yawned and tried to lift his arm to rub his face, he found it pinned by a body. That was when he recalled Ginny coming to his room.

After his fury flared through him again, he remembered her crawling up against him and pressing herself into him. That memory was enough to erase everything negative from his thoughts. His wife had shared his bed with him again. She'd chosen to share his bed with him.

Lifting his head off the pillow, Shane expected to see his wife and he did. Ginger was there, curled on her side, on top of his outstretched arm.

But she wasn't the only one.

Cam was in the space left between Ginger's curled body and Shane's straight one. His son's little mouth was open, and his eyes blinked at the ceiling like he'd woken in unison with his father. Rocky was on the bed too, stretched out behind Ginger.

Shane decided he'd have to get a bigger bed.

As he exhaled a whisper of a laugh, Shane slapped his free hand on his cheek. Had he really gone to sleep alone, missing his son, desperate for a glimpse of his wife?

He'd literally gone to sleep with nothing and woken up with only a small fragment of the bed beneath him, but he didn't care that the littlest member of the Warren clan was kicking him, trying to claim more space.

It was the dream. Shane's ultimate fantasy. Except he was definitely awake. That was his reality.

Cam rolled over to his front.

Ginger whimpered. "Boo," she exhaled.

"I've got him," Shane said, steadying Cam as he rose onto all fours and then sat up between mother and father.

"No," Ginger said and opened her eyes a sliver. "I can do it."

Cam's presence proved that Ginger must have gotten up in the night. That made the morning all the more special. His wife had gotten up and had the chance to leave him. Instead, she'd returned and brought their son with her.

"You're too beautiful to wake up."

And he didn't want to lose the moment.

Ginger smiled and curled tighter, clasping her hands beneath her chin. "I'm not beautiful when I'm awake?"

God, what was she doing to him? He fell in love with her all over again. Though the moment was shattered when Cam bopped her arm.

"Ma! Mama!"

"Yo, buddy," Shane said, flipping onto his side to prod Cam's belly. "Pick on someone your own size."

"It's okay," she said and straightened her legs in a stretch.

Ginger's toes touched his shin. Shane glanced down to see that her legs were beneath the sheet he was using while Cam was on top of the sheet with his own smaller blanket. Although her eyes were closed, Ginger knew what she was doing by making contact with him. Shane could read that sly little smile on her lips when she wiggled her foot between his shins to slide her leg up between his as her other curled over the top.

Cam was still on the bed between them, playing with his mother's hair. Her locks slid from her elbow down to her breast that was teetering on the edge of sliding free from her satin slip. Could he be aroused by the sight and feel of his wife when his son was in the same bed? Shane wasn't sure on the rules.

"Dada!" Cam called.

Snapping out of his selfish desire, he looked at his son. "Yes, buddy. You hungry?"

"Num!" Cam said and threw himself forward.

Wriggling up, Cam pushed his face between Ginger's breasts. "That better be Cameron," she murmured and grinned.

Shane combed his fingers into her hair to move it over her back. It was so long and silky; it felt amazing. Mesmerized again, he almost didn't notice his son squeezing his hand into his mom's top.

"Mama!"

Cam was trying his best to get his mouth to the right place. Shane understood the struggle.

"No, Angel," Ginger said, easing Cam back and sliding his hand away from her breast.

She tried to roll onto her back, but Rocky was in the way.

Shane leaned over her to give the dog a shove. "You shouldn't be up here. Down, boy."

Ginger relaxed onto her back and stretched again. Cam climbed on top of her and grabbed both her boobs.

"Gentle," she said.

Cam fell face first into her cleavage. "Mama! Num."

"No," she said, using her mommy voice. "Daddy doesn't want to see that."

Her feeding his son? Was there anything more natural? If the accident hadn't happened, he'd have seen it already, it would be a common sight for him.

"Actually," Shane said, watching his son roll about on his wife. "Daddy would be honored."

Her eyes popped open, showing her surprise. "Really? You'd let me feed him? Here? In your bed? It wouldn't gross you out?"

"Hell no. Why would it?"

"Well, I…" she said, pushing up to a slouching sit. "Calvin never liked to see it… In fact, he was completely against the idea of me feeding Cam myself… I had to really fight for him to let me do it."

Why wouldn't someone want what was best for anyone's child? If she'd chosen not to do it, fine. If she'd had issues and been unable to nurse, he'd have supported her. But if it was her choice to feed their baby the natural way, why should anyone object?

Just when Shane thought Bishop couldn't slide any further down in his estimation, he outdid himself. There was enough drama on the horizon and Ginger was all too aware of how he felt about Calvin.

So instead of adding to the aggravation, Shane bowed and kissed her cheek before whispering in her ear, "I'm not Calvin Bishop."

"Da!" Cam hollered and pushed his shoulder. "No! Dadeee!"

Urging his father away, Cam was wearing the

cutest intense frown when Shane eased back.

"What? We can't share mommy?" Shane asked.

With wide arms, Cam pressed himself to Ginger and babbled. "Ca, mama!"

Ginger was laughing but Shane was in shock; he'd just been cock-blocked by his own son.

"What?" Shane asked.

"Aww," Ginger said, ruffling Cam's hair. "I love you too, Angel. He's only doing what you told him to do, Daddy. He's protecting me from your dishonorable intentions."

The urge to carry on with the banter left him when Ginger shifted to sit up straighter and stole his pillow to put it on her pulled up knees. Turning Cam to his side like a pro, Ginger bent to kiss their son's plump cheek and then like it was no big deal, she slid down the strap of her slip and exposed her breast. Right there in front of him, without any modesty. Scooping a hand around Cam's head, she guided him in, but his boy knew where he was going and latched on like a pro.

Her smile was so warm and loving as she gazed down at their feeding son. With her free hand, Ginger stroked Cam's face and when the baby fumbled for her hand, she gave him her thumb.

"There, my love," she whispered. "Mommy's angel... so handsome."

That soft mommy voice split Shane in two and poured fire into his soul. He'd never felt so... primal before. That was his woman and his son, vulnerable, together, and they needed him.

Words burst out of him. "Marry me," he said.

Ginger's attention rose and she whispered out a laugh before holding up her hand to show him her rings. "We're already married, Shay."

God, she was still wearing them, and it was actually real... Maybe he'd slipped into a coma in the

night and everything since was just a delusion. Except…
it wasn't… he pinched himself to check.

"I know, but…"

Clambering closer, Shane didn't know what he
wanted, he just wanted to be near. Cam was slurping and
gulping. He reached over to touch him, but hesitated.

"It's okay," Ginger said.

With Cam's hand still attached to hers, she
managed to use her fingers to guide Shane's hand to
Cam's face.

"It's amazing," Shane said. He didn't know why
watching his son enjoy his breakfast was so incredible,
but it was. "I… I don't know what to say."

It wasn't such a big deal to Ginger; she was a
veteran. "He shouldn't really be getting this," she said.
"I'm supposed to be weaning him off."

"Why?" Shane asked, wishing he could see the
same sight every morning.

"He can drink regular milk when he's one and
the breast becomes a comfort."

"I get that," he said, transfixed by the natural
sight.

Cam let go of his mother to push Shane's hand
away, except that pressed his father's knuckles into the
cushion of Ginger's breast. He shouldn't touch her there,
but Cam's hand stayed on his and Shane didn't want to
disturb breakfast, so he froze.

Ginger laughed again. "Boo, are you blushing?"

The mother with the child was confident. That
was it! That was the key! She was confident and
comfortable when Cam was around.

"No," Shane said. To combat his discomfort, he
stretched his thumb so the edge grazed her flesh. Except
he hadn't expected the contact to be so combustible. At
the same second their eyes collided, she shivered.
Recognizing that tremble and the interest in her eyes,

Shane lowered to kiss her, but stopped before he got there. "I don't… I don't know the rules here."

"Cam's feeding," she smiled and uncurled her arm from over Cam to hook it around his neck. "When he's eating, my boobs belong to him."

"And when he's not?" Shane asked, with a hopeful brow raise. "Who do they belong to then?"

Laughing relaxed her. He loved to see her glow; it reminded him of the first moment he'd seen her.

"Do you really think you'll ever be turned on by my breasts again after witnessing this?"

But he was actually more aroused by them knowing they'd sustained his son. This woman had borne his son. Her body had given his seed life. Literally, she was his mate. He hoped last night was the watershed that meant she was his again.

Someone tried his bedroom door handle. Thankfully, the door didn't give. He hadn't locked it, so Ginger must have. Smart.

Panic seized her, her worried gaze bounced from him to Cam and back. "If I take him off, he'll shout," she whispered.

"So would I," Shane said. Her unimpressed expression conveyed that it wasn't the time for jokes. He was going to get up, so he started to toss back the covers. At the last second, Shane remembered he wasn't wearing anything. "Uh, I'm naked."

Ginger's lips curled; she stifled a laugh. "Are you asking me to avert my eyes?" she whispered.

"Nope, giving you tickets for the show," he said, moving to the edge of the bed.

"Shane? Are you awake?" Owen hissed through the door.

"He can't know I'm here," she said. "We can't tell anyone what happened last night."

The part where she found the rings or the part

where she spent the night in his bed? Shane didn't have time to ask. Instead of going to the drawer for underwear, he went straight to the door and unlocked it to open it an inch, keeping his hips on the inside of the door. Ginger would have a view of his naked ass, but Owen would see nothing more than a bare hip.

"Geez, are you still in bed?" Owen asked, and glanced down then held up a flat hand to cover his below-the-waist view. Not that there was anything to shield his eyes from. "You're naked? Why are you still in bed naked at this time?"

Shane didn't even know the time, but slid a hand up the door and shrugged. "Well, you know, it's been sixteen months… and being around Gin all the time…"

"What?" Owen squawked. It was funny to see his brother-in-law's blinking surprise. It kind of reminded Shane of Ginger's, especially when he got pissed off straight after. "While you're in there jerking off, Julianna is expecting you for brunch."

"What?" Shane asked.

"Is jerking off worth ten billion dollars to you?"

No, but sharing the morning with his wife and son was.

Shane didn't say that, instead he went with, "Brunch wasn't on the schedule."

Owen sighed. "I know, she brought the later meeting forward. She has some conference call this evening or something. Does it matter?" He backed off a step and gestured. "Get changed. We think Gin is out with Cam, but if you're quick, you'll make it back before his naptime."

"Naptime?" Shane whined.

That was in the afternoon. He didn't want to spend all day dealing with business when he'd just got his woman and his boy in his bed.

"Yes, come on now, chop, chop."

Owen clapped his hands and took another step back, so Shane closed the door and locked it again before he turned. Ginny's grin dropped in and flash and she lifted a hand to cover her view, not unlike what Owen had just done. Apparently, she was fine when he was giving her the ass view, but full-frontal was too much.

Lumbering back to the bed, Shane sat on the edge, facing her, and pulled the sheet over his lap, which uncovered Ginny's legs, so he stroked her calf.

"I have to go to work."

"I heard," she said.

"Your idea to bring Julianna here wasn't so great after all."

"It was if it strengthens your business," she said, admiring their son again.

"Means I might miss therapy... and I don't want to leave you alone with... him."

Shane didn't even want to refer to Bishop by his last name anymore.

How Ginger could be so calm was a mystery to him. "We'll be fine," she said. "I have my new computer to play with. Doctor Guinness wants individual sessions today anyway, so I won't have to confront... anyone."

"Are you going to tell Guinness?" Shane asked. "You said you didn't want to tell anyone, but—"

"I won't tell him," she said. "I won't take the risk of anyone else knowing, not until Julianna is on a plane. I said it last night, I meant it. So if you're in with Doctor Guinness, I'd appreciate it if you held off on sharing your feelings about last night... I know I'm not supposed to tell you to withhold, but—"

"I won't say a word," Shane said. "If we have feelings to talk about, we can talk about them after she's gone... My feelings are all positive, I'm not repressing anything evil that might leap out."

"All positive?" she asked. "You're happy that

Calvin misled me and lied to us all? That he—"

Showing her his palm, he silenced her. "Don't remind me of that part," he said. "I'll do my best to keep my head down, but I already didn't like the guy. This new information makes it harder to... be patient."

"I have faith in you," she said, finger-combing Cam's hair. "Have you ever seen such a beautiful boy?"

Crawling up the bed, Shane turned and sat right up beside her so his dick was pressed to the satin covering her hip.

"Never seen such a beautiful sight," he said and kissed her shoulder. "If you have feelings you want to share... you can share them with me."

He hadn't meant for that to sound so non-subtle. Ginger smiled at him like she thought he was referring to the obvious. Them. Except they'd been talking about the doctor. So he was actually thinking about feelings she might share in therapy but couldn't because they were keeping a secret. Instead he came off sounding like a clingy girlfriend looking for an affirmation of love.

"Anything that's on your mind I mean," he said. "That you might want to share with Guinness but can't."

Ginger inhaled and got serious. "To be honest, there's only one imminent thing I'm worried about."

"What's that?" Shane asked, kissing the soft skin of her shoulder again because she hadn't objected last time he'd done it and he couldn't restrain himself. His wife tasted amazing, like him and her and sleep... like the old days.

"Calvin agreed to give me two more days on the divorce papers, Boyd's updating them apparently... which means he'll come at me with them tomorrow."

"And what are you going to do?" he asked, trying to remember he was playing shrink and not outraged husband.

"I'm going to... I'm going to... I don't know,"

she said and thought about it for a minute. "It depends when he brings it up."

"Before or after Julianna leaves?" he asked and Ginger nodded. Sure, because after they could tell Bishop to shove the papers up his ass and kick him out. But Bishop wasn't patient, he'd pressure her if he thought he could get her alone. "What if it's before?"

"I guess it's not as much my problem as it is yours," she said.

Joy and pride made his chest swell and he felt himself puff up. "That's right, baby. Your man takes care of business. I'll make him eat the damn things."

Again, she was laughing as her hand covered his cheek. Shane loved it when she did that, touched him like that, and he turned his head to kiss her palm. No objection. In fact, she was still smiling.

"I didn't mean that," Ginger said. "I meant because he has to get you to sign too. If he corners me and I end up having to put pen to paper, it won't mean anything unless he gets you to do it as well… You have to keep your cool if he asks, no fighting in front of Cam."

Cam turned his head away from her breast when he heard his name. His drowsy eyes took a minute to focus on his mother. But Shane was more interested in the nipple his son had just liberated, plump and glistening, Ginger had never seemed more whole to him, more womanly.

"Ca!" Cam said and shoved away from his mother to climb off the bed.

"I better get him dressed," Ginger said and was about to get up when Shane put his arm across her body to pin her back.

Her arm was crooked beneath his with the strap of her slip in her hand, breast exposed. Cam was still in the room, climbing over Rocky, busy on the floor. Shane was a man alone in bed with his woman, he was a bit clearer on the rules and the aroused intrigue in her eyes fired him on.

"My turn," he grumbled and dipped his head.

Before he could make contact, Ginger's hand caught his forehead and she curled her fingers into his hair. "No," she whispered. "I'll be too sensitive for your mouth. It'll feel… weird." Damn. He'd never been more disappointed, but it was worth a try. He'd learn that kind of stuff as they went along, and he'd put up with whatever she needed, even if that meant he was on emergency rations. Except, instead of getting up, Ginger peeked to make sure Cam was busy. Interesting. Shane was intrigued by his wife's thoughts and grew even more intrigued when she slid down to her back and bit her lip. Curling her other arm, she hooked the other strap of her slip around her finger and drew it down. "You can play with this one."

His woman was a vixen, a hot viper coiled to tease him. Shane ducked forward to kiss the tip of her nipple and that was enough to make her gasp. Sliding his hand up her ribs, he cupped the breast she'd offered to him and squeezed, being gentle as he opened his mouth and circled it with his tongue.

He didn't remember her being so responsive. Her reaction to his mouth was incredible. Writhing beneath his tongue, she was gasping and whimpering little breaths that were hardening his dick beyond anything it had known before. He needed her. Now.

"Oh, God, Boo. No, you can't," she said, grabbing his hair to pull his mouth away from her breast. "I don't know what I was thinking, I'm sorry."

She tried to push away to free herself, but Shane caught her to put her on her back again. Pressing his body against her side to hold her down, he explored her face.

"You can say no, baby. You don't need to run

away. Just say no and I'll stop."

Was she scared? Sad? Guilty? There was so much going on behind her eyes that he struggled to pinpoint the cause of her panic.

"It feels too good," she breathed and managed to give him the ego boost he'd waited sixteen months for. "You feel too good… this feels too good."

"Listen to me," Shane said, stroking her hair from her face because as she gave him what he needed, he had to return the favor. "You're not gonna marry him, right?" Ginger shook her head. Her teeth went into her lip again as she fumbled to finger her hair. His hips thrust into her of their own involuntary will. His dick wanted to be inside her and that was as close as he'd come since she disappeared… Except their son was on the floor, so he had to keep his cool. "You are married to me. You are my wife." She nodded again. "So we're gonna work all this out, together… It's supposed to feel good. Being with someone you care about, someone you love, it's supposed to feel like this. This is why we deal with the downs and stick together, we do it for moments like this. You deserve to be happy and that's what this morning is, this is our happy." Clearing his throat, Shane wanted to give her perspective, but wasn't sure he wanted to hear her answer to his next question. "Did it ever feel like this with him?"

The chewing on her lip got faster, either she felt guilty because of what she was about to confess to him or what she was going to confess about Calvin. When Ginger slowly shook her head, Shane's heart almost leaped out of his chest. Yes, he had her. He knew it. This woman was the key to his happiness, the key to his joy, and she was back in his bed.

"Four," she whispered and he had no clue what she was on about. "I think I want four children." Shane upgraded his thoughts of dreams or delusions and began to consider that he might be dead because that was as close to heaven as he could get. "Not right now, there are things… other things to deal with first and I…"

He soothed, hoping to keep her from descending into a panic. "What, baby? You can tell me anything."

Ginger blinked before confessing her secret. "Watching you with Cam turns me on too. I'm so grateful that you're his father and… I never said thank you to you for giving him to me. He was a gift. The piece of you that I carried with me through all of this, even if I didn't know who you were. Thank you… I wouldn't have gotten through it without him… without you. I know now that he was the only truth I had."

"I love you, Bit," Shane said, running his fingers over her face to come to a stop on her lips. "I don't want you to say anything… I'm not forcing your hand. I'm telling you I love you because I can't give you happiness like this, I can't give you as much happiness as you give me… Anything I can ever give you will only be a fraction of what you do for me. You never have to say thank you."

If they weren't back together after that, Shane figured he didn't know anything about how the world worked at all.

"Da!" Cam was standing at the side of the bed, trying to pull himself up.

Shane reached over to offer a hand and Cam pulled himself up only to climb onto his mother and shove his father away.

"Hey," Shane said.

Cam was concentrating on trying to cover Ginger's breasts. Laughing, she helped their boy put them away, then scooped him into her arms.

"Come on, you three. The world is waiting for us."

The world could keep waiting as far as Shane was

concerned. He'd spend the rest of his life in that room and never see another soul as long as he lived and he'd be happy.

But he followed Ginger into the bathroom and watched her turn on the shower, she felt the spray while Cam shouted at it. His girl retrieved a towel from beneath the vanity and brought it over to him. Neither mother nor son seemed bothered about his nakedness anymore. Their acceptance inspired him. The life he wanted was starting to come to life.

Cam wriggled from his mom's arms, so she put him on the floor.

"Do you need anything, Boo?" Ginger asked. "You have to get to your meeting. So if I can help with anything…"

"In the shower together?" he said because he couldn't help himself even though he knew she wouldn't join him.

She smiled and caught sight of Cameron sitting on the floor by the bathtub dumping his ducks over the edge into the tub.

"Oh no, Angel… Daddy needs to get clean now."

Rushing over to take the ducks out, Ginger was hindered by Cam throwing them straight back in. Then Rocky trotted in and sniffed Cam. The dog picked up a duck in his mouth but instead of running off with it, he put it in the bathtub then sniffed the shower spray.

That was his family, crazy and disorganized, sometimes working against each other, but they were his and Shane had never been happier.

TWENTY-EIGHT

YAWNING, GINGER STRETCHED out on the bed and listened for Cam. She didn't hear her son but did hear male voices downstairs. From the rush of cool air on her shoulders, she guessed the front door had been opened.

It was late in the afternoon already. Everything was pushed back because Cam had gone to bed late and overslept. She, herself, shouldn't have given in to sleep while Cam was napping, but that ship had sailed. Ginger sat up and wiggled her toes. Being in Shane's bed didn't feel weird. It should, but it didn't. It hadn't even felt weird the first night she'd slept there when Shane was in her bed.

Forcing herself to get out from under the cozy sheet, Ginger went through to her bedroom to check Cam was still in his crib. Brushing her fingertips on his cheek, she smiled at her angel and retrieved his monitor.

She headed downstairs to find out who was home and was happy to learn that Calvin was still out. He'd had some emergency business thing with Boyd, and they'd run off to the lodge over an hour ago. The living room was abandoned. Rocky had been asleep on the hearth when she went upstairs; he wasn't there anymore.

The sound of a hearty bark coming from the back yard widened her already beaming smile.

Murphy was in the kitchen. It took effort to calm herself to exchange a nod with her brother-in-law. He seemed curious, but she drew her eyes away and her smile took over again. Tiptoeing through the screen, she paused to watch Owen throwing a stick for Rocky on the grass. Hooking her thumbs into the cuffs of her oversized cardigan, Ginger ignored the man on the swing at her side. For a second anyway.

Sidestepping, she swayed her hips on approach to the swing and lowered onto it beside him. Although she could feel Shane admiring her, she played it coy and kept watching her brother and the dog.

"Murph's getting drinks, you want something?" he asked. Ginger shook her head and tried, but failed, to subdue her smile. "We not talking?"

Drawing her feet onto the swing forced him to brace it. Ginger curled her arms around her bent knees and let one slide up so she could catch her thumb nail in her teeth through her sleeve. They were supposed to be playing it cool. They weren't supposed to be letting anyone know what had happened last night. Discretion was key. Yet, she was overwhelmed by the urge to share.

"I thought of you today," she mumbled.

"I think about you constantly," Shane said like it was any normal conversation.

To her, it wasn't. The flirtation could get away from her, she was a novice after all. Ginger was excited by the idea that it might overwhelm both of them. The possibilities were so enticing.

"Thinking of you… made me naughty," she whispered.

He did a double take at her profile. "Made you…" It only took him a second to catch on to her implication, maybe because her tone was so saucy. She noticed the curl of his lips in her peripheral vision as the air began to crackle. "Oh, baby," he groaned.

Nodding, Ginger pouted and twisted herself toward him. Hooking an elbow over the back of the swing, she skimmed her thumb nail along the seam of her lips.

"You were incredible," she purred, enlivened by the ability to share her dreams with their subject. Shane groaned again and his eyes grew heavy. "In your bed… all by myself… I was lonely… so I had to pretend you were with me…"

She pouted again and glanced at the yard to check Owen was still busy. Boosting up a little, she checked Murphy was still in the kitchen before raising her bare foot over Shane's thigh to press it against his groin. He slouched until his head bumped down on the back of the swing.

His hand curled over her foot to press it harder against the solid lump behind his fly. "Bit…" Shane exhaled, a growling edge in his voice. "Did you dream about me?"

Parting her legs so she could lean between them, Shane tipped his head to accept her lips against his ear.

"I've been dreaming about you for days," Ginger breathed.

He shivered.

Sliding his hand up her bare shin, he curved it to the inside of her thigh. "Your guy likes to hear that…" With one shin resting along his outer thigh, her other foot slipped away from his groin to settle on the arm of the swing by his opposite thigh, so her knee was on his chest. Resting her temple against the back of the swing, his turned head meant their faces were within a couple of inches of each other; so much for being discreet. "Did it get you wet, baby?"

Biting her lip, Ginger twisted the edge of her thumb between her teeth and nodded. "It got me off," she murmured. Shane blinked; his surprise overtook his desire for a second. "In your bed." His grip on her knee tightened; there was something intoxicating about exploring their connection. Walking her fingers up his torso, Ginger pressed the pads of her first two fingers to his lips. "Do you think I'll taste the same?"

His eyes flared, aflame with burning need. She could feel the tattoo of his strong heart beneath her knee. She was desperate to slide herself into his lap, but a grumble from the monitor on the swing seat behind her gave her a cue.

"Only one way to find out," Shane growled and seized her wrist.

"Ah," Ginger said and slid off the seat as his lips parted. "Duty calls."

Picking up the monitor, she shook it at him, forcing Shane to let her hand slide free from his grip as he grunted.

Smiling, Ginger sashayed away, peeking at him over her shoulder. He was distracted while fixated on her. Knowing that he had only one thing on his mind, and that she'd put it there, Ginger had never felt so powerful, or so close to the woman she'd seen on those videos.

Murphy was on his way out as she was going in. She laughed at the confusion in his expression that was still there from before. Cam was making more noises in the monitor, so she tried to forget about teasing Shane and focused on being a mommy. She was only two stairs up when there was a knock on the front door. She paused, considered ignoring it, but then spun around to run over and answer it.

When she opened the door, she saw the same lodge employee who'd delivered the apples, holding another clipboard.

"Ah, Mrs. Warren. We have another delivery."

He gave her the clipboard. As she signed Cam screamed through the monitor at the top of his lungs. Yes, her baby was impatient. She backed away from the door.

"Dump it there," she said, pointing just inside the door. "Thank you."

Turning around, Ginger sprinted up the stairs and picked up her baby. She changed his diaper and bounced him on her hip. Rocky barked outside, so Cam began to babble at the window. Ginger took him onto the upper balcony and her son screeched at the sight of Rocky who barked up at him.

Boy and dog had definitely bonded.

Ginger had some tidying up to do, but Cam would do better playing. So she took him out of the bedroom with intentions of handing him over to his father. Shane hadn't connected with his son since before he'd left the chalet for his brunch meeting that ran late.

Halfway down the stairs, Ginger noticed the boxes stacked high just inside the door. There wasn't just one parcel, there were at least twenty. Everything was brand new. There were all kinds of toys and accessories for Cam. Everything was for Cam. There were trains that ran on a track, cars, a ball pool, a bouncy chair, a brand-new top of the line changing table carved from solid oak. It was more than her son had received all year.

A flare of anger made her squeeze Cam tight against her although he tried to struggle free. A large trampoline that required assembly stood in a box behind the others. And there was a motorized police car behind that. A fortune lay there in boxes and bags. While Cam was trying to clamber down, she held him tighter still.

Huge boxes from baby clothing stores were at the base and more bags of toys circled the castle.

The shock wasn't enough to dampen her anger; in fact, it enhanced it.

"Shane Warren! Get your butt in here now! And bring your buddies with you! Shane!"

A few seconds later she heard the scramble of feet and the rush of heavy bodies hurrying through the kitchen. The screen door bumped closed after the scratch of claws scrabbled on the kitchen floor. All the boys were coming to her, even the furry one.

Supporting her baby on her hip, Ginger met the men in the shadow of the stairs. "Who is responsible for this?" she asked, glaring at them all. "Come on, don't be shy, which one of you is responsible?"

"Responsible for what, Bit?" Shane asked, reaching for her.

Whipping around, she walked away from his outstretched arm to march toward the hoard. Halfway there, she stopped to spin on them and thrust her arm toward it.

"This! Who is responsible for this and why the hell didn't you—"

"Cool!" Owen declared, his gasp and expression a picture of excitement. "Trains! I love electric trains!"

He came to try taking Cam, but Ginger spun her son out of his uncle's reach.

"No! No, you are not going to encourage him." Her anger dwindled and hurt took over when she turned to Shane. "How could you think that we're like this? How could you believe that you have to buy our love? Am I so shallow? Is Cam? Do you think we need this ridiculous display of wealth to—"

"It wasn't me," Shane said, slipping his hands into his pockets as he glanced at Murphy and Owen. "If I check the accounts, will I find receipts?"

Murphy turned out his lip as he lifted his shoulders.

Owen shook his head furiously. "It wasn't me," Owen said. "I kind of wish it was because look at his little face."

Cam was grinning, kicking and trying to buck down. Owen thought that the baby wanted the toys. In truth, Cam was probably more interested in exploring what to him probably looked like a cardboard castle.

Ginger was confused. Shane could be lying, but would he risk doing that after what it did to them before?

She sighed and gave in. "Can you move the boxes so they're lined up? We can't have a tower of heavy packages with a dog and a baby in the house... One of them will get hurt."

All three men began to move toward the packages. Shane didn't get far, Ginger sidestepped into his path, stopping him in his tracks. She moved right in close until their bodies touched.

Searching her eyes, he stroked a hand over the back of Cam's head. "It wasn't me, baby," he said, reading the question in her eyes.

Ginger hoped that was true. As angry as she was at the extravagance, she'd have gotten over it. But if he was lying to her, that would do more damage than they might be able to repair.

"If it was, please just tell me," she begged. "Please... Spoiling him I can get over, okay? I'll get over it. But if you lie to me again... it won't be such an easy fix and I... I really don't want us to be broken again. It's been easier today... it's easier when we're a team."

He cupped her cheek. "It wasn't me, Bit... I'll check the accounts, make sure nothing came from his uncles or the company... I did tell Nell the new place should be kid proof, but..." He looked over her head to scrutinize the parcels. "Everything there looks roughly age appropriate… except maybe the car and trampoline. And it looks like there are clothes… she'd have no way to know how old the kid was to buy those."

"Boo—"

"Hey," he said, curling a finger beneath her chin to make sure she saw his smile. "You always loved big romantic gestures… but they rarely had anything to do with money. That's not what you value… We're the same that way. And shit like that…" He nodded at the bags and boxes. "That's why you have credit cards. If we need clothes and toys or furniture, buy them. But as far as me buying him things? I know you're not comfortable with the money yet. Course I've been tempted to go nuts, but I figured that it's his birthday in a few weeks, I was going to wait until then to spoil him." He scowled at the packages. It was a relief to see him as confused as she felt. "And there's no point having all this stuff here. We're on vacation, how will we transport it when we leave?"

There were courier companies that would transport it, but that was inconvenient and meant more cost. Another waste of money. It made no sense.

"Did you tell Julianna about him?" she asked. "Maybe your business associate—"

"Uh, guys," Owen said, picking up a document from the top of a box. "I have a delivery notice."

"Let me see it," Shane said and edged her aside to go to her brother.

Paling, Owen tried to move away, but there was a wall behind him. "I don't think I want to show you," he said.

Shane snatched the papers from him. As he read it, his confusion became anger. "I'm gonna rip his fucking face off."

"Language!" Ginger said, resting her lips on Cam.

"It's from Calvin," Owen said as Shane went through the pages. There were so many that he was still reading while she processed. "Diane's name's on there as a contact too."

It could only mean one thing.

"Oh no," Ginger said and took Cam to Murphy.

She passed her baby off to his uncle and went to grab Shane's sleeve. Ginger pulled him across the room, ignoring Murphy and Owen's questions.

Dragging him into the dining room, she rounded him to close the door. "He knows," she hissed and turned to drop back against the door.

"Knows what?" Shane asked, coming over to stroke her face, hair, and shoulders.

A smile brought on by his affection broke her tension. "You're always touching me," she said. "Why are you always touching me?"

"I'm terrified you'll tell me you don't want to be touched again."

If she needed proof that she'd hurt him, there it was.

Picking up his hand, she kissed his palm. "I like how your hands feel on my body... the way you touch me... your hands don't feel like anyone else's."

They didn't feel like Calvin's. Her fiancé had never been tactile. She hadn't known what she was missing until Shane came into her life.

"Good," Shane said, getting closer to take her hips and align their forms. "Now you gonna tell me why Bishop did this?"

She worried her lip, coiling a tendril of hair around her finger. "He has to know."

"Know what?"

That was what she didn't know. It made her nervous to think Calvin was just waiting to confront her about something. She didn't know why, but her anger didn't quite trump her anxiety.

"I don't know," she whispered. "Did you see him today? At the lodge? You were in the function suites at about the same time that he was there."

"What do you think I said? 'Hey, asshole, my wife knows you're a scumbag liar. She spent the night in my bed, we're back together. Ha. Ha. You lose.' Don't you think I'd have told you that? You told me not to say anything and I didn't. I'm not going to do anything to wreck this, trust me on that."

Searching him, she had to wonder. "Are we?"

"Are we what?"

"Back together?" she asked. "We didn't have sex or—"

"I told you, sex can wait until you're ready," he said, brushing her hair from her temple with a fingertip. "I love you and yes, we're together. As far as I was concerned, we were never split up."

Her stomach did a flip. She wasn't going to remind him of her other wedding day.

"Outside on the swing, I… I'm sorry. I took that too far. I got carried away and—"

He bent his knees to align their eyes. "With us, there is no too far, okay? Anytime you want to flirt or torture me with thoughts of you touching yourself… or touching me… you go for it, Bit. It doesn't mean I expect you to have sex with me next time we're alone. All of this is at your pace, okay? All of it. You're leading the dance."

Touching one of his shirt buttons, she watched herself circle it. "And touching you? Is touching you okay? I never asked I… I climbed into your bed last night without permission… I pleasured myself in your bed this afternoon and I… on the porch, I was in your lap."

He growled again and kissed her jaw.

Rubbing his cheek on hers, he smelled her hair before whispering, "That coy thing you do drives me wild, Bit… You know damn well I want your body on mine every minute of the day."

"Really?" she asked, sucking on her lower lip as she turned her innocent eyes up to his. "I… I've never flirted or played these sex games before."

Her chaste tone made him grumble. It was working. Playing up the naïve act was turning him on.

Grabbing her waist, Shane thrust her against the door so hard that she gasped… he wasn't the only aroused one.

"You've played me before, baby, you just don't remember. We'll play 'em all again, sweetheart. I've got all kinds of fun lined up for you."

"Shane," she whimpered, stroking his chest. "I… I do want you."

His forehead bumped on her hair when he ducked to try to kiss her and she lowered her chin. "Oh, you got me, Bit. Got me all to yourself."

Turning her fingers in as she stroked his body, she wanted to test that and learn everything he had to teach.

Her last thread of control was taut and close to breaking. "We have to back off."

That cooled his arousal. "We have to… what?"

"Calvin, he has to know… out there, those toys, he's never… He's always accepted Cam, but he's never been interested in fatherhood. He gave us everything we needed, but Cam was never showered with gifts, not like this. He has to know I slept with you."

Shane thought about this for a second, examining her as he did. "You told him about before? About us kissing?"

She nodded. "He went insane. He was shouting and… he wanted to confront you. Doctor Guinness explained it was natural for me to be curious and how you have residual feelings for your wife."

"Residual… Wait, what the hell? There's nothing residual about my feelings."

"Don't get defensive," she soothed, wrapping her arms around him. Ginger had figured out that his blood pressure seemed to be directly related to how many inches of her body were touching him at any given second. "He said my feelings for you are… new. So it's only right I get swept into the initial pangs of romance." She frowned. "But I…"

"What, baby?" Shane asked, stroking her back.

"Sometimes when I look at you, I feel like… like there's something so…" As she struggled to explain it, he smiled and stroked her face. "I'm sorry, I can't explain it."

"It's okay," he said and kissed her head. "I understand, like no one else can."

"Da!" came a shout from beyond the room.

She tightened her hold on Shane. "He loves you so much… He's never connected with anyone the way he connected with you. He recognized you. He'd never met you but…" Leaning back, Ginger gazed up at him. "He knew you."

Sensing her melancholy, Shane cupped her face, trapping her hair against her cheeks. "We're going to be okay. We're a family; we're going to stick together."

That wasn't enough, she needed more from him. Even if it wasn't fair to ask, she had to push, something in her told her that it was important. Her encroaching dread might be paranoia, or maybe it was some kind of sixth sense foresight.

"Promise me you'll always look after him," she said, "that Cam will always be your priority."

"Gin—"

"Please," she said. "Listen to what I'm saying and take me seriously, I need you to hear me. Cam, he has to be the most important thing in your life, over me, over the money, the business, the—"

"He is the most important thing in the world," Shane said. "Him and every other baby we're going to have."

Just like him to break an intense moment with his arrogant humor.

Tutting at him, Ginger pushed his chest. "I need to be sane before I can bear more children."

"Sane?" he asked. "You've dumped the ringer and got back with the star pitcher. Baby, you're well on the road to recovery."

"Dada! Dadadadada!"

Ginger smiled, hearing her son calling out for the man who'd protect him with his life pleased her. It excited and aroused her too. Overwhelming pride in their son was enlivening.

"He's really got that down, hasn't he?" she said. Instead of being jealous of their bond, she admired it. But they still had an issue to deal with. "I could ask Calvin to take me away somewhere for a couple of days. Away from here."

Shane tensed. "Why would you do that?"

"If he knows we spent the night together and he bought all those things… he's playing us. I don't like him doing that when you have business on the table."

He wasn't the best at hiding his emotions; he exhaled an irritated groan. "Would you forget about the business?" he said. "And I think you're paranoid. There's no way he could know. It's possible he knows you found the rings."

Considering it, she angled her head. "Possible, but unlikely. They were in a place he doesn't use much. So unless he was looking for them… Why wouldn't he confront me if he knew?"

"He didn't say anything?"

She shook her head. "No, and today he was

wearing the same cufflinks he always wears. He wore them yesterday. He just tosses them on the nightstand and then uses them again the next day. I doubt he's even opened the box."

He scowled. "Let's not refer to you being anywhere near his bed again."

It was a reality whether he liked it not, whether she liked it or not. "Calvin can't suspect anything from today because he hasn't seen us together today. You left the bedroom before Cam and I did. When we got downstairs everyone else was out. They assumed Cam and I were already out. So no one knows we weren't up until late… I won't be keeping Cam up late again, let me tell you. His sleeping in threw off the rest of my day."

She didn't expect his kiss on the end of her nose. "I saw the pictures in my phone… that was an amazing surprise, baby. Thank you."

Oh, that felt like a lifetime ago. She hadn't even thought about Shane finding the images when he was at his meeting.

"Just Cam and me playing," she said. "I was trying to distract myself."

"You should've told me about the rings before I went to the meeting."

She shook her head. "Now I'm beginning to think you're the crazy one in this relationship. You were already late."

His frustration was aimed at himself. "I could tell there was something wrong when you put my cufflinks in. I should've pushed harder."

In an attempt to calm him, Ginger softened her voice. "You'll have to learn to trust me. If I say I'm okay, then I'm okay… And if I say something can wait, then it can wait."

"Yes, mistress," he hummed and nuzzled the side of her neck.

"Dada! Dadee!"

Ginger couldn't keep him all to herself, so on an inhale, she pushed Shane back. "Cam missed you at dinner, didn't see you at bedtime and he hasn't had you at all today," she said. "He's been spoiled with your attention… don't deprive him now. We still have some time before dinner although…"

"You're still worried about Bishop."

Typical that Shane could read her like an open book. "I just don't understand the presents, I—"

"Why can't you go with your gut?" he asked.

"Meaning?"

"You thought I was trying to buy your and Cam's love. I think he's trying to do the same, or at least guilt you into thinking he's the better option. Like you said, I've been spending a lot of time with Cam and he knows Cam is the way to get to you. He's trying to buy you by buying Cam."

When he put it like that, Ginger could see his point. It had been her instinct to assume the shallow gesture was some form of manipulation. Why shouldn't it be the same coming from Calvin?

"You think that's it?"

Shane nodded. "Yep. The question is, what are we going to do about it?"

The answer to that question was damn easy. "I'm going to tell him to send it all back," she said, certain of that if nothing else.

"Even though you don't want to raise his suspicions?"

As far as she could figure, it would be suspicious to have no reaction to this bizarre behavior. "I won't be bought," she said because it was true, but then lowered her volume. "We can't take all that stuff one day and then dump him the next day. What does that say about me?"

"If you want Cam to have it, I'll reimburse—"

She hit his chest. "If we want Cam to have those things, we'll order them ourselves. We'll buy them for birthdays and Christmases and as our baby needs them. We will not take from another person. Not one like…"

Oops, she was beginning to sound bitter.

Shane loved it. "One like him? Oh, baby, I'm loving you more every minute. You're right, I don't want my son touching anything from him."

"Cam will want to play with the boxes, I'll do my best to cover them up. Maybe…"

"What?"

"You could take him to the gift shop? Just get him something small to distract him otherwise he'll think I'm a mean mommy stealing his toys."

"Okay, baby," he said and kissed her jaw. "Do you need anything?"

She shook her head and fumbled at her back for the door knob. "Something small, Shane. If it's practical, all the better." Ginger opened the door an inch. "You hear me?"

"Yes, ma'am," he said. "And what are you going to do while we're out?" His brow wiggled. "My bed will be free if you want to—"

Touching his lips to quiet him, she grinned and whispered. "If I keep taking care of myself all the time, what will I ever need you for?"

Pulling the door open, Ginger tried to run away as Shane swatted her ass. Cam was just a couple of feet from the door, eating his fist, blinking up at her as she laughed. When her son saw that she was laughing, he laughed too, but immediately went to his father's feet.

"Dada!"

Tugging on his jeans leg, Cam demanded attention. Shane picked him up and tossed him onto his shoulders, holding him in place with two hands flat on the baby's back. Cam draped forward to drool and bury his face in his father's hair. She'd never seen anything so amazing, and while admiring Shane, she thought that she might be forced to go with his suggestion.

Until Owen spoke up and reminded her of their problem. "So can we unpack?" he asked. "Murphy said we shouldn't accept this stuff? What's going on?"

Murphy might just know his brother well enough to assume his feelings or maybe Shane had confided in him. Ginger couldn't read any clue in his expression as Shane crossed the room with Cam still on his shoulders.

"We're going to the lodge; Ginny needs some alone time. Come on, uncles… let's entertain the most valued member of our boys club."

TWENTY-NINE

GINGER WAS TRYING hard not to think about what might be going on at the lodge, and what Shane might be buying for Cam. They'd been away for quite a while. Maybe he hadn't heard her when she'd said something "small." Shane's hearing did tend to be selective.

Sitting on the porch swing with her legs stretched along it, Ginger was enjoying reading a book on Owen's Kindle. So much so that she didn't hear anyone approach.

"Good read?"

Glancing up, she saw Calvin standing at the end of the swing, leaning against the exterior kitchen door.

"Yeah," she said, smiling. "Surprisingly."

"Anything I'd know?"

A few days ago, she'd have said no. Ginger had no idea if that was true anymore. "It's Shane's book," she said. "Weird that it turns out he did write a book after all."

"Probably ghosted," Calvin said, coming to lift up her legs so he could sit beneath them. "It's a biography?"

"Kind of," Ginger said, sitting up to cross her legs facing him so that she didn't have to keep her legs over him. "It's a kind of insider look at the corporate world of software engineering." Smiling at Calvin's frown, she shrugged. "It's not as dry as it sounds." Calvin would probably love to read anything written by such a successful man… any *other* successful man. He was never going to like anything from Shane's hand. "He tells it through his own experience, names have been changed, but it's littered with anecdotes and jokes… it's funny."

"Hmm," he sneered, resting his hand on her knee. She was grateful for the skinny jeans she'd put on before coming out, they meant she didn't have to tolerate skin-on-skin contact. "Don't you want to come inside? It's cold out here."

"I'm fine," she said. "I'm cozy."

His scowl turned to her torso. "Whose sweater is that?"

She hadn't thought anything of snagging the hoodie and hadn't for a second thought it might offend anyone if she wore it… except maybe its owner.

"Uh, Murphy's I think. It was just lying on the back of the couch."

"If you're cold, you should come inside."

"I'm not cold," she said and was reminded of the reason she'd wanted to come outside, other than it being Shane's chosen spot. "I'd prefer to be out here than sit and look at that extravagance in there."

The angle of his head shifted. "I thought… I assumed Cam was out with Warren, that you were waiting until he got back to unpack."

So he'd come outside for praise? Had Calvin assumed she'd leap up and throw herself at him in gratitude?

"No, Cam's seen it. They've all seen it. I told them not to touch anything."

"But… why?"

"Because you're going to send it all back, Calvin," she said, putting the Kindle up on the exterior kitchen windowsill behind them. "Why would you think Cam needed all that stuff? Why would you have it sent here? Why didn't you discuss it with me first?"

"It was meant to be a surprise," he said, going on the defensive. "Some business associates of mine arrived at the lodge today. They'll be staying while we complete our deal. I don't know how long it will take. I didn't want you to be lonely and feel neglected. I'll be spending more time up there with my associates while Boyd and I hammer it out. I was trying to be considerate. You were supposed to be happy. You're always talking about how important Cameron is. I proved to you how seriously I take that."

Funny how as soon as Shane had important business, Calvin did too. "By spending a fortune on him? I don't want him to be raised like that. I don't want him to think that every time there's a bump or someone's trying to prove something that he'll be used—"

"Used? Buying him things he needs, that's using him now?"

"He doesn't need—"

"You're using the top of a dresser as a changing table. That's not its purpose. Why shouldn't we have something functional?"

The only function of a changing table was to be a safe place for the baby to have his diaper replaced. "I can change his diaper on the floor or on the bed," she said. "We don't need something so expensive… and so heavy, when we're only here temporarily."

Calvin was offended, more than that, he was angered by her reaction. "So you want me to send everything back?"

"Yes," she said. "I—"

"Mama!"

Cam's voice echoed through the kitchen. Shane came out the back door a minute later, carrying Cam. When she saw what he was wearing, she leaped to her feet. Her adrenaline had already been high, but she hit a major spike when she saw her baby's outfit.

"What is that?" she asked.

"We got him swimming shorts," Shane said. Murphy and Owen came out onto the porch carrying other bags. "I thought I could take him in the lake while the sun's still out."

"The lake?" she asked. "Swimming shorts?" Calvin snickered. Ginger ignored him to reach for her baby. "Give him to me."

"What?" Shane asked.

He and his boys had been proud of themselves for their purchase. All Ginger felt was chilled to the bone. Her hands were already shaking; her throat was closing. Panic pulsed through her arteries.

"Give Cameron to me, Shane. Now!"

"Okay, okay, it's okay," he said, handing Cam to her.

Running her hand over him, Ginger found herself checking for injuries even though he'd only been gone for an hour. When it was clear her son was fine, she took the packet of water wings he was chewing on from his tiny hands and tossed it at Shane.

"What the hell were you thinking?" she barked. "Water? You want to take him into the water?"

"Yeah, I—"

"No! You should've asked my permission! There is no way in hell that my baby is going anywhere near the water!"

Calvin stood up and put an arm around her. "We'll reimburse you for your... expenses, Warren," Calvin said, looking down his nose at the shorts Cam was wearing. "Really, you should be more sensitive. You were told how she felt about water."

"Now wait a fucking minute," Murphy said. "If his father says—"

Ginger couldn't contain her burning rage. "His father can kiss my ass!" She rarely swore with such vicious anger, so everyone was taken aback by the outburst. "There's not a chance in hell I will let anyone risk the life of my child."

"Risk the—Shane has his lifeguard certification," Owen said. "He'd never let—"

"Didn't do her much good when she needed him," Calvin sneered. "Where were those certificates when the boat they were on went down?"

She couldn't… Shane was saying nothing. He seemed so stunned, but her irrational terror wouldn't allow her to feel sympathy.

"Cameron is to never go near water," she said to him, to all of them. "Never, you hear me?" Storming forward, she pushed through the men to get to the kitchen door. "If any of you even think about going against my wishes on this…" Her anger disgusted her. "I swear you'll never lay a hand on my baby again." Her focus went to Shane's as Cam began to cry. "I don't care who you are."

THIRTY

AT FIRST, GINGER thought she'd never calm down. Pacing in the bedroom, kissing her baby, she kept the door locked and fumed silently on her own. Cam was upset for quite a while. She hated herself for losing her temper in front of him. He wasn't used to hearing arguments and he'd always been good at sensing her mood. When she was upset, he was upset. It wasn't fair that she let her panic scare him.

But the exchange worked the other way too.

As she focused on calming her son down, Ginger changed his clothes and played with him by blowing bubbles. They folded all the laundry too, though Cam preferred to wait until she was almost done so he could crawl through it and mess it all up again.

He was fun. Hanging out with her baby levelled out her mood. As soon as her thoughts evened out, Ginger took a more rational look at her reaction.

Her reflection wasn't positive.

She'd acted like a crazy person; there was no way her final comment hadn't hurt Shane. The one thing she'd promised was not to keep him from his child and then she'd threatened to do exactly that.

The time for dinner had come, but Ginger couldn't imagine sitting around a table with the people who'd watched her make a fool of herself.

Using the internal phone in the room that only connected to the lodge, she ordered food for herself and Cam. To make it fun for him, she laid out a blanket and used his plastic, pre-sterilized utensils to lay a table for him. Their picnic wasn't ready until they were.

Doing her hair, Ginger put on her best dress and styled Cam's hair using Shane's hair wax in the bathroom. It smelled so incredible her eyes watered. She doubted that Shane would object to Cam using his products, even despite her craziness that day.

Because he hadn't used it yet, she put Cam in the little suit that they'd brought in case he needed to be smart. He'd grow out of it soon, and Ginger didn't want it to be wasted. Cam laughed and played with her cosmetics bottles as she made an effort for her baby. She expected the food to take a while so was surprised when there was a knock on the bedroom door as she was putting gloss on her lips.

"Room service!"

Ginger smiled at the sound of her brother's voice and hoped he wouldn't be too pissed at her. Cam was sitting on their picnic blanket laid out on the floor at the end of the bed, hitting two plastic bowls together, entertaining himself.

She went to open the door. "Hey," Ginger said.

Owen held up a tray. "I guess you're not joining us for dinner," he said, examining her apparel. "Wow, I never knew there was five-star dining up here… You got a hot date?"

"Yep," she said, pushing the door further open to reveal Cam sitting up in his waistcoat and bowtie.

"Isn't he handsome?"

Owen swooned. "Oh my God, you have to show Shane!"

Her brother turned and inhaled as if he was going to shout, but she put a hand on his chest. "I can't," she whispered.

He frowned. "Why not? You're still pissed about—"

"I acted like an idiot," she said.

Taking the tray from her brother, Ginger carried it over to the floor and put it down away from Cam.

Owen came in and closed the door. "Everyone was shocked," he said. "But no one thinks you were an idiot… Well I do, but Shane and Calvin are so desperate to get into your underwear that they'd never say it."

His humor was appreciated, but she still felt like shit. "I would never keep them apart, Shane and Cam," she said, sinking onto the rug next to her boy. "I just… I didn't mean what I said."

"He knows that," Owen said, sitting down beside her. He straightened a plastic fork and Cam bopped his foot. "It never mattered how much you two fought, you always loved each other. Shane isn't angry… he's worried about you."

Ginger groaned and flopped onto her side. "That makes me feel worse. Why does he have to be so… sweet?"

"You trained him well," Owen said. Cam bopped his foot again. "Ow, what is with this kid?"

"Our restaurant is barefoot only." Owen looked at her feet and Cam's, she had proper dress shoes for her baby, but he sat better without them, so she'd foregone shoes too. "Besides, you know he likes to hit things," she said. "Maybe Shane can teach him to box instead of how to swim."

Owen took off his shoes. "Only you would

prefer a full contact sport over something completely passive like swimming."

Yes, she was an idiot, they'd established that. "Is he upset?" she asked. "I know I was irrational."

"So apologize."

How could her brother act like it was that simple? Ginger felt awful, like she'd crossed a line.

"I don't know if he wants to hear it…" she said on a sigh. "Where would I even begin?"

"Ask for a minute alone, toss him on the bed and ride him hard. I guarantee he'll forgive you after that." Owen was teasing. Still, the idea was completely outrageous. "It worked for you for years."

"It did not!"

"You always resolved fights with sex… well maybe not resolved them but…" He tilted his head and peered at her like he felt sorry for her. "I don't think you get the level of intimacy you two had. It was… complete, like nothing I've ever seen before. You were always touching. Like always. You never got over the fun sex part that most people only have at the start of their relationship. You used to play all these games, like role play and dressing up. You fed off each other. Sometimes he was so rough with you in public that people got worried… then two minutes later, you'd be alone, hiding in some dark corner and Shane would be on his knees pledging his undying love and devotion to you… You were best friends. Really. Absolute best friends. You just seemed to like being around each other, you liked hearing each other talk. You were so in love and—"

"I am in love with him," she said. When her brother didn't respond, she let her gaze rise. Ginger had never seen a person so in shock. Climbing over the picnic, she sat right beside her brother to pick up his hand. "You can't tell him. You can't tell anyone. But I… I thought it was attraction and curiosity. I guess part of it is. But that thing I see when I look into his eyes, it's not some big secret about him, it's a big secret about me… My heart, my soul, everything I am, gets it… It's my mind that holds me back. My frustration."

Squeezing her fingers, Owen mouthed silently. "And Calvin?" Before finding her rings, she'd have felt guilty. Right then, Ginger only felt resolve as her head began to shake. Owen hissed, "Oh my God… You love Shane? I have to tell him, you can't—"

"You said we had brother-sister privilege," she said, holding up a stern finger. "You can't—"

"But why?"

"I'm scared."

He dismissed her with a huff. "You don't have to be afraid of Shane. He'd turn himself inside out for you."

"I'm not afraid of him, I'm afraid of…" It was as she'd stood looking out over the lake that afternoon that she figured out the root of her discomfort. "I'm used to our life here. We see each other all the time, it's just us, it's quiet. Everyone's under the same roof, it's safe. I'm not… I'm not ready for corporate offices and big empty houses and living with a CEO. I don't even know what that means. I don't know what will be expected of me, of how people will react to me."

Owen stroked her hand, sympathizing. "You don't want to go home with him." She shook her head, chewing her lip, and coiling a finger round a loose strand of hair. "You know it's funny, when it was you and Shane in a small group, you were the most confident person. In bigger groups, you only ever wanted to be in the background. All that mattered to you was being the focus of his attention. You were never gregarious, but… you've always been like this. Always shunned any kind of spotlight, hated being the center of a group."

That Ginger was becoming more like herself was

reassuring. It didn't help her figure out how to tell Shane she planned to stay behind.

"He can't stay here forever," she said. "I feel like I still have work to do with the doctor. But after Julianna goes tomorrow—"

"She's not going tomorrow," Owen said. "There was no time to tell you earlier, but there's been an adjustment to their availability, which means we may be increasing our acquisition." She didn't even know what that meant, so shook her head at him and he explained. "There's more to negotiate. They're staying an extra day… but they'll be leaving early the day after."

She might not be able to picture the distant future, but the immediate future was clear. "Oh God, this is going to be awful," Ginger said and took a turn filling her brother in. "Calvin has associates at the lodge too, they're doing some sort of deal."

"So both of them will be holding warring conferences?" Owen said and grinned. Cam put the plastic fork in his mouth and she pulled it back so he didn't push it too far. Her son argued with her and she continued to wrestle it from him as Owen carried on. "That will be fun. You're like a gauge for who's the most powerful in a room, whichever one you want to jump after the meetings, he'll be the one with the biggest dick."

"Shane's is bigger," she said as Cam let go of the fork.

Replaying her words, Ginger lifted her head and gaped at her brother whose shocked grin became a snicker.

"Did you just have a memory or do you have something salacious to share, sis?"

She had something salacious in her mind, but not anything shareable. "Let's forget I said that," Ginger said.

Owen kept prodding until she laughed.

"It's nice to hear you laughing and…" Owen

said, making a show of leaning forward to pull something from the back of his waistband. He held up a legal envelope and waved it at her. "This was with the boxes, under the delivery notice. I guess it was at the front desk and they brought it down with everything else. Maybe they thought it was part of the same shipment. Anyway, I didn't think it was the right time for Shane to see it. With you yelling at us and all."

Oh, yeah, the other time she'd been a crazy person that day. Maybe she was losing her mind.

Ginger didn't know what her brother was holding up, so she took it from him and unfastened the top. Emptying it out, she was awed and excited and overwhelmed all at the same time.

"This is…"

"Cam's official name change documents. His birth certificate and passport… it's official."

"It is," she said, staring at the curves and lines of the letters that made up her baby's new name… his real name.

Owen's voice got all soft. "You should show Shane."

Shaking her head, Ginger put her fingertip on the words and then took a breath before putting everything back in the envelope. "I can't… I didn't do this to win brownie points. If I show him now, he'll think I'm trying to distract him from the horrible way I acted today. This was supposed to be special, an important statement, not a cover for my behavior."

"Trust me, he won't care about how or why," Owen said. "He'll be ecstatic… He'll forget—"

"That's the point," she said, annoyed that her brother didn't get it. "I shouldn't use Cam to get myself off the hook."

Her sibling was as irritated her. "Shane wants to see this," Owen said. "I've been desperate to tell him.

Now it's here. We can't hide it from him. A surprise is just a secret if you don't share it. Why would you want to—"

"I can't show him. I can't… Geez, Owen, I'm hiding up here eating dinner alone with my baby 'cause I can't face him. If I can't look Shane in the face, how can I show him this?"

"Then I'll show him," Owen said. "He'll want to see it. You don't know what it will mean to him."

All she seemed to do these days was argue with people. It was exhausting. "Won't it mean more if I tell him when we're friends?"

"We're not friends?"

Both she and Owen turned toward the doorway to see Shane draped against the doorframe.

"Dada!" Cam screamed and flopped into a crawl to scurry toward his father, right over the top of the picnic blanket, scattering everything.

THIRTY-ONE

"MAKING A BREAK for it top man?" Shane asked, crouching to catch Cam who was on a mission. "Wow, check out the duds." His grin got wider as he held his son up and turned him left and right. "I'm underdressed in here… You're on it, buddy, looking almost as hot as your momma over there."

"I crashed their barefoot date," Owen said, putting the envelope on the floor and eyeing her. "Show him." Her brother grabbed his shoes and went to the door. Shane sidestepped, but lowered Cam when Owen nuzzled his face. "I think the biggest competition you have for Gin's affection is this stunner."

Owen kissed Cam again and slipped out, closing the door behind him.

Shane lifted Cam high on his forearm. Ginger felt his eyes on her though she couldn't meet them. Cam leaned forward to smudge his mouth on his father's jaw.

"How's that tooth coming, buddy?" Shane asked, sliding his finger into Cam's mouth.

"It broke," she said, tidying up the picnic blanket.

"Show daddy your teeth, Angel."

Cam opened his mouth in a big grin that made both parents laugh. Ginger reached over to pull the tray toward her so she could scoop some food out for Cam.

"Well done, little guy," Shane said, letting Cam pull his finger deeper into his mouth to chew on it again. Shane began to move closer; her heart sped up so she focused on the food. When he got to the picnic, he crouched, putting Cam on the floor between his legs. "Do you want me to leave you alone?"

Picking up the bib she'd put on the floor, Ginger leaned forward to fasten it around Cam's neck and scooped some of the food into his mouth. She didn't want Shane to go, but she didn't want to fight and didn't know how to apologize.

"It's carbonara sauce. They made it with this non-dairy, baby-friendly sauce apparently, but it's nice, not… like it sounds. You probably don't remember, he had it at the lodge one night… Cam really likes spaghetti, can you believe it?" Cam tried to put his fingers in the food. She moved it away but picked out a piece of spaghetti and put it on his fingers. "How does that feel, Angel?" she asked Cam, then spoke to Shane. "It's good for him to learn the texture, he'll make a mess, but—"

"Bit," Shane said, sliding his hand beneath her chin to draw her head up. "I love you."

Oh, God, why did he have to say that? Shifting to her knees, Ginger married her eyes to his. Just when she was falling apart, feeling awful for what she'd said to him, he came in there and made her feel good.

Touching her fingertips to his lips, she smudged the sauce on him. "Does it taste good?"

Opening his lips, Shane sucked her fingers; the vibration of her ragged breath stung her throat. It wasn't enough. Rising higher, she forced her mouth over his before her fingers even slipped free. Clutching his shoulders, Ginger balanced herself over her son and pushed her mouth hard against her husband's and he didn't retreat.

Easing up enough to keep her lips brushing his, she whispered, "I'm sorry. Boo, I'm so sorry. I would never keep you from Cam. I was crazy and—"

"Baby, much as I hate to say it, Bishop was right. I was told and I didn't give your fear enough thought... I don't need an apology... You know all I need from you?"

She'd give him anything.

"Ma!" Cam called out and pushed her legs that were probably crowding him.

Ginger stayed fixated on Shane. "What do you need from me?" she whispered.

"Faith," he said. "I need you to have faith in me. In us. That's it. If you can do that for me, I promise we'll get through this. We'll conquer your fear together." Linking her fingers at the back of his neck, Ginger felt slimy baby fingers on her leg betraying that Cam had to be feeding himself. Yet, she couldn't withdraw from Shane's mesmerizing gaze. "I promise not to take Cam near the water... but will you give me the chance to help you?"

"You are helping me," she said.

"Will you have faith and let me help you?"

"Dada!" Cam shouted out. Shane glanced down. "Dada!"

She looked down to see Cam rocking back and forth, lifting and dropping his legs. Ginger could see that ending badly, so she lowered to her son and grabbed his waist.

"Daddy's face can take a blow from mommy's head. His boy bits aren't as hardy."

If Cam kept rocking like that he'd have fallen back and head-butted Shane right in the jewels. Shane shifted to sit on the floor properly and put a hand on Cam's head as he stroked her hair and spoke into her crown.

"And Mommy wants more kids."

Picking up Cam, Ginger moved him to the opposite side of the picnic blanket and sighed. "What a mess baby made," she said.

There was carbonara sauce smudged on his clothes, his hands, his face, it was all over her dress and as she rose, she saw it was on Shane's pants too. Cam didn't need time to make a mess, just opportunity.

Grabbing the wipes, she went back to Cam. Stripping him down, she wiped his hands and face and kissed his head.

"Mama!" Cam said, babbling as she scooped food into his mouth.

She handed him a spoon and an empty bowl, which gave him something to do as he banged them together.

"I love watching you be a mom," Shane said.

He was sitting on the floor with his legs stretched out in front of him, his arms straight behind him holding him up.

Cam was chewing his food and happy with his instrument. She was so disappointed that his suit was a mess. In consolation, he grew so fast that he'd need a new suit soon anyway. Dressing up to date a ten-month-old was a bad plan. Standing up, Ginger unzipped her dress and stepped out of it. There wasn't a dry-cleaners at the lodge, but there might be one in the city.

Bending to spoon more spaghetti into Cam's mouth, he grinned at her. "Look at those teeth, Angel," she said, kissing his sauce smudged mouth. "So handsome."

With her son happy, Ginger moved the bowl out of his reach and crawled over the picnic to kneel by

Shane. Unfastening his belt, she undid his button and drew down his fly. Shane raised his hips for her to lean forward and grab his waistband. It wasn't until her body bumped his that she paused, realizing what the hell she was doing. She was undressing him like she had Cam… or like a wife would undress her husband.

Shane's hips were braced off the floor, his weight balanced on his extended arms and heels. His brows rose above his smile. "Keep going, baby," he said.

Sinking back onto her heels, she exhaled. "Can this really belong to me?" she whispered, caressing his solid thigh. "Can it really be okay for me to do…"

"Whatever the hell you want with me?" he asked. "Yes."

She might still be uncomfortable with some of the sex stuff, but the only way to get used to it was to push through. Maintaining eye contact, she pulled his jeans down over his ass and shuffled down to take them off over his feet.

"This is a barefoot picnic," she said and tugged off his socks as well.

"You never let me keep my socks on," Shane said.

Ginger bowed to kiss the top of his big toe making him laugh.

She gathered up the dirty clothes and took them to the changing table where she put Cam's suit back on its hanger. When she turned around, she saw Shane pulling off his shirt.

"Is that dirty too?" she asked, wondering how on earth Cam had reached his torso.

"No, I just felt overdressed," he said.

Somehow their barefoot picnic had become an underwear picnic. She was in her bra and panties, Shane was wearing boxers, and Cam was bouncing on his diaper in only a vest. He was babbling to himself, then flopped forward with the food bowl in sight.

"Shane!" she called, pointing at the impending disaster.

He flipped around and snatched up the bowl like a pro before Cam could reach it.

Cam berated his father for being so quick and spoiling his fun. Going back to join them, she stepped over Shane and sat down between him and the blanket. Taking the bowl from Shane, Ginger bent forward with her knees and elbows on the floor so she could reach her son and scoop more food into his mouth.

Shane's warm rough hand slid over her ass and she froze. It was her impulse to sit back and slap him away because she hadn't been touched in that way.

Being on all fours with Shane behind her, it was a vulnerable position, and an intimate one. But she was feeding her baby, so she kept her attention on him, replying to his blathering and feeding him in time, while Shane became more handsy.

He stroked her ass cheeks, down the back of her thighs and back up to the line of her thong. When his fingers slid down over the crotch of her panties, Ginger sat up, finding herself nestled in the crook of his body, in front of his hips.

She caught his hand. Taking it off her ass, she coiled it around to her opposite hip. "You can't touch me there," she whispered.

"I love your body," Shane said. "I always did."

"Mama!" Cam called out.

"Would you like some spaghetti?" she asked Shane. "There's plenty for all of us to share."

Admiring her for a second, he said nothing. He cupped her cheek and rose enough to kiss her. "I have never been happier than I am right now," he said. "Sitting here in our underwear with our baby, it's perfect."

"In the almost dark eating cold, baby-friendly carbonara?" she asked.

"Exactly," he said, leaning forward to kiss her again. "Are we friends again?"

Ginger wanted them to be friends, but it was Shane who had the right to deny her, not the other way around.

"I don't know, are we?"

"Yes," he said before nodding past her. "Now do I get a peek?"

"A peek at?" Glancing back she saw the legal envelope on the floor. She'd forgotten about it. Given what he'd just said, it had become a good time. Reaching for the envelope, she pulled it over to them, pausing to feed Cam the last of his carbonara on the way. "I'll show you. But I… I haven't told anyone else about it. Only Owen knows."

"This is what you were talking about in the bathroom?" he asked, taking the envelope to open it.

He took the first item out to read it. His serious eyes lightened, he took out the other and his smile grew.

"How do you feel?" she asked.

"Baby," he exhaled. "It's the… this is amazing."

"It's what we signed for… I just thought—"

He snatched her to push his mouth over hers. His tongue delved deep and she struggled to catch her breath, but it was made harder when he yanked her close.

"Thank you, baby, this… it means everything to me. You're fucking incredible."

"Dada!" Cam hollered. Shane kept kissing her, sliding his hands down over her body. "Dada!" Shane stopped kissing her when Cam crawled over and pulled his hand away. "Mama!"

Cam used her to pull himself up and squeezed between his mother and father to babble his anger.

"Is he pissed at me for touching you?" he asked,

lying back again.

With Shane lying on his side, she was leaning against his torso, her arm on his ribs which let her caress his muscles. Cam was still between them and Shane put an arm around him to rest a hand on her knee, giving Cam support to stay put.

"I think he's pissed that we're not looking at him," she said. Both she and Shane kissed his opposite cheeks at the same time. Cam turned to put both arms around her neck and Shane slid his arms up to copy him, squeezing Cam between his parents.

"I take it back," Shane said. "This is the happiest I've ever been. Only one thing would make it better…"

"One thing?" she asked. "What's that?"

"If you were pregnant right now."

"What?" she asked. Cam wiggled until he had enough space to sit down and crawl away. "Don't be premature, Boo."

Shane nuzzled against her ear. "Never. That would be a waste of my swimmers and I want them all in there."

He spread his hand on her belly, it was large enough to span her and she looked down to admire his caress.

"We should get dressed," Ginger said. "The door isn't locked… and you're too easily distracted."

"By your body, true," he said, rolling onto his back to link his hands behind his head when she picked up his tee-shirt and put it on.

Cam pulled a pot of chocolate pudding from his diaper bag and held it up to babble. "Mama!"

Leaning in, she kissed Shane's cheek. "Will you give him his pudding? I'll get his sleepsuit."

"Isn't it early for his pajamas?"

"If I put him in clothes, he'll think he's going out again," she said.

Shane went to retrieve son and pudding, as she got everything ready for his bed and put on the water for his bath.

"We can have a slumber party," Shane said. "I can bring a TV upstairs; we can watch a movie."

Sounded great, but impossible. "We can't leave Rocky downstairs all night alone," she called from the bathroom, tying her hair back.

Ginger came out of the bathroom to find Cam sitting in Shane's lap on his crossed legs. Eating chocolate pudding. The carbonara bowl was still uncovered and it smelled great. She went over and sat down to sample the pasta. It was good, so she twirled some around the fork and offered it to Shane who finished putting pudding in Cam's mouth before accepting the pasta from her.

"It is good," he said.

They kept on eating with Shane feeding Cam and her feeding both the adults. It was a strange, but intimate experience. The new kind of bonding was important for father and son. It was important for both parents and their baby… they were becoming a family.

THIRTY-TWO

CLOSING THE BEDTIME book she'd just read for Cam, Ginger glanced at the boys lying on the other side of her bed. Shane was flat on his back with Cam lying on his belly on top of his father. Cam was fast asleep; Shane's eyes were closed too, so she guessed he'd succumbed to his own tiredness.

Leaning over to kiss the back of Cam's head, she hesitated for a moment before kissing Shane and was surprised to feel him respond. But when she looked at him, he still appeared to be asleep. Maybe it was autopilot to kiss her back. That was a nice idea, one which made her smile.

Leaving the bed, she put the book away and prepared Cam's crib. She retrieved him from his father and laid him down believing it best for him to start the night in his own bed even if he didn't end there. The adults hadn't eaten dessert. So when she picked up the diaper bag to begin packing away the utensils they hadn't used, Ginger also pulled out a pot of chocolate pudding from inside.

"Do you want me to move?" Shane mumbled from the bed.

She hadn't expected to hear his voice. Just the sound of it put a smile on her lips. She turned and leaned on the dresser.

"Nope," she said, peeling the lid from the pudding pot and dipping one of Cam's plastic spoons into it.

"What you got there?"

"Pudding," she said and went to the bed.

Crawling on her knees toward him, she spooned some pudding into his mouth.

"Mm," he said, "that's amazing."

She laughed in a whisper. "Babies get all the best food."

Shane tried to ease up, but she pushed his shoulder with the ball of her spoon-occupied hand to put him on his back again. Sliding her leg over his hips, she sat on him and ate more of the pudding. His hands curled around her hips as she admired the planes of his incredible chest.

Smearing the back of the spoon with pudding, she smudged it against the nook in his collarbone at his throat and bent over him to lick it clean. Brushing her lips against his Adam's apple, the vibration of his groan heated her mouth and raised her hips as the bulk of his erection grew against her soft center. He grasped her hips tighter to urge her down against him, keeping her there so he could grind his pelvis against hers.

"I'd still prefer to be eating you," he said, sliding his hands around to her ass. "This is the best fucking restaurant in the world."

Moaning on his lips, Ginger kissed him again and eased up to circle her hips on his as she spooned more pudding into her mouth.

"I've got the best seat in the house."

"Always reserved for you, baby. Only you."

Working her hips, she spooned more pudding into his mouth. Ginger loved the way his eyes rolled and his throat shook when he groaned.

"Last one," she whispered, scraping the last of the dessert onto the spoon.

She put it on his tongue and expected him to seal his lips to swallow. Instead, he pulled her down and slid his tongue into her mouth, sharing the sweet dessert with her in a delectable kiss that made her drop both spoon and pudding pot.

If that was what being intimate with Shane was like, Ginger was in trouble. Her body was fizzing and bubbling. She couldn't keep still, couldn't stop her mind from filling with heat that blurred her thoughts.

She didn't even think about acting before she did. Covering his hand with hers, she slid it up her body, around to her breast, giving him permission to squeeze and caress her. Like a pro, he unclipped her bra with his other hand and cast it aside to allow the heat of his large palm to meet her flesh.

"Shay," she whispered, "I love your hands on me."

As if in contradiction to what she'd said, Ginger took his hand away from her breast. He grumbled in protest, but she wasn't taking it away, she was just relocating it. Lifting her hips, Ginger pushed his fingers down the front of her panties, earning her a grumble of satisfaction from his throat.

When his fingertips grazed over her clit, she froze, her mouth a breath away from his, her eyes wide, fearful with curiosity and satisfaction.

"Feel good, Bit?" He kept massaging, circling and she could feel herself swelling and softening for him. "Relax, baby, just relax for me."

The bark of a dog broke through the haze and

there was male shouting, then another bark. She tensed and grabbed his wrist, but Shane put his other arm around her to hold her against him.

"Boo, there's—"

"Just a minute, baby. I'll make you—"

"No," she said. "No, Shane, let me go."

His arms opened and she leaped up. Rocky had taken her out of her dream, she should never have gone that far with Shane. What was she thinking? It was so easy for her to forget herself with him and be swept into the moment.

"Bit?" Shane asked, pushing onto his elbows. "You okay?"

"Yeah, I... I..." She wasn't sure how to put herself back together after... that. She didn't know if she should be offended that he'd been persistent or galled at herself for being so forward. "Rocky needs his walk. Can you take him out for—"

"You better put some clothes on first or I'll never get rid of this boner," he said, gesturing to the pronounced lump in his underwear.

"Shay, I..." She squeezed her eyes shut. "God, you're too hot to be my husband."

He laughed. "All yours, baby, and you're all mine... come back to bed."

"No," she said. "You have to get up and walk Rocky. I have to... I have to..."

"What, baby?" he asked. If she was more together she'd be offended at how amused he was by her bewilderment. "What do you need, Bit?"

She balled her fists. "Stop it. You're screwing with my mind. Stop... being all you... and hot like that. Get out of bed, go walk the dog."

"Okay," he said, snickering as he rose. He came to her and with a hand on the back of her head, he pulled her forward and kissed her forehead. "I'll do your bidding, my sweet."

"Good," she said, pushing at him, trying to put some distance between them because if she didn't, she might get carried away again. Trouble was, he didn't budge. "Thank you. And I'll… I'll clear up the food."

"Okay, Bit," he said, kissing her temple and her cheekbone.

He bent his knees to lower and kiss her jaw, then beneath, sliding his lips down her neck.

She exhaled. He was doing it again, distracting her. Was it for her benefit or because he couldn't help himself?

Pressing her hands on his chest, Ginger smiled. "You're insatiable," she said, deciding to be more forceful. Grabbing his waist, she turned him, rather he allowed her to turn him, and she pushed him backwards, walking with him toward the bathroom. "You go to your bedroom and lock the door while you're getting changed."

"Why?" he asked, running his hands up her shoulders to her neck where he tried to angle her head back again.

"Stop," she laughed, trying to pull his hands down. "Shay, please—"

"I love that you're calling me that again. You're the only one who ever shortened my name like that… turns me on."

"I get that," she said and reached beyond him to open the bathroom door. "Please, baby." Rocky barked again. "You have to take him out."

Shane groaned as he turned a hundred and eighty degrees. "You drive me crazy, baby. Drive me crazy."

THIRTY-THREE

APOLOGIZING TO CALVIN was becoming a habit that Ginger didn't like. Shane took Rocky for a walk while she took their dishes down the stairs to wash. Being domestic gave her some alone time to think and there was a lot to reflect on.

Ginger didn't know how long she'd been in the kitchen by herself, it was a good while, probably close to an hour as she tidied up and made plans. When Calvin came to join her, she was disappointed by the interruption.

"You've been in here a while," Calvin said. "You're not still obsessing about earlier, are you?"

"No," she said, washing her hands. "I still feel bad for what I said to Shane but—"

"He should've paid more attention to what we told him," Calvin said, coming over to lean on the counter beside her as she picked up a towel to dry her hands. "I don't want to talk about him."

Good, because she didn't want to talk to Calvin about Shane, that was too risky a subject right now.

"Okay," she said, watching him put his hand in his pocket. "What do you want to talk about?"

"This," he said and picked out her engagement ring.

Uh-oh. She hadn't even thought about that ring, not since she'd taken it off. "What about it?"

"I want you to wear it. I understand that you were angry and confused when you took it off. But I think it's time we refocused on our future, don't you?"

"Our future," she said, pleased that her hands were still tangled in the towel because as long as she was drying them, he couldn't put the ring on her. "Calvin, I don't know what's going to happen tomorrow, let alone next week or next month."

If she offended him, they might argue. If Shane came back to see that, he'd jump to her defense and there would be a fight. She knew it.

"Are you saying that you don't want to wear it?" Calvin asked, his expression becoming severe. "I see no reason why you shouldn't. If you're worried about offending Warren, I'll speak to him."

Yeah, because that would be a smart idea. "No, I don't want more fighting," she said, trying to be diplomatic. "I just… I think we should all be cautious and, you know, focus on one thing at a time."

Calvin took her hand, pulling it free of the towel to hold it out flat. "It would mean a lot to me if you would—"

The back door opened and Rocky came racing in. He ran over and circled her, pulling her away from Calvin as he nosed her and barked.

"Oh, baby," she said, sinking into a crouch. "Where's momma's baby? Who's a good boy?"

Rocky barked again and she laughed.

"It's a nice night," Shane said. She looked up to see him just inside the back door. "Rocky really went for a run out there."

"Did you?" she asked Rocky, scrubbing her fists behind his ears and kissing his nose. "Did you have a good walk with daddy? Good boy, who's a good boy?" He barked again and she laughed. "Shh, sweetie, if your baby brother hears you, he'll wake up and want to play… Do you want to play with Cam?" Rocky barked and she looked up at Shane. "He knows him."

"Course he does," Shane said, rubbing his knuckle between Rocky's ears then going to the sink to get a drink of water.

"Does it have to bark all the time?" Calvin asked.

She looked over her shoulder. "Sorry, that's my fault, I encourage him."

Calvin said nothing but rolled his eyes and turned away. She stood and made eye contact with Shane who was gulping from his glass.

"Thank you," she mouthed and he winked at her.

He had to have heard, or seen, what was going on before he came in. Interrupting, without starting a confrontation, was considerate of him and probably not his first impulse, which meant he'd done it for her.

"Took your time, bro, come on!" Murphy called from the living room. When she turned, Ginger saw all the men, minus the doctor, heading toward the dining room. "We've been waiting for you."

"What's going on?" she asked Shane who went to pull a box of beers from the fridge.

Rocky dashed off after Murphy.

Shane slid an arm around her as he walked in the same direction as the dog. "Poker. You in?"

"Poker?" she asked, turning against him to block his path. "Do you think that's a good idea?"

"I promise not to break the bank," he said and kissed her hairline, but she eased back a step.

They were just out of view of the dining room

door, unless someone was deliberately peeking at them.

Ginger dropped her volume. "That's not what I'm worried about."

"What are you worried about?"

"Murder and mayhem," she said. "All of you are competitive. Someone has to lose and… Cam is asleep upstairs, if there's a fight—"

"There won't be," he said. "I promised you Cam would be my priority and he is. Anyone gets out of line, I'll put them outside before I'll endanger you or our son."

"Calvin hates to lose," she whispered.

But that wasn't going to sway Shane's opinion. "Well he better get used to it, 'cause he's going to find out soon that he lost the biggest prize."

Narrowing her eyes, she didn't back away when he got closer. "I am not in the pot, Shane. He'll goad you into promising to back off and if you do…"

He laughed. "You think I'd do that to win a hand of cards? I don't think so, Bit. You have nothing to worry about."

Worrying about Cam's wellbeing was hard enough on her nerves. Worrying about Shane's too had the potential to break her. "I don't want you to kill each other."

Shane didn't seem worried. "If you're that worried, play."

She scoffed. "That will make it worse. Besides, I don't have a clue how to play."

"We'll teach you."

"I have nothing to bet."

"I'll spot you."

She smiled. "You have an answer for everything, Mr. Warren."

"Shane!" Murphy and Owen called out from the dining room.

"Put my sister down and get in here!" Owen

shouted.

Calvin would just love Owen for saying that.

Shane gave her another chance. "Coming?" he asked and she shook her head. "Okay. I won't push. You know where I am if you change your mind."

"I'm going to bed. Please, Shane," she said, curling her hands in his tee-shirt beneath his jacket. "Please, please, please keep it together. I don't want a riot."

"Scouts honor," he saluted and leaned down to kiss her.

Ginger stepped away wearing a smirk. "You play nice with the other boys and then we'll see if you get one of those," she whispered.

He smiled and she gave him a wide berth to head for the stairs. "Rocky!" she called. "Come with momma."

"He can stay down here," Shane said. "You don't need to look after both our kids."

"It's a mommy's job to protect her babies from madness like this," she said, touching Rocky's head as he bounded past her, up the stairs. And she didn't want Rocky getting the blame for any tension, if there was a fight, the dog would want to protect his master.

She carried on up the stairs, Shane watched her the whole way. At the top, she glanced at him and they shared a smile. He was in a good mood, she just hoped it would last until the next day.

THIRTY-FOUR

"DOCTOR GUINNESS, HOW would you like a drive into town with Cam and me?" Ginger asked, coming out of the kitchen with Calvin in her wake.

He'd just asked her to go to dinner with him, alone, but she'd already had another idea that should save her from that encounter. Calvin seemed sure he'd get points for having all the gifts removed from the house that morning, but it had been his fault that they were there in the first place.

The doctor was seated in the living room, reading. "Yes," he said, closing his book. "That could be interesting."

"With this bunch all going off to do business at the lodge, I thought it might be nice to get out and run some errands." Going around the coffee table, Ginger sat down on the floor in front of Rocky, next to Cam who was banging his wooden blocks together. "We can take Shane's truck… It would help me out if you'd come because I don't have a driver's license."

Cam took a block to his father and struggled to

stand up while holding it, Shane bent over to pick up his boy who handed over the block. All of the men were seated in the living room, except Calvin who stood behind the couch.

"Absolutely," Doctor Guinness said. "I have a few things to do as well."

"Why his truck?" Calvin asked.

Ginger hadn't expected the question or the abrupt tone. "It's not fair to ask the doctor to use his gas," she said. "And Cam will like sitting up high, he's never been in a pick-up before… And Shane is the only one with two vehicles in the parking lot; he still has that rental too. So if he needs to go anywhere, he still has access to a vehicle. You don't mind, do you, Shane?"

Taking her eyes to him, she wasn't surprised to find that Cam was already holding his father's keys.

"What's mine is yours, Bit," Shane said.

Cam took the block away from him to throw it at his uncle on the seat beside them.

"No!" she said. "Cam, no throwing blocks."

He pushed away from his father and slithered onto the floor, still holding his father's keys in his soggy fist.

"What do you need in town?" Calvin asked her.

"I have some dry cleaning," she said. "And I thought I might make dinner tonight."

"Cook?" Calvin said like it was a repulsive thought. "You're going to cook?" She nodded. "Why?"

"I don't know, I just… I thought I might like to give it a try. You aren't obliged to stay and eat. You can go to the lodge if you want to, you too doctor." She looked at Shane, Murphy, and Owen. "You three are obliged."

"Why are they obliged while Boyd and I are not?" Calvin asked, sneering at the other men.

"Because Cam is obliged. I'll need Shane to be

on Cam duty while I prepare and serve. My brother is required to be supportive of my new ventures and Murphy's not going to eat alone with you guys… and someone has to do the washing up."

That was the truth.

Owen clapped. "This is fun, you were always a great cook. Do you remember how?"

She shrugged. "I've been reading recipes on the internet. I looked online, there are some nice food stores in town… It will be fun to try and if I screw it up… well there are a couple of jars of baby food upstairs."

"I'm sure it will be delicious," Shane said. "I look forward to it."

"How much do you think you'll need?" Calvin asked, reaching to his inside pocket for his money clip.

"Oh no," she said, glancing around at the others. "It's okay. I… I got my old cards back. I have money in my accounts."

Calvin stopped in surprise and drew his eyes to Shane. "You did that?"

Shane smiled and looked at Murphy. "I love how he's pissed at me for giving her financial freedom. Man, aren't I just a prick?" Then his glare landed on Calvin. "When you're secure in a relationship, you don't have to work overtime to control someone."

The tension was beginning to rise.

Ginger was aware of her baby being in the room. "Okay," she said. "I don't want a fight."

Cam picked up another block and when he turned to crawl toward his father with it, he left the keys on the floor.

"Are you ready to leave?" Doctor Guinness asked, probably sensing the same friction in the room that she did.

"Yes," she said, leaving the floor. "I'll grab our stuff. Shay, can you put on Cam's shoes and jacket, please?"

"Sure thing," Shane said, sweeping up his son who was at his feet again. "You going out with mommy, buddy?"

"I can get him ready," Calvin said.

Shane laughed and turned a sneer on Calvin. "Really feeling threatened today, aren't you, Bishop?"

"Guess that's what happens when you lose your wad at poker," Murphy said.

They didn't need the mocking. It didn't help anyone or anything.

"Shane," she murmured and he turned to look at her. His smile slid away when he saw how serious she was and he nodded once. "Thank you… Calvin, I'll need your help getting Cam's car seat from your car."

Ginger went toward the stairs but heard what was said next. "What was that?" Murphy asked in a hushed tone as Calvin went to retrieve his own car keys.

"Nothing," Shane said. "Forget it."

***

THEY ALL HEADED to the parking lot in front of the lodge as a troupe. Cam was in his stroller, shaking his father's keys. Calvin walked ahead with Boyd, keeping Ginger's hand so she had to keep pace with him and leave Cam with his father and uncles.

When they got to Calvin's car, Boyd carried on to go into the lodge.

Calvin unlocked the car, but his phone rang, so he answered it. "One second," he said to her and walked away to talk into his phone.

Ginger bent over to unfasten the seatbelt from the baby seat. A second later, two hands slid onto her hips and she looked over her shoulder to see Shane behind her.

"I'm sorry," he said. Ginger went back to doing her work. "I can make it up to you right here."

"Good," she said. His hand slid lower, but she straightened and turned to dump the heavy car seat in his arms. "You need to learn how to put this in properly anyway."

He nodded in acquiesce, wearing a knowing smile, and turned to take the seat to his vehicle which they'd passed on the way there. Calvin was wandering toward the lodge, still on the phone. Cam was with his uncles and Doctor Guinness in the middle of the parking lot.

"Put it behind the driver," she said when they got to his pick-up. "That way I can turn around and get to him from the passenger side."

Shane did as told and she slid in between him and the back seat to show him how the straps slid into place.

"Are you going to let me make it up to you?" he asked when they were done.

"By screwing me in the parking lot? No."

Ginger turned around. He trapped her against the frame of the car, the door still open at his back.

"I'm sorry," he said into her eyes.

She wanted to stay mad, but like she'd told him, it was easier when they were communicating. "Don't you get that you've won?" she asked. "Why do you have to keep goading him? And Cam was right there, what if an argument had started?"

"I know, you're right, I'm sorry."

"Cam adores you. He worships you… but if he sees you shouting and, God forbid, getting physical with anyone… you'll scare him, Shane. I don't want our baby to be afraid of you."

While he was searching her gaze, it hurt her to see him so scared of that idea. "I just… the guy gets on my nerves. The way he treats you and what you've been through… I want to knock out his teeth."

She could understand that, but that wasn't what they'd agreed on. "We're playing this cool, remember? We're supposed to be on the same side. I don't want us working against each other—"

"We're not," he said, scooping his hands up to her face. "I promise, baby, I'm sorry. But you do know if I suddenly start being super nice to the guy, he's going to know something's up."

Fair point. Still, she wasn't expecting them to be best friends. "I'm not asking you to be nice to him, just… ignore him. That's all. Just let it slide."

"As soon as this business stuff is done later… We're going to have to tell him it's over."

She straightened enough to spread her hands on his ribs. His hand was on the roof above her head, his whole body slanted toward her, shutting her into the enclosed space.

"I'm going to have to tell him. You won't be anywhere near it. You're going to be with Cam, protecting him with your life."

"Murphy and Owen have our backs. They can be with Cam while—"

"Having you there will just be antagonistic," she said, thinking about where they were and the day ahead. "We can talk about this later. Julianna doesn't leave until tomorrow morning, so we won't be telling Calvin a thing until after she's gone."

"Okay," he said. "I'll put Cam in the car."

Ginger nodded and Shane twisted, but she slid her hands to his sides, increasing her grip to stall him.

Returning to his post, he lowered. "Something else?" he asked, his attention heating.

Biting her lip, she was too tempted to be self-conscious, especially when they were going to be apart for most of the day. "He's not watching, is he?"

Shane looked over the roof of the car. "No, his back is to us."

"Just a little one?"

"You got it, Bit," he said, stooping to touch his mouth to hers. "The only way I know you've forgiven me is if I get a kiss… Sometimes it's like you remember everything."

"Some things just feel natural," she said. "Go get Cam for me."

The dry cleaning and stroller were put in the truck as Cam was strapped in by his father. Everyone said their goodbyes and then she was off for her day with the doctor. Leaving the men to their business should be safe, unless any of them ran into each other. But that would happen whether she was at the chalet or in town. At least with her and Cam in town, she could be confident her son wouldn't witness any carnage.

THIRTY-FIVE

TYPICAL THAT GINGER should gear herself up to try something new only to collapse at the first hurdle. Her day with the doctor had been great. They'd had lunch; Cam had slept a little in the car on the way home, but he hadn't had his full nap, so she worried how that would impact his mood for the rest of the day.

It didn't help that she'd had to rush up to the lodge in a panic when her brand new laptop decided to screw around on her.

Walking along a corridor on an upper floor, she was trying to find the specific office that the receptionist had directed her to. Pushing the stroller along the narrow space, Ginger came to a door and leaned over the stroller to pull it open as she tried to angle herself through it.

"Oh, let me help you."

The redhead on the other side of the door pushed the door from her side allowing Ginger to navigate through. "Thank you," she said.

The woman didn't move aside. "I'm sorry, do I... Do I know you?"

The redhead was beautiful, taller than Ginger, more refined in her expensive clothes and complete with perfect makeup.

Ginger smiled. "No, I don't think so."

But the woman was really peering at her. "You look familiar to me, but I… I'm not sure why," she said. Cam kicked and babbled, getting the woman's attention. When the stranger smiled, her beauty became more striking. "Hello, little one." The woman crouched to touch Cam's head. "Aren't you precious? How old is he?"

"Almost eleven months," Ginger said.

She was in a hurry, but never really minded when anyone commented on her perfect boy.

"He's gorgeous."

Well, duh. "Thank you," Ginger said.

"Are you lost up here or looking for something specific? There are only conference rooms and offices down there."

Maybe the woman was a manager or employee and that was why she was so smartly dressed. "No, I asked at reception. They sent me up here to find their IT guy, I'm having some computer issues."

Ginger touched the laptop resting in the folded hood of the stroller.

Cam began to kick and pant again, getting himself excited. Ginger hoped he wasn't going to throw a hissy fit because he was tired. She needed him to stay calm while she spoke to the IT guy, if she ever found him. He might not want to help her if she brought a screaming baby into his office.

The woman narrowed her eyes as she peered up at her. "Are you sure we don't know each other? You look really—"

"Dada!" Cam hollered.

Ginger looked up as the redhead turned.

There at the opposite end of the corridor, just coming through the double doors was Shane, Murphy, and Owen with a couple of suited men. Cam must have seen them through the glass panel in the door. Great, she hadn't thought about being in the business suite. The woman on reception had just said second floor, right and then left to the end of the corridor.

All of the men's expressions were serious as they spoke in hushed whispers.

"Is that what he calls all men?" the redhead asked, surprised as she rose to stand up straight.

There was no time to answer or retreat.

"Dada!"

Shane immediately stopped talking and his staunch expression lightened in an instant. "Hey, buddy!" he said.

Ginger was as shocked as the redhead whose jaw fell. Shane sped up as he headed toward them.

"I... I—"

"This is a nice surprise, Bit. You okay? You looking for me?" Shane asked and actually leaned over the stroller to kiss her temple before he hunkered down to blow a raspberry on Cam's cheek.

Cam laughed and kicked again. "Dada!"

"You... you're his father?" the redhead stuttered.

"I sure am," Shane said, tickling his son before glancing up at the women. "Sorry, Ginny, this is Julianna. Julianna, meet my wife, Ginger."

Shane was curious about Julianna's reaction. It was obvious from how he looked at the stunned woman. Maybe that was why he'd told the truth. They could've made excuses; he didn't have to introduce her when their lives were so complicated.

Julianna gasped. "You're... you're... Oh my God, you're Ginger Warren!"

"Yes," Ginger said, offering her hand.

Julianna was still gaping when she shook her hand.

Shane ruffled Cam's hair. "Are you okay, Bit?" he asked her. "We're just finishing up."

"When she said she was looking for an IT man, I had no idea she meant *her* IT man," Julianna said, though she still blinked at her like she was looking at a mythical creature. "I'm sorry, I'm amazed. Everyone thought you were—"

"She's stronger than ever," Shane said. "It's been a journey."

"I'm sorry, but… where have you been?" Julianna asked and looked down at Cam. "And your baby… you have a baby."

"*We* have a baby," Shane said.

Ginger identified the thread of irritation in his voice.

"Dada!" Cam said, straining to try to see up over the back of the stroller.

Her boy wasn't going to be patient for much longer.

"I'm sorry," Ginger said. "I have to get going."

"Oh, sure, sure," Julianna said and waved to the suited men hanging back with Murphy and Owen. "We should have dinner, when you get back to California. I'm sure you have quite a story to tell."

Ginger just smiled because she didn't want to commit to anything. "It was nice meeting you."

"I'll get that paperwork to you," Julianna said to Shane, then she and her colleagues stepped over Cam's stroller to get to the door.

Ginger backed away as much as she could, squishing herself into Shane who was at her back, to give Julianna and her colleagues space to pass.

When the door was closed, Ginger swatted his stomach. "You got defensive."

"I did not," he said, rubbing his stomach. He put his hands around onto hers on the stroller handle when she tried to move away. "I just didn't like the way she said—"

"You'll have to get used to it," Murphy said, coming over with Owen. "Ginny disappears for a year and a half and comes back with a kid? Suspect much?"

"People will think I faked it?" she asked. "You think they'll think I disappeared to have some other guy's kid?"

Murphy shrugged and she didn't like that.

"No one will think he's another guy's," Owen said. "The math works, it easily works."

"And how many people really pay attention to math when there's a scandal?" Murphy asked.

Scandal, fantastic, that was never a fun word.

Sighing, Ginger couldn't handle stressing about one more thing right now. "Okay, well now you've brightened my day, Murphy, thank you. I have to get going. I'll see you back at the chalet."

"Whoa, wait, I'll come with you," Shane said, picking up one of her hands to link their fingers as he bowed to put his mouth on the back of her ear. "Where are we going?"

"You want to come when you don't even know where I'm going?"

"Maybe she's going to meet Bishop for some afternoon delight," Murphy said.

Thinking the jibe served Shane right, Ginger smiled up at him. "Yeah, maybe I am."

"Then I'm definitely coming with you," Shane said. "He'll get the shock of his life if I walk in there first."

Murphy and Owen laughed until Murphy cringed. "Oh, nasty visual. You could walk in there and see more than you ever wanted to, know what I'm saying?"

They were venturing toward mocking that she didn't want to become habit when everyone's moods were frayed.

"Shane," she murmured, tipping her chin to her shoulder.

"Right, yeah, sorry, baby. Enough, guys."

"What is with that," Murphy said. "How does she tell you off just by saying your name in that soft way?" He looked to Cam. "You've got your work cut out, dude. Momma's gonna be strict with you."

"Cameron is an angel," she said. "It's his daddy who needs to learn to behave." Murphy and Owen jeered. She rolled her eyes, thinking that it was typical for them to take her words in a dirty way. "Can I go now?"

"I thought you were looking for me," Shane said. "Julianna said you wanted your IT guy."

"No, I said I was looking for *the* IT guy, the lodge's IT guy. He has an office around here somewhere."

"Problem?" Shane asked.

She nodded. "Something with my computer, I was looking up my recipes and it just… I don't know, went weird on me. I hope he'll be able to fix it."

"Use mine," Shane said. "That's a piece of junk anyway."

She didn't appreciate him being glib. "Because you didn't pick it?" she asked.

"Because you deserve better. Either way, I can fix it or you can let me give you something of higher performance," he murmured, getting closer and wrapping his arms further around her as he hummed the words in his bedroom voice. "Something that won't ever let you down, something customized and designed to fulfill your every need. Dedicated to you and your needs every minute of every day."

"Mm," she purred, like she was considering it. "That sounds like an interesting proposition… but that doesn't help me tonight."

She tried to walk, but he drew her back again and lowered to whisper through her hair into her ear so the guys wouldn't hear. "I'll make it worth your while, Mrs. Warren… Let me do this for you and you can have my hands all to yourself all night, directed by you, devoted to your pleasure, anywhere you want them. Just you and me…"

Ginger leaned back to look him in the eye. "And chocolate pudding?"

His smile was adoring. "And chocolate pudding." So she handed over the laptop to him. He wanted to kiss her; she saw it in the way his eyes glittered. Their audience was too close for them to get away with that. As if to remind himself, Shane turned to his brother. "We need to buy shares in the chocolate pudding company."

Murphy paused, his hands half in his pockets as his brow rose. "Say what? You mean, Cam's chocolate pudding? Why would we—"

Shane pulled his phone from his back pocket. "'Cause, brother, I'm about to place the largest order for stock that the company's ever received."

"We're going into retail?" Murphy asked.

"Nope, just satisfying the Warren family needs," Shane said.

Laughing, Ginger pulled the phone down before he could put it to his ear. "Let's go home."

THIRTY-SIX

DINNER WAS GREAT. Ginger actually managed to cook for everyone without burning the chalet down and because she was busy with dinner, she didn't stress as much about what was going on around the table.

Everyone had stayed, either in support of her effort or because they didn't want to be excluded.

Everyone except the doctor who had chosen to go to the lodge to eat alone. It wasn't too much that he wanted a night off from their craziness. She was surprised he hadn't requested more time away from the madness.

The empty, but dirty, plates were still on the table. Cam was banging his spoon on his highchair tray in time with the beat provided by his father, who was at his side as usual.

"Dinner was wonderful, thank you," Calvin said and other noises of appreciation went around the table. Father and son stopped making music and she began to think about clearing the table. "While everyone is present, there is something I would like to do."

Twisting toward him, Ginger wondered what he was talking about. "You want to do…"

To her horror, Calvin slid off his seat onto one knee and held up her engagement ring.

"I want you to recommit to being my wife."

She'd thought she'd got off the hook with him not bringing up the divorce papers. Except as Calvin kneeled next to her, she spied Boyd retrieving a stack of papers from beneath the unused placemat next to his. Only one thing those could be.

Ginger didn't feel panicked or guilty, she lowered her gaze to the ring and tried to contain the burst of fury that exploded within her. "You're doing this now?" she murmured.

"Yes, I—"

"You're doing this in front of my child?" she asked, her volume spiking on the last word.

Calvin was stunned. "I… I…"

Her anger snapped, infusing her every cell, but she kept her voice to a crackling hiss so as not to scare her baby. "Cam doesn't see this. He doesn't get involved with any of our relationship issues. I would protect my child with my life… We do not do this in front of him."

"But—"

"No!" she said.

Calvin wasn't even accepting her rage; he had the gall to act offended.

Screw it! Julianna was leaving at six a.m., that's what Owen had told her when she was cooking. Six a.m. was only a matter of hours away. They were close enough.

Ginger would never get through to Calvin with subtlety and she'd come to the end of her rope. Her head snapped to the side to fixate on Shane who had a hand on Cam's head as he observed the scene.

"Bit?" Shane asked, noticing her attention.

He was probably expecting her to tell him to take over or maybe to take Cam away. She did neither.

Tilting her chin, Ginger's determination grew. "Call, raise, or fold."

"Excuse me?" Shane asked.

Murphy hissed through his teeth as Owen "Ooo'd."

But she kept her eyes on her husband. "Call his offer," Ginger said, knowing he wouldn't fold. "A ring for a ring."

"You think Shane just happens to be packing a ring?" Murphy asked.

Shane's brows rose in time with his smile, because they both knew something that no one else did.

"You sure, Bit?" he asked.

Ginger nodded, so Shane stood up to put his hand in his pocket.

Calvin sputtered. "He is not going to offer you—"

Shane slapped the velvet pouch on the table. "Raise. I see your ring and raise you another. Two for the price of one."

Calvin was speechless again and bounced into his chair to look at Boyd. "I... I..."

"What's in there?" Owen asked.

"Where did you get that?" Calvin asked.

Ginger turned her focus to him. "In your drawer," she said and he had the decency to pale. The conversation was happening whether she wanted it to or not. "Shay, will you take Cam upstairs for his bath, please?"

"Uncle Owen will do it," Shane said. "Murph, get the—"

"No," she said. "I need to talk to Calvin alone."

Shane was hesitant, but Cam squealed and began to bounce. He was only going to have energy for a while, it would dwindle and he would get grumpy fast.

Shane unbuckled their son from the seat and lifted him up. "Shout if you need me," he said and lingered over eye contact before side-nodding at Murphy and Owen.

They left, but Boyd stayed and she eyed him. "Can we have a minute alone?" she said. "Please?"

Boyd waited for Calvin's approval before standing up to leave the room, closing the door after himself. "I can—"

"I don't know what explanation there can be for this," she said, staring into the man sitting beside her, unable to find a redeeming quality. "I was… devastated Calvin. I know Shane gave you a narrative, he told me about it in therapy and… I went nuts, I told him he was crazy."

"Then you went snooping and—"

"I didn't go snooping," she argued. "I went to get cufflinks from your drawer to let Shane borrow them. It wasn't meant to be a big deal. But you… I found the rings by mistake. Calvin… You can sit there sneering at me all you like, but this… it proves… I don't even know what it proves. Is it true? Did you know… Did you know the whole time?"

"This is what Warren wants," Calvin asserted. "You're letting him into your head! I don't see what two little trinkets have to do with our future!"

"Goddamn it, Calvin," she hollered. Thrusting to her feet, she slammed the side of her fist onto the table, making some of the plates jump. "Just for once, show me a bit of respect and tell me the truth!"

He sealed his lips tight. It was odd that looking into his eyes gave her nothing. Reading Shane was innate, she didn't know how she knew his mood, she just did. But with Calvin, she was at a loss. Was he going to keep avoiding the issue or be a man and face up to what he'd done?

"I…"

"Please, Calvin," she said. Sinking into her chair, she picked up his hand. "Please, just be honest with me."

It took him another minute, but when he spoke again, he wasn't so defensive. "I hit you with my car," he said and she straightened a fraction. "You came running out onto the road like a lunatic and I couldn't stop. There was just no time!" She'd always believed he'd found her at the side of the road like a wounded animal. Ginger hadn't thought for a second that Calvin had injured her in any way. "I panicked. When I got out, you were unconscious, white as a sheet." Did he consider leaving her? Was that why he was getting frantic? "I took you to the hospital, I thought it was the right thing to do. They asked if you were my wife… I said yes." He was quick to follow up. "I promise you, I hadn't even seen the rings or put anything together, I just… was so worried about you."

He touched her face but she pulled away. Searching the room, she was oblivious to its features, she couldn't get over the shock. He'd known. All along. He'd know that she'd been married at least, even if he didn't know who it was too.

"Calvin, I… why would you propose… Spend all that money on a wedding and—"

"Because I loved you and it had been so long… I just assumed that whoever he was, he didn't love you, not really, or maybe he'd been the one to hurt you. How did I know who you were running from? You were so scared when you ran out onto that road. Terrified."

Yeah, because there was a massive vehicle hurtling toward her at a great rate of speed.

"I don't… I don't even know where to begin."

"Think about it," he said, squeezing her hand tight. "Even if I'd known that you'd been in an accident before I met you, how was I to know that the man who gave you those rings wasn't dead already? By keeping you from investigating, all I was doing was saving you pain."

Turning to look at the pouch over on Shane's side of the table, how would she have felt knowing she'd been married? If Calvin had told her the truth about the rings. Except, if she'd known, she would have understood more about Cam's parentage.

"You should've told me," she said. "Why did you hide the rings from me?"

"The hospital gave them to me with your effects. I put them in my pocket and didn't think more about it… I was worried for you. They couldn't tell me if you'd wake up."

Her perspective on their initial meeting changed. The picture he was building was of something much different to that of the kind Samaritan doing another human a favor. The revelations made her wonder if he'd paid for her treatment, not out of altruism, but fear that he could be convicted of hurting her if she didn't make it.

"But I did wake up," she said, realizing he must have known about Cam long before she did.

If Shane was right about Calvin's want for child support, he must have figured out who she was early. Like while she was unconscious at the hospital.

If the hospital assumed he was her husband, he could've been making all kinds of medical decisions for her without her knowledge or consent. It made better sense why they allowed Calvin to transfer her to a private facility without follow-up. The hospital thought they were a married couple.

"Yes. You were exhausted and dehydrated," Calvin said. "Seeing you weak was very difficult for all of us and I… All I wanted was for you to get your strength back and as you got better… I started to care for you…

I fell in love with you, Ginger."

He sounded like he meant it and there was a tenderness in his eyes that actually made her want to believe it. So the next time he cupped her face, she stayed put to accept the caress.

"I'd never have known," she said. "If Shane hadn't come to find us, Cam would never have known his father."

"I knew I could offer you a good life and given your medical condition I knew we couldn't be faulted for assuming we were free to marry," he said. "We fell in love, no one can blame us for that."

And if Calvin had decided their relationship wouldn't work before Shane found her, he could void the marriage and not pay a cent to her in the divorce. He could even have brought bigamy charges.

Ginger still didn't understand his need to keep her from her past. How could one person do that to another person? Shane had said if they were secure in their relationship there was no need for one person to have all the control, but Calvin had all the control in their dynamic. Maybe that was something he liked and just the way he was with women, or maybe he was scared, if she found out the truth she'd leave him for her original husband.

If he loved her, she couldn't fault him for being afraid to lose her. But how could he love her and keep such a secret?

She was still thinking about it and about all the times she'd believed in her feelings for Calvin when he leaned in and touched his lips to hers. How could he think about kissing? Calvin pushed and coiled his fingers around her upper arms to draw her closer to him. Ginger turned her face and tried to pull away, but he kept hold of her.

"I love you," he said, "think about the life we had

together, the life we can have together… I know this has been confusing for you, but it's time to stop with the games. Stop playing Warren and I off each other. We're going to get married. That is your future."

Her future. Standing at the altar with Calvin was supposed to be the beginning of a future she wanted. But since being at the lodge, she just couldn't see it anymore. Ginger couldn't imagine going back to Calvin's house with Cam, eating dinner with Diane and being told what was expected of her over the course of the week.

Ginger wanted choice. She wanted to make her own decisions. She didn't want her wants to be questioned and scrutinized.

"No," she breathed out.

Uttering the single word lifted an invisible burden from her shoulders.

Calvin's hands fell from her arms. "No?" he asked like he didn't understand. "No, what?"

"That is not my future," she said, meeting his eye. "I'm not going to marry you, Calvin." And because she wasn't completely heartless, she added, "I'm sorry."

But her apology meant nothing to him; the rage that had subsided earlier came back with a vengeance. His jaw moved to the side and his eyes got dark as they filled with disgust.

"It's him. It's because of him you're saying this."

"No," she said, shaking her head. "This isn't about making a choice between you and Shane. This is me making a decision about what's best for me and my son. I don't believe that a future with you is what's best."

Calvin shot to his feet. "Have you been having sex with him? Have you?"

"No," she said. "This isn't about sex either." Standing up, Ginger didn't feel beholden to him anymore, she felt liberated. "I don't know what's going to happen with me and Shane. But I do know what will happen with you and me and it's this… we're over."

Sucking in a breath, Calvin huffed and grumbled a bit before backing away from her and striding to the door.

"This is not over! I won't give up! I don't lose!" he said, throwing open the dining room door. But his words weren't desperate or filled with love, they were just… angry. "You'll be sorry. You'll all be sorry."

Spinning around, he marched out. From her position, Ginger could see him cross the living room and storm out the front door.

It was a numbing experience to watch him leave. It felt wrong to be relieved and yet, she did feel lighter. Ginger stared at the closed front door for a while, but eventually exhaled. That was it. Over. The only man she'd known for months, the man she'd thought was her savior, was gone. Out of her life.

There was no time to reflect on her decision and she was too emotionally tired to try and make sense of what she'd been told. Ginger had to be present, in the moment, and as her eyes drifted to the side, one conclusion was easy to reach. The table was still a mess; they'd need to do dishes.

Her focus landed on the velvet pouch. Without really thinking about it or shirking her numbness, she began to move toward it. Picking up the soft fabric from where Shane had slammed it down, Ginger opened the drawstring and tipped the jewelry out.

They were beautiful, both of them, and probably expensive too; not that she cared about their price tags. Sliding her wedding ring onto her ring finger, she followed it with her engagement ring, then looked at her hand.

That was it. They were back where they belonged.

She still felt numb.

Dropping the pouch, she wondered if it would be wrong to burn the velvet prison that had kept her rings from her and hidden the truth.

Shane would be worried, but it was Cam she needed to see. Looking into her baby's eyes would prompt her to start feeling again.

Migrating from the dining room, Ginger was clutching her ring finger in her hand as she fixated on the front door. Was Calvin coming back? His things were there, Boyd was there, or maybe he wasn't, she didn't really know.

When Ginger reached the back of the couch, the hairs on the back of her neck prickled up. Instead of being fearful, another emotion began to ooze through her. Love.

"You're supposed to be with Cam," she said, projecting her voice.

Although she could feel him watching, though his exact location was a mystery.

"He's giving his uncles a crash course in bath time," Shane's voice carried from the mezzanine above her. A smile curled her lips as her eyes closed. He'd been watching over her, without being too close to cause aggravation or eavesdrop, he'd just hung around in case. "I'm right outside the door, if he needed me I'd have been there for him in a second."

So he was watching over both of them, standing just closer to their son but in shouting distance of both of them. And just like that, all the angst slid out of her. Leaving the couch, Ginger didn't bother to look up, she walked to the stairs and began to ascend. She saw his shadow in her peripheral vision and as she reached the top of the stairs, he emerged into the light to meet her.

Going straight into his arms, she exhaled and held herself close to him. "How did I ever survive without you, Shay?" she asked because it was like he'd given her the gifts of clarity and peace.

There were so many things they had to deal with, but she wasn't afraid to make decisions. Shane made it okay for her to act. No matter what, he'd always have her back. Her tears warmed her cheeks before she realized they'd flooded her eyes. When she sniffed, he drew back, sliding his hands to her face.

"Hey," he said, crouching to look into her eyes as he wiped the moisture away. "Why the tears? You're sad that it's over with Bishop?" Was that what he thought? That she was crying for the end of her relationship. "You did end it, didn't you?"

She nodded and sniffed again as her nose was running. "I told him it was over."

"Here," Shane said. Offering her a shirt sleeve for her nose, he managed to make her smile again. "I'm sorry you're hurting. Tell me how to make it better and I'll make it better."

"No," she said, shaking her head and wiping her nose on her hand. "I'm not hurt."

Putting her arms around him again, she clung to him, forcing him to hold her. Stroking her hair, he cupped her skull and kissed the top of her head. "I'd rather get kicked in the balls than see you cry, Bit. Please, baby, help me to help you. If you're not hurt, why are you crying?"

Why? For a million reasons, but only one thing came out of her mouth.

"I'm in love with you," she whispered.

Shane stopped stroking her head, but his grip got tighter. "You're... you're in love... with me?" She nodded and sobbed out a wail. He squeezed her tight like he didn't know what the hell else to do. "It's okay. It's okay. We'll... we'll work it out." Shane did his best to soothe her with kisses and murmurs of comfort and eventually her tears began to dry. "Feel better?" She nodded against him. "Good." He kissed her head again and she relaxed into him. "Babe?"

"Mm hmm?" she said, rubbing her face on his shirt just to absorb the smell and security of him.

"Don't take this the wrong way, but I have to ask… Why does being in love with me make you cry?"

"Because it's complicated and terrifying and overwhelming and… I don't know, Shay, I… I have so much more to lose now and I don't know how the hell I'm going to keep it together."

Ginger damned him for asking because her eyes began to heat again. Except before her tears could restart, he took her head to tip it back so he could graze his lips on hers.

"You're not going to lose a damn thing, my precious wife. This is just the beginning," he whispered on her and kissed her again. "I know what will make you feel better. I know what to do now."

What to do? He linked their fingers and led her through her bedroom and into the bathroom where Cam was laughing and splashing both his soaked uncles who were hunkered down on opposite sides of the tub. Owen and Murphy had their arms in the soapy water up to their shoulders and neither had ever looked so frazzled.

"Oh, Cam, Angel, what did you do to your uncles?" she asked, rushing past Shane to get to her son.

"Your kid's a maniac," Murphy said just as Cam launched a duck at him and got him square in the middle of his forehead.

"Cam, no throwing things at Uncle Murphy," Ginger said, urging Murphy aside to stroke Cam's head. "What is it about you that makes my angel want to throw things at you?"

"He can take it," Shane said and clapped his hands. "Right, uncles out, mommy needs some Cam time."

"Have you been crying?" Owen asked her, reaching over the tub to touch her chin with a wet hand.

"Yeah," Shane said. "'Cause us bastards let this beauty cook and walked out without doing the clean-up. Move, both of you, we're going to make this place sparkle."

Murphy went toward Shane and Owen kissed his nephew. Shane stepped back to hold the door.

"Shay," she said, "wait with me a sec."

Murphy stopped in the door. "Oh, hey, nu-uh, bro, you're not sending us down to clean up while you stay up here to have fun with the ball and chain," he said, shoving Shane's shoulder.

Ginger took over holding Cam so Owen could join the others. "Just a sec, Murph," she said, "I promise I'll send him down in just a minute."

Murphy drew an unimpressed, but comical, eye off both of them as Owen nudged him out the door.

"What's up, Bit?" Shane asked when the brothers were out of the bedroom.

"Hold Cam for me," she said.

"Oh-kay..."

Although his eyes went one way as his body went the other, displaying his confusion, Shane came over and bounced into a crouch to take over supporting Cam. Making a face at his son earned him a laugh. Cam held up a duck to his father for a kiss, for some reason that one was special.

True to her word, Ginger was going to send Shane down to help the others, so she leaped to her feet and pulled off her top. It didn't take Shane long to notice her stripping down, but it wasn't an attempt at seduction, she just needed someone to hold Cam. She didn't want to take him out the water just to put him back in when she joined him.

As Shane held a supporting hand around Cam's

back, his eyes travelled up to watch her taking off her clothes.

"Thank you," Ginger said, and lifted a leg to slide it into the water at Cam's back. "Can you grab Raa and toss him in the crib for me? He's downstairs on the couch I think."

Her baby didn't seem to notice her at first then she lifted him to sit on her and he squawked when he dropped his duck. Ginger soothed him and scooped water up over his hair while examining his wound to see how it was healing. Thankfully, it looked good.

"If I split whatever we have in the bank down the middle and transfer it to our brothers," Shane said. "Will you let me get in that water with you two instead of going down to help clean up?"

Reaching past Cam, Ginger gathered up his ducks. "The water's starting to cool," she said. Cam yawned before putting a beak in his mouth. "We'll only be in a few minutes."

Ginger took the duck from Cam's mouth and noticed that Shane didn't seem to be going anywhere.

"It would be worth it for thirty seconds," he said, resting his forearms along the edge of the bathtub and lowering his chin to them.

Turning Cam, she lifted him. "Give Daddy a goodnight kiss, Angel," she said and the boys both did as told.

Keeping hold of Cam with an arm around his torso, she slid toward the middle of the bath and curved an arm around Shane's neck to pull him in for a kiss of her own.

"Will I see you again before bed?" he asked. "Or is Mommy giving me her goodnight kiss too?"

Sometimes when it had been a long day, she just locked her door and stayed in her room to read before going to sleep early.

"Depends how long it takes you to clean up downstairs," she said.

Cam began to wriggle and complain as he set his sights on one specific duck. Ginger moved him through the water to let him get it.

"I could just watch," Shane said.

Laughing, she gave him a shove. "Get downstairs! Stop slacking."

"Right," he said, standing up to straighten his jeans. "Clean up… that's so what I want to be doing now."

Bending over, Shane curled a finger under her chin to kiss her again, then kissed the top of Cam's head.

Shane went toward the door, but stopped to look back at them. "Perfect," he said and departed.

How could Cam be so oblivious to what they had? Ginger rubbed her face in her baby's wet hair and just breathed him in. Life wasn't supposed to turn out that way for them. They were supposed to be married to Calvin and living a life that was opposite to this one in many ways.

Shane hadn't just found her when he walked into the church to stop the wedding, he'd rediscovered their family and they had to find a way to hold it together.

THIRTY-SEVEN

HOLDING IT TOGETHER was going to be easier said than done because she was starting to freak out. Cam had been sleeping for less than an hour and Ginger felt like she was going insane already. What had she been thinking telling Calvin that their relationship was over, just like that? And Shane, what about him? She'd just slid her rings back on her finger like accepting a role as his wife wasn't the biggest decision she'd ever made in her whole life… that she remembered.

And what had Calvin meant about them being sorry? What was he going to do? Was he desperate? She shouldn't have acted on impulse. She should've been more thorough. Arguing and upsetting him could lead to someone getting hurt and it was hanging over their heads, all this emotion, no resolution, just… anger.

Needing to take control, she'd marched into Shane's bedroom and begun to pack his things into the suitcase she found in his closet.

"Am I going somewhere?"

Ginger spun around to see Shane standing in his

bedroom doorway. "Uh…" she said, glancing at the suitcase she had open on the end of his bed. "I… uh…"

"Babe?" he asked, coming inside and closing the bedroom door.

He put a hand on the bathroom door handle as if he planned to close that door too, but she leaped forward.

"No," she called and saw how her panic intrigued him. Tucking her hair behind her ear, she tried to play it cool. "Cam is sleeping… I won't hear him if you close the door."

"Our boy has a healthy set of lungs," he said. "But if it will make you feel better, I'll get his monitor."

"No," she said and dashed forward to catch his wrist to stop him.

Shit. He was looking right through her again. There was more than intrigue in his eyes, he was downright worried.

"Bit, what's going on?"

"Nothing, I… Just go sit with him, will you? I'll be done in a minute."

"Packing my things?" Shane asked, glancing from the open dresser drawer to the half-full suitcase on the bed.

Ginger couldn't stand under his scrutiny any longer. So she busied herself by going to the terrace door to check that it was locked, even though she'd already checked it twice. With Shane in the room, she could lock his bedroom door too, so she went past him to do just that.

Taking a deep breath, Ginger spun around to sink against the door. "I want you to move in with Cam and I," she said.

His face blanked. "I'm sorry, did you just say you were fulfilling my ultimate fantasy?"

Some of her tension ebbed as she exhaled a

laugh. "Not for sex," Ginger said, though she struggled to figure out how she could be part of anyone's fantasy. "It's about safety in numbers."

"Safety?" he said and lost his edge of teasing to rush to her. "You're worried about your safety?" He didn't let her answer. "Pack everything and we can be back in California before sunrise."

Damn, she'd scared him. "No," she said, moving forward to put her arms around him. "Doctor Guinness is in his room. We shouldn't disturb him; he requested the night off."

"Sorry, Bit, but I don't give a damn about the doctor. If you feel unsafe here, we're leaving, it's as simple as that."

No, it wasn't. They had responsibilities to think of… and she wasn't ready to leave yet. Rather, she wasn't ready to be in California yet.

"Cam is sleeping," she said. "If we wake him up, he'll be scared."

"He won't be scared, not with us, he knows we protect him. Besides, I'll bring the truck down the hill, right to the door, and if I lift him carefully, he won't wake up."

Admitting her actions were part of her illness, Ginger tried to control her paranoia. "Shay," she sighed, pinching his shirt to bring him closer. "This is just me freaking out… I don't like knowing that Calvin is out there upset."

"You think he might try to hurt you? That's why you're checking the locks?"

"I'm just being paranoid," she said. Just having his body against hers was starting to relax her. "You're right, forget it, you can stay here."

"No, no way," he said. "You can't take it back now, you already asked me."

Pushing her back to the door, Shane bent his

knees to line his mouth up with hers. After a breath, he teased her lips with his, taking his time about raising the simmer within her to a boil.

"You never answered," she said, gasping for oxygen as she freed herself from their kiss. "I can withdraw the offer before it's been accepted."

"Not with me, wife. I accept," he said, kissing her left, then right. Pressing his palms into hers, he threaded their fingers together and raised her hands to push them into the door. His eyes flicked to the side. "You're wearing your wedding ring."

"I put them back on downstairs," she said. The pulse of her blood was stretching her veins; she did her best to push onto her tiptoes. It wasn't fair that he was constantly coming down to her level, but Ginger didn't want to part her mouth from his. "I'm thinking maybe I was premature."

"No," he said, dismissing her with a scowl and sliding his tongue into her mouth. "You said you loved me."

Tracing his lips along her jaw, Shane let them descend over the fading bruise he'd put on her skin.

"I'm not sure I'm ready… that I'm prepared to be your wife."

"Prepared?" he asked. "You are my wife, that's all the preparation you need. And you are all I need, Bit. You and Cam, that's it."

His next kiss brought him lower still and when his lips made contact with her throat, he slid his hands beneath her ass and lifted her up. Ginger wrapped her arms around him, letting him carry her over to his bed. Because of the case, they couldn't lie the right way, so he put her on her back parallel to the headboard in the middle of the bed. The reassuring weight of his body pressing her down made her feel safer straight away.

The glide of his hands on her thighs reminded

her that she was only wearing her satin jammies, shorts with a lace-trimmed vest in smooth gray fabric. He adjusted the angle of her pelvis so he could rock against her, stimulating them both with the ridge in his jeans.

As his need grew, so did the pressure of his hips. He skimmed his hands up her sides to stretch her arms up high above her head, keeping her at his mercy. It was interesting to have her wrists stacked, locked inside the grip of one of his large hands as the other slid back down her body, over her breast and… oh… she gasped when he pushed his hand under the waistband of her shorts to cup her sex.

"Where do you want me, baby?" he asked, toying with her clit. He kissed her lips with such delicate pressure that she almost forgot to breathe. "Do you want me inside you?"

"I…" she inhaled, elevating her head for another kiss. "I'm not ready for…"

"Not my dick," he said, "like this."

Extending his fingers, he caressed the circumference of her opening and then pushed his digit inside. Her mouth opened wide, but she forgot to inhale and instead just squeaked. Her eyes fixed on his, heavy and enamored, he appeared ensnared.

"Boo," she managed to murmur.

"I love it when you forget to breathe like that," he said, nuzzling her cheek. "Tells me I've got you right where I want you." His finger moved deeper and he wiggled it, testing the limits of her passage. That was the most intimate she remembered ever getting with any man. It felt more than good, it was… sublime. "I'm going to take your shorts off, okay, Bit? My mouth is going to feel so good on your pussy. You're going to—"

"You… you can't do that," she said.

Panic and arousal were fighting to take over her heartbeat, but his implication only made her pulse skyrocket.

"I won't hurt you. I want to make you feel good."

"You do," she said, trying to find his mouth, but he chose to nibble and suck on her neck instead. Damn, why did he do that? When he did that she wanted to sign herself over to him heart and soul. "Do you have condoms?"

Shane rose to look into her eyes. His finger slid free of her body, but stayed in her folds. "What?" he asked. "No, I said to you—"

She sagged. "We can't have sex without a condom. I'm not on birth control, breast feeding works as a natural contraceptive, kind of, but it's not reliable. My cycle is back to normal and if my math is right, I'm ripe right now. We can't have sex without birth control or you'll knock me up." He grinned. "No." Even though she used her stern mommy voice, she wasn't sure he heard her. "We're being patient, Boo. We're not rushing things."

"Are you saying… Are you saying you're ready to have sex?"

Was she? No, not exactly. When she could think clearly, Ginger knew it was a bad idea to rush into having sex with her husband. God, that sounded so dumb. He was her husband. If she was going to rush into sex with anyone, he was the best bet.

"Maybe," she admitted. "I don't know. I just know that when you touch me and kiss me… it feels good. So if something were to happen naturally, you know, without any pressure… I might be okay with that."

It was like his whole body clenched. Like he was a teenager trying to contain his excitement in front of his friends. That didn't last long. Turned out, Shane wasn't so good at playing it cool when it came to her and sex.

"We'll get you on the pill. I can have it couriered

here tomorrow and—"

"Great, but I have to take it for seven days before it works," she said. If they both knew the boundaries, they could both be responsible for respecting them. "So we'll have to hold off for seven days."

He thought about that for a second. "I can go ask Murphy, see if he has any rubbers."

She laughed and tugged on her arms. "Try explaining that one to him."

"We'll just tell him the truth… It's not like I'd be using them with anyone except you," he asked, moving onto his side, though his hips didn't go far. His long, strong legs stayed between hers, pinning one down and scooping the other over the top of his knees. "They probably have them in the lodge—"

"What's the urgency?" she asked, teasing while at the same time wishing she hadn't been so honest about her availability.

"For sex?" he asked. Ginger was horrified when he touched his fingertips to his lips. The fingers that had been playing with her. "I believe the word you used was 'ripe.' Since I heard that, I feel it's my duty to—"

"No, it's not," she said, pulling his hand away from his mouth as he was about to slide his fingers past his lips. "Don't do that."

"Your sweet taste is mine now," he said and tried to lean forward, but she called out and pulled harder, while throwing herself onto him. "Do you want some?" He made contact with her lips. "We can share."

"Shane!" she said, trying to push his hand down.

"Ah, you want me to finish," he said, taking their playfulness to a new level. "Open wide for me."

Somehow, he managed to scoop both hands into her inner thighs and open her legs wide as he rolled onto his back and pulled her on top of him. "I don't—"She battled with his playful hands as they tried to creep into her shorts. "I didn't—Shane! Stop!"

Her face hurt with the breadth of her smile and her chest ached as she gasped for breath through her laughter. He was persisting, trying to get his way, but he wasn't really fighting her or using his full strength. If he wanted to force her to submit, he could, he'd had her pinned down just a minute ago. As it was, she was on top of him, so technically, to get him to stop, all she had to do was stand up and leave him on the bed.

"Okay, I see I'll have to come at this a different way," he said and tugged his hands out of hers to grab the cleavage of her flimsy top. Pulling hard he ripped the fabric apart, right down the middle. Ginger was so stunned that she froze, her mouth open, her top hanging from her shoulders in tatters on its spaghetti straps.

With wide eyes, Shane was waiting, without breathing, for her to react. "Too much?"

"Definitely too much," she gasped in and bowed over him to grab his face, forcing him to kiss her.

It was too much because it was perfect. It was too much because it aroused her and tested the limits of her restraint.

Inhaling hard, Ginger squeezed his face and growled against his mouth. "Play with me," she asked and dug her teeth into her chin.

"You got it," he replied and sat up.

It was a scramble to get him out of his tee-shirt and shed her torn top from her shoulders. A flash later, Shane had his strong arm locked around the small of her back. Lifting her up, he twisted them around to put her beneath him. They were going to do this. She was going to have sex!

With hot, wonderful, sweet, delectable Shane!

Pulling on the buttons on his jeans, she tried to get her hands on him, but was stopped by his belt. While trying to keep up with the urgency of his kiss, she fumbled for the buckle.

"Shane," she panted. "Shane, please, Boo. I need you!"

"You got me, baby. You got me," he said, pushing up to grab for his own buckle to help her out. There was a knock on the door. "Leave it."

Without finishing with the buckle, Shane flattened himself on her and drove his tongue into her mouth again.

Oh, she wanted to leave it, to ignore the knocking even as it came again. But the sound reminded her of where they were and why having sex would be a crazy decision.

"Wait," Ginger said, pushing on Shane's chest. "We're not meant to do this, not here like this tonight."

"We're not?" he panted, his skin flushed, his eyes crazy in their swamp of desperate need. "But you're ripe."

It was intoxicating to have such an effect on Shane. While he couldn't be accused of being calm and reasoned when it came to sex and his wife, Ginger was seduced by his dedication to her.

"Maybe that's why…" she said. "Maybe the time isn't right for—"

"Shane!" Owen called through the bedroom door.

"Shit," Shane said. "Fuck! Shit!"

"Shh," she whispered, half-subduing her giggle and running her hands up his sides. "He can probably hear you."

Her smile didn't help his irritation. "If I tell him I'm getting laid he'll fuck off!" Shane said, whispering until he got to the last two words, which he tipped his head back to yell.

"Shh," she said again, pressing her hand to his mouth. "Cam will hear you, and please don't swear at

Owen, it's not his fault that I'm frigid."

"Oh, baby, you're anything but that," he said behind her hand and tried to pull it away to kiss her, but she switched it with the other. "Let me show you how sexually liberated you are."

Hooking his hands under her thighs, Shane wrenched her legs up and open, tightening them over his hips.

"Please talk to Owen," she said, using her arms to balance her weight as she rose to kiss his shoulder. "I can't relax with him right outside the door. And you have to take Rocky out anyway."

"Murph took him out before I came up," Shane said, but exhaled and bolted from the bed to storm over to the door.

He thought he'd covered his bases and then they were interrupted anyway. The poor guy must think the whole universe was conspiring to ensure he didn't get any. Shane unlocked the door and yanked it open so abruptly he might have broken the hinge if he hadn't stopped it less than a foot later.

"My sister been leaning on you again?"

Ginger didn't get it, but Shane looked down and she guessed he was sporting the evidence of what they'd been doing. "You come here to tell me something or stare at my boner? I'll send you a picture, it'll last longer."

"I guess she shut you down," Owen said, enjoying Shane's irritation too much. "Dick pics don't really do it for me, but thanks for that terrifying offer."

"What do you want, Owe? I'm not in the mood to play."

Funny, he had been a moment ago. Shane propped a horizontal forearm on the door and rested his forehead on it. The poor guy was probably ragged from the emotional rollercoaster they'd been riding. Ginger hadn't taken enough time to consider his feelings throughout everything.

"We thought that with the doctor in his room and the two stooges gone, we might sit down as a family and figure this out. Is Cam okay?"

"He's sleeping," Shane said. "I'm kinda beat, can we do it tomorrow?"

"It's eight thirty, Shane," Owen said, not falling for the tiredness excuse. "Either my sister is in your bed now or you're hoping to climb into hers, whichever it is, it can wait… We need a strategy. Murphy and I are swinging in the wind. We don't have a fucking clue what's going on. Bishop or Boyd could come back any minute, are they welcome? Are we letting them back in here? And what about the doctor? What are we telling him? He's going to want to know what's going on… And, hey, I got a bonus for you, I can't knock on Gin's door this late, I don't want to wake up Cam. So I'm giving you an excuse to go through there and talk to her."

"Okay," Shane said. "I'll talk to my wife tonight. The rest of you bastards can wait until morning. Gin has been through enough today. I'm not asking her to go through more drama this late. We'll have a session tomorrow, around the fire like the early days."

"Us? Or everyone?"

"Us," Shane said. "Bishop won't come back here tonight. I'm damn sure on that. He's all bark and no balls. He's a prick, but he's not stupid. You think Murph and me would have any trouble taking him and that dipshit lawyer on if they threatened us?"

Ginger shivered. It was wrong that she was turned on by how adamant Shane was about taking control and protecting his family. But damn it, his vehemence scorched her.

"Okay," Owen said, giving up. "But if you're wrong—"

"Lock all the doors, keep the place secure,"

Shane said. "If he comes back, come find me."

"And you'll knock him out? How will Ginger feel about that?"

"I'm about to ask her, ain't I?" Shane said. "Goodnight, Owe." Shane closed the door. Ginger pushed onto her elbow when he started to walk, she held up a hand to stall him, so he stopped. "What?"

Putting a finger to her lips, Ginger waited until Owen had time to leave the hallway and then she got to her feet.

"I might need your credit cards after all."

"Why?" he asked. "I mean they're yours but—"

"Calvin was paying for all of this, wasn't he?" she said. "The doctor, the chalet, the whole retreat and without—"

"Don't think about money," he said, holding out a hand for hers.

Ginger went over to give him her hand and he used the connection to tug her body to his. "Do we need to talk?" she asked, nestling against him.

"All you have to do is tell me what you want me to do if Bishop comes back," he said and rubbed his mouth in the top of her head to murmur. "Can I knock him out?"

She couldn't tell if he was joking or if that was genuine hope in his voice, either way it made her smile.

"No, you can't. We're going to be civil, no gloating or crowing, be magnanimous."

"Magnanimous, right…" Shane said, his chin moving in her hair as he nodded. "How do I do that?"

"By not mentioning me if at all possible, or Cam. You're walking away from this with a wife and child. Whatever way you look at it, his house is going to be emptier when he goes back to it."

"I'll send him a hooker," Shane grumbled.

While he probably meant that as a polite gesture,

she turned it into a tease. "Oh yeah?" she said. "Is that all it takes to replace me and my beautiful son? A quick roll in the hay with a stranger? Thank goodness Cam is young enough not to be influenced by your lack of sentimentality... yet."

"You better be grateful to my sentimentality," Shane said, sliding his arms up her back and beginning to sway like they were dancing, except there was no music. "It's my sentimentality that's stopping me from putting you on your back again right here."

"Oh yeah?" she asked, smiling as she lifted her chin to see his smirk. "You think you could make me give it up?"

"Sure," he said, pulling her tighter to him to keep on dancing. "Sorry to tell you this, but you're easy, Bit."

"Uh, you're talking to the woman who's coming up for seventeen months celibate."

"You're not the only one," he muttered. "I might need some alone time in the shower tonight before we go to bed."

"We?" she asked, kissing his pec. "Who said 'we' are going to bed together?"

"You did, when you asked me to move in with you."

She had asked that before he'd helped to relax her. "How about a compromise," she said. "The bath... you wanted to join us earlier right, will you settle for just me?"

"Every time," he said. "Will you let me help you come?"

"Maybe," she said. "If you promise to be patient about the other stuff."

"Deal," he said and gave her ass a squeeze with both hands before letting her go so she could run the bath. Before she got to the bathroom door, he spoke again. "You're still going to let me sleep with you."

He hadn't even turned around and although his voice was playful there was also a command in it that made her inhale her arousal. Hugging herself against the doorframe, Ginger admired how perfect his muscular back was and wondered what they'd be doing if she'd gotten his belt off on time. Could that be the difference between giving their second child life and not?

"Probably," she whispered, then turned her mouth to the back of her hand that was supporting her against the wood.

Shane turned and looked over his shoulder at her. "I love you, Bit. I'll push you sometimes and I'll piss you off, but don't underestimate how much I love you and how far I'd go to keep you and Cam safe."

Slowly, Ginger let herself grin and took her mouth from her hand. "Smooth," she said. "Though I told you you're not getting laid, Warren."

He scoffed like he was all innocent and offended. "A husband tells his wife he loves her and suddenly it's sinister."

"A husband," she muttered, smirking as she turned her back to sashay into the bathroom to fill the tub.

Yes, her husband was a pro at pushing her buttons, but she was getting wise to his tactics and playing with him was a lot of fun.

THIRTY-EIGHT

SO MUCH FUN that she actually struggled to stop doing it. After breakfast the next morning, Cam was out back playing with Murphy and Rocky while Shane washed up the dishes. Ginger had just come down the stairs and rounded the banister when she noticed her man with his back to her, his hands in the suds.

Oh, that back, she loved that back, so broad and strong. Recalling the lines of his muscles and the texture of his skin, she bit her lip and tiptoed forward. He was her husband, right? No one cared what they did with each other. No one was around to care anyway. They'd asked Doctor Guinness for a fireplace session before lunch, so they still had some time.

Shane didn't notice her, or at least he didn't turn around. Using the element of surprise, she grabbed the hem of his shirt and pulled it up over her head to press her face against his spine. He laughed, but she pulled the shirt down over her shoulders and traced her lips on his skin. Letting her hands snake around to spread on his ridged abdomen, she slid them up to his chest, and stuck out her tongue to trace the tip upwards.

"Is that my sister inside your tee-shirt?" Owen's voice came from not too far away.

Damn, she was busted. With the damage done, she figured there was no need to stop rubbing herself on her husband.

"I hope so," Shane said and then raised his voice to call out. "Gin! There's a woman in my shirt with me. If it's not you, you better get down here and kick her ass!" Purring, she opened her mouth wide and dug her teeth into him. "Yeah, it's her."

"I know that 'cause I can see her… some of her," Owen said. "How do you know it?"

There was a casual joy in Shane's voice when he spoke like a content man. "You think I don't know how my wife's mouth feels?" he asked. It seemed he was still just washing up as if this was behavior he expected from her… and remembering how the blonde had approached his sleeping form, maybe it was. "The way she smells? How she wriggles and presses herself into me like that when she's horny?"

"I'm not horny," she objected, her voice breathy.

Her lip ran across one of his back muscles and both of her hands descended to cup his package through his jeans.

"Yeah, Bit, you're not horny," Shane said.

Just to make him feel some of her pain, she began to rub his dick through the denim.

It was his fault that she felt so good. He'd made her come with his hands in the tub and again in bed when he snuck between her sheets after she said no. Though she hadn't really meant no and was grateful that he knew that.

Then that morning, she'd been feeding Cam when Shane woke up and maneuvered her forward so he could sit at her back, nestling her and Cam between his thighs.

With his arms around her, Ginger felt invincible. The pride she had in her little family was doing things to her, and making her feel things, that weren't motherly at all. She'd been a mother for months; being a wife was still new to her.

"I guess your talk last night went well," Owen said. "Did you talk at all or did you just have sex?"

"Just sex," Shane said. "We're paying the doc for the talking. Sex is free, so we do that on our own time."

Tugging his shirt over her head, Ginger backed away, running her fingers into her hair to straighten it.

"We did not have sex!" she said to his back and then looked to Owen who was just inside the back door. "We didn't."

"Murph and I just want to know what's going on," Owen said. "We came all this way to…"

She didn't like the way her brother trailed off or looked at Shane as if he needed to be bailed out. "Fix me," she said. "And I'm still broken… I don't have my memories back." Shane emptied the water from the sink and began to wash his hands. Owen was still looking at her with a pity that made her feel inadequate. "I'm sorry I'm such a disappointment." Taking a step back, Ginger started to get annoyed with herself. "I've done it again, haven't I? I got caught up in my attraction to Shane and I… I forgot that's not the point." Tugging a length of her hair in one hand, she twisted it with the other. "Oh, God, I'm being a hussy and not thinking about my baby and what's best for—"

"That's not what he was saying," Shane said, coming to her to cup her elbows. "You know I'm a good father, don't you?" Ginger nodded. "You know that I love Cam more than anything. I'd protect him with my life." She nodded again. "And you've seen the paternity; I am his biological father. There's no doubt about that, right?"

"Right," she murmured.

"So if you're going to fall in love with any guy, I'd say I'm the best candidate for the job."

Looking past her husband, Ginger met her brother's knowing eyes. "I told Owen I was in love with you," she whispered. Owen's shock matched Shane's, probably because she'd told him it was a secret. "On carbonara night, before I... before I ended my relationship with Calvin."

"That's okay," Shane said, smoothing a thumb over her cheek as Owen's jaw fell. "I'm happy that you were sure before you told me."

"You told him!" Owen gasped and rushed forward a few steps. "When did this happen?"

Panic made her frantic gaze seek out Shane's calm one. "I've messed this up, haven't I?" she said.

Shane smiled. "Messed what up? Us? I told you it wasn't possible for you to lose me and Cam's great. You haven't messed anything up, Bit."

"This therapy thing, I've messed that up," she said. "I was supposed to make decisions about the future based on what was best for Cam."

It was amazing how patient he was with her. Her husband didn't show restraint with any other adult.

"We are best for Cam," Shane said. "His mother and father together and in love, that's what's best for Cam."

"But I'm still... broken."

Shane didn't argue with her, but he did consider her for a second. "Remember you told me you'd have faith?" he asked. "On carbonara night?"

"Yes."

"I need you to have faith now and trust me," he said. "I want to show you something... something I bought for you." The last part was added as if he knew

Owen might turn the first part into something kinky. "And if you're willing to trust me, I want to go back to the start of this… I want you to get in the water with me."

Taking a reflexive step back, Ginger immediately tensed. "I can't… I can't do that. Calvin tried to—"

"I'm not Calvin," Shane said. Understanding why he was doing the patient thing, she realized he was trying to manipulate her. "I know this is a big deal for you, for both of us. I got you a swimsuit the same day we got Cam's. But he's going to stay here on dry land with his uncles—"

"And if something happens to both of us out there, he'll have no parents—"

"Nothing will happen," Shane said, stroking her arms. "We're only going to stay in the shallow water, okay? You know how close the shore is. We're only going to go as far as you're comfortable with, you don't have to do it all at once."

Ginger didn't think she could. Any time she tried to get into external water she'd failed. She'd got as far as getting a toe wet and then she tensed and freaked and ran away from the danger.

"Shane, I… I don't think I can."

He dipped to kiss her. "All I want you to do is try. If you can't do it, that's okay. But there's nothing dangerous about changing into a swimsuit and walking to the edge of the water with me, is there?"

Not technically, but her anxiety was soaring.

Ginger tightened her grip on her hair. "It scares me," she whispered. "The water… scares me."

"I know," he said, cupping her jaw. "But I'm going to be with you and you have to think about Cam… You want to get over this for him, don't you? Just like you said."

She had to fix herself. Ginger was tired of being

broken. Even if she could never jump in and swim like she apparently used to, continuing to have the same extreme reaction to the idea of Cam going near water could be damaging to him. He'd probably go swimming at school or with clubs. His friends would want to have pool parties and go to the beach. If she was too scared to let him near those events, her anxiety would transfer to him. Ginger didn't want her baby to feel that way. Never.

Steeling herself, Ginger pushed back her shoulders. "I'll get changed," she said and both men exhaled rushed sounds of relief. "I'm not making any promises, Shane. I'll just… I'll try."

"That's all I want, Bit," he said and moved in to kiss her head. "That's all I want."

THIRTY-NINE

IT WAS A BAD IDEA.

A terrible idea.

Ginger was already cold as she stood on the pebbles that made up the lake shore. Shane was in the water up to his knees with his back to the lake and his arms stretched toward her.

"You've done amazing," he said and his beaming smile was genuine. Ginger felt like an idiot, at least, she would if she could slow down her heart. "And you look fucking hot."

Trying to control her breathing, she didn't want him to distract her. "Please don't flirt with me," she said, eyeing the water behind him. "I can't concentrate when you flirt with me."

She'd tied her hair up on top of her head, though why she'd bothered was a mystery. There was no way she had a chance in hell of getting in further than her ankles.

"I know what you mean," Shane said, wading back another few feet. "I can't concentrate with that hot figure wrapped in spandex right in front of me."

It wasn't spandex, but she wasn't going to correct him, not while he was still getting deeper.

"As you keep reminding me over and over, you've seen me naked, Shane."

"I have, so if you want to skinny dip," he said and stuck both thumbs into the waistband of his shorts. Gasping, Ginger took a step forward intending to stop him. Except when she felt the water on her feet, she squawked and retreated. Shane laughed. "You make the same sound Cam does when he gets a fright."

"This isn't funny, Shay," she said, pissed off that he could smile. "Life might be one big joke to you, but I'm actually not laughing right now."

Shane straightened his face. "I'm sorry, baby. You're right," he said, walking toward her. "I wasn't laughing at you. It was nice to see him in you, that's all." When he got near the edge, he held out his arms again. "Will you take my hands?"

She didn't want to take his hands. Doing that would mean dropping her arms from their embrace of her body and trying to combat her irrational craziness.

"If I take your hands, will you let me go back to the house?" she asked. "Can that be enough for today?"

"If you want," he said. "Or you could try taking a step toward me."

Cam was approaching the age when they'd be trying to guide his steps. At the moment, he was a crawler who could pull himself up on furniture as long as the angles were right. Her baby struggled every day, he had to push himself to learn new things and had to keep going even when he fell down time and time again.

Loosening her arms, she slowly let her hands rise until they slipped over Shane's. "Don't let go of me," she said.

"Not a chance in hell of that," he said and squeezed her hands. There was an odd kind of pride glowing out of him. All laughter and amusement was gone. "Now just walk forward, Bit. One step at a time, slow as you like."

Swallowing didn't help her dry mouth, but she did it anyway and fixed her eyes on his. "Maybe if I pretend we're in bed my crazy heart rate will seem normal," she said, putting a smile on his face. "Usually you're the only one who gets it going this fast."

She'd told him not to flirt and there she was doing it. Kind of.

Shane didn't point out her hypocrisy, he just returned her teasing. "If you come over here, I'll make sure you get a reward usually reserved for the bedroom," he said.

Flirting and fighting were sort of their specialties. "Have we ever done it in water?" she asked, edging forward to let her toes get wet.

"A bunch of times," he said. "We have a—or maybe had, I guess, a pool on the roof of our building."

The roof Owen had said Shane owned. The lake water was cold as it lapped over her feet. No big deal, she told herself. She got wetter when she was in the bathtub. The bath-water was never that cold, but yeah, it was just water, just like being in the tub. Ginger inched forward, forcing herself to take steps until the water was over her ankles.

Looking into his eyes and talking helped her to forget about the movement of the cold water on her legs. "You said I used to like the water."

"You did," he said, still holding her hands tight. "You took part in triathlons all the time, it was your thing. And we used to have endurance battles."

"We seem to battle a lot," she said, doing her best to keep moving a tiny bit at a time.

Her teeth began to chatter either because of the temperature of the water or the adrenaline coursing through her.

"In good fun," he said. "If I let you win, I got lots of sex."

"And if you won?"

He grinned. "Then you got lots of sex." Seemed like a win-win. She squeezed him hard when the water sloshed over her knees. "You're doing good, baby, amazing. Just keep those eyes on me."

"Something's been bugging me," she said, letting him guide her forward again.

"What's that, Bit?"

"What did we fight about?" A flash of concern crossed his features, maybe it wasn't smart to be talking about it, given where they were and what they were trying to accomplish, but she had to know. "The night the Gem went down… what did you say that upset me?"

"Bit, I—"

"I want to know," she said. "I did this for you, and you said in the church that you'd tell me anything I wanted to know. I want to know this."

Shane had said that and must've remembered, because although his jaw ticked, he answered, "I said you were distracting me on purpose… That other men's wives knew their place and didn't get in the way of their men while they were doing business."

If they'd been anywhere else, she'd have pulled away from him. Although he'd been reluctant, it actually worked out for him that he was telling her there because she couldn't run away from him.

"Knew their place?"

He nodded. "Mistresses, call girls, they can wave their tits in the guys' faces and get their attention. Wives are supposed to sit down and shut up. They're not supposed to wear skimpy little bikinis that make their husbands, and all his buddies, think about sex. They're not supposed to smile and flirt and tease like tempting little sexpots whose joy in life is to tease cock." Ginger's anger burned in her chest, her mouth opened, then it closed, she glared until she was spitting fury. How dare he? Who the hell did he think he was to speak to her that way? To speak to her like that! She was his wife. She deserved respect! "I told you the other guys wives stayed the fuck out the way and let their husbands do men's work. But with you strutting that stacked little body around the deck all day I couldn't form a fucking sentence let alone make a deal."

"You bastard!" she said. "How dare you speak to me that way!"

Just as Ginger was about to pull her hand away, he yanked her forward and pinned her body against his to steal a kiss that tipped her head so far back her neck hurt. His tongue went deep, it was warm and solid in stark contrast to the cold, fluid water lapping her chest. Her chest!

Shoving away, Ginger looked left and right. They were in the water. She was in the water!

"Oh my God, Boo!" she screamed with overwhelming delight and leaped up onto him with such force that she knocked him backwards.

Ginger wrapped her legs and arms around him and kissed him with everything she had. He'd brought her out there, distracted her, tormented her with the story of how he'd been so disrespectful and riled her with that despicable language and…

Breaking the kiss, she blinked at him. "It was foreplay," she gasped and his smile was quick. "We were fighting, but… You were talking to me like that to make me mad… it was foreplay."

"You always did like smacking me down in the sack," he said and curled his hand around the back of her head. "You would've put me in my place damn fast if you'd had the chance to reply… If we'd really been fighting that night, like for real fighting, I don't think I'd have gotten this far."

"The guilt," she said, moving her hands to his shoulders. "Boo, it wasn't your fault. It was never your fault. And I don't care what happens to me in the future, or to our relationship, you should never hurt yourself, never even think about it."

"Would've been easy for a guy like me to go into the mountains and never come back... accidents happen."

"It wouldn't have been an accident, though, would it?" she asked, curving one arm around his shoulder as she ran her other fingers through his hair. "Why didn't you give up on me?"

"It never occurred to me for a second that you weren't out there, somewhere," he said. "Other people thought I was nuts, law enforcement, the media, everyone. But I just... I couldn't comprehend a world that didn't have you in it. That would be like a world without gravity... a world without oxygen... It wouldn't be possible to survive without those things. Just like it wouldn't be possible for me to exist in any world without you. You are my oxygen. I knew, as long as I was still breathing, you were still breathing."

Her love overflowed and as she searched inside of him she was seared by the heat of his. "I love you, Boo," she whispered and brushed her lips over his. "I love you... Thank you for this. For sticking by me. For finding me. For giving me Cameron. For everything."

Typical Shane, he played down the enormity of what he'd done for her. "It was an endurance battle, that was all," he said, squeezing her. "All I had to do was keep going. Every day. I had to keep going. Just one more step, one more inch... You got me up Everest, baby. Thinking of you has kept me alive in the world's harshest climates. You think I couldn't handle a little game of hide and seek when you were the prize? You were the ultimate summit, Bit. The only one that ever mattered."

Her eyes and her heart were warm as her skin froze. Being in his arms, Ginger got it, she understood, the love, the intimacy. It was a connection so deep that there would be no limit, no stretch too far. He would never have given up on her. Never.

She couldn't give up on him. "Boo, you make me strong, give me confidence, make me whole. I want to make you happy."

"You want to try to swim for me?" he asked. It seemed like the least she could do, but Ginger tensed around him. "I'm not asking you to swim far, just enough. I need to know, Bit, for my sanity… I need to know that you can do it."

In case anything happens again. He didn't say it, but she saw it in his eyes. His greatest fear was anything happening to her.

"I'll try."

Sliding down his body, Ginger found the uneven surface of the lake bed and stood on her tiptoes in the deep water. Shane kept her hands as long as he could but eventually only their fingertips were touching and he paused, making eye contact for the longest time before letting their hands part.

Without him there, she panicked, and when he sank back to tread water, she began to fear what might happen to him. She wouldn't be able to save him if anything went wrong, she wouldn't be able to pull him out, he was too heavy.

"Come on, Bit," Shane said, gesturing to her. "You can do it."

It was only a couple of meters. Two or three strokes should be enough to do it. Clenching her jaw, she thought of Cam. He needed to see his mommy do it. He needed to know he'd be safe; that the water was fun and not to be feared.

Telling herself just to go and to stop overanalyzing, Ginger lunged forward in the water, trying to stretch herself flat and kick her legs. She went under. All the way under. Shock opened her mouth, so her lungs took a shot of water. In a flash, she was out again, breaking the surface with a strong arm hooked around her waist.

Coughing the water from her lungs, she sputtered and clung to the buoy that had pulled her free.

"Breathe for me, baby," Shane said, his voice stern. "Take a breath in; breathe in."

Blinking her webbed lashes, Ginger found his eyes and the fear in them made her cling tighter. "Shane," she gasped.

"I've got you, baby," he said. "Shit, I'm sorry. Shit! Fuck! I'm sorry, Bit. Please, breathe for me."

She was breathing, just not evenly. When he began to drag her back toward the shore something in her snapped.

Ginger pulled away. "No!" she said and dropped her feet onto the bottom.

"We're done, Bit. I'm taking you back to the chalet," he said. "We need to get you warm and—"

"If I go inside now, I'll never come back out here."

Determination gave her limbs heat and her mind purpose.

Shane pulled her body close to his. "I should've been there to pull you out that night too," he said. "This is what should've happened then… I should've been beside you to pull you up, to keep you safe, to protect you."

It was what should've happened, but it didn't. Her demons weren't the only ones in the water with them. Something flashed in her mind, the blackness, the icy bite seizing her skin…

"I was pulled down, into the black water," she whispered, sensing the emotion that had plagued her. "I kept thinking of you, of love, that was what made me kick and… by the time I broke the surface… I was alone and exhausted. But I swam, Shane, I called out for you and I… I swam."

"You remember?" he asked, his guilt sidelined by surprise.

It was like a flashback, pictures in her mind that made sense, but… didn't. "I swam for as long as I could… I was pulled out of the water by… men… I… I don't know when or who they were. They took me back to shore, they weren't speaking English, I don't know who they were… I don't know what they were planning, but they put me in a truck. Something didn't feel right so when they stopped… I ran… I don't know why, I just… ran. I was in a forest… I was there at night. I was cold and scared and… I kept thinking of how scared you'd be… and I…" Her eyes rose to his as she recalled the ball of grief in her gut. "I was terrified that I might have lost you. That maybe you hadn't made it out the water."

"If you remembered me then… the amnesia didn't happen in the water. It was the trauma or…"

Calvin hitting her with his car had knocked her unconscious, that could've been it, or maybe it was a culmination of the physical exertion and the psychological trauma. Whatever it was, it didn't matter. Shane kept his arms around her even when her own hands fell to her belly.

"What if something had happened to him," she whispered because her thoughts were never far from her baby. "What if I had lost him and… lost you."

"You didn't lose either of us, you have both of us," he said. "Let's go back inside and—"

"No," she said.

Sweeping an arm out to move him aside, she fixated on the vast expanse of water in front of her. Ginger was terrified. She hadn't suddenly lost her fear. The memory of going under and breaking the surface remained with her. That terror followed by the relief. But she breathed in deep, ignoring her aching lungs. In a more controlled manner, she fell forward, pushing off the lake bed with grace that had to come from muscle memory.

She had to swim. Had to prove it was possible and… she did.

Focusing on the line where the lake met the mountains, Ginger glided through the water, kicking and moving her arms in practiced moves that felt familiar.

The further she got the more she pushed and her motion became less clumsy and more finessed. Taking a breath before she turned her head into the water, she counted silently and turned her face to take another breath. Yes, somehow her body remembered and she was doing it.

It wasn't just relief that flooded her when she finally took stock of what was happening, it was joy and pride. Everything that she'd battled dwindled to a manageable load. What couldn't she face? That was her greatest fear, and there she was, taking control.

Slowing down, she eventually stopped, but had to tread water because the lake bed wasn't under her feet anymore. When she turned, Ginger saw that Shane was just a few meters behind her. When she stopped, so did he.

"You can't tell, but I have the boner of the fucking century going on over here," he called to her.

Somehow she doubted that in the cold water, but she laughed and thrust up to sink down onto her back, letting the water take her weight. Ginger stayed that way until Shane got to her; then she draped an arm around him and began to tread again. Their limbs collided and they sank lower in the water; but they made it work and kept each other up.

"Mama!"

The sound tensed her for a second. It was loud, echoing off the mountains, so it seemed close. Shane must have felt her clench because he brushed his fingers across her jaw and moved aside to point back to shore. There he was on dry land. Cam was in Owen's arms with Murphy and Doctor Guinness at their side too.

"I'm ready to go home," she said, watching her son wave frantically at his parents with his uncles' encouragement.

"Home?" Shane asked. "You mean—"

"I want Cam to meet my mom," she said. "If you don't want him near your parents, I'll accept that… They hate me, don't they?"

Shane couldn't even lie because his expression said it all. "How did—"

She shrugged. "It's not a memory as much as it's common sense. You went on the offensive, which is what you do when people hurt me. Your childhood was fine. No problems through your teen years. I've been paying attention in therapy, you know." She smiled and kissed his cheek. "If they'd just been awful people, you'd have told me. *There's something wrong with them, they're not capable of loving anyone except themselves.'* That's what you said. Owen said, *'Everyone told him that screwing with young underlings was a bad idea, and his family thought he could do better…'* So I figure… they hate me."

"A little bit," Shane said, genuine in his contrition.

Ginger tossed her head back and laughed. "Oh, Shay, if that's the worst we have to deal with bring it on."

Kissing him again, she shifted into a static, half-backstroke and lifted her feet to his hips. He kept treading but gripped her toes and his brows went up.

"What game you playing, Mrs. Warren?" he asked when her toes hooked into his waistband. "Our son is watching, you know?"

She knew that but dug her toes in and wrenched his shorts as far down his thighs as possible before using his strong body as a push off point to glide back toward the shore.

"Race you back," she called over her shoulder and swam with everything she had toward the shore and her boy, leaving her husband behind her, eating her spray.

FORTY

GINGER HAD WON, but it hadn't mattered because everyone was so ecstatic by the time they got back to the shore that no one was keeping score. If she'd thought about it, she'd have known that Shane would never have raced past her and left her out there. Her husband was always going to follow, never lead. In the water at least. He kept Cam while she showered and then they switched for him to wash off.

Ginger was pumped, ready to fight, ready for action, ready for something. Murphy came to say he was taking Rocky for a quick walk before therapy, so she passed off her son to his uncle who agreed to take him in his stroller.

She'd just closed the door behind them when Shane came out of the bathroom, rubbing a towel in his ear.

"Where's our prince?" Shane asked, scanning for Cam and peeking into the crib to only find Raa there.

"I'm not mommy right now," she said.

"Okay." Shane tossed the towel from his

shoulders toward the door next to her, but the other stayed around his hips. "Who are you?"

Strutting toward him, Ginger said nothing and planted both hands on his chest to thrust him back onto the bed. While he was still in shock, she shimmied her panties down her legs, slid the straps of her dress from her shoulders and climbed on top of him.

"I'm your wife," she said on his mouth a breath before she kissed him.

Shane was as ready as her for the kiss. His arms closed around her body, but she wouldn't let him flip her over, wouldn't let him take control. Ginger fought to stay on top, driving both fists into the mattress at either side of his head.

With her freshly-shampooed hair tumbling around their faces, Ginger licked her lips. "I don't want to wait," she murmured. "Say it, Boo. Tell me that you love me."

"I love you," he said, his strong hand sliding up her spine and disappearing into her hair to clasp the back of her neck to try for another kiss. "I do, I love you."

"Now tell me I'm allowed. Give me permission."

"Permission for what, sweetheart," he asked, dazed by her kiss, drugged by the passion and the strength of their need.

"Everything. Anything. Permission to do whatever the hell I want with you."

The corner of his mouth curled. "Damn right you have permission. You are—"

Yanking his towel open, Ginger seized his dick and held it tight. He muttered out a curse, but she wasn't done. Sitting up, she took him into her body in one slick, confident move, which had to be another example of her muscle memory coming in to play.

Shane crunched up, his torso coming half off the bed as he groaned and sputtered. "Shit, fucking holy hell!

Fuck!"

Thank God Murphy had taken Cam out of the house; she just hoped they were gone already. It didn't really matter, she was enjoying the sensation of riding her husband. As the rhythm took over, she picked it up, moving faster as she slid her hands over his hard abs and squeezed the girth of his cock in her pussy.

"Oh, fuck, baby. Slow it down," Shane panted, his hands skimming her back and clutching her hair. "Fuck, Gin!"

"Come," she said, pressing her hand into his groin and using her thumb to stimulate her clit. She didn't want her hands, she wanted his. Grabbing hold of one, she pressed it to her abdomen, low down, right at her pubis. "Come here, Boo. Come deep inside me. Right here... Oh, Shay, your cock is amazing."

Bouncing up and down on him, she closed her eyes and panted toward the ceiling begging to feel him inside her like that forever more.

"Bit," he hissed out through his teeth.

"Rub my clit," she said, turning his hand to push his fingertips against her. "Yes, baby, oh like that... I'm so close... yes..."

Pushing his fingers harder with hers, Ginger yelped and screamed, squeezing him hard with the power of her unparalleled release.

Shane reared up. His hips bucked from the bed and he pumped himself into her as he dragged her down for a kiss that left her breathless.

Their bodies were still connected when she finally relaxed and rested her cheek on his chest.

"Boo," she whispered, trailing her hand up and down his rib cage. "You were... incredible." He didn't say anything and his hands weren't on her body. Ginger was too lost in her own endorphins to think too much about it at first. In time, as she cooled and began to return to reality, she panicked and sat up... Except he was still inside her so they both flinched. Trying to find his eyes, she worried when she saw they were fixed on the ceiling. "Shane... did I do it wrong?"

Another score of seconds passed before his gaze lowered and landed on hers. He looked so stunned that her heart began to race again as fear edged in.

"There are no fucking words for what just happened," he said, his voice barely above a grumble.

"Oh, I did it wrong, did I hurt you? I—"

Ginger tried to lift her leg, but he grabbed her hips and held her on him.

"I've missed you, Bit," he said and breathed out, emptying his lungs. "There's no distinction anymore... you are her. No doubt about it."

The confident woman in the videos, the one who took control of her man, who played and tested him.

Ginger blinked at his belly button. "But I... I don't remember so much."

He laughed and sat up, taking her neck in one hand and her ass in the other. "You are my Ginger, that's all that matters to me. You are the woman I fell in love with. The woman I love. The mother of my child."

Gasping, she looked down. "We weren't careful."

"You told me to come and I came." Yes, she'd actually ordered him to do it. Her cheeks heated while recalling her words and commanding nature. "I like the blushing thing, we should keep that," he said and leaned in to kiss her neck.

Ginger was laughing as his tongue tickled her ear lobe when there was a call from downstairs. "Therapy!"

They kissed again, but it couldn't last. Before she got off his lap, Ginger laid her fingers on his chest.

"I did it right?"

"Perfect," he said, making her grin as she got off

his lap and ran to the bathroom.

They should really shower again, but there wasn't time, so she figured it would wait. They'd just finished cleaning up and dressing when there was another call for therapy. Great, that meant they were holding everyone up.

Running down the stairs together, Shane came up short behind her when she stopped abruptly behind the couch that Owen was seated on.

"I just had sex with my husband."

Why had she said that? Why had she declared it like that? Ginger didn't know, but it felt important and she felt better for saying it. Owen twisted to look over the back of the couch. Instead of looking at her, her brother looked over her head at Shane, just like Murphy and Doctor Guinness did.

"Why are you all looking at me?" Shane asked and put his hands on her shoulders. "I didn't know we were going to declare it like that, but, yeah... she did."

"You had sex with him or you had sex with each other?" Doctor Guinness asked.

Ginger went around the couch to sit next to Owen who had Cam on his lap.

Shane went to his brother and dropped onto the couch in his usual position. "Does it matter?" he asked. "I definitely did my bit... at the end."

He and Murphy fist-bumped as she moved Cam from Owen's lap to hers.

"It's been an emotional day for Ginger," Doctor Guinness said. "An emotional few days actually. Owen and Murphy have been filling me in on what they know about last night... with Calvin."

"Yeah, we were down here doing the therapy thing while you were upstairs getting laid," Murphy said. "Does that mean she's cured?"

"I do want to go back to California to see my

mom," she said, letting Cam rest back against her, giving him a forefinger in each hand. "I think maybe it's time Cam and I went to see what life is like out there."

"That's progress," Doctor Guinness said.

"I feel like this is wrong," Owen said, frowning at them all. "Shane, switch places with me."

Owen got up and went over to Shane, shooing him off his couch. He gave Shane little choice but to join Ginger on hers. There was a free couch, but Ginger didn't mind having Shane at her side. Especially when he sat so close that their thighs touched and one of his arms stretched along the back of the couch behind her.

"I should get Cam something to eat," she said, thinking about her baby who she'd neglected that morning.

Passing him to Shane, she went into the kitchen to get him a banana. It only took her a minute to mash and mix it up. Ginger brought it back into the living room to find that Shane was lying on the couch with his ass up close to the arm so his legs dangled off the end. Cam was using his father as a seat, leaning against his thighs, his baby butt on Shane's abs.

There wasn't much space for her, so she scooped a hand under Shane's head and he lifted his shoulders enough to let her sit and then dropped his head into her lap. Scooping up some banana, she leaned over Shane to slip it into Cam's mouth and rested the bowl on her husband's shoulder.

"Wow, this is some kind of fucked up," Murphy said.

"Language," Ginger and Shane said at the same time.

Her husband stopped playing with his son's feet and lifted his eyes to hers. She bent down to kiss his mouth.

"Look at them," Murphy said. Everyone turned

to see him holding an open palm toward the couch that she and Shane were occupying. "They're a little fucking Warren family."

"Language!" she and Shane said at the same time again.

That time, Shane stretched an arm off the couch and pointed a finger at his brother. "Do it again and we'll have a problem."

Rocky, who had been lying on the rug in front of the fireplace, lifted his head to bark.

"Lie down," she and Shane said in unison.

Owen laughed. "Oh, this is too funny."

Cam saw his uncle laughing and laughed too, spitting banana goo all over his father's tee-shirt.

"Thanks, Cam," Shane said, tickling the baby's feet.

"What a shame I have an excuse to get you out of your clothes again," Ginger teased, sliding a hand into the neckline of his tee-shirt.

Shane grinned and bounced Cam's feet together. "I gave you permission, remember? Anything you want to do, any time."

"Do you think underwear picnics are going to be a regular thing in the Warren house?" she asked.

Shane laughed. "Until Cam is old enough to notice, sure, then I think they might become a Warren mommy and daddy thing."

"They'll just end up being naked picnics," she said.

"True," Shane nodded, lifting one of Cam's feet then the other in a rhythm as she fed the baby more banana. "And let's be honest, who needs the food?"

"The food?" she asked, cleaning Cam's chin with the spoon. "We can skip the entrée, but I'll have to insist on dessert."

His eyes were smiling when they ascended to

hers.

They said together, "Chocolate pudding."

"What else?" she asked. They shared the laugh.

They both stopped when Doctor Guinness stood up and closed his binder.

"What's up, doc?" Shane asked.

Doctor Guinness looked stern and Ginger thought for a second that they'd done something wrong.

She kept on thinking it until he smiled. "Our work here is done. You have my card if you need any follow-up; I'd be honored to come to California to work with you some more." Doctor Guinness moved to the couch and stood in front of her. "You don't need a retreat now. You need your family… and you have them right here."

The doctor shook Shane's hand and walked away up the stairs. Ginger was stunned as the men exchanged looks. Cam broke the silence with a babble. He tried to lunge forward to steal the banana bowl from his father's shoulder, but Shane grabbed it up just in time. He picked up his son too and sat up on the couch at her side.

With the baby on his lap and the banana bowl in the same hand that held Cam, Shane curved his hand around the side of her neck. "Bit?"

Turning to him, she was… astounded. "We… we're a family."

"Yeah," Shane said, his smile was slow as was his hand in slithering onto her belly. "Maybe a growing one."

And that wasn't a scary thought, it was exhilarating. "Yeah… maybe." Still, she had to be wary. "But Calvin and—"

"I already called to file protective order paperwork," Owen said. "I told Boyd at the lodge this morning, he and Calvin took their business associates and split not long after… They don't want the truth of what he did getting out, it would be devastating for his business."

Calvin was gone. Out of her life. She was safe. She was happy. In love. A mother. A wife.

Shane was still holding his breath, waiting for something from her.

"Let's get married," Ginger said in a rush of breath.

"What?" Murphy asked. "You're already married, how can—"

"Shh!" Owen swooned though she and Shane couldn't take their eyes off each other. "It's romantic, you idiot."

"Yeah, Bit," Shane said, scooping his hand under her ear to pull her to him. "Let's get fucking married."

And before Ginger could chastise him, he sealed his mouth over hers, taking control of the moment, their lives, and their family. After all, he was the daddy.

Thank you for reading this tale!
If you can, please take the time to review.

~

Ask your local library for more Scarlett Finn novels!

~

For all things Scarlett Finn
check out:

www.scarlettfinn.com

CHECK OUT BILLIONAIRE ROMANCE

SCARLETT FINN

AVAILABLE NOW!

www.ingramcontent.com/pod-product-compliance
Lightning Source LLC
Chambersburg PA
CBHW061612210726
48287CB00001B/101